NO CHERUBS FOR MELANIE

Other Inspector Bliss Mysteries
by James Hawkins

Missing: Presumed Dead (2001)
*Nominated for the
Arthur Ellis Best First Novel Award*

The Fish Kisser (2001)

To Harvey,

NO CHERUBS
FOR MELANIE

An Inspector Bliss Mystery

Happy Xmas

James Hawkins

James Hawkins

A Castle Street Mystery

THE DUNDURN GROUP
TORONTO · OXFORD

Copy-editor: Steven Beattie
Design: Jennifer Scott
Printer: Transcontinental

Canadian Cataloguing in Publication Data

Hawkins, D. James (Derek James), 1947-
   No cherubs for Melanie / James Hawkins.

(A Castle Street Mystery)
ISBN 1-55002-392-6

I. Title. II. Series: Castle Street mystery.

PS8565.A848N6 2002   C813'.6   C2002-902277-0   PR9199.4.H38N6 2002

1   2   3   4   5   06   05   04   03   02

THE CANADA COUNCIL | LE CONSEIL DES ARTS
FOR THE ARTS | DU CANADA
SINCE 1957 | DEPUIS 1957

Canada

ONTARIO ARTS COUNCIL
CONSEIL DES ARTS DE L'ONTARIO

We acknowledge the support of the **Canada Council for the Arts** and the **Ontario Arts Council** for our publishing program. We also acknowledge the financial support of the **Government of Canada** through the **Book Publishing Industry Development Program** and **The Association for the Export of Canadian Books**, and the **Government of Ontario** through the **Ontario Book Publishers Tax Credit** program.

Dundurn Press
8 Market Street
Suite 200
Toronto, Ontario, Canada
M5E 1M6

Dundurn Press
73 Lime Walk
Headington, Oxford,
England
OX3 7AD

Dundurn Press
2250 Military Road
Tonawanda NY
U.S.A. 14150

To my dearest Amanda — my elder daughter.

With all the love that only the
proudest of fathers can understand.

This is a story of relationships;
where love, hate, good, and evil meet.
It is of men and their daughters.

"Ye shall reap what you sow."

chapter one

Death was very definitely in the air, yet not one of the hundred or so designer-clad women in the restaurant's grand dining room — and only one of the overdressed men — felt the slight shift in ambience that signalled its presence.

The cognizant man, sitting alone beyond the gleam of the chandelier, could have been a public health inspector, but his suit, though aging, was too sharp, his shoes too shiny, and he had a robustness about him that said he'd done more with his fifty years than poke fingers into U-bends and grease traps. Sitting, he seemed tall, but his length was in his trunk; his legs had let him down an inch or two. In deference to the August heat, he'd slung his jacket carelessly over the back of his chair and loosened his tie with casual contempt. However, he meditated over each morsel of food with the morose dedication of a culinary critic. Other guests, uneasily noticing the man's introspective countenance, and feeling the scrutiny of his nervously watchful hazel eyes, might have quite wrongly imagined that he was the one preparing for the grave.

Heads snapped around as a fat man erupted into the room through a panelled door. A whisper swept across the room, swiftly gaining strength, and was carried by waiters past the lone diner into the bustling kitchen, where it became a cacophony that drowned out the clash of pots and the hum of extractor fans. The chefs tried to pretend nothing was happening but the lower echelon gravitated into a grumbling huddle. "The old man's pissed again!"

Out in the grand dining room, beyond the sound-proof swinging doors, the fat newcomer navigated drunk-enly from table to table and an excited murmur spread from mouth to mouth: The sideshow had started, the evening's entertainment had begun. Whom would he ridicule tonight? What would he shout? *"Are you mad, woman? Champagne with pheasant! Never! I will not permit gastronomic suicide in my restaurant. Mon Dieu!"* *"Fork! Moron. Yeah, you. You don't eat oysters with a fucking fork!"*

But not tonight. Tonight he was too far gone for repartee, however abusive or one-sided.

A foreign tourist, American judging by his tie, grabbed the arm of a passing waiter and drew his atten-tion to the drunk with a concerned nod.

Without a second glance the waiter leaned for-ward. "It's alright, Sir, he's the owner," he said with confidence, as if recommending the plat du jour; as if such behaviour should be expected of all London restaurateurs.

The pantomime continued as the slobbering clown fell from table to table, grasping at imagined safety rails, steadying his hand on expensively manicured heads. "Mind the wig, old chap, cost a bloody fortune," they laughed.

Around the room, twitchy fingers reached for cellphones. Whom to call? The police or the *News of the World*? The police, probably. Although the owner's antics may at one time have smudged a column or two in the tabloids, the paparazzi and the public had long since found greater interest in other, more ridiculous, characters.

With a wry smile and without a hiccup, the tuxedo-clad pianist twisted his bow tie drunkenly and swung from Dvořák's "New World" to the drinking song from Romburg's *Student Prince*; few noticed.

Spouting gibberish, insisting that he should be heard, the owner clutched his throat. "Ah ... urg ... argh," he gurgled and was misinterpreted by a wispy model-type. "Do you think he wants us to leave, Roger?" she asked her companion in a stage whisper.

"Bloody scandalous ... Absolutely disgraceful," echoed around the room, but to some the drunk's behaviour was consoling: those able to point and snigger, "Well, at least I'm not as bad as that!"

"Wish I had a camera," exclaimed one diner, and got a dig in the ribs from his skimpily clad female escort. ("We'll have to be discreet," she'd whispered saucily as they'd slipped away from her husband's dismal book launch party. "Discreet!" he'd cried. "Wearing that!")

Another diner was suitably armed, toting a video camera brought to record a momentous family occasion. But the celebration of forty years of undying matrimonial fidelity couldn't stop the husband's camera eye from roving.

"Please don't!" implored the man's wife, feeling the heat from guests at surrounding tables, but, shaking off her admonition, he continued filming.

In less than a minute the bulky figure had reeled his way from one side of the room to the other, leaving a trail of bemused, disgruntled, delighted, and offended patrons. His goal, the kitchen, lay directly ahead of him, and diners on the far side of the room were already losing interest, returning to more mundane matters: platters of undercooked, undersized, and overpriced culinary creations.

The padded service door to the kitchen was flung open and the slobbering owner filled the void like a marauding alien in a movie. A wave of silence spread through the kitchen; whisks, spoons, and knives ground to a halt as one of the monster's pudgy hands gripped the door frame with white-knuckle force, his other hand grappling to loosen the clothing around his neck like a struggling lynch-mob victim. A burble of voices began to penetrate the silence, but the owner exclaimed, "Chef!" in surprisingly clear tones and cut the babble as cleanly as if someone had pulled a plug. Then he slumped to the floor with a soft thud.

Less favoured guests — those seated at tables closest to the kitchen — sat mesmerized, their eyes riveted to the creature on the floor. And the expressions on their faces were mirrored in the wide eyes of the kitchen staff who stared, jaws dropped, like toilet sitters when the stall door unexpectedly flies open.

A doctor, attending his daughter's engagement party at a nearby table, braced himself to rise. His wife's hand and steely glare dissuaded him.

"He's drunk again," he mouthed, his conscience easily assuaged.

The chef de cuisine, ex-army by the trim of his moustache, took control. "Quick, get him in," he commanded, his voice sharp with annoyance. Three sous chefs grabbed at the owner while the chef turned his attention back to the kitchen and donned his sergeant major's persona. "*Mis en place*," he bellowed, emphasizing the order by slamming a silver serving platter onto a metal table with enough force to buckle the oval dish beyond repair.

The pensive lone diner watched in silent consternation as the macabre tableau unfolded before him, then slid on his jacket, dropped enough cash on the table to cover the bill, and slipped from the room unnoticed.

"Crap!"

The shout pricked the ears of the old ginger cat. He tensed, sank deeply into the knotted shag-pile, and readied himself to pounce. The flying paperback missed by more than a chair's width and landed with the sound of ripping paper.

"Sorry Balderdash," his owner called. "I wasn't aiming at you, old mate. It's that damn book. Load of bloody —" The doorbell interrupted his apology and, rising slowly from the comfortably decrepit armchair, Detective Inspector David Bliss muttered disgruntledly. "It's bloody Sunday afternoon." Then he stumbled as his unbuckled trousers slipped halfway down his thighs. "Who is it?"

The only answer was a second peal of chimes; same chimes, different silly tune. God, how he hated those chimes; his ex-wife's final kick in the teeth. "You keep the door chimes, Dave," she had said with a leer, "I know how much they mean to you."

Still struggling with his zipper, Bliss shuffled to the door, flicked the catch, and was flung backwards by the force of his commanding officer marching into the room.

"Bliss old chap. Hoped I'd catch you. Been phoning for days." Detective Chief Inspector Peter Bryan kept walking, on a mission, making the old cat leap out of the way as he headed for the far side of the sparsely furnished room. "Your phone's not working," he continued, and swept the phone off the glass-topped side table, holding it aloft — a trophy, as the unconnected cord dangled accusingly in mid-air. "Do you want to talk about it Dave?" he asked, eyebrows raised — a priest visiting to enquire why a parishioner has converted to the other side.

"Not particularly, Guv," replied Bliss, slumping into a chair that could have been chucked out by Oxfam; hiding an obvious rip with his left elbow; missing a couple of nasty cigarette burns. "What do you want?"

DCI Bryan, looking decidedly unpolicemanlike in Sunday jeans and golfing shirt, scanned the room with a scrap merchant's eye: one dilapidated leatherette armchair, a small dining table that the previous occupiers hadn't considered worth a struggle down the stairs, a television set that looked as though it may have been installed for the Queen's Coronation, a couple of other bits, and a pile of tired cardboard boxes. Five quid for the lot.

Bliss saw the look. "The wife cleaned me out," he protested, making no attempt to clear a space for his senior officer to sit.

"Thank God for that. I thought you'd had burglars," said DCI Bryan, dropping the telephone onto the table. He checked his fingernails for dirt and selected his most serious expression. "Murder, Dave. It's murder."

Bliss relaxed into the enveloping security of the well-worn padded chair and felt the tension drain from him. This was not exactly what he'd been expecting and he joked in relief, "That's the trouble with Sundays, Guv. Wife, kids, gardening, traffic, being polite to the neighbours. It's murder. Bloody murder."

Bryan let him finish. "Very funny Dave. But this is a real murder and I think you'll be interested."

Randomly selecting a glass from several on the floor by the side of his chair, Bliss drained the syrupy dregs then stared into the empty vessel, puzzling. Where did that go?

"I've decided to quit," he said finally, as if the DCI had not spoken — as if murder no longer intrigued him.

Peter Bryan studied Bliss's face for the first time since entering the apartment and shuddered at the realization that only six years separated them. You can count me out if this is what marriage and divorce does to you, he thought, seeing the chaos of the unkempt room mirrored in the older man's face — unshaven, unwashed probably, and sagged under the twin weights of middle age and carelessness. The sad glaze of hopelessness in Bliss's eyes startled Bryan. He'd seen the look before: prisoners, lifers usually, resigned to their fate, with nothing worth anticipating beyond the possible introduction of in-cell flush toilets and the certain visit of the HIV nurse.

"Why quit?" Bryan ventured with an upbeat lilt. "You've got at least ten good years in you for a full pension, and you are — well, you were — a damn good detective." Bliss gave a 'couldn't-give-a-shit' shrug, and slumped fully into the chair. "I wanna get on with my life."

"I didn't know you had a life to get on with," Bryan retorted, immediately trying to bite back his words.

But Bliss took little notice. "You said I'd be interested in this case. Why?"

Did Bryan detect a glimmer of curiosity in the other man's dark brown eyes? "Have you seen the papers?" he asked, but one glance round the room told him, *Not*.

"Guv, is this some sort of party game or did you bugger up my Sunday afternoon for a reason?"

"Inspector!" the DCI began, then checked himself. What is there to bugger up, he wondered. If this is life, it can only improve. But, Bliss was off duty after all. "OK, Dave. I'll be straight with you." He stabbed a finger at the whisky glass. "Word has come from above that unless you stop pissing away your life on gut-rot and get back to work, you're finished."

Bliss sneered, "I was right. That's what I thought you came to tell me. So why give me the whole spiel about a murder?"

"Huh! Well, you were wrong. I was only supposed to tell you about the murder, to see if you had enough bottle to pull yourself together long enough to take the case."

He's lying, thought Bliss, but couldn't avoid looking sheepish. "Try me then — let's see if I've got any bottle left."

"Does the name Martin Gordonstone mean anything to you?"

"Yeah. He's that posh geezer who owns a fancy restaurant. Usually pissed as a rat, swearing at customers, chucking them out if he doesn't like 'em, that sort of thing."

"*Was* that posh geezer," corrected Bryan. "Anything else?"

Bliss missed the innuendo. "Are we back to twenty questions?"

"Sorry Dave. I was hoping you'd remember."

"Remember what for Chrissake?"

"Nineteen seventy-seven. You dealt with the death of his daughter."

Bliss's face went through a contortion that could have been mistaken for heartburn as his mind exploded with memory. "Melanie Gordonstone?" he queried in a disbelieving whisper, "You mean ..."

The other man, eyes wide in agreement, nodded quickly. Bliss got the picture, found himself sinking into his mind, and his eyes blanked as he focused on the images that sprang up behind them. A child's white, lifeless body drifted into view, floating face down in a pond, like a scuba diver scouring a reef. Only this diver was wearing neither a snorkel nor a mask. Time hadn't diminished the memory. His first child fatality as a policeman. His first child fatality, period.

"You'll always remember your first dead 'un," the training school instructor had said. "'Specially a kid." How true, Bliss thought, how true.

He pulled himself back to the present and stumbled over his tongue. "I ... I didn't realize it was him ... I had no idea it was the same bloke. I ... I didn't think he was into restaurants."

"He wasn't back then," replied Bryan. "He was a stockbroker. Made a mint and got out years before everyone else lost their shirts on Black Monday. Very lucky or bloody good timing, who knows?"

DCI Bryan was still talking, unaware of the maelstrom raging in Bliss's mind as he fought to disengage his thoughts from the image of the dead six-year-old, arms akimbo, embracing the water, while a halo of dark auburn hair floated around her head and a school of koi carp curiously inspected the newcomer to their world.

"Accidental drowning wasn't it?" Bliss looked up. "Sorry?" he said, realizing he'd missed the question; the haunting image was still there, overpowering all his thoughts.

"His daughter's drowning. Accident wasn't it?"

"That was the coroner's verdict."

"It *was* an accident wasn't it?" Bryan asked, his tone lifted a half pitch in surprise.

Bliss pondered for a second then nodded firmly. "Yes." But his expression wouldn't have fooled a social worker and he knew it.

Bryan caught the look and tried to make eye contact. Bliss quickly dropped his head for a close study of his left thumbnail but only found the deadpan features of a lifeless little girl. "Was it an accident?" he began quietly, hiding behind the softness of his words. "I don't know. It was just a bit suspicious at the time, but I couldn't put my finger on it." Bliss paused, then added with calculated casualness, "I've often wondered if her father did it."

"Why?"

"It's difficult to explain, but he was sort of funny, uncooperative almost."

"No. I meant, why would he have done it? Why would he have killed his own daughter?"

Bliss levered himself out of the chair, fighting against the images in his mind, needing space to think. "Do you want a drink, Guv?"

"Tea would be fine."

"There's no milk," Bliss explained, not apologizing. "I've got some of that powdered stuff."

DCI Bryan pulled a face. "I'll take it black. So tell me about the daughter."

Bliss reached the kitchenette in two strides and fiddled unnecessarily with the kettle. He would have been out the back door, if he had one, gulping lungfuls of fresh air and searching the sky for a bird or aeroplane's contrail, anything to take his mind off the dead little girl. Both hands shook — it could be the whisky, he reasoned, but knew different as he hunched over the sink and stared out the window at his bleak concrete neighbours. Seconds later, dark images of Melanie Gordonstone blotted out the September sun and dragged him down into the sink of scummy washing up water. Plunging his hands in he hoped to find a cup, but felt only a clammy child's body with stiff matchstick arms and legs — all the elasticity of life gone. Suddenly, the water seemed to boil; he whipped out his scalded hands and found himself confronted with an image of her body, her wet summery dress clinging opaquely to her skin, the thin fabric creased into a fold between her spindly legs. Twenty years later, but he could almost feel the wetness on his mouth as it enfolded her unresponsive lips in a desperate fight to revive her.

"Breathe please," he had implored, and a bubble of snot had inflated from one of her tiny nostrils.

"Breathe," he had shouted, as he frantically compressed her androgynous chest, willing the heart to beat, the lungs to inflate, the mouth to suck.

"Where's your keyboard, Dave?" the chief inspector called, still scouting around the small flat looking for signs of life. "You do still play don't you? I hope you haven't given that up ..."

But Bliss couldn't hear. The images in the murky sink water wouldn't let him go, trapping him in a whirlpool of images that rekindled the panic and fear and left him feeling as helpless as he did at the time.

"Breathe damn you, breathe," he was still yelling inside when the singing kettle eventually broke the spell. Swiping his hand across his forehead he swept the images away and smeared beads of sweat into his hair, but his voice cracked with emotion as he tried to continue the conversation. More than twenty years and he still choked up at the thought of that floppy little body lying in the sunshine on the pond's grassy bank.

"I tried mouth-to-mouth ..." he called from the kitchenette, his voice trailing off, then, after a moment, he turned abruptly and demanded. "Have you any idea what it's like, Guv?" He knew the answer and didn't wait for a response. "How *could* you know? She was only six for God's sake. Only a year or so older than my girl at the time."

DCI Bryan put on a reassuring voice. "Kids are always the worst, Dave. You know that. Give me some clapped out old beggar who kicks the bucket and it doesn't put me off me steak and kidney; but a kid ... "

Tea in hand, Bliss returned to the main room, shaking his head, interrupting. "No. This one was different. She wasn't just any kid. She was so pretty. She looked like a little stone angel. What do they call them?" He delved into his memory, came up with another image of the little girl, and answered his own question. "Cherub. That's what she was like. One of those marble cherubs you see on gravestones." He paused, and a vision of a stoneless little grave flitted through his mind — a pathetic grave, just a little mound with a numbered marker. But just how big a mound can you make when you're only six years old, he wondered. "She was the first real dead child I'd seen," his monologue continued, eyes fixed firmly on a carpet stain, the origin of which he'd long since forgotten. "She didn't look dead. Just asleep. I kept thinking, She'll wake up in a minute." Twenty years worth of guilt bubbled to the surface and his words were hushed as if he were alone with his memory — a memory he would rather not share. "The body was so cold — as cold as marble. She felt like a ... like a big plastic doll. Later, much later, I began to think, Why was she so cold? The water was cold but no one ever challenged the time of death."

"What are you suggesting?"

Bliss looked up sharply, almost caught unawares by he presence of an audience. "I often wondered. What if she'd been dead longer?"

"Why did you think that?"

"According to the parents — her father anyway — she had been missing for no more than ten minutes or so, and his wife backed him up; well, at least, she didn't contradict him. According to them, Margaret had come running, crying, saying she'd lost Melanie."

The chief inspector cocked his head, "Margaret?"

"Her older sister."

"So, they called the police. What's wrong with that?"

How many times over the years had Bliss asked himself the same question. What's wrong with calling the police? Nothing. But why not go and look for her first? Why call the police straight away? And, more significantly, why had he never asked those questions of the parents? He had never asked, not really, although Martin Gordonstone had clearly anticipated the questions as he and his wife had greeted Bliss on the front steps of their country retreat, looking like Mr. Snobby Stockbroker waiting to welcome the Porches and Jags of dinner guests.

Bliss took up the conversation again as if the chief inspector was somehow privy to the images in mind. "'We thought it best to wait for you to arrive,' Gordonstone said, or something like that."

"So why didn't they look for her?" queried the DCI. Bliss shrugged. "I don't know." But he was lying. Inwardly he knew only too well — his twenty-year-old conversation with Gordonstone was replaying in his mind with the clarity of a digital tape recording. And he clearly remembered the way that Gordonstone, in doeskin loafers and designer jeans, had lorded over him at the time. "We're absolutely certain she can't be far away," the stockbroker had pompously whined. "You shouldn't have any difficulty finding her." Leaving Bliss thinking that the other man felt himself above searching for missing persons, even one of his own.

"It only took me a minute to find her," continued Bliss. "I remember walking across the lawn into the woods, calling her name, and there she was, face down in the pond. They could have found her if they'd looked."

"But they didn't look?"

"Obviously not."

"And you didn't find it strange?"

Strange? His mind shuttled back to the pond and the lifeless little bundle of flesh as he picked at a split nail until it broke off and jerked him back to the moment.

"Strange? Not at the time. Afterwards, sometime afterwards, I started wondering about a lot of things but I didn't know what to do. The coroner's verdict was clear. No hint of foul play. No unresolved issues. Accidental drowning." Bliss squeezed the remains from a bottle of scotch into a glass and took a gulp before continuing. "Look, Guv. I've never told anyone before but I'm pretty sure he killed his daughter."

"That's just your imagination, Dave. Time has a way of distorting things."

"And sometimes it makes things clearer."

"True. But why the father?"

"You know how it is, Guv. Sometimes you just have a gut feeling something isn't right."

"What do you mean?"

Trying to think beyond the tenacious image of the dead little girl, Bliss closed his eyes and sank back into his chair, leaving the other man with his backside propped against the windowsill. "Gordonstone never really pushed; he was always happy to accept that it was an accident, that she just fell in. If she'd been my six-year-old, I'd have been jumping up and down demanding explanations. I'd have been at the police station every day, banging on doors, shouting my mouth off, wanting to know what was happening, wanting action, wanting answers."

"And he wasn't demanding answers?"

"No," Bliss shook his head with earnestness. "He took it all too calmly for my liking, and I'll always remember him saying, 'Well officer, these things happen.' I think I was more upset than he was." He took a slow swig, changing his rhythm, buying time to deliberate before deciding to reveal his trump card. "Then there was the sexual thing." The DCI raised an eyebrow interestedly, and waited.

"The pathologist couldn't be certain but he thought she may have been interfered with — somebody playing doctors and nurses, mommies and daddies, you know the sort of thing."

"And you think it was the father?"

"Who else?"

"You tell me."

"According to the parents they never let her out of their sight except for when she was at school, and even then the mother took her and picked her up."

"It could have been the mother," the DCI chipped in, his voice loaded with experience. "It's not without precedent, although they usually go for boys. And the parents must have let her out of their sight sometimes or she wouldn't have drowned." Bliss massaged his forehead with both hands trying to work the knots out of his mind. "According to them she was supposed to be with her big sister, Margaret. The two girls had gone exploring together, and the pond was just behind the house. They'd rented the place for the summer holidays to get the kids out of the city. They'd just arrived and the girls went off to explore while they unpacked."

"So what did the big sister say?"

Bliss hesitated, staring into his drink and searching for an answer; but all he could see was the little six-year-old cherub with long dark hair and a white marble face.

Peter Bryan prodded, "Well?"

Bliss made a performance of finishing his drink, lighting a cigarette, and checking out a small rip in the knee of his trousers. Finally he threw the empty cigarette packet toward an overflowing rubbish bin and admitted, "I didn't interview her."

"Who did?"

Bliss didn't answer right away, knowing there was no satisfactory answer, and that his brain would always shut down altogether whenever he tried to fabricate something plausible out of nothing.

"Dave, it's not too difficult. All I've got to do is dig up the file." Bliss held up his hand to silence the other officer and then, in a barely audible whisper, said, "No one interviewed her."

The DCI dropped his cup onto the windowsill, splintering the atmosphere with an audible *crack*, then leaned closer to Bliss, his face screwed into a blend of curiosity and confusion. "But surely she was the prime witness. You said the two girls were together. *Someone* must've interviewed her." The old cat shrank into the carpet again and held its breath as Bliss tried to conjure an image of the elder sister out of thin air and came up in the middle of an impenetrable fog. The chief inspector was still waiting for him when he came out the other side with no sign of relief on his face, and the senior officer picked up the vibes.

"What's that look for?"

"What look?" said Bliss, trying hard to take the pain out of his face.

"That look that says, 'Can I trust you?'"

"OK. Can I?"

"Depends."

"Depends on what?"

"Depends on what you say."

"In that case I ain't saying nothing."

DCI Bryan pushed himself off the windowsill and took up a headmaster's stance, hands knotted behind back, head craned forward questioningly. "Dave, if you want to get something off your chest, particularly if it might affect this case, you may as well tell me. It happened more than twenty years ago so I don't suppose anybody will be too worried about it now."

Bliss feared the sting of the cane hidden behind the encouraging words and appealed to the other officer with eyes wide. "I didn't do anything wrong, but I'll be honest I've had something on my conscience ever since that case. It might have something to do with Martin Gordonstone's murder, it might not. I really don't care anymore so I may as well tell you."

"Oh, shit. Don't tell me Gordonstone coughed to murdering his own daughter."

"No, Guv. Far from it. It wasn't what he said, it was more the things he didn't say that bugged me."

"What the hell do you mean?"

"He kept saying, 'If there's anything you want to know just ask.' I'd ask but he never really gave a straight answer."

"Be specific, man."

Bliss gave it a few seconds thought. "Well, I remember asking him how long the girls had been gone, and he was sort of vague. He said something like, 'Difficult to say precisely, officer. We were unpacking and I don't remember when they left the house for sure. It could have been ten minutes, but it may have been fifteen, possibly longer.' So I suggested that I ask the sister but he said, 'That won't be necessary. I've already asked her and she doesn't have any idea.' I told him I should still like to ask her and he said, 'I've told you that won't be necessary.'"

Bryan studied Bliss's face closely. "So you never interviewed the other girl."

Bliss shook his head. "Never even saw her. Looking back on it now, I feel bloody stupid. It's obvious he kept her out of the way, but at the time —"

"What did his wife say?" cut in the chief inspector, like an interrogator keeping a suspect off balance. Bliss got up and started wandering around as if he'd lost a hip flask in the tangles of the shag-pile.

"You did interview the wife?" Bryan asked.

"Oh yes." Bliss looked up defensively. "Of course I did. Although I never got her on her own. He was always hovering around ... comforting her, that sort of thing. What was I supposed to do? She'd just lost her daughter — she was distraught. Plus, it appeared to be an accident, and there were no obvious signs of dirty business. I could hardly insist on interviewing her on her own could I?"

"So what did she say?"

"Guv, this was twenty years ago."

"I realize that. But you're right, it could have some bearing on the old man's murder. Do you remember anything she said?" Bliss's eyes drifted to the ceiling and became entangled in the intricate pattern of a cobweb as he sought to unravel his memories. "I remember she kept referring my questions to him," he began slowly. "I'd say, 'What time did you realize Melanie was missing?' and she'd turn to him and say, 'What time was it, Martin?' Even when she didn't ask his opinion, she'd look at him while she answered, like she was waiting for a clue, a nod or a wink perhaps, I don't know. But she never really spoke for herself; never gave a straight answer. She even looked at him when I asked her bloody name."

"Did you tell anyone about your suspicions?" Apparently confused by the question, Bliss snatched his eyes away from the cobweb. "What suspicions?" he asked, peering into the DCI's blue eyes.

"That the father killed his little girl." Bliss thought hard and found himself staring at charges of neglect of duty — perverting the course of justice, even — and he gave his reply the most favourable spin he could. "At the time I didn't have any suspicions. I was more worried about filling out the forms, doin' sketch plans of the scene, having the body identified, arranging the post-mortem: all the admin crap. Anyway, Gordonstone had a pretty good alibi. He was in the house unpacking with his wife while the two girls were playing together in the back garden."

"You don't know that. How do you know the girls were together?"

"He told me."

"Precisely."

"Look, Guv. I've tortured myself to bloody death over this case. I've asked myself a thousand times why I didn't pull him in for questioning. Why didn't I bang him up in a cell for a few hours? I could have softened him up a bit; maybe a few threats, arm up his back, good cop–bad cop. You know the routines."

"Why didn't you?" Bliss sheepishly studied the back of his hands, searching for a clearer memory of the now dead man. The bastard bullied me, he thought, remembering Gordonstone's haughty attitude. But this memory had been with him for twenty years and he still found it painful, if not impossible, to articulate. He nearly blurted out, "He bullied me," but stopped himself, realizing how pathetic it sounded, and knowing he would be asked to cite examples. Turning his hands over, he searched the palms for evidence to support his accusations but drew a blank. Innocuous phrases sprung to mind — innocuous phrases with implied threats. I'm a good friend of Judge so-and-so. I know quite a few of your bosses; we're in the same lodge. It was obviously just an accident. I'll give the coroner a ring, let him know; I'm sure we were at school together."

Leaving his hands, Bliss looked up at his senior officer, seeking understanding, or perhaps compassion. "Gordonstone sort of threatened me with things that sound stupid now. And they weren't even threats, really. Just by the tone of his voice he somehow pulled rank on me ... made me feel uneasy. I remember asking one question he didn't like, and he stuck his nose in the air and said, 'Please address any further questions through my lawyer.' As if he were saying, 'I'm too busy to deal with a little bit of shit like you.' Like I said, I've never told anyone before, but I've often wondered if he killed her. I was just a rookie at the time and didn't really know what the hell I was doing. But now he's gone perhaps the wife will talk."

"Maybe. Although there's no mention of a wife on his sudden death report. He's shown as being single."

"Divorced, probably. I wouldn't be surprised, the way he bossed her about. What about the elder sister? I often wondered if she knew what was going on. Maybe Melanie told her what her dad was doing. Maybe he was touching her up as well, that's why he kept her out of the way. Maybe he was screwing them both."

"I don't think you'll get much out of her."

"She isn't dead —"

The DCI held up his hand. "No. But she lives somewhere in the wilds of Canada. She didn't even come back for the funeral."

"Any idea why?"

"Maybe you're right. Maybe he was playing around with both of them. Maybe she wanted to keep out of his way."

"Why Canada?"

"For Christ's sake, Dave, stop bloody grilling me. Just come back to work and you can ask all the questions you want."

Bliss stared vacantly into his empty glass. "I don't know if I can. Ten months is a long time."

"Course you can. It's like riding a horse. Once you know how, you never forget. You'll just have to see the Force trick cyclist, get an OK from him. What did your own doc say was the problem?"

The well-rehearsed prognosis rolled off Bliss's tongue, accompanied by an appropriately miserable expression. "Post-traumatic stress syndrome."

"The plane crash?"

"That and other things."

"What things?"

"Divorce."

"So you're a bit depressed."

"Depressed is hardly adequate, Guv," Bliss began, but laboured to find an alternative way to express the pain of divorce and sat in silent consternation for a few seconds. How can you explain to somebody that your mind has been torn apart? How can you carry on after such a trauma; why would you try? Death is at least final; divorce lingers. Death can be buried but divorce keeps coming back to smack you in the face. "Twenty-five years investment — hard bloody work ..." he explained, "then whole bloody lot gets flushed down the pan."

DCI Bryan softened his voice in sympathy. "Why did she leave, Dave?"

"She'd had enough, I suppose. I think it was the job mainly. She never understood; reckoned I loved the job more than her."

"Did you?"

The admission stuck in his throat for a few seconds. "Probably."

"If I had a missus she'd probably say the same. But you can't hide out here for the rest of your life. You've still got your daughter and you've still got a job — barely. Who knows, you might even find someone else."

"I've had a couple of tries. I really thought I'd cracked it with the last one ..." He paused briefly as a dark memory passed, then brightened himself up for the other man's benefit. "Anyway, I'm getting too old to try again."

"Rubbish. I know dozens of men who'd love a second chance. There's plenty more fish."

"It's too much effort. I can't be bothered any more. At first I thought, 'Great! Free again, and still young enough to enjoy it.' Who was I kidding?" He paused and ferreted down the side of the chair squab, suddenly recalling the hiding place for a badly pulped packet of Benson & Hedges. The match shook noticeably as he lit one of the squashed cigarettes, and he stared into the flame for several seconds before blowing it out. "I got so bloody desperate I even started smoking again."

A smirk spread across DCI Bryan's face.

"It's not funny, Guv. Have you ever tried giving up?"

"Never started."

"You wouldn't understand then. Took me two years. Always wanting one, always tempted."

"Oh well. Life goes on."

Bliss's reply was loaded. "It doesn't have to."

"For God's sake pull yourself together man."

Bliss shrugged and gazed silently into the dirty grey cloud of exhaled smoke as if looking for inspiration; searching for a more hopeful future.

Bryan gave him a few moments, then enquired again about the electronic organ that Bliss had played to a rapturous crowd at the pensioner's concert.

"In the bedroom, Guv," said Bliss, his eyes immediately lighting up. "I've got a new one actually. Cost a bloody fortune." In an instant he was out of the chair and guiding the DCI to another room, another world — a world of music.

The single bed looked under siege, squashed against a wall surrounded by Yamahas and Technics that, combined, could outperform a thousand-piece orchestra. Bliss waved the DCI to the bed while he flicked a couple of switches and started playing.

"Recognize it?" he asked after a few bars.

Bryan nodded, "'Time to Say Goodbye.' That's beautiful Dave. You're wasted in the police force."

"Yeah, I know, Guv. Too bloody sensitive, that's my problem."

He finished the song and they wandered back to the main room.

"Look, I'm not going to get on my bloody knees," said Bryan, "But if you think this act of being round the twist is going to let you retire and draw a cushy disability pension, you're wrong. You're as sane as I am. I know that doesn't necessarily mean a lot in the police force, but you're one of the best blokes we've got and I don't want to lose you. Got it?"

Bliss nodded.

"OK. I'll give you twenty-four hours. Either see the doc tomorrow and tell him you're as fit as a bloody fiddle, or damn well resign and stop pissing everybody about."

Bliss's eyes found the stain on the carpet again as his senior officer unlatched the front door and stepped out. But Bryan paused on the threshold, jammed the door open with his foot and turned back into the room. He looked as though he was having second thoughts as he called, "Dave."

"Yes, Guv."

"Interesting case, eh!" he suggested cheerily. "Who murdered the murderer?" Then his eyes swept the room. "Oh, and get this place cleaned up before the council declares you a health hazard." The door slammed, and the old cat cringed again.

chapter two

An untidy queue in the police station lobby blocked Bliss's access to the enquiry counter the following morning. An old lag, well known for spending more time in other people's houses than his own, was last in line, waiting to report to the police as a bail condition. He spun lazily to view the newcomer; a hint of recognition animated his keen eyes for a second, then faded under the force of Bliss's black stare. Bliss knew the lag's face well, and he had no intention of striking up a conversation.

Bypassing the disparate line-up of criminals, victims, and bloody nuisances, he reached over and tapped lightly on the enquiry desk window.

"Stop that," yelled the elderly woman clerk, accustomed to dealing fiercely with irate and impatient people. She hadn't looked up from where she was painstakingly recording the details of an errant motorist's driver's licence, but Bliss recognized the blue-rinsed thin white hair and precariously balanced spectacles. He considered thumping harder, but decided to wait until she had finished. He'd tangled with her before — a crusty crone, the sort of woman who could cause a stink in Harrod's perfume department.

A mumble of annoyance swept through the habitués at the prospect of someone barging in, and a balloon-chested spinster with a fistful of charity raffle tickets buddied up to a bailed rapist to make it clear that Bliss would have to wait his turn. Half a dozen pairs of eyes stung the back of his neck and he smiled to himself, avoiding eye contact by casually studying the notice board. Little had changed in ten months, he thought, scanning the few 'Wanted' posters, several legal aid lawyers' business cards, and a 1960s Ministry of Agriculture poster warning of the ravages of the Colorado beetle. Little had changed outside either, he had noted on his way to the station from the doctor's surgery. But what was there to change? The west London landscape, where grime-encrusted red bricks — Victorian terraces of a bygone suburbia — met the limestone Georgian mansions of the City, had not changed for over a hundred years, and would not change without another war or a new motor-way. He found it somewhat disconcerting that the people, sights, and sounds, had not changed either. During his ten-month absence, the world had apparently got along perfectly well without him.

The clerk slipped the driver's licence back through the contraption under the window and took a breath to shout, "Next," through the metal sieve. Bliss banged hard on the Plexiglas with the side of his fist. A gawky young man, next in line, bumped him roughly out of the way. "Oy. Wait your turn."

Frightening the youth off with a vicious stare, Bliss defiantly banged again. The frosty-voiced counter clerk took off her glasses, preparing for a fight, and glowered at him from behind the safety of the armoured glass. "Stop that. What do you want?" Flipping open his wallet he fished out his ID and slapped it against the glass.

"Detective Inspector Bliss. I work here!"

Understanding flooded her face. She smiled, and sympathy sweetened her tone to a sickly whine. "Oh, yes, Inspector. Of course. I'm terribly sorry — I didn't recognize you."

She knows, he thought with swift realization. Damn. I hope they're not going to treat me like a bloody invalid.

The latch on the side door clicked open with an electronic buzz. "Please come through, Inspector. Are you feeling better now?"

"Thank you," he replied, his worst fears confirmed.

Stepping into the corridor, he cringed under the onslaught of ghosts from a thousand old cases. Complainants, villains, and witnesses — distraught, violent, supercilious, and contrite — seemed to spring to life in front of him and he dragged his feet, fearful of confronting the ghosts. He was fearful, too, that doors would jerk open to reveal the faces of his colleagues reproachfully asking if he were better, mindful that they had been slaving while he had luxuriated in his sorrows.

Three chatty secretaries swanned past without recognition or acknowledgement, leaving him a trifle disappointed. Scornful indifference might actually be worse than condemnation, he thought, stopping outside the chief inspector's office to straighten his tie and flick a few cat hairs off his jacket.

DCI Bryan had cleared away for action. A couple of potted plants, a brass desk lamp, and a black plastic pen rack were grouped geometrically at one end of his desk, and a couple of telephones had been pushed off to the other end, while a thin file marked "Gordonstone. M."

sat squarely and solely in the middle as if it were the only case for which he was responsible.

"Pot," suggested Bliss, noisily sniffing one of the plants, knowing it wasn't, but still surprised that an unmarried, relatively young, university-type high flyer like Bryan should spend so much time rooting about in his garden.

"*Rosmarinus officinalis*, actually," Bryan said, pulling it from under Bliss's nose. "And, no, you can't smoke it."

"How did you know I would come back?" Bliss asked, pointing to the file as Bryan motioned him to sit.

"Easy. The doc called. Surprise, surprise. Apparently you're as fit as a dog with two pricks."

Bliss's confused expression showed that he wasn't satisfied. "But you didn't know I'd come back today."

Bryan slid the file toward him. "I would have bet my next pay packet you'd be dying to have a go at this case."

Bliss fingered the folder and cocked his head, waiting for the truth.

Bryan smiled like a kid caught with his hand in the cookie jar. "OK, OK. I watched you on the security camera trying to use your old code on the back door. We changed the codes last month, so make sure you get a new one before you leave."

Satisfied, Bliss relaxed and flicked through the slim file. "Not much here. What's the story?"

A spiky-haired clerk clutching a bunch of files wandered halfway into the room. Bryan gave the interloper a fierce look and barked, "Not now."

The young man froze; his lower lip trembled.

"Oh for Christ's sake, get that ring out of your nose and shut the bloody door behind you," Bryan shouted, not waiting for the man to leave before rolling his eyes and venting his feelings. "Where do we get them from?

Anyway, where was I?" He paused, arranging his thoughts, and plucked a few leaves off the little rosemary bush, rubbing them under his nose for a few seconds, before picking up where he'd left off. "Like I told you, Gordonstone's dead and buried. Classic symptoms of heart attack: red face, short of breath, clutching his chest — you get the picture. No one really questioned it, and the staff at the restaurant didn't call an ambulance for nearly three hours, thinking he was just paralytic, as usual."

"That wasn't very thoughtful."

"Especially as he was such a natural for a heart attack. Fat geezer, drank like a fish, smoked bleedin' great cigars, and he was always up in the air over something."

"Could one of the staff have done it, then?"

"Quite probable, I'd say. The problem is it took a few weeks for the toxicology boys to get round to running some tests on a few bits of Gordonstone's innards the pathologist put aside at the post-mortem. They called me at home yesterday ... No, make that Saturday. Anyway, turns out it was poison. Some unpronounceable, exotic stuff that attacks the nervous system. They would have done the tests sooner but there didn't appear to be anything suspicious; nothing obvious like a knife in the back."

"So theoretically it was a heart attack, then."

"Yeah," continued Bryan scanning the pathologist's report. "Though there was nothing natural about it."

"So where do we go from here, Guv? This happened weeks ago."

"Well, it's too late to turn up mob handed and pull the place to pieces. Whoever did it has had plenty of time to clean up anything remotely embarrassing. That's why I wanted you on the case."

Surprise lifted Bliss' voice. "On my own?"

"Just for starters." The chief inspector raised his eyebrows. "Unless you don't think you're up to it?"

Flattery or blackmail, wondered Bliss. Probably a bit of both. "I can handle it."

"Good. I was hoping you'd say that. To be honest we're a bit stretched at the moment. I need someone to get the ball rolling and I'll give you some help later. Start with the staff at the restaurant and be ever so subtle. Tell 'em it's just routine. Don't let 'em know what we know."

"They're bound to guess something's up if I start nosing around after all this time."

"Let 'em guess all they want. You never know, somebody might let something slip. Might say something weird, drop themselves, or someone else, in it. Give 'em the idea you're just tying up a few loose ends, a bit of background work just for the record. Let 'em think they got away with it."

"Let who think they got away with it?"

"The staff. It must've been one of them."

"Have you forgotten your basic training, Guv? Remember: never assume anything, never dismiss anything."

DCI Bryan shook off the suggestion that his intuition might be misplaced. "It must've been an inside job. He lived in a flat above the place; the only people who had access were the staff."

"Guv!"

"OK, OK, I get your point," conceded Bryan. He snatched the file back from Bliss and shuffled through it. "Look, here's a statement from the head waiter. Took Gordonstone his dinner at seven-thirty as usual and said he was right as rain. Thirty minutes later he was dead."

"The head waiter could be lying. He could have been the one who did it."

"Granted. But if he were, that would still make it an inside job wouldn't it?"

Bliss gave way on the point with a grudging nod. "So what was the poison?"

"Like I said, it sounded pretty exotic; probably organic according to the egghead who called me. I haven't got his report yet. They're still running tests but he thought we should know straight away. Apparently there's dozens of possibilities and he was asking if we had any control samples that they could try to match it against."

Bliss shuffled through his rusty memory bank of training courses and came up with very little on the subject of poisons — just a couple of lectures from a doddery old doctor shaking with Parkinson's disease, and a few photocopied sheets of common symptoms.

"Apparently, this type of stuff comes from mushrooms, jellyfish, even plants," continued the DCI. "It paralyses fairly quickly — in maybe ten to fifteen minutes — but the brain keeps working as the nerves go haywire. The last few minutes seem like forever, and he must've been screaming for help, but his mouth wouldn't have been working right. Everyone in the restaurant thought he was being his usual obnoxious self — thought he was pissed."

"I know the feeling," admitted Bliss.

Pretending not to hear, the chief inspector continued, "He was almost certainly dead when he hit the floor."

"And no one called an ambulance?"

Bryan shook his head. "Probably fed up with him. They'd seen it all before."

"Surely this was different?"

"Apparently the restaurant was full. The staff just wanted him out of the way. A couple of flunkies dragged him into his office and shut the door on him. Nobody realized he was dead until they were locking up and somebody thought to check on him. They were just grateful they'd had a peaceful evening."

The chief inspector continued leafing through the file. "The investigation went pear-shaped right from the beginning," he snorted. "Looks as though a green-horned uniformed lad asked just enough questions to fill out the sudden death report, then he copped a quick statement off the head waiter and the head chef — the last people to see Gordonstone alive — and left it at that."

"I don't suppose he had any reason to suspect murder ..." said Bliss, his voice trailing away as his eyes were drawn by a scuffle in the car park outside the office window. Several officers were struggling with a runty youth whose frenetic kicking and squirming made him slippery as an eel. A burly policewoman stepped in, grabbed the kid's long greasy hair, and hauled him across the tarmac to the cellblock door. Bliss lost his focus and found himself confronted with an image of Gordonstone — not the revolting, fat drunk who died in his restaurant, but a slim, polished man who, even in the midst of questioning about the death of his daughter, carried himself haughtily and spoke with an arrogance that made Bliss want to get his investigation over and flee back to the police station as quickly as possible. Rushing to fill out the pre-printed forms on the life and death of Melanie Gordonstone, he had summarized in a few dozen words an entire lifetime of hopes, fears, successes, and failures. Name, date of birth, last known address, next of kin; time, date, and place of death. Witnesses.

Witnesses, he mused to himself, remembering the simple form with Melanie Gordonstone's name on the top line. None, he had written, knowing the untruth of the word, knowing that Margaret, Melanie's older sister, must have seen or heard something. But he had calmly written, *None*, and, at the time, had been thankful to escape from Gordonstone's clutches without having to ask too many questions.

Bliss broke out of his reverie and pretended he'd been admiring a bowl of cacti in Bryan's window. "What about his wife?" he asked, having no idea how long his mind had been adrift.

Bryan scanned the report, apparently unaware of the hiatus. "There's no mention of his wife. He was definitely married wasn't he?"

"Yeah, I told you. I interviewed her after her daughter's death."

"I dunno then," the chief inspector added vaguely. "It says here the next of kin is the daughter, Margaret."

"That's the older girl. The one I never got to see. So what happened to the wife."

"Probably divorced him after what happened."

"My money would be on her then."

"Now who's jumping to conclusions?"

"It would make sense, especially if I'm right and he did kill the girl. If someone murdered my daughter, I'd sure as hell find a way to get him, particularly if he'd been touching her up as well." Bryan gave a nonchalant shrug. "It's possible. Follow it up."

Bliss reached forward to take the file then hesitated "Wait a minute, Guv. You only found out about this on Saturday, and you came to see me yesterday. So that whole spiel about the bosses giving me an ultimatum was a load of porky pies just to get me back to work wasn't it?"

DCI Bryan suddenly found his attention drawn to one of the little plants, which he pulled toward him, searching for whiteflies amongst its slender leaves while debating his response. Finally, he looked up, somewhat sheepishly. "Dave, I know you've had it rough recently, but it's time to get on with your life. I want you on this case, and you need something to take your mind off the other stuff."

Seething, Bliss spat through clenched teeth, "You crafty bastard."

"Inspector?"

Rising hurriedly, he scooped the file off Bryan's desk and turned back as he reached the door. "Sorry. I meant: You crafty bastard, Sir."

Bryan responded with mock fury as Bliss disappeared into the corridor. "Keep me informed! I expect results!"

chapter three

Bliss missed Gordonstone's restaurant at the first pass, and got stuck in a one-way system as he tried to backtrack. Several left turns later he opted to search out a parking space from which he could walk. Providence, and an amiable traffic warden, found him slotted into a spot normally reserved for visiting diplomats, and he was pleasantly surprised to find he had landed directly opposite his goal. As he waited to dart in between the constant stream of traffic, he glanced over his shoulder and noticed that his old green Ford Escort, another legacy of the divorce, looked distinctly out of place amid the BMWs and Volvos parked in front of the imposing Georgian terraces.

The restaurant's facade was shielded from the road by a barrier of ornate wrought iron railings and a row of pollarded plane trees heavy in summer leaf. A couple of bronzed fibreglass gargoyles, looking remarkably genuine, graced the projecting edges of the stained-glass canopy and a discreet brass plaque announced, *L'Haute Cuisinier*. Nothing else distinguished the elegant building from others in the terrace. It was, thought Bliss, the sort of place you could drive by a hundred times without ever noticing. The sort of place found only by reputation. No need for gaudy advertising, no golden arches, no menu in a shiny brass frame. Anyone needing to ask the prices probably couldn't afford an hors d'oeuvre.

Bliss took the two polished stone steps in a single leap and was surprised to find the huge black lacquered front door ajar, and unmanned. A door like this demands a butler, or at least a footman, he decided as he entered; he felt as if he were trespassing.

Once inside, an archway from the entrance hall led directly to the main dining room where he stood, slack mouthed, staring at the enormous chandelier high above the centre of the room. It looks more like a theatre than a restaurant, he mused, with its terraces rising around a central auditorium: ideal for anyone wanting to be seen eating publicly. A theatre of culinary arts, devoid of the cast. The props — empty tables, piles of crisply starched tablecloths, stacks of plates, and trays of cutlery — awaited a stagehand to meticulously dress them in place before the arrival of the actors and audience.

'Noises off' alerted him to the presence of a back-stage crew. Actors preparing in the kitchen for the next performance, he assumed: KPs in striped aprons peeling potatoes, chefs in whites cooking, jacketless waiters in open-necked shirts polishing cutlery, a sommelier in a snazzy waistcoat carting wine up from the cellar in a frayed wicker basket, mindful not to disturb the accumulated dust on the bottles.

A strange smell immediately caught his attention and he screwed up his nose in disgust. A strong whiff of yesterday's cigar smoke had mingled with stale alcohol and a waft of garlic — somehow managing to turn the olfactory ingredients of ambience into an unpleasant stink in the fresh morning air. Standing alone in such a large space made him uncomfortable and he was almost overwhelmed by an illogical temptation to turn and run. He knew he should follow the sounds to the kitchen, but the prospect of encroaching upon the personal space of the staff caused him to hesitate. Someone will come out in a moment, he guessed, acclimatizing himself to the atmosphere, and reminiscing nostalgically about the time he and his young wife-to-be were early arrivals for a first night performance of a little-known play by an even lesser-known amateur theatrical group. Sarah, whose tendency to be fashionably tardy often led Bliss to introduce her as "The late Mrs. Bliss," had been early for once. There was no hint of a problem at the box office, and the usher, a sixteen-year-old aspiring Gielgud, made a majestic performance of sweeping aside the blackout curtains leading into the auditorium to reveal that they were the first members of the audience to arrive. By curtain time another dozen or so had sneaked into the rear seats. "They're probably relatives," sulked Bliss after Sarah insisted on staying.

"We can't leave," she whispered. "They probably know who we are. They'll come after us."

"Rubbish," said Bliss, feeling as nervous as the lead actress, whom he spied peeking through a crack in the curtain.

He'd regretted his faint-heartedness at the end of the first act when they were forced to applaud madly to save the cast's total demoralization. Sneaking out during the intermission they found a local pub where they sat giggling with relief, and a touch of guilt. Ten minutes later they were forced to abandon their drinks and dash for the emergency exit when the play's entire cast turned up to drown their sorrows.

"I told you they'd come after us," laughed Sarah breathlessly as they ran to the bus stop in the rain. Then some of the other audience members turned up and they'd run again...

Smiling to himself at the memory, Bliss looked around and noticed a couple of kitchen porters eyeing him up. He could feel the weight of their stares as they peered through the small oval windows in the kitchen's swing doors.

"He ain't a customer. It's too early, an' he's not dressed proper," said one.

"Prob'ly a health inspector looking for more dead bodies," joked the other, known for his bad taste.

The well-muscled head chef pushed the young men out of the way with a growl and swept through the door. "Can I help you?"

Bliss tried to respond, but found that he was unable to tear his eyes away from the other man's mouth. As if he were ruminating on a particularly tough morsel of meat, the chef's jaws and lips were in constant motion; the facial idiosyncrasy was accompanied by wet clicking sounds as he spoke — like a dripping tap. This could get annoying, thought Bliss, as he tried to get past the nervous habit and ask to speak with the manager.

"I'm in charge at the moment," the chef said, adding two clicks to the comment. "We could sit over here." His starched white clothing rustled with every movement as he swept a hand toward one of the unlaid tables. A tieless waiter hustled toward them at the crook of the chef's finger. The pecking order was clear.

"Coffee, Inspector?"

Bliss was miles away, fascinated by the constant mouth movement. "Inspector?"

"Oh! Coffee. Yes, please — white with sugar," he replied, after delving back through his memory to resurrect the question.

"Make that two," said the chef without looking at the hovering waiter. "I know it's early," he continued, addressing Bliss, "but can I tempt you with a *tranche* of *Plateau Seville*." Catching the quizzical look on Bliss's face, he explained. "It's a gateau topped with orange segments, soaked in orange brandy, and served with a sauce absolutely laced with Grand Marnier." He leaned forward with a wink and a click. "I've just made it — highly recommended."

"Thank you, I will. Sounds great."

"I've probably been watching too many cop shows; I somehow expected you to say you're not supposed to drink on duty."

Bliss leaned forward conspiratorially. "I don't call *that* drinking. I call it eating."

The chef smiled and sent the waiter away with an order for one. "You not having any?" Bliss enquired.

"I never eat on duty," the chef replied with a ring of humour in his voice and an extra couple of clicks. "Have you worked here long?"

The chef relaxed back in his seat, accompanied by much rustling and a prolonged bout of lip clicking, while he considered the question. "Pretty much since the place opened. I made myself indispensable, you see. Of course I've had a few challenges from the odd spiky-haired nouvelle cuisine types straight out of catering college, but they didn't last. The owner was — how shall I put it — a bit difficult."

"Difficult?" Bliss jumped at the prospect of a motive.

"He could be a bit awkward ..." the chef began, then paused and ruminated for several seconds, apparently deliberating as to whether or not he should be betraying the deceased owner. Then he shrugged and continued: "I was all right. I trained in the Army Catering Corps, so I'm used to having somebody's boot up my jacksy most of the time. You learn to do what you're told, keep your mouth shut, and get your own back later. What goes around, comes around, an' I guess someone finally got their own back on him."

Bliss shot him a look that queried, What do you know? but the chef didn't wait for the question. "Inspector, I'm not stupid. He's been dead nearly three weeks. You can't tell me you just popped in to see how things are going."

"Well, there are one or two things that don't quite add up," Bliss admitted. "If someone had done him in ... Don't misunderstand me, I'm not saying he *was* killed, but hypothetically, if it did turn out there was more to this than a straightforward heart attack, the first question I'd have to ask would be, What was the motive? Who had a reason to kill him? Who's he upset?"

"Have you got a phone book?" responded the chef in a flash.

"OK. So he's pissed off a few people."

The other man scoffed, "A few. You are kidding aren't you?"

"Well. What I mean is, just because he upset someone doesn't mean they would kill him."

"I could have."

Bliss viewed the man through slit eyes. "Are you serious?"

"Deadly," the chef replied in a relaxed manner. "You should put me first on your list, although I can tell you for nothing that I didn't do it."

"At the top of the list ... That's honest of you. But why? What reason did you have to want to kill him?"

"Same reason as hundreds of others. The man was a pompous self-righteous bastard who didn't give a shit about anyone. He bullied his way through life, crapped on everyone, treated people like dirt. As far as I'm concerned he got what was coming."

The culinary creation arrived — an oversized portion swimming in an alcoholic sea of orange sauce and swirled with cream.

"Tell me what happened," said Bliss, digging in.

"We thought he was just drunk at first, as usual. Dead drunk as it turned out," the chef continued after a taste of coffee. Bliss lifted a finger, intending to speak, but the chef carried on without waiting for him to empty his mouth. "Like a bear with a sore head when he was drunk, which was most of the time. Quite honestly, I didn't want to wake him up. I thought he'd sleep it off."

"So he was awkward when he'd had a few?"

"You could put it that way," chuckled the chef. "The trouble was he couldn't see it himself and nobody dared tell him."

I can understand that, thought Bliss. How can you convince an unreasonable man he's being unreasonable?

"He could be quite amiable at times, but you were never sure where you stood with him. Everything was a competition, you see. He probably got like that working in the stock exchange. He always had to win. A simple handshake could turn into a trial of strength. He always had to have whatever he wanted."

"What about women?"

The chef thought for a second then shook his head. "He never seemed particularly bothered."

"Men?" enquired Bliss, in a disapproving tone. "He wasn't . . ." "Oh no," laughed the chef. "Definitely not. He tried it on with a female customer from time to time, although I don't think he got very far. He usually had a severe case of distiller's droop by the end of the evening. Anyway he was so bleeding fat he probably couldn't have found his whatsisname even when he was sober."

Bliss smiled. "So what happened that evening?"

Both men knew which evening he was talking about.

"I didn't have time to deal with him. It was right in the middle of dinner. Two staff off sick with ..." He glanced up at the chandelier then gave his head a quick shake. "I don't remember now. Anyway, a couple of juniors just dragged him to his office and dumped him on the floor. Nobody had time to deal with him. Nobody wanted to deal with him. He had a nasty habit of firing people on the spot."

Bliss glanced around the unprepared dining room. "What will happen to the place now?"

"We don't know. The lawyers and accountants are working on it but haven't said anything. We're still being paid, but trade has gone down the tube since the publicity over his death. Of course the lying bastards who dine here all said how nice and quiet it would be without him, but the truth is many of them only came to watch him making an ass of himself. Rich snobs, nobody would even fart in the same room as them usually. They'd go to the opera or ballet, wouldn't understand a bleedin' word, say it were absolutely wonderful, then come here and he'd give 'em a right mouthful 'Fuck this,' he'd say, and, 'Fuck that,' and they loved every minute of it. They could understand it; it took them back to their roots. But they'll soon stop coming altogether unless something happens."

Bliss nodded sagely, doubtful they would easily find another obnoxious drunk capable of running the place. Then he checked his notes. "So what did he have for dinner that night?"

"Nothing."

Bliss looked confused. "I thought ... Wait a minute." He clicked open his briefcase, selected the thin file and searched for a handwritten page. "I've got a statement here from the head waiter."

The chef jumped in: "Malcolm, the head waiter. He took his dinner up to him — the boss had an apartment upstairs. But he didn't eat anything. He didn't touch it. It was quite common. He'd order dinner, but would start on the bottle and forget all about the food. It used to piss me off, especially when he ordered something special. I'd spend bloody ages making it perfect just so he couldn't complain, then it would get chucked in the bin."

Bliss persisted; he'd already set his line of questioning and couldn't easily change tack. "Who could've tampered with his dinner that day?"

The chef replied slowly, carefully emphasizing each word by liberally interposing clicks, and insisting by his tone that Bliss should comprehend. "Like I said: he didn't touch it. He didn't eat anything, and the only stuff he ever drank came out of a bottle — his own bottle."

Bliss studied the chef's face critically asking, "Is there anything else you can tell me?"

The chef fidgeted noisily and ruminated under Bliss's stare, but then spread his hands and shook his head. "Nothing."

"All right. I'd better talk to Malcolm then," said Bliss, trying to pick a sliver of orange peel out of his teeth.

"He quit."

Bliss shot him a surprised look.

"It was nothing to do with the old man's death," the chef added quickly. "Well I suppose it was in a way. Once word got out that the old man had kicked the bucket, the buzzards gathered and picked off the best staff. Malcolm went to the *Faison d'Or.*"

"You're still here though," said Bliss, stating the obvious.

"I had a few offers, but I figured I might have a chance of taking full control with the new owner. I've been running this place for years anyway. You could never rely on the old man."

A high-heeled waitress, with a bum that stuck out like a small shelf, and nicely formed breasts hidden by a virginally opaque white blouse, leant provocatively over him to refill the coffees. Bliss chased an errant thought from his mind, then reflected and let it back.

"So who does own it?" he continued as the waitress drew his eyes in her wake.

"I guess his daughter. She's a strange girl — woman really, I suppose. She must be in her thirties now. She went abroad to live — Canada — just after her mother died." The chef glanced at his watch and rose. "And now, Inspector, I wonder if you'd excuse me. I've got a kitchen to run."

Gordonstone's wife — dead! thought Bliss, but he kept quiet, unwilling to admit his ignorance of such a basic piece of information. "I'd like to have a nose around, and talk to any of the staff who were here the night Gordonstone died ... if that's OK."

The chef nabbed a passing waiter and turned to Bliss. "Jordan will show you around."

"I'll need a list of everyone on duty that day, and also a customer list if you have one," Bliss said, before the chef could get away. Wandering around the dining room, Jordan in tow, ostensibly searching for evidence, Bliss soon found himself staring up into the giant chandelier, expecting its myriad glass eyes to offer some sort of clue. The crystal prisms swayed and tinkled slightly, wafting in the draft from an open door, and an eerie feeling swept over him, causing him to step away, irrationally fearing the whole thing might suddenly come crashing down on him. Then Jordan dropped a bombshell: "That's what killed her."

"Killed who?"

"Mrs. Gordonstone."

Bliss's head jerked around in surprise. "The chandelier killed Gordonstone's wife?"

"So they say. It was before my time. It was years ago."

"What ... It fell on her?"

"I don't know. You'd have to ask Chef. He was here then."

Bliss's eyes followed the thick white rope from the top of the chandelier as it wound its way up through a pulley and down the wall, to where it was tethered in a figure eight around a huge brass cleat that might have once graced the deck of a schooner. He imagined it might take two, even three, strong men to lower the giant chandelier to the floor for cleaning, and walked over to examine the rope. The chef, returning from the kitchen, noted Bliss's interest. "They had the rope shortened after the accident with Mrs. Gordonstone."

Bliss stared at the chandelier as if expecting it to divulge some crucial piece of information. What accident? When? Mentally asking, demanding of it, "What happened?" The chandelier knew. It was a giant all-seeing eye that had peered down on the great room for over two hundred years. One giant fly-like eye with a mass of crystal lenses each absorbing images from the room below. Locked in its crystal gaze were the secrets of thousands of spies, philandering husbands, and shady businessmen. And the secret of Betty-Ann Gordonstone's death.

It was the fifteenth of October, 1987, just before the great hurricane. The creaking floorboards, a natural security system of all old houses, alerted Betty-Ann Gordonstone to movement outside her room; the room in which she had lived alone for nearly ten years. She peered at the bedside clock: almost two o'clock. A door hinge squeaked with a familiar sound — Margaret's door. *He's going to her ... I know he is.*

Whispers in the hallway confirmed her suspicions. She lay, immobile, as she had on a hundred other nights, listening to the furtive sounds: hushed whispers, doors opening and closing with a careful hand, moans, groans, and an occasional muffled cry.

Would the torment never end? *I saw you*, she longed to say to Martin. *You touched her didn't you?* If only she had the courage to confront him, to tell him: I know what you're doing to her. You could have gone to a prostitute. Not Margaret. You didn't have to touch Margaret.

She dug her head into the pillow. "It's none of my business."

A voice deeper inside countered, *It is your business. She's your daughter. He's your husband.*

They're both adults, she reasoned, knowing full well that was no justification.

Why don't you stop him? said that other, inner voice.

The painful memory of a bruised cheek reminded her why. There was no point in even trying to talk to him, to tell him that she knew, to demand that he stop.

Noises in her head augmented the sounds from Margaret's room. Cries for help — Melanie's cries. A six-year-old's screams, which had lasted for ten years in her mind and had grown ever more persistent.

Sleep, when it came — if it came — offered no respite. Nightmares merely replaced the anguish of reality. And in the morning there was more pain. Having to face her daughter as she bounced into the room: "Hello Mummy. How are you today?"

What was there to talk about? What, she often wondered, did other mothers talk to their daughters about. So many times over the years she had been tempted to ask, "So Margaret, just how was Daddy last night? Was he good?" What would the young woman say?

But she would never find out. Some unspoken agreement, some taboo, would always get in the way. Do other daughters confide sexual experiences to their mothers? Betty-Ann sometimes wondered. But Margaret was not like other daughters.

Margaret was a tease, taunting her with innuendo, revealing little secrets in tidbits, never once admitting anything specific. She dropped hints, even an occasional conspiratorial wink, as if craving her mother's approval, wanting her mother to be pleased for her, whispering excitedly: "Daddy's been really nice to me." No details, nothing specific. Betty-Ann would turn away, wanting to know — to be certain — but, at the same moment, not wanting to know.

Unable to protect one daughter, she now watched the other being slowly sucked through a gauze curtain into a place she could see but never touch.

Awake, as usual, she glanced at the bedside clock: two-thirty now. Night or afternoon, she wondered. Does it matter? Not really. Although she guessed it was night. It was always night when she heard the sounds. The noises of the night, noises familiar to any prisoner: cries of anguish in the dark, lover's whispers, creaking bedsprings, and an occasional shout of alarm from an inmate tortured by a nightmare. Every day in prison was the same: the same people, the same cell, the same view from the same window, the same smells from the slop bucket, and the same boiled cabbage. The only difference between day and night was the sounds.

Betty-Ann lay for a few moments ticking off the years in her mind. Ten, she counted, with the backhanded pride of a hunger striker. Ten years of self-imprisonment, ten years flagellating her mind, ten years of refusing to give in to temptation. Tormented during the day by the clamour of people in the restaurant below and at night by the sounds in her mind, she even denied herself the lush dreams enjoyed by most prisoners. How easy it would be, she often thought, just to walk out and rejoin society. But what punishment would that be. How much more challenging it was to stay, without guards, bars, or locks.

She slipped out of bed and shuffled to the window, easily avoiding the furniture in the familiar surroundings of the dimly lit room. The blue-white light of a street lamp painted deep shadows as she opened the curtains a fraction. "Night." She had been correct. "Another night," she mused. Another day successfully completed. Another day of punishment, bringing me closer to what? Ten years of what? Waiting for what? There must be something at the end. Some reward. Forgiveness perhaps.

Who is there to forgive?
Me?
Who can ever forgive me?
Myself?
Never.
Melanie then?
Melanie could. Melanie, still alive in her mind, still six years old — forever six years old. "Forgive me Melanie," she implored, knowing inwardly that it was not enough. It would take more than Melanie's forgiveness to wipe away all her sins.

It wasn't just that Betty-Ann had devoted part of herself to the memory of Melanie in the way that other bereaved parents might, a corner of their minds forever blackened by the loss. Betty-Ann had become the lone member of a devout religious sect formed solely to perpetuate and worship the memory of her daughter. Everything must remain exactly the same, she had decided within days of Melanie's death, fearing that any change might cause Melanie's spirit to flee. In the beginning she had concentrated all day, every day, on thoughts of Melanie. In this way the flame of Melanie's life was not extinguished by her death, but was merely reduced to a glowing ember that only waited to be rekindled. Initially she used a photo in an ornate gold frame as a focal point for her hushed deliberations. Then, almost subliminally, she began muttering incantations: "Melanie, grant me, I beseech thee, pardon and peace, that I may be cleansed of all my sins and may serve thee with a quiet mind," she would recite, sometimes aloud, but often silently, in what was left of her mind; over the years she developed an accompanying set of eccentric gestures and postures to match the words. Before long each day, and most of each night, was filled with devotions. Like a fanatical follower of a charismatic religionist, Betty-Ann attended her pious ministrations at precisely the same time each day, staring into a candle's flame, reverently fingering Melanie's clothing with as much devotion as a Christian might caress the Pope's cassock or the Shroud of Turin.

The candle at Melanie's sepulchre was flickering precariously close to extinction now. Betty-Ann left the window and shuffled to the dressing table where Melanie's remains were precisely arranged. She poked a few shards of wax into the flame, until it burned steadily with an ochroleucous light. The candle was, she knew, her greatest achievement.

Martin had tried to stop her at first, confiscating her supply and ordering the staff to lock away all the candles at the end of each evening. But she had beaten him; making nightly foraging raids on the dining room, scratching even the tiniest of wax drips off the candelabra to feed her habit. And every now and then a careless waiter would accidentally leave a partly consumed candle on a table; she would seize these treasures with the gratitude of a starving man finding a potato. She was proud of her achievement, proud of her self-determination, and proud of the fact that, in some strange way, she had defeated Martin. She had robbed him of his power; her actions were beyond his control. I decide what to do, she thought, I make the decisions in my world — in Melanie's world.

Every day she had the same inviolate routine. Every action, every movement, was choreographed; she was like a one-woman film noir destined to run eternally. One character going through the same motions, wearing the same costume, saying the same lines, moving to the same blocking. A solitary pitiful character played with passion and energy, but played without any desire for acclaim.

Betty-Ann had broken her routine on very few occasions, and then only for a specific purpose. Once, not long after Melanie's death, before being fully committed to a lifetime of self-immolation, she had left her room to stand on a railway station platform, fully resolved to commit suicide. Twenty or more trains had passed and each time she pledged that the next would be her executioner. But when each train arrived, she shrank back from the edge of the platform, promising herself that the next one would be the one. Eventually she was harassed by an elderly shrew of a ticket inspector who nastily told her to either buy a ticket or leave. "What a country," she had mumbled. "You even need a ticket to die."

But she couldn't kill herself — it was too easy. Death is not a punishment, she convinced herself. Death is an escape from punishment.

Punishment for what?

For what you did.

No. Not what I did. What I didn't do.

Bliss's eyes were still rivetted to the chandelier.

"How did it happen?" he asked the chef without looking around.

"Suicide they said. Something official like ... 'The balance of her mind was disturbed.'"

That's possible, thought Bliss, recalling the frail frightened woman whose obvious good looks were marred by the ravages of grief following her daughter's death. But something in the chef's tone suggested he thought otherwise.

"When?"

"It must have been almost ten years ago; could have been more. She kept herself to herself, never came down to the restaurant. Stayed in the apartment all day. Apparently she had one of those phobias ... What do they call it?"

"Agoraphobia," suggested Bliss.

"Something like that."

"What about her daughter?"

"Lumpy girl ..." the chef stopped and thought. "Young woman really, I suppose. She was about twenty but you wouldn't have thought it. Always bouncing around the place bumping into things. Used to bring half-dead animals and birds into the kitchen asking for food for them. I soon put a stop to that. Health regulations, and all that."

"So tell me about the suicide."

"From what I could make out it happened in the middle of the night. She came down and tied the end of the chandelier's rope around her neck. Then she must have unhooked the rope from the cleat and the weight of the chandelier . . ."

Bliss stared up at the monstrous silver and crystal bauble, trying to gauge its weight. "And it was definitely suicide?"

"So they said, although more than one person thought he'd done her in. You see there was no note or anything, but she'd been funny for years. Her other daughter drowned you know, when she was three or four."

"Six actually."

"So you knew about that then?"

"Done my homework."

"Well, apparently she was never right after that. Round the twist they said, that's why the old man kept her out of the way. Some people reckon he kept her locked in her room from that day on."

Suddenly everything became clear and Bliss swore under breath, "Shit."

"Inspector, are you all right?"

"Yes," he said, but inwardly he was feeling some of Betty-Ann's pain. She had known all those years, he realized. Known her husband killed her youngest daughter and lived with that torment every day. No wonder her body language was wrong when I interviewed her, he thought. That's why she couldn't look me in the eye, why she couldn't answer any questions without checking with her dear husband. It wasn't surprising he kept her out of the way all those years. He didn't want her breaking down in front of the staff or the guests, saying, "Oh by the way, did I mention my husband drowned my little girl?"

chapter four

The Grand Marnier in the gateau had started him drinking early, and the chef's revelation that Gordonstone's wife had committed suicide didn't help. If ever there was a woman with a reason for murdering her husband, thought Bliss, she was it; but being dead and buried for ten years gave her a fairly convincing alibi. He would just have a single scotch he kidded himself. The news about Betty-Ann's death gave him a convenient excuse, as if he needed one. A toast to a woman he'd met briefly twenty years earlier — a woman with whom, in some ridiculous way, he suddenly felt an affinity.

He selected a pub as opposed to a liquor store. Home held too many bad memories, and he didn't fancy drinking alone there. Anyway it was early, very early. Too early to start in earnest; he would have to drive home from the pub, so he couldn't afford to risk drinking much.

A sullen twenty-year-old in a baseball cap and Grateful Dead T-shirt was attempting alcoholic suicide at a nearby table. "I wuz up all night, thinkin' about my life," he said to a similarly dressed companion. "Where I am? Where I'm going? What I'm gonna do?" he added, with the rhetoric of a depressed pop singer. As if he had a choice, as if fate had not already laid out its plan. "That's the story of my effin' life."

Bliss was tempted to tell him, from experience, that he may as well get used to it, when a fierce-faced young woman stormed up to the young man and casually dumped his beer in his lap. Punch-up, thought Bliss, readying to leave. But the man didn't flinch; just turned to his companion with his voice so full of controlled anger his jaw was quaking, and said, "I guess it's over then." Bliss sat back, wishing he could have ended his relationship with Sarah so succinctly.

An hour and three drinks later he sat contemplating the smoke-stained ceiling, trying to make out familiar images in the dirty brown tar. Mother Teresa's profile swirled into view, but vanished as a commotion at the bar attracted his attention. The landlord had grabbed the phone and was semaphoring to Bliss with his free arm. "Excuse me mate someone's just stolen your car," he called across the bar as the emergency operator answered.

Bliss spun to look out of the window. His car was gone. "What? Who the hell would want my car?"

"Joyriders," the landlord replied, after he asked for "Police."

"How did you know it was mine?"

"I saw you drive in. Anyway, that's the spot they usually pinch 'em from."

Bliss put on a crestfallen look. "It'll probably be wrecked."

The landlord gave him a look which said, I've seen your car, then spoke into the phone as he was connected to the police operations room.

Catching the bus to work the following morning, Bliss was grateful the rain had eased. In the circumstances he would have been justified in asking the duty officer to send a car, but he didn't want to give anyone the satisfaction of having a laugh at his expense. The early shift are probably pissing themselves already, he assumed, rightly.

"Did you hear about poor old Dave Bliss," one of them had said, "Someone nicked his wife, he gets into a plane crash, goes sick for nearly a year, then someone half-inches his car.

"When?"

"Last night outside the Four Feathers up Dalton Road." They laughed. "I'd rather someone nicked my missus than my car," said a wag.

"I wouldn't go sick for ten minutes if someone nicked my missus," said another.

"Who would want to nick your missus?" asked a third with a malicious twist...

"She's not that bad," he replied, paradoxically defending her.

There was a message waiting for Bliss on his desk; a response from a George Weston to a small article in the morning papers revealing that a police spokesperson had refused to confirm or deny that the death of Martin Gordonstone was now being treated as suspicious. But first he had to deal with another note — hand scrawled in an obvious attempt to disguise the writer's identity. "This is the best we can do but it's worth more than your old one," a joker had scribbled, and left it attached to a battered dinky toy, hurriedly borrowed, Bliss guessed, from the lost property office. Dropping the toy and the note straight into a waste bin, and ignoring the guffaws of the assembled pranksters, he read the other message. It advised him that Weston had phoned to say he made a videotape of Gordonstone collapsing in the restaurant the night he died.

The vultures drifted away after one of them fished the toy out of the trash bin, leaving Bliss to contact the videographer and arrange to collect the tape.

A succinct third message awaited him in his pigeonhole. *Report to Superintendent Edwards at 11:30 a.m. today.*

A pep talk, assumed Bliss, immediately feeling more depressed than ever. He could guess the format if not the actual words. Welcome back, tidy yourself up, pull yourself together, lay off the booze, and stop farting about.

Central records opened at eight-thirty. Bliss strolled in at nine-fifteen and found the three clerks still clustered around a copy of the daily nude.

"Not disturbing you, am I?" he asked as sarcastically as possible. Two of the three men drifted languidly in different directions without comment, leaving the third to carefully fold the newspaper as if it were a precious manuscript.

"Yeah Mate. What d'ye want?"

"Detective Inspector to you," shot back Bliss, resolving to bring up the question of uncivil civilians at the next divisional meeting.

The Betty-Ann Gordonstone file had been shredded, the clerk pronounced after a brief search through his records.

"Shredded!" cried Bliss.

"That's right, Inspector. It was non-suspicious sudden death according to my records."

"Suicide," said Bliss.

"Maybe it were. It don't say here. But it were destroyed in 1999."

"Why?"

"You should read standing orders, Mate," suggested the clerk, then he quoted the relevant order verbatim in an affected official voice. "Destruction of documents: non-suspicious sudden death files to be destroyed after seven years, unless the officer in the case specifically requests otherwise."

"I know that," replied Bliss untruthfully, but with sufficient conviction that most would have believed he was fully conversant with the standing order on the subject. "But I also know that files often hang around for years before they are shredded."

"Not this one. Like I said, it's gorn."

"Are you sure?"

The civilian clerk took the enquiry as an affront. "Ruddy coppers," he mumbled aloud, but kept the rest of his outrage under his breath. "Think they should be treated like ruddy God. I could run rings around most of 'em." The phone rang, providing him with an opportunity to make Bliss wait while he took a lengthy message. Undeterred, Bliss waited; there was more to the Betty-Ann Gordonstone case and he wanted answers. Finally, the clerk put the phone down and looked at Bliss as if to say, Are you still here?

"Do you expect me to check my files again?"

His files? Bloody cheek. "Yes please."

That wasn't the correct answer; not the answer the clerk was expecting. A polite, "No, that's all right, I believe you," would have sufficed. The clerk slowly took off his spectacles and made a performance cleaning the lenses, contemplating various ways of thwarting Bliss's request. In the end he simply opted to make a song and dance about finding the right book and after several false starts eventually slung the open book on the counter between them,

"There you are," he shouted triumphantly, "See for yourself."

Betty-Ann Gordonstone
Born 23rd June ,1955
Deceased15th October, 1992
File Location. Destroyed 15th October, 1999

"That's seven years to the day," said Bliss, more to himself than the clerk.

"Told you," the clerk replied in a childlike manner.

Someone hadn't wasted much time in destroying the file, Bliss noted, and reread the 'Cause of Death' column: suicide. Then he spotted the name of the investigating officer in the far right-hand column: Detective Inspector Edwards.

"Is that Superintendent Edwards?" he enquired.

"How should I know?"

"Is there any way of checking?"

"Yeah," said the clerk, slamming the book shut with unnecessary force. "Go and ask him."

Superintendent Edwards pretended to be absorbed in a file on his desk when Bliss arrived at his office at 11:30 A.M. "Shut the door," Edwards shouted, apparently equating brusqueness with authority. "Nice to have you back," he added, removing his spectacles, although something in his tone suggested he didn't consider Bliss's return to be at all welcome. "I hear you've taken the Gordonstone case."

"Yes, Sir. Actually I wanted to talk to you about that." Edwards looked up quickly. "Shoot."

"Well, it's early days yet, but I suspect the motive may have been revenge. You see I now suspect he murdered his wife in 1992—" Bliss would have continued with his theory but Edwards' dismissive wave made it clear that he should stop.

"Officer, let me put your mind at ease. I can assure you Betty-Ann Gordonstone's death was definitely suicide."

"Suicide," echoed Bliss.

"That was the verdict. Do you have a problem with that?"

"You bet I do, Sir. It wasn't suicide. It was murder. He killed her."

"Inspector ..." "Sir ..." Bliss tried interrupting, but was silenced by the forcefulness of Edwards' response.

"As I was saying Inspector, it was suicide. You're not questioning my professional integrity are you?"

Now what, thought Bliss, already feeling the senior officer's bite.

"I'm sorry ..." he began. "But ..."

"Before you answer, just remember, Inspector Bliss, you weren't involved in the case. You probably haven't even seen the file."

"I'm aware of that ..." Bliss fumbled to find conciliatory words but failed, and his voice drifted off.

"Good. I'm glad you understand."

"But you may not know he'd already murdered his daughter, sir."

Edwards jerked forward in mock surprise. "I understood it was an accident."

Bliss was passionate. "Believe me, sir, Melanie's death was no accident. It was murder. Her father drowned her."

"Not according to the coroner."

"The coroner was wrong."

The superintendent's squinted eyes pierced Bliss. "And not according to the copper who did the investigation. He had it pegged as an accident. In fact there was never any mention of foul play."

"It was me, sir. I was the investigating officer." Edwards pretended he hadn't known. "So are you telling me you committed perjury? Is that what you're saying? You stood in front of a coroner's jury, stuck your hand on the Good Book and deliberately perverted the course of justice."

"No. It wasn't like that."

"Good. Because as far as I'm concerned the case is closed. The girl died accidentally and her mum committed suicide ten years later 'cos she couldn't stand the strain anymore."

"But that's not what happened."

"It is as far as I'm concerned, and it better be as far as you're concerned as well. Personally I don't give a monkey's fart whether he done her in or not, all I care about is keeping the records straight and if some prat like you starts stirring up shit from the past I shall take great delight in stomping all over you. I trust I make myself clear, Inspector Bliss."

The onslaught forced Bliss to retreat somewhat, but he had no thought of total capitulation. "But you must admit it's possible he killed his wife."

Edwards slowly and deliberately pulled himself up to his full sitting height behind the oversize leather-topped desk, and fixed Bliss with a defiant stare. "I admit nothing of the sort. The case is closed, Inspector. It was suicide ten years ago and it will remain suicide today. Do I make myself clear?"

Although Bliss was nodding he couldn't get his face to

agree, so Edwards drove the point home with the hint of a threat. "Just remember, it may not be in your best interest to make waves. You need all the friends you can get at the moment."

That went well, thought Bliss sardonically as he slunk out of the superintendent's office and found DCI Bryan hovering in the corridor. "How are you getting on, Dave?"

"Brilliant, sir. You gave me a murder, I've ended up with three, and now I've got the superintendent on my back. Just brilliant. Thanks a lot."

DCI Bryan tipped his head queryingly. "Three murders?"

"Gordonstone's kid and his wife," continued Bliss. "I'm almost sure they were murdered as well."

"Almost, Dave?"

"Well, all right. Personally I'm sure. I can't prove it yet, but I will."

"So how have you upset the super?"

Bliss filled him in quickly. The chief inspector glanced up and down the corridor then caught hold of Bliss's sleeve and dragged him toward the washroom. "In here," he said. "I need a pee."

As the door shut, he started. "Dave. Let's get this straight. If the other two were murdered, who did it?"

"He did, of course — Martin Gordonstone."

"So what's the point in fannying around trying to prove it? It's too late to prosecute him now and nobody's going to thank you for dredging up old cases and proving your mates wrong."

"You mean Edwards isn't going to thank me."

"*Superintendent* Edwards to you, Inspector, and ... Yes, I do mean that."

"Well, I don't really care what he thinks. He's no mate of mine. Anyway, I believe it's important."

"Why for Christ's sake?"

"A motive of course. I've got to start somewhere and it seems to me that the family cupboard might be a good place to find a skeleton.

DCI Bryan stood at the urinal and spoke over his shoulder. "You're looking in the wrong place, Dave. Lots of people had a motive from what I can understand."

"Lots of people had a motive to bop him on the nose or kick him in the goolies, but if everyone who's ever been insulted by a restaurant owner bumped them off, there'd be a huge shortage of restaurants in this country."

"What about business partners?"

"Weren't any, as far as I can tell. The staff say he owned the place outright."

"Disgruntled staff then. Didn't mean to kill him, just give him a bellyache for a few days."

"It's possible," conceded Bliss grudgingly.

"Do you know how he was poisoned yet?"

"I've absolutely no idea — why?"

"Just a thought, Dave, but I don't suppose Gordonstone could have been a suicide as well?"

"Not a chance."

"Wait, Dave. Think about it. His daughter drowns —"

Bliss interrupted quickly. "Was *drowned*."

The chief inspector wrenched up his fly and turned to give Bliss a hard stare. "Let me finish. His daughter drowns accidentally. Ten years later his wife commits suicide and for another ten years he's a lonely, fat, old drunk. I'd have thought suicide was a strong possibility in such circumstances, wouldn't you?"

Bliss opened the door to leave. "I'll think about it, sir. But suicide would be totally out of character for

Gordonstone. He was too pigheaded, too —" Bliss broke off, momentarily frozen. He stood half in and half out of the washroom, his hand seemingly glued to the brass handle on the door. There, disappearing down the corridor, was Sarah, his ex-wife. He wanted to call out, but her name stuck in his throat. His mind, trapped in a continuous loop, kept asking, What's Sarah doing here? A tense tremor started in his hand and shivered through his body. Then, as if feeling the force of his stare, the woman turned. Bliss's heart sank — it wasn't her. In fact, the secretary didn't look anything like Sarah. The illusion, conjured by the woman's familiar hairstyle, vanished. The DCI, stuck in the vestibule behind him, misinterpreted the cause of Bliss's hesitation. "Dave, do you need some help with this one?"

Bliss rapidly pulled his thoughts together. "No. Not at the moment anyway."

"OK. But stick with the program, Dave. Gordonstone was murdered by a person or persons unknown, and I doubt it has anything to do with his wife or daughter. So stop digging up old skeletons and move on."

Easier said than done, thought Bliss, as he turned and ran smack into Superintendent Edwards, marching solidly down the corridor toward them.

Edwards spoke right through him. "Ah, Chief Inspector Bryan. Can I see you in my office in five minutes, please?"

Bliss cadged a lift home, deciding one bus a day is enough for anyone, then he rooted through his life's remains in the pile of cardboard boxes stacked untidily against one wall of the apartment. "It's got to be here somewhere," he muttered, searching for Melanie's file — a copy of it anyway, from twenty years ago. She had always been in the back of his mind and he had never been able to let go of the thought that he had somehow failed the little girl, so he was certain he had kept the paperwork.

A school photograph of his own daughter fell out of an old exercise book and jogged his memory. Samantha! Maybe it's in that pile of stuff I stored in her attic after Sarah threw me out, he mused, and scrabbled to find the phone which was buried beneath piles of law books, LPs, and a bundle of love letters he'd sent to Sarah during their courtship. "You keep these," she had said while they were cleaving apart their intertwined lives, making it clear by her tone that neither his love nor his letters were any longer her concern.

"Hi, Dad," Samantha said, answering her phone the moment it rang. "That's a coincidence, I was just going to call you. How are you doing?"

He considered explaining, but chose not to. "I'm back at work."

"Great."

"Not really. They've given me an impossible murder just to keep me occupied, and fed me a load of garbage about being the only one who could solve it."

"Oh."

Bliss picked up a distinct lack of surprise in her voice. "Did you know about this?" he asked, suddenly suspicious.

"What?" she replied guardedly.

A penny dropped. "You had something to do with this didn't you?"

Her tone was mischievous, "What, Dad, murder? You know me better than that."

"No. You know what I mean. You spoke to DCI Bryan, didn't you?"

"Who me?"

"Yes, you."

"I might have."

"Huh. You bloody lawyers are all the same."

"What do you mean?"

"Always interfering in other people's problems."

"That's what we lawyers get paid for. Anyway, it's reassuring to hear you admit you have a problem."

Bliss tried bravado but his voice lacked conviction. "I could have sorted it myself."

Samantha moved on. "Tell me about the murder."

"It's three murders, actually."

"Three. I didn't know."

"Neither did the DCI. Anyway, as you dropped me in it, you can buy me dinner and give me some free legal advice while I tell you about it."

She laughed. "Tonight?"

"Can you?"

"Sure. Pick me up at eight. If I'm paying for dinner you can drive, deal?"

He immediately sussed out her plan: he who drives, does not drink. "I'd like to lodge an appeal ..."

"Take it or leave it."

"OK. I'll be there." He'd half put the phone down before he remembered. "Sam," he shouted into the mouthpiece, and caught her just in time. "I just remembered. I can't drive. Someone's nicked my car."

"A likely story," she laughed.

"Still smoking I see," she chided as he clambered into her car two hours later.

"So?"

"I wouldn't mind, Dad, but you used to be so fucking sanctimonious when we were kids."

"Samantha! Do you have to swear?"

"All lawyers do. Anyway, don't change the subject, I'm not going anywhere until you've got rid of that awful stink."

Bliss took a long drag then tossed the barely smoked butt out of the window.

"Litter lout."

"I can't win, can I?"

"It's not a competition, Dad. I just worry about you that's all."

"How's your mother?" he asked as they drove off.

"Dad, do you really care?"

"Of course I do."

"Maybe if you'd shown her how much you cared she wouldn't have left."

"Don't rub it in, Sam. Do you think I don't know that?"

They drove in silence while Bliss relived the pain of his separation. The denial: "This isn't happening." The misplaced optimism: "She'll come back." The pleading, the crying, the begging: "I'll change." "No you won't." "I'll try."

Bliss broke the silence. "What does she see in him Sam? How is he different from me?"

"Dad. He's there."

"What do you mean?"

"Do I have to explain?"

"Yes."

"You were never there — not when she needed you."

"Is that what she says?"

"C'mon, Dad. You were always working; or that's what you said you were doing. That or playing your keyboard with your headphones on."

Bliss defended himself indignantly. "I *was* working."

"All right, Dad, I believe you. Anyway, it doesn't matter."

"It does to me."

"I said I believed you ..." She paused, then added softly, "But Mum didn't."

Bliss sulked. "Well she should have. Anyway, how is whatsisname?"

"George, Dad, his name is George. As if you could have forgotten."

She's right, he thought, how could I forget George? Gangly George. Hairy-nostril George. Closing his eyes he let his mind wander and found himself arguing with his conscience. "Poor me. Poor cuckolded husband. Last to know as usual."

Are you sure you didn't know? his conscience chimed in.

Did I know?

Perhaps it was comfortable to pretend it wasn't happening.

I'd never admit it.

Who would admit it?

What do you expect me to say. "I say old man, my wife prefers some other chap."

Be honest with yourself at least.

OK. Of course I knew. Not the details. Not his name. Not his hairy nostrils. I thought it was a passing phase, just a fling. Put a bit of sparkle back into her life. I'm not stupid. I saw through the pathetic excuses, the poorly disguised lies, the extra shopping trips. New clothes never worn, not for me anyway. The expensive necklace: "Just felt like treating myself, you don't mind do you?" How stupid did she think I was? So why not admit it? I thought she'd get over it. Come running back with her tail between her legs. Only she didn't come back. And it wasn't a tail between her legs — it was George.

"Hold tight, Dad!" Samantha's shout of alarm jerked him back to the present. He grabbed the dashboard with both hands and stabbed at an imaginary brake as his daughter swerved around an unlit parked truck with inches to spare.

"Stupid place to park," he shouted, as if anyone could hear, then turned to Samantha. "Do you want me to drive?"

"You're kidding — you lose your own car and now you want to wreck mine?"

"I didn't lose it," he protested but, conceding she had a point, relaxed and let his mind drift back to thoughts of Sarah.

Deep down she had wanted to be caught, he'd realized. Tempting him with obvious little clues, little Freudian slips which grew bigger and bigger as her guilt egged her on to make mistakes. And then there was the farce with the underpants — George's semen-stained underpants, left in her car following one of their most intimate moments, either by accident or, as Bliss later began to suspect, by design. She had tenderly washed, dried, and folded them, then placed them in *his* underwear drawer. By accident or by design?

He hadn't noticed. He'd even worn them — the other man's underwear. He'd even laughed later, much later, when she taunted him with it. "You didn't even notice you were wearing his bloody underpants did you?"

Talk about walking a mile in the other man's shoes — he'd driven to Bristol and back in the other man's Y-fronts. The memory still brought a wry smile to his lips.

And when, finally and inevitably, he'd actually caught them together he still wouldn't acknowledge the fact. It was a hurried lunchtime rendezvous. Sarah — his Sarah, the mother of his daughter — enjoying a romantic moment with George over a greasy pork pie, a shared packet of crisps, and a couple of lagers in a sleazy bar.

He was at work, following a suspect. But how serendipitous deception so often turns out to be. He would never know what hand of fate, ill or otherwise, persuaded his target to enter the same obscure back-street bar as his wife and George that day.

He'd discovered them *inflagrante,* but had remained oblivious for some moments, his attention entirely devoted to watching his target, a beak-nosed anorexic sixteen-year-old who was trying to fence a pocketful of hot watches that one of his mates had liberated at gun-point from a jeweller's safe. Sarah half rose from a dimly lit nook, flustered into motion like a pheasant put up by a beater. He might never have noticed if she had remained seated and kept quiet. But her conscience was pulling the strings.

"Hello David," she said, catching his eye.

That greeting alone should have alerted him. Not, "Hello Love," or, "Hello Dear." "Hello David." So formal. Businesslike almost. Twenty-odd years of using the same toilet and sleeping in the same bed and she said, "Hello David," with as much familiarity as she may have used to address the butcher.

"This is George," she continued, with a nervous hand gesture, as if she expected him to know who George was.

Bliss looked puzzled, but his right hand automatically stretched toward the stranger expecting a shake. The stranger shrank back, anticipating a punch, and Bliss sought an answer in his wife's face.

"George is ..." she started at last, but her face said: Surely you recognise him. You're wearing his bloody underpants.

"Yes, Dear," said Bliss, urging her to finish the statement. But he knew — of course he knew. Who was he kidding? But his pride wouldn't let him make it easy.

The silence between them may have lasted eternally had not George summoned courage from somewhere. Pushing his chair back with a teeth-clenching screech, he stood. "David, I think it's time you knew that Sarah and I have decided to move in together."

"That's nice for you, George," Bliss said stupidly.

Sarah clearly thought it was stupid as well. "Is that all you can say?"

What did she want him to say? What's expected of a man in a situation like this? Did she expect him to fly into a jealous rage? Was he supposed to invite George outside and bop him?

"You can do what you want," was all he could think of saying as he stalked away, beginning to feel the itch of the George's underpants. The young villain had pocketted the hot watches and scarpered, so Bliss headed for another bar.

It sank in about an hour later as he sat drowning his sorrows. I should have smashed his face to a pulp, he decided. That's what she wanted. That's what a real man would have done. Then I should have dragged her home and given her a right seeing to.

He swallowed his drink in a single gulp and, holding the empty glass in the air, spoke to the barman as if he were aware of the entire situation. "She was waiting for me to prove I still wanted her enough to fight for her."

"They all do mate," he replied knowingly, refilling the glass. "They all do."

Sarah had gone when he eventually got home. Just one hurriedly packed suitcase, replaced with a scrawled note: "Sorry David. I've told Samantha."

The ground opened beneath him and he started to plummet. She had walked away with twenty-five years of his life — the best twenty-five years. Twenty-five years of accumulated memories. More importantly, she had stolen his hopes and dreams for the next twenty-five. *Their* hopes and dreams, he had thought: the ivy covered cottage near the sea, long walks on the beach in the sunset, reliving simple childhood pleasures with the grandchildren. *Their* grandchildren. Not step-grandchildren. Not confused grandchildren enquiring, "Are you my real Grandpa?" *Their* grandchildren playing in *their* garden; *their* grandchildren opening Christmas presents in front of *their* fire. Gone. His dreams — *their* dreams —snatched away by George and his hairy nostrils.

Why? Why? Why? His head was going to explode. All the hurt, anger, loneliness, and love swirling around in his brain was too much. Too many thoughts. Too many synapses firing simultaneously and sending out contradictory signals.

Some form of telepathy between father and daughter alerted Samantha to his distress.

"Are you all right, Dad?"

Her question snapped him back to the present. "Yeah," he replied, but his voice was shaky.

"You said on the phone you wanted some advice."

He took a few seconds to push Sarah and George to one side, then said, "I want to know how a man could kill his own daughter."

"I hope you're not thinking of practicing on me."

"Oh, Sam!"

Her face shone in the gleam of oncoming head-lights. She was joking.

"Maybe," he said with a serious tone, joking back

She laughed, "You don't need a lawyer. You need a psychiatrist."

You could be right, he thought to himself, but said, "You don't understand. It's serious. I let a murderer go free twenty years ago and he killed again."

Her voice took on a critical, lawyer-like tone. "Did you have sufficient evidence to prosecute?"

He shook his head. "I didn't look for any evidence. I broke the cardinal rule. I assumed it was an accident instead of assuming it was murder."

"And now you believe it was murder?"

"I'd bet my pension on it."

The trattoria, a favourite lunchtime haunt of Samantha and her legalist friends, was brash, noisy, and big. Big tables for big families, big plates, big steaming mounds of pasta, and the constant din of Pavarotti belting out pop operas. Bliss made a point of seeming disappointed with the menu. "Don't they have any real food?"

The waiter, Italian by necessity, overheard as Bliss had intended. "What would sir consider real food?"

Samantha stepped in. "Ignore him, he's in a bad mood. He's lost a murderer."

Bliss shot her a look of alarm but the waiter shook his head, laughing lightly. "You lawyers," he said.

"We'll both have the penne Alfredo with a couple of skewers of the lemon garlic prawns. Thank you, Angelo," said Samantha, figuring her father was in no frame of mind to make a rational choice. Bliss considered protesting but instead asked for a very large scotch.

"You can't," Samantha asserted. "You're driving us home."

Feeling thoroughly defeated, he settled for a small scotch on the condition that he could have a glass of wine with the meal.

As Angelo moved away Samantha whispered, "His name's Godfrey really." Bliss blurted out a laugh and she shushed him noisily with a finger to her lips. "So tell me about your murderer, Dad."

"Murderers," he said, and briefly recounted the circumstances of the three Gordonstone deaths and Betty-Ann's missing file.

"So what's your plan?" she asked when he had finished. "Go to the powers that be and confess everything? Confess you screwed up? There was no evidence. You said so yourself."

"The evidence was probably there, I just didn't find it."

"Legally speaking, that's immaterial. If there's no evidence of murder how can there be any proof you screwed up. Even if you're correct about the girl, there was only one witness, his wife, and she's been dead for ten years. You won't get much of a statement from her."

"But he killed her as well."

"Dad. It was suicide, the coroner said so."

"He was wrong."

"You don't know that, and in any case without a witness ..." She left the sentence hanging; she had made her point.

Bliss gave her a sly look, as if he were holding all the aces. "What if I found a witness?"

"You're a bloody lawyer's nightmare. A client who insists on confessing the truth, even when there isn't a shred of evidence to back up the prosecution's case."

"But there is evidence ... at least I think there is."

Samantha peered over the top of her wine glass and her wide brown eyes urged him to continue.

"What about the other daughter," he said. "She must have known what was going on. I'm sure they kept me away from her because she knew her father killed her sister."

Putting the glass down slowly, Samantha considered her reply, then jabbed a spoke into his wheel. "Dad, she was only a kid. This happened twenty-odd years ago.

Whatever she says now, a good lawyer would punch a dozen holes in her testimony: False memories, survival guilt, revenge against her father for precipitating her mother's suicide. Not to mention the fact that although she's been beyond his control for the past ten years she hasn't found it necessary to come forward and point the finger at him."

Bliss was not easily deterred. "I bet she was terrified of him. Everybody else was."

Samantha studied her father carefully. "Were you frightened of him?"

He contemplated his answer carefully and found himself walking through a mental minefield. Frightened? he asked himself. Was I? And should I admit it, even to myself?

"No ..." he began, then started again. "Yes. In a way, yes. Not physically, but he had a sort of aura. Like a ..." Bliss found himself stumped for a simile.

"Like an Old Bailey judge," suggested Samantha.

"Yeah. You know the feeling."

"Doesn't everyone?"

It must be part of every judge's training, Bliss thought. Somebody must give them lessons in how to scare the pants off you with just a look.

Dinner arrived. Bliss checked his watch: twenty-five minutes. Giving the pasta a poke he grumbled, "What were you doing Godfrey, making it?"

Samantha tried killing him with a look, but failed.

"It's Angelo, sir. And yes, we make it fresh for each customer."

"That was spiteful," Samantha said as soon as the waiter left.

"Sorry. I'm just fed up with everyone dumping on me all the time. I've got no one else to take it out on, besides the cat."

They began the meal in embarrassed silence, then Samantha started thinking aloud about Margaret, Gordonstone's eldest daughter. "Let's just say she did play ball and spilled the beans about her father killing her sister. What good would that do you? What are you going to do, insist they prosecute you for perjury?"

"Neglect of duty," he suggested, his expression making it clear he had given the prospect careful consideration.

"Come off it, Dad, you're just trying to get rid of the guilt. You just want someone to absolve you of your sins. Shit. If you're that concerned why not go the whole hog: become a Roman Catholic, go to confession, say three Hail Marys, and you'll be right as rain."

"Don't be funny, Sam, I'm quite serious."

"So am I, Dad."

Undeterred, Bliss insisted on laying out his thoughts about Gordonstone's eldest daughter. "I reckon she went to Canada to keep clear of him. Put yourself in her place. He'd killed your sister and convinced the police it was an accident, then he makes your mother's murder look like suicide. You'd be scared to death."

"She wouldn't be scared now he's dead," Samantha mused, then saw a look of triumph spreading across her father's face and acted quickly to dispel it. "Dad, I'm not saying you're right. I'm not agreeing with you." His face clouded again as she continued, "What I am saying is, even if she was scared to come forward earlier, there is nothing stopping her now, so why hasn't she?"

"Maybe she's waiting for someone to ask," he replied, his tone and expression indicating he had every intention of being the one to do it.

Bliss declared himself full when Samantha toyed with the desert menu and said she was considering the Tiramisu.

"How do you stay so slim?" he laughed, reaching over and giving her a prod. Her eyes dropped automatically to her belly. She looked up, a worried frown across her forehead. "Actually, Dad, there's something I've been meaning to tell you." Her expression warned him to keep quiet. "I think I'm going to have a baby."

It took a few seconds to sink in. "You think ...?"

A smile spread back over her face. "Oh, don't worry, it's probably a false alarm. I don't expect you want to be a grandfather, not yet anyway, not at your age."

Without giving him an opportunity to reply she slapped down enough money to make up for Godfrey's hurt feelings and was on her way to the door.

The meeting between Superintendent Edwards and DCI Bryan had started cordially, with Edwards pouring the chief inspector a coffee.

"What's this I hear about Bliss ferreting about in central records, nosing into the Betty-Ann Gordonstone case?" Edwards said.

"He thinks it may be linked to Gordonstone's murder somehow."

"Rubbish."

"That's my view. I've told him to lay off and concentrate on finding Gordonstone's killer."

Edwards waved Bryan to a chair. "Look, I think it might be a good idea to yank him from that case. Put somebody else on to it."

"Oh no, sir." Bryan said. "I think he's the right man for the job as long as he stays focussed."

"And if he's not up to the job?"

"I believe he is, sir."

"All I'm saying, Peter, is don't stick your neck out for him. He isn't worth it. A man who can't separate his personal life from the job is a liability. You know that."

Bryan gave a noncommittal nod. "He's also a damn good copper who happens to have been through a rough time. That last case nearly got him killed."

"Don't get sentimental, Chief Inspector, that was nearly a year ago. We're running a police force not a bloody kindergarten."

"I know that, sir. But we all have problems from time to time."

"Yeah. And we leave 'em at the door."

The chief inspector wasn't going to argue and contented himself with mumbling, "We all make mistakes."

Edwards heard. "Humph. The only time people say that is when they've just made a bloody great balls-up."

"Are you saying it was a mistake to give Bliss the case?"

Edwards need not have answered, his expression made his feelings clear. "Let me put it this way: it was your idea, so I'll hold you personally responsible if he screws up. If you want to keep him on the case, on your head be it."

"That's a risk I'm prepared to take, sir."

"Right, well keep him under control. Give him two weeks at the most, and for God's sake keep him focussed. You know me, Peter, I like to give a man a fair shake." I know you, thought Bryan, staring at his feet. A pompous toad who'll jump on anyone if it makes you look good. The secretaries know you as well — I've heard them warning newcomers, "Don't bend over in front of Edwards, 'cos he'll whop a finger up your fanny as soon as look at you." And how come you drive a filthy great Mercedes and holiday in Fiji? It's a wonder Internal Investigations aren't camped out on your front lawn. Oh ... I know you, all right.

"So," said Edwards, his tone indicating he'd had the last word and the meeting was over. Bryan was half out of the door before he realized he hadn't even started his coffee.

The pavement was still damp from an overnight shower when Samantha answered the front door to her neat, terraced house, half a slice of dry toast sticking out of her mouth.

"Sorry I'm late," said her father, slipping into the barely furnished hallway. "Busses," he muttered, without need of further explanation.

She waltzed past him down the short hallway, stepped into her shoes, slid on her coat, and swallowed the toast in a single fluid motion. "I've got to get going," she called, half out of the front door. "Your stuff's in the attic." she added sourly, "And don't mess my place up."

"Would I?" he called, genuinely offended.

She turned. "I've seen your place, remember."

Bliss ignored the innuendo and pointed a finger at her belly. "Have you told your mother about … ?"

She dismissed the question with an unconcerned, "Not yet," and quickly changed the subject as she made for her car. "Must dash. I've got an indecent assault at Snaresbrook Magistrates."

"Prosecuting?" he asked, hopefully.

"Defending," she replied over her shoulder, knowing how much it would aggravate him.

"Hm," he grunted, but refused to be drawn.

Swinging a bulky brown briefcase onto the rear seat, she leapt behind the wheel and shouted, "Don't forget to lock up behind you," as the engine burst into life. She was gone before Bliss could object.

Samantha's whirlwind exit left an uncanny stillness in its wake. Bliss felt Melanie Gordonstone's ghost calling him. He knew she was there, in the attic — it was the reason for his visit — yet suddenly he found himself stalling. What was he scared of? What harm could she do him now? Was she seeking revenge?

The only coffee in Samantha's kitchen — instant decaffeinated — compared favourably with the stuff available in the police canteen, but then, so would used engine oil, he thought. But at least she had fresh milk. He drank two cups before venturing to the loft.

The time-worn buff folder with nibbled edges, creased corners, and faded green treasury tags jumped out at him and he did not need to read the label. He stared blankly at the file; opening it was unnecessary, he already knew every detail, even the stain made by a wayward tea cup in 1983, and he was unable to explain, even to himself, why he had bothered to search it out.

Back downstairs, in Samantha's living room, he dropped the unopened file on the coffee table and scanned through the contents in his mind. He could recall every word with almost the same precision as he could recite the Lord's Prayer or take the Oath in court. There was, he knew, a statement headed 'Martin Gordonstone, father of deceased,' together with statements from Betty-Ann Gordonstone, née Miller, mother of deceased, Dr. Mohammed Akbar, GP, and Dr. Eugene Finestein, pathologist. There was also another statement, the first one in the file, had he chosen to look. He knew it was there but his mind worked hard to blot it out, to pretend it didn't exist — to pretend it had never existed. It was the statement of twenty-two-year-old Detective Constable David Anthony Bliss.

He escaped to the kitchen, threw open the window, lit a cigarette, and made himself another coffee. It was no better than the first two, but its preparation filled time and occupied his mind.

The temptation to open the file eventually nagged him back into the room. Melanie's spirit was demanding action; not retribution — it was too late for retribution now, he knew, but not too late to excavate the truth and satisfy the poor girl's soul, not to mention the balm it might apply to his conscience.

The file still lay accusingly on the table despite his prayers that it might have vanished. Tearing his eyes away from it, he deliberately distracted himself by scouting around the room for signs of Samantha's pregnancy. What had changed? Nothing, as far as he could see. The little house looked the same as usual. Like Samantha, he thought: neat, clean, and compact. More books than a junior school, less furniture than a squatter's pad.

"What do you expect to find?" he said to himself and tried casting his mind back to the time that Sarah had been pregnant with Samantha. But he shook his head after a few seconds realizing that the memories had faded beyond recognition and he questioned whether the images of his beautiful young wife he managed to summons were recollections or fantasy. Thoughts of Sarah, still young and still his wife, triggered a flood of emotion and his face started to crumple. "Stop it," he ordered, and managed to pull himself together.

Perhaps Samantha has bought a book on childbirth, he thought, changing the subject away from Sarah, scanning the bookshelves crammed with legal texts. But there was little room on Samantha's shelves for such trivia as the birth of a baby. What else, he wondered. A pregnancy testing kit in the bathroom, a fridge full of peanut butter, or a cupboard full of Fry's chocolate creams. He searched fruitlessly. No cuddly toys, no photos of herself when she was a baby — nothing.

Maybe it is a false alarm. Damn, he thought, realizing he'd been so preoccupied with his own problems he'd never asked the obvious: Who's the father? He scolded himself for his lack of interest, but noted that she hadn't volunteered the information. She would have told me if she'd wanted me to know, he reasoned. What would she have said if I had asked? Mind your own fucking business, probably, he thought with a smile. Then quite irrationally he became angry. "It *is* my business," he declared out loud. "A quarter of the poor little sod will have my genes." The idea tickled him, twenty-five percent of his identity going to make up a new life and marching off into the future.

The thought of a young child dragged him back to the file on the table. There were, he knew, photographs of a child in the file. Death-scene photographs, taken to show the coroner every gory detail of the unfortunate incident. He sat slowly, and picked up the file, picturing every detail of the photographs. They were, he recalled, not at all gruesome. Not like the usual murder pictures. No blood, no faces contorted in agony, no jagged wounds, no severed body parts with protruding bones, no brains and skull fragments splattered all over the front of an express train or patterned across a wall. Just a little girl sleeping peacefully in a hospital cot and the same little figure, naked, sculpted out of polished white marble, as she lay on the mortuary table awaiting the mortician's knife.

He continued to resist the temptation to open the file. There is no point, he thought, defying the power of his own conscience. Why punish yourself again?

You deserve to be punished, said his conscience, playing Devil's advocate.

"Don't open it."

Open it.

"Don't open it."

Punish yourself.

"Don't punish yourself anymore."

Temptation won. He opened the file. The photographs lay on top and he slowly shuffled through them sad nostalgia. The little stone cherub had not aged. One of the photographs was missing, although he could not remember where it had gone. But he was able to conjure it up from memory: the light blue lake dappled with touches of white from a few passing clouds, some trees — bushes really, hawthorn and elder, he recalled — tiny pink splotches of water lilies hiding amongst a raft of greenery, the shadow of a taller tree falling across a patch of water and muddying it with a deep grey tint. And there, in the centre, was a shoe forming a tiny red speck that looked more like a glitch in the film than something tangible in the water.

It was the cameraman, the scenes of crime officer, who spotted it through his lens and called Bliss's attention.

"Did she have her shoes on?"

He hadn't noticed, he had been so wrapped up in his frantic efforts to breathe life into her.

A phone call to the emergency room soon answered the query. "Yes, one of her shoes was missing, the left one."

She must have kicked it off when she was struggling in the water, they had decided. He remembered the semisubmerged shoe vividly. Wading out to retrieve it with his trousers rolled knee high. A red sandal, Clark's, size ...? He'd forgotten the size and tortured his brain for a full half minute before deciding it was immaterial.

Although he had forgotten the shoe size he remembered the ambulanceman, a gentle giant of a man who tenderly scooped the little body off the grassy bank with hands as big as shovels and swung her onto the stretcher. Bliss still had his lips affixed to hers as the man carried the stretcher to the waiting ambulance, he was still blowing, still breathing movement into her chest, and his tears still trickled onto her tiny cheeks. Within moments a plastic oxygen mask had replaced his mouth and the ambulance drove away, a mechanical respirator now pumping air into the lifeless lungs, the little chest heaving futilely, mocking life. Her tiny heart no longer even trying to beat. Each future page of her life's passport now stamped with a single word, "Dead"

And under the photographs in the file lay *the* statement. His statement. The statement headed, "This statement of David Anthony Bliss, consisting of two pages, each signed by me, is true to the best of my knowledge and belief and I make it knowing that if it is tendered in evidence I shall be liable to prosecution if I have wilfully stated in it anything which I know to be false or do not believe to be true."

He didn't read the statement, he had no need, but the final paragraph leapt off the page accusingly. "I believe that Melanie Ann Gordonstone, aged 6 years, wandered away from the house and accidentally fell into the lake while her parents, Martin and Betty-Ann Gordonstone, were otherwise engaged." Those words, those exact words, had reverberated confidently around the Coroner's Court twenty years earlier, in the clear calm voice of the young policeman standing in the witness box. And the voice of the coroner, an older, gravelly voice filled with quiet authority and a lifetime's experience, invited him to confirm the statement so there should be no doubt in anyone's mind. "Is that your honest belief, Officer?"

"It is, Sir," Bliss had replied.

"Thank you, Officer. No further questions."

He had faltered leaving the witness box and looked at the faces in the sparsely peopled room: the stoic face of Martin Gordonstone; the dishevelled face of his wife, a poor crumpled figure who had snivelled throughout the twenty minutes of the proceedings and had been excused from giving evidence by the coroner on the basis that she had no material facts to offer; the impassive face of a reporter from the local paper who'd seen it all before. He'd seen the sad faces, heard the sorry stories and the guilt-ridden excuses: "I only left her for a minute, I don't know how it could have happened." It happens, he thought, all too often it happens. And, at the back of the courtroom, Bliss spied a huddle of grieving relatives awaiting the next inquest, an inquest into the death of a ninety-three-year-old victim of road accident.

There was no sign of Margaret. No twelve-year-old weeping tears for her little sister. In fact, as far as anybody in the courtroom was concerned, Margaret might never have existed. Gordonstone had hardly mentioned his surviving daughter as he recounted his well-rehearsed story. Bliss, in his evidence, though not in his statement, had carefully avoided making reference to Margaret; he had no wish to explain why he hadn't interviewed her. Everybody, it seemed, had avoided mentioning Margaret.

With no further witnesses to be called, the grey-haired coroner removed his half-spectacles and, doing his best to inject as much sympathy as he could into his voice, pronounced that Melanie Ann Gordonstone had been the victim of a tragic accidental death. But he'd seen it all before, as well.

"We thought it would be too upsetting for Margaret to attend," explained Gordonstone loudly in the foyer outside, after the verdict had been handed down. It seemed a reasonable assertion at the time; it was only later that Bliss wondered about the true meaning of the statement. Would it have been too upsetting for Margaret, or would it have been too upsetting for her father if she had used the opportunity to blurt out that he had killed her sister? And, Bliss thought, why had Gordonstone found it necessary to make such a loud and public declaration about Margaret's absence? Isn't it usually the guilty who most vociferously protest their innocence?

chapter five

The man who shot the videotape had not been impressed with *L'Haute Cuisinier*, even before the episode with the owner. Bliss, anxious to view the tape, found himself standing on the threshold of George Weston's apartment listening to a catalogue of complaints about the restaurant, which included the prices, the parking, the service and, amusingly, the height of the food.

"Why is it," the man demanded, fiercely stretching his bright red suspenders in a show of annoyance, "Why is it, that some chefs believe indifferent food can be improved by giving it a vertical aspect?" Weston strongly suspected that they were pandering to the American tourists, whom, he believed, were far more likely to applaud an audacious culinary balancing act than a subtle gastronomic conjuring trick. "Even the names signify loftiness," he whined nasally, his affected Oxbridge accent overlaying a Cotswold twang. "Gateau Mont Blanc, Mile High soufflé; A stack of ... Whatever." The only thing higher than the food was the price, he moaned. "Even the name of the place, *L'Haute Cuisinier* . . ."

Bliss managed to stop him momentarily by suggesting they should go inside, but Weston's griping began again as soon as the door was shut. "Why?" he continued loudly, thumbs still tucked into suspenders. "Why is it so necessary to set fire to everything in front of the customers?"

At this point Bliss cut him short and more or less demanded he hand over the tape. But he was determined to have a final all-encompassing grumble and, sounding like a newspaper's restaurant critic, he summed up *L'Haute Cuisinier* as, "A high class brothel for gourmands: piles of trashy food plastered in cheap perfumes and tarted up with gaudy cosmetics to make it appealing."

Finally consenting to get round to the tape, he apologized that he only had a copy. The original, he claimed, had been given to a television reporter who had called earlier. Bliss's black look left Weston in no doubt that he should not have disposed of the original, especially to a reporter.

"You should have come first thing this morning, when I called, if you wanted it that badly," he said defensively, leaving Bliss stumped for a reply.

Bliss would have viewed the tape there and then, but felt a visual reminder of the restaurant would only be inviting a further critical tirade. "Thank you very much, Sir," he said quickly, as he headed toward the door.

"I say. Could I have a receipt?"

"I'll mail you one," replied Bliss over his shoulder, with absolutely no intention of doing so.

"I've picked up that video of Gordonstone kicking the bucket," Bliss said lightly, poking his head into Detective Chief Inspector Bryan's office following a pub lunch and a whole packet of Polo mints. "Do you want to have a shufty?"

Bryan appeared taken by surprise. "Oh! Hang on, Dave. Come in a second will you, I need to have a word."

Bliss strolled in, noticing a recent addition to Bryan's already extensive assortment of houseplants. "It's beginning to look like a greenhouse in here."

The chief inspector idly fingered the leaf of a plant that, to Bliss, may just as easily have been a rose as a rhododendron. "I'm thinking of starting a gardening club. Interested in joining?"

"In my poky place — you're joking. I couldn't grow a decent-sized bacteria."

The DCI forced a laugh. "It looked as though you were trying."

"I've had a good clean up since then," Bliss replied sheepishly.

DCI Bryan picked up a wire paper clip he'd been using as an earwax remover and began fiddling with it, flexing it back and forth. "Dave, there's no easy way to say this," he began, his eyes glued to the paper clip. The wire snapped with a click; Bryan flicked the bits toward a waste bin and looked Bliss in the eye. "I've decided to take you off the Gordonstone case. I'll find you something else."

"What's going on, Guv?"

"It was my mistake. I think it would be better if we eased you back in with something smaller. A burglary or fraud perhaps."

"This is crap. The day before yesterday you were pleading with me to take it. Now you want me off it?"

"It's Edwards," the chief inspector admitted.

"What?"

"He wants you off the case. Right now."

"Why?"

"This isn't a murder enquiry, Dave; this is politics. I warned you to play it quietly; you went in like a bull in a china shop; now the press are onto it and he's furious."

"The press were bound to find out sooner or later. Anyway, it would have looked funny if the first time the public knew it was murder was when we announced it at the inquest. There must be more to it than that."

Bryan fidgeted with his fingers. "There is. I told you to leave the past alone. He doesn't want to get involved —"

Bliss cut in with irritation. "But he was involved. He was in charge of Gordonstone's wife's case."

"Quite."

"So why does he want me off the case?"

"Think about it, Dave. If you proved Gordonstone killed his wife it would make him look a fool."

"He doesn't need me to make him look a fool. In any case, whoever takes over is just as likely to come to the same conclusion."

"Leave it alone, Dave."

"Damned if I will," shouted Bliss, starting to rise.

Bryan switched tack and attempted persuasion. "Dave, don't do anything rash. If Edwards had his way you'd be off the force."

"On what grounds?"

"He mentioned psychological unfitness."

"The psychiatrist gave me a clean bill."

Bryan spread his upturned hands in a throwaway gesture, which was reflected in the nonchalance of his tone. "You know what psychiatrists are like, Dave. They blow with the wind. One day they'll say you're as sane as ..." he shrugged but couldn't think of anything sufficiently sane to prove his point. "And the next you are only fit for the loony bin."

"You mean they'll say what they are told to say."

"Something like that."

"They wouldn't do that," cried Bliss, then added somewhat uncertainly. "Would they?"

Bryan's sly look implied that they would. "Don't take it personally ..." he began, leaving Bliss thinking that whenever anybody said that he could be sure they were about to be exceedingly personal.

He wants me off this case for his own bloody reasons, Bliss thought, and shot out of the chair. "It's too late. You gave me this case and I intend finishing it," he said as he made for the door. "If he wants me off the case he can damn well tell me himself." •

Bryan tried to mollify him. "Look Dave. He told me that if you didn't drop the case I should suspend you pending a full psycho—"

"I'll see about that," he shouted, clipping the chief inspector off mid-sentence.

Bliss's footsteps pounded down the corridor, shaking furniture and rattling ornaments in adjacent offices. His face, set firmly in Edward's direction, was growing angrier by the second and he burst into Edwards' office, fuse lit and primed for detonation, but was unprepared for the salvo of verbal shrapnel fired in his direction by the expectant senior officer.

"How dare you just march into my office? You're an incapable lout, not fit to scrub the shithouse." Scruffy, drunken, and stupid entered into the tirade, each preceded by a liberal assortment of foul expletives and he climaxed with, "You incompetent bastard." Edwards wound down with, "You even lost your car," as if that were Bliss's own fault and stabbed in a final, deeply wounding, sneer. "No wonder your wife left you," as if that were Bliss's own fault as well.

Some clerical workers in surrounding offices found themselves physically ducking the barrage, while other police officers pulled embarrassed faces at each other and winced in mock pain.

Bliss started to leave. "I'm not going to listen to this."

Edwards was at the door in a flash, stretched to his full height in his built-up shoes and puffed out like a predatory beach bum.

"Sit down!" he yelled with vehemence just short of hysteria. His booming command energized the atmosphere and deluded Bliss into believing that the substantially shorter officer was towering over him. Losing both his momentum and his nerve, Bliss sat. But his firing pin had been pulled, the fuse within him was burning — the fuse which had smouldered for ten months now fanned into flames by anger, resentment, guilt, and fear. Anger against Edwards, the world, and whomever had stolen his car; resentment against Gangly George for usurping his wife; guilt for letting Gordonstone off the hook; and finally — the fear of an uncertain future.

Edwards reached his chair on the other side of his leather-topped mahogany desk and sat, incognizant of the explosion building in the man opposite. He completely misdiagnosed the symptoms of Bliss's pent-up frustration, mistaking his angry fixed stare for insolence and his tensed posture for defiance. Three words from Edwards, delivered quietly but with meaningful venom, were all it took. "You fucking disgrace."

The fuse torched the detonator, the detonator blasted the dynamite and Bliss erupted with a ferocity few would have believed possible of the usually mild man. Leaping to his feet and shouting, "You bastard!" he hoisted the immense desk and hurled it in Edwards' direction. Edwards fell from his chair as he scrabbled to get out of the way and was hit by a storm of paper cascading from the drawers as hundreds of heavy files burst open. A computer screen imploded as it crunched on the floor. Telephones, lamps, photographs, and an assortment of stationery flew all around him. Edwards, on his back on the floor, disappearing under the flying debris, flung out his hands in defence and there was an audible *crack* as his right wrist gave way under the weight of the heavy wooden desk.

For the briefest of moments there was calm in the turmoil, like the patch of clear blue sky in the eye of a hurricane, and then, in a kind of delayed reaction, a weighty onyx ashtray slid slowly down the inclined leather surface of the desk and smacked Edwards firmly between the eyes.

No one rushed to investigate. Herd instinct cautioned against involvement in a solitary victim's struggle for survival. In any case, violent noises from the direction of Edwards' office were not uncommon. He was frequently heard angrily stamping around, raging about this or that, and viciously lashing out at the furniture. Rumour had it he'd even kicked the odd policeman, although none had ever put his masculinity on the line by publicly complaining.

Bliss, stupefied but not wholly unimpressed by the result of his action, stood back for a fraction of a second, examined his hands in disbelief, and seriously wondered, Did I do that? Life changed so radically in those few seconds that his brain initially refused to comprehend the consequences, then he found himself sharing the desire of a million other victims of self-inflicted suffering: the desire to go back in time just one minute and select a different route. But the deed was done; there was no going back.

Edwards pulled his thoughts together, struggled unsuccessfully to release himself from the weight of the desk using his undamaged arm, then reached for the phone which had fallen beside him. Bliss made a grab for it, got there first, and yanked the cord out of the wall. He fought the instinct to run and actually bent with the intention of raising the heavy desk off his senior officer. He would have continued had Edwards not started screaming, "Help, help!" like a drowning man.

Bliss was out of the door in a flash.

"Stop that man!" The cry followed him out of the room.

"I've just resigned," he explained to several heads poking cautiously out of adjoining offices, and he slammed the door on the helpless superintendent.

Heads nodded with sympathetic understanding.

"Stop that man," yelled Edwards.

Bliss walked quickly down the corridor. "I don't think he wants me to leave really."

The understanding nods broke into smiles.

"Stop him!"

"I never knew he cared so much."

Smiles turned into laughter as Bliss boarded the world's slowest elevator and descended to the lobby, expecting at any moment that the building would crash on top of him.

The story streamed through the grapevine at Internet speed, reaching the divisional commander and the constable's locker room simultaneously. However, the furrowed frown of the commander contrasted sharply to the buzz of delighted excitement in the lower ranks. Any poke in the establishment's eye was cause for celebration among the grunts and, according to several wildly exaggerated accounts, Bliss had certainly poked Edwards' eye.

An ambulance had, strictly speaking, been unnecessary for a broken wrist and a bump on the forehead, but Edwards insisted. This was one molehill he was determined to turn into a mountain.

"Dad, where are you?" asked Samantha in response to Bliss's call.

"Sam, I can't talk, they may have bugged your phone."

"Can they do that?" she asked with a sudden chill.

"Legally ... no. But I wouldn't put it past them.

"You only broke his wrist for Christ's sake. It's not murder."

"There's more to it than that."

"Don't be silly, Dad. You're being paranoid."

"They want me off the case."

"I know ..." she paused. "Dad," she continued kindly, "Maybe they're right."

He couldn't believe it. She was on their side.

"What d'ye mean ... Maybe they're right? Edwards has been on my back for years. He'll love this. Broken wrist, that's GBH you know: grievous bodily harm. An indictable offence in case you've forgotten."

"But Dad, I hear you were provoked."

"How do you ... Who told you?"

"Chief Inspector Bryan was here looking for you. Said you should turn yourself in. He gave me the usual crap about making it easy on you."

"And what did you say?"

"I told him I was representing you and would advise you accordingly."

"And your advice would be?"

"Are you going to pay me for this?"

"Samantha ..."

"OK, Dad. But maybe you should consider going back. They're just worried, that's all. After what you've been through recently they were worried you might flip and ..."

"And I did. Is that what they're saying?"

"Dad. You broke his wrist for fuck's sake,"

"Samantha!"

"I know, I know, don't swear. But is it true? Did you?"

"Possibly," Bliss admitted grudgingly. "But he deserved it."

"He's still at the hospital shouting his mouth off about charging you."

"All I want is justice."

"You know as well as I do that justice is an intellectual concept unrelated to the truth."

"Jesus," he blurted. "Where the hell did you get that?"

She laughed. "Law school probably, but it's true Dad."

A faint buzzing alerted his already heightened senses. "What was that?"

"I didn't hear anything."

Bliss slammed the receiver down and walked quickly away from the payphone, slipping back into the pub where his half consumed drink still sat under the watchful eye of the barman. "Thanks," he said, sinking the rest of the double scotch in a single gulp, then slinking out of the bar with his head down. Twenty minutes later he was back on the phone. Another call box outside another pub. This time he called her mobile phone.

"It's me." he whispered, before she could even say who she was.

"Where are you?"

"Not telling."

"Don't be so childish."

"You might be working for the enemy."

"I'm not."

"I need you to do me a favour. Several actually."

She was very noncommittal. "What?"

"I need clothes, money, and my passport."

Genuine concern filled her voice. "Look, Dad. Why not just talk to Peter Bryan? It's not too late, it can all be sorted out. I don't think Edwards will press charges."

"Samantha, I'm not fleeing the country, I've just got to sort out a few things."

"Dad," she started crying. "It's OK. Everyone understands. You've been through a lot."

"Sam, I'm fine. There's nothing wrong with me. I think Edwards set me up deliberately. He wants me out for some reason. Do what I ask, please. Clothes, money, and passport in a suitcase. I'll call you in a couple of hours, OK?"

"I don't know, Dad," she replied, her tone suggesting it was unlikely — that she didn't think it was a good idea.

"Please," he begged.

"I'll think about it, but I'm not making any promises," she said as she slowly put down the phone and wiped a droplet from her cheek.

"What did he say?" enquired DCI Bryan, creeping up from behind and causing her to physically leap.

"How the hell did you get in my house?" she screamed, more in fright than anger.

"You left the door open. I said I'd be back."

"How long were you ... ? What did you...? How dare you ...? she said, starting three questions consecutively without expecting a reply to any of them.

"I knocked," he protested weakly, then continued without giving her room for contradiction. "Anyway, you shouldn't leave the door open. So, what did your father say?"

Samantha pulled herself together and lied calmly. "He said he'd be in your office at nine tomorrow morning."

Bryan smiled in relief. "Thank God for that."

"Now, if you'll excuse me, I have to get ready. I have a date."

"Nine o'clock?"

"That's what he said."

Bryan looked serious again. "Make sure he's there Sam."

"Roger Wilco," she replied, putting on her best impression of a colonel and throwing a salute.

He called again less than thirty minutes later, his impatience fuelled by nervousness. Samantha reacted angrily, refusing to help, citing her reputation, her career, even her freedom.

"They won't be watching my place," he assured her.

"Why don't you go yourself then?" she responded forcefully.

She had a point, he conceded, but persisted anyway. "Well, they might be—"

She cut him short. "Dad. I still think you should give yourself up and plead insanity."

She was joking, wasn't she? He laughed, but wasn't altogether sure why. Maybe she was right, he thought, maybe he was insane. Quickly dismissing the notion he was nevertheless left with a nagging thought buzzing in his mind. Does a crazy man know he is crazy?

An hour later a tartily dressed young mother manoeuvred her rummage-sale pram through the street doors of Bliss's apartment block and shrieked at the sight of a man, all in black, crouching under the concrete stair-well, the pram's usual parking spot.

"Police," he said quietly, pointing to the badge on his shirt. Another officer was creeping up behind her.

"What's going on," she demanded loudly, hoping to attract someone's attention.

"Shhh," the officer behind her shushed soothingly. She leapt round with a start. "There's nothing to be worried about, Madam," he said, but the fear in her eyes told him that she thought differently. "Just come with me," he added, gently placing his hand on her arm.

Ripping her arm from his grasp she started backing away, pram in tow. "I ain't going nowhere wiv you ..." she started, but he blocked her path, all six-feet-two-inches of his frame filling the doorway.

"What's going on?" she repeated.

He smiled reassuringly. "You can't go in at the moment."

"Why not? What about the kid's tea?"

The kid's tea would have to wait, he explained, then frightened her half to death by telling her the place was surrounded by armed policemen.

She agreed to go, to her mother's she said, just around the block, and no, she didn't need any help with the pram. "Bloody coppers," she mumbled as she passed another darkly clad figure squatting behind a rubbish bin in the backyard. Then she paused, struck by the unusual peacefulness: no screaming kids, no revving motorcycles, no traffic — not on their street anyway. And in the stillness she heard the cooing of a pigeon and mistook it for a cuckoo.

The plan for a stakeout of Bliss's apartment had been hatched by Superintendent Edwards and was being orchestrated from his hospital room. Despite his injuries he had insisted on taking command, his adrenalin overcoming the grogginess from the painkillers, and he was like a tornado, whipping up a storm, flattening everything in his path. A tactical support unit, a plainclothes surveillance team, and a dog handler had already been dispatched to back up the three detectives initially posted to watch the apartment.

Now a small gathering of unit supervisors and commanders shuffled awkwardly around the end of Edwards' bed, staring at the pastel walls, inhaling the aroma of disinfectant and floor wax, trying to ignore the performance of pitiable suffering that Edwards was putting on for them. Gritting his teeth, he squeezed his eyes shut and caught their attention with a woeful, though distinctly masculine, whimper.

"Thank you for coming," he exhaled, in a voice shot through with anguish. "It is essential that Bliss be found quickly, for his own safety," he continued, in a voice now loaded with sympathy. Many in the small group nodded knowingly, although DCI Bryan kept his head up and his face straight, determined not to be railroaded into anything that did not involve fair play for Bliss. The divisional commander, Edwards' immediate superior and usually a reflective, considered man, found himself being swept up and hauled along in the scheme without good reason to resist.

Embarrassment was another consideration, and Edwards sought agreement in the face of the divisional commander as he gravely intoned, "It is also essential for the good of the force that we find Bliss and keep the bloody press from becoming involved." Edwards naturally failed to mention that it was also in his personal best interest to stop Bliss from talking publicly. Tabloid headlines screaming, "Inspector Bops His Boss," would, he might have guessed, cause a great deal of sniggering behind his back.

Finally, deflecting the spotlight from himself completely, Edwards shone it directly on DCI Bryan. "Adverse publicity could seriously damage DCI Bryan's career," he said, staring straight at the other officer but talking as if he were persona non grata. "After all, it was DCI Bryan who encouraged Bliss to return to duty and assigned him to the Gordonstone case."

Bryan went beet red. Was he supposed to be grateful? Did Edwards expect to be thanked for trying to protect him from the media? He started to protest, but Edwards waved him away with a flick of his good hand, then reached across to the bedside table to pick up his radio.

"Where is Inspector Bliss now?" he asked one of the detectives at the scene.

"There's no change, sir," a female voice replied. "He went into his flat about half an hour ago and he's still there."

Edwards turned back to the small group. "He's violent, psychologically disturbed, and he may have suicidal tendencies."

This was too much for DCI Bryan. His jaw dropped. "Sir, I don't think we should go overboard. It's not as though he's a dangerous offender."

Edwards glowered at him. "You mightn't think so Chief Inspector, but look what he did to me." The plaster cast on his wrist and the inflamed swelling on his forehead certainly seemed to back up his assertion.

Bryan found himself feebly defending his own words. "He's been under a lot of stress recently, that's all."

Edwards rolled his eyes for the benefit of the others and continued with his impromptu briefing. "He may be armed —" Bryan, exasperated, tried again. "Sir, I don't think there is any evidence of that."

"You also thought he was fit to return to duty."
Edwards hissed.

"The psychologist said —"

Edwards cut him short. "Shut up and listen for
once. I warned you he wasn't fit. I told you it would be
your fault if anything went wrong. Well it bloody well
has gone wrong, so I suggest you leave this to me."

Bryan's resolve more or less collapsed, but he
made one last attempt. "I still don't think he'll be
armed," he mumbled.

"Well, I'm not going to take any chances." And,
pausing for effect, Superintendent Edwards added
solemnly, "We don't know what he might do."

Twenty minutes later the early evening gloom had faded
to darkness. A small bank of floodlights faced the apartment building but remained unlit, waiting, like everyone
else, for the right moment. Darkly clad figures scuffled
around the unkempt grounds seeking a clearer view of
Bliss's third floor apartment window, where shadowy
movements behind the curtains signalled the presence of
life. Others sought somewhere secluded for a snatched
cigarette.

A classroom at the back of the infant's school had
been hastily turned into an evacuation centre. One disgruntled resident, forced out of his home for the
evening, chose the local pub instead of the school and
tipped off the local newspaper with an anonymous call.
A press cordon of orange crime scene tape, patrolled by
a few tight-lipped uniformed bobbies, was set up half a
block away. Another of the evacuees had escaped from
the school and was blabbing to a small contingent of
scribbling journalists. "There's coppers swarming everywhere," said the publicity seeker, but he could offer no

further explanation. Neighbours in nearby apartments were quickly hunted down, cameras and microphones stuck in their faces. They knew nothing either.

The remaining evacuees, lounging reminiscently on desks, leafing through books with once familiar stories about naïve pigs and grumpy billy goats, rediscovered a sense of childhood camaraderie. Neighbours who had only ever nodded suspiciously, or complained about each other's kids, discovered commonalities transcending their racial and social backgrounds. Their petty grumbles temporarily forgotten, if not altogether forgiven, they conversed freely, anxiously debating what was happening. Told little, they imagined a lot. A fundamentalist's bomb factory was a favourite explanation, but the rumour evaporated with the arrival of the apartment building's only Muslim family. Attention switched to the 'dirty old man' who lived on the top floor, but no one gave any thought to the reclusive man from the third floor who, it was rumoured, was a policeman.

A dozen children, uncaring and largely unaware of what was happening, tore around the classroom, playing noisily and happily together, irrespective of colour or beliefs. They always had. They weren't old enough to be frightened of each other.

Outside, in the street, DCI Bryan informally briefed a huddle of sergeants under a streetlamp, well away from the frustrated press, and re-iterated his own beliefs forcefully. "We're concerned for DI Bliss's welfare, that's all."

"He is suicidal then?" suggested one, in the form of a question.

"I don't think so."

"Why are we here then?" asked another, his tone making it clear he had made other plans for the evening.

Don't ask me lad, Bryan felt like saying, but merely shrugged off the question with a blank face and an open-handed gesture.

"What if he starts shooting?" enquired a sergeant, mindful of Edwards' warning.

"He won't," said Bryan with a scornful laugh.

The sergeant, a stickler for protocol, wouldn't be fobbed off and insisted on knowing the rules of engagement. "But what if he does?"

DCI Bryan wouldn't be drawn. "Nonsense," he replied, refusing to consider such a possibility, but then he slipped quickly into the mobile incident van to avoid further awkward questions.

The converted van, sprouting antennae and buzzing with radios, phones, and computers, offered Bryan no haven; half a dozen pairs of eyes turned questioningly in his direction. Ignoring them, he tuned out the buzz, blanked his eyes, and thought: What if he does start shooting? What was Bliss waiting for? he wondered. Was he waiting for someone to shout, "Come on out with your hands up!" An old memory brought half a smile to Bryan's face. He had once used those exact words, in a public toilet in the middle of the night. Just for fun, for the amusement of a new recruit. "Here's how it's done lad," he had called, and marched straight into the vestibule shouting, "Come on out with your hands up!" To his utter amazement a stall door slowly opened and a renegade wanted for murdering his wife shuffled out, hands held high, crying, "Don't shoot! Don't shoot!" Bryan didn't shoot — he couldn't shoot, he didn't have a gun. But now half a dozen guns were trained on Bliss's windows and door. What if . . .?

"Sir, sir," a fuzzy-haired policewoman was addressing him; she may have been there for a second or a minute.

He shook himself out of his thoughts. "What's happened?"

She gave him a critical look. "Nothing, sir. Are you all right?"

"Fine," he replied, feeling anything but.

"Tea," she offered and scuttled off to get him a cup without waiting for a response.

He delved back into his thoughts. Why are we doing this? Why not just knock on Bliss's door? No one had even considered it. Everyone assumed he wouldn't come out. Why? he asked himself. Why had everyone assumed that? Edwards, he realized. Edwards had spooked them into believing Bliss was dangerous. Edwards the puppeteer; Edwards with his hand up your backside, making you dance and sing to his tune. Then, if something goes wrong, he'll whip out his hand and be first in line to point a shit-covered finger. Bliss wouldn't shoot — Bryan knew him too well. Then he had an awful thought. What if Edwards *wants* Bliss to shoot? What if he wants him shot?

Tea in hand, he kept his thoughts to himself and sidled up to the hostage negotiator, a civilian hunched over a phone in one corner; a man trained to talk, wanting to talk, ready to persuade, to cajole, to say anything to avoid bloodshed. "Pick it up. Pick it up," the man was murmuring, his headphones buzzing to the tune of Bliss's unanswered phone. Talking, negotiating, was difficult enough; not being able to negotiate was even more nerve-wracking. A dribble of sweat ran down his forehead and he brushed it aside. "Answer the bloody phone," he pleaded.

Bryan caught the man's attention with a gentle touch. He looked up and his eyes said there was nothing to report. No communication, no demands, no threats to harm hostages. But this case was different:

there were no hostages, unless Bliss himself was considered a hostage — a hostage in his own home, a hostage in his own mind, a hostage to his own misfortunes. Misfortunes largely self-inflicted.

Ten minutes later, just as the nine o'clock news on the television in Bliss's apartment was winding down with a brief mention of the siege, there had been no change. Then one of the communication officers thought the unthinkable, aloud: "Maybe he's already done himself in."

"He's definitely not answering," added the negotiator from his corner, conveying the premise that only dead people leave their phones unanswered.

DCI Bryan choked on the tea dregs, cleared his throat with a loud cough, and unwittingly attracted everyone's attention.

"He wouldn't do anything silly ..." he started, realizing he was expected to make a statement, but then he paused in reflection. Bliss had lost his wife and, possibly, his job. He was probably facing a criminal charge; disciplinary charges surely. He had certainly attacked Edwards. Had he? Edwards said so. Whatever happened to the presumption of innocence? Anyway, bopping Edwards was hardly a good reason for doing yourself in; there were many who would think he should be congratulated. Bryan stuck his head out of the van door, peered thoughtfully up at the faintly glowing window of Bliss's living room and mused. "Living in a shithole, wife gone, car nicked, job on the line ... Maybe he has flipped."

With a panicky voice he radioed one of the marksmen on the roof.

"I haven't actually seen him," came the reply. "Just the lights. Perhaps he's slumped in front of the telly . . ."

The word "slumped" finally jolted Bryan into action. "I'm going in," he announced, turning back into the incident vehicle

"We'll cover you," said one of the sergeants.

"That won't be necessary."

A couple of minutes later, heavily protected in a bulky bulletproof vest, and feeling somewhat traitorous for it, he sidled along the third floor landing toward the familiar door. Tapping lightly with a shaky hand he found himself edging to one side. There was no reply. The shotgun blast he half expected didn't come either.

Counting off ten seconds he tapped again, adding softly, "Dave, please answer."

Nothing. He wasn't surprised; he guessed that Bliss would be anticipating an ambush. Then, thinking he heard a movement inside, he gingerly laid his ear against the door and tapped again. Silence ... Wait! Was there a noise from in the room or was it his heart pounding? He took a deep breath and listened hard. The sound he heard was coming from inside the room: a moaning, no, a murmuring, a faint mumbling. "Dave," he called anxiously, thumping hard with the flat of his hand. "Dave, are you all right?"

A minute later, breathless, he was back inside the incident post. "He's there all right. We'll have to go in, and quickly."

Then Edwards arrived, his newly plastered arm picked out nicely by the bright florescent lighting in the vehicle. "I discharged myself," he proclaimed proudly, as if it were some kind of achievement. "What's happening, Chief Inspector?"

Bryan brought him up to speed.

"Well, you must do what you think is best," Edwards said, craftily lobbing a grenade into Bryan's court.

A blast with the force of a thousand firecrackers rocked the air less than a minute later and a freelance photographer who had sidestepped the police cordon smelt a champagne dinner, while the other journalists bulged forward against the orange tape with IRA on their lips. The pigeon's coo turned into a shriek of alarm as a pulse of dirty grey smoke ballooned out of Bliss's window and signalled the start of controlled mayhem.

Floodlights pierced the shattered window. Security systems in neighbouring apartments paused for a second in electronic thought, then screeched in alarm. The sledgehammer team, poised in readiness on the landing, swung a heavy iron head into Bliss's door. The locks held but the frame gave way. The crash-helmeted assault team swept over the door and through the gap, guns first, crouching, ducking, weaving, leapfrogging from one doorway to the next through the apartment.

It was over in less than four seconds. Shock tactics practiced in heavily furnished multiroomed buildings proved superfluous in the cramped starkness of Bliss's apartment.

Bliss's television, his sole sleeping partner for the past ten months, had taken the brunt of the blast. The old set — which had rocked with bomb blasts over Hanoi, Excocet strikes off the Falklands, and Scud attacks on Tel Aviv — had fallen victim to friendly fire. A youngish constable looked down at the smoking remains. "Christ, it still had valves!" he exclaimed, his voice full of nostalgia.

Bliss's tiny apartment was suddenly crammed with personnel jammed embarrassingly together, as if waiting for some unacceptably intimate act to occur. Then someone moved the old leather armchair and discovered Balderdash. The terrified cat, ticking off yet another life from its roster of nine, hissed like a burst bicycle tire, puffed himself up into a cartoon character, and prepared to pounce. One policeman's hand, offered in comfort, took a vicious swipe. Its owner shrieked in pain and another policeman's boot crashed into the old cat's skull — Ten!

Superintendent Edwards stepped out of the lift and viewed the carnage from the landing. "Well where is he then?"

The concerned look on DCI Bryan's face alerted the senior officer to the bad news.

"We definitely saw the lights go on," protested the woman detective who had been watching from a car in the street below.

DCI Bryan spun on her. "Did you actually *see* Inspector Bliss come home?"

"Not exactly," she admitted.

"Not exactly!" Edwards flung his head back in disbelief and cried out in genuine pain as the sling yanked at his broken wrist. "Well if he's not here where the bloody hell is he?"

chapter six

Bliss was riding on a tube train, sorting through the contents of his suitcase, wondering how many fugitives in history had used the Victoria line for their getaway. Samantha said she had done her best to find clean clothes; the stale smell emanating from the suitcase suggested failure. A blue uniform appeared in his peripheral vision, and his heart skipped a beat.

"Tickets, please."

He scrabbled through his pockets. The ticket inspector eyed him suspiciously. Wraparound sunglasses more suited to a rap singer with dreadlocks only served to accentuate his stature as a slightly balding, beer-gutted, grandfather-to-be. He ditched them under the seat as soon as the inspector turned away.

Every glimpse of a uniform spun his head. He tried not to react, telling himself not to be so foolish, reminding himself of the number of offenders he had personally caught only because they had reacted to his presence by attempting to run or hide. Had they played it cool, he might never have shown any interest.

Half a world away, and twenty-eight hours later, he was still nervously avoiding uniforms as he wandered around the terminal at Toronto's Pearson International Airport in a daze, half wondering how he got there and what he should do next. He checked his watch for the umpteenth time, comparing the result with the giant hands of the terminal's skeletal clock, which was as much an engineering exposition as a functional timepiece.

The clock's giant minute hand showed 10:01 P.M. and he drifted away, wandering idly around the terminal, trying to clog his mind with a plethora of irrelevant deliberations that would shut out Edwards and Sarah. It would be another hour or more before the sun would make its way up the Thames and over London's horizon so that he could call Samantha and make sure she was all right.

He had worried about her ever since their meeting in the bustling refreshment room at King's Cross station where she had passed him the suitcase, together with a small bundle of cash, with all the furtiveness of a cocaine dealer. She was concerned that she may have been followed. A suspicious-looking couple was sitting in a car outside his flat, she had told him, but he assured her that such events were common in the area in which he lived.

"Anyway," he said, "It's me they're after."

Clearly anxious, she kept her voice to a low whisper. "They might have been waiting for *you*, but they could have caught *me*."

"Since when has it been illegal to take a few things from your dad's flat?"

"I seem to remember an obscure offence of knowingly aiding a wanted criminal to escape justice."

"Samantha, be serious. I'm hardly Ronnie Biggs or Lord Lucan."

"I *am* being serious, Dad. You must have arrested people for a whole lot less than breaking someone's wrist in your time."

He was indignant. "It was an accident Samantha."

She was adamant. "That's what they all say. Anyway it won't stop them arresting you."

"Whose side are you on?"

"Yours," she replied with little conviction. "Anyway, where are you going?"

"I'm not telling anyone."

Her tone suggested she was genuinely hurt by his lack of trust. "Why? Do you think they are going torture it out of me?"

He ignored the sarcasm. "I'll call you when I get there."

"You could lose your pension over this."

"Never mind. I've got a successful daughter to support me."

"Forget it," she said harshly, then she softened. "Dad?"

"Uh huh."

"Do be careful."

"Who's being paranoid now? Anyway it's quite exciting being on the run. Funny, after all these years seeing it from the other side, at least I know what mistakes not to make."

"I have to go," she said with finality as they hugged for the fourth time, then she was swept away into the rush-hour crowd. He wiped the trace of tear from his eye as he approached the booking office window, then had to duck behind a cast-iron pillar to do so again before he could face the clerk.

It was nearly midnight at the airport and Bliss still felt close to tears as he stood by a bank of payphones watching the cleaning staff sweep and mop with a flamboyant furiousness that hinted it was time for all passengers to be somewhere else. Feeling out of place he picked up a phone and had an imaginary conversation while keeping his ears tuned to the cleaners as they vociferously decried the filthy habits of the travelling public.

"Look at this," bitched one, pointing to a glob of chewing gum stuck in the carpet and giving Bliss such a glower he almost felt responsible.

"I know," replied the other, in a voice weighed down by a lifetime's experience of misplaced chewing gum. "I know."

Every piece of dirt, every scuff mark and every full litter bin invited a further derogatory comment from one or other of the men, causing Bliss to speculate on the obvious. Without dirt, who would need cleaners? He had on many occasions applied the same principle to the police force. Without criminals, who would need the police? It was an argument he had, in the past, used to mollify fellow officers lamenting the loss of a case. "It's like fishing," he would say. "You have to let some get away otherwise you'll have nothing to catch the next time."

He put the phone down, picked it up again, and dialled Samantha's number. She answered almost immediately, her grumpy voice complaining it was still dark, then enquiring, "What's the time?"

"What's happening there?" he retorted, deliberately ducking her question.

"Peter is pretty pissed off with you."

"Peter now is it?"

She ignored him. "He promised Edwards you'd give yourself up yesterday morning. Edwards is threatening to charge him with neglect of duty if you don't show up soon."

"That's hardly likely."

"Are you sure you're doing the right thing?" she enquired, a mixture of concern and censure in her voice.

"Who knows, but it beats sitting around in that poky flat waiting for the world to end. I'm quite enjoying myself really ... Oh my God!"

"What!"

"The cat. Balderdash; I forgot all about him."

"Don't worry, I'm taking care of him."

"There's some tins of his favourite stuff in the cupboard over the sink."

"OK."

"And he likes milk in the ..."

Samantha knew all about Balderdash. Using her key to get into the small apartment the previous day, before DCI Bryan and his demolition squad arrived, she had soothed the old animal with a stroke and emptied a full can of Whiskers into his bowl. Then she had rounded up her father's passport and clothes before turning on the television to keep the animal company. "The cat's fine Dad, stop worrying," she assured him, unaware that the unfortunate creature had later died under a size 11 boot in the act of protecting his home, although she had been very conscious of the unmarked police car parked in the street outside as she prepared to leave.

"He likes a bit of chicken sometimes," Bliss was saying, but Samantha wasn't listening. Her mind was still on the two young detectives in the car, pretending to be a courting couple as they had watched for her father. Fearing they might recognize her, she had slipped lightly down the fire escape at the back of the building. Warily searching the shadows in the scrub below, she saw only an abandoned car, a rusted rubbish skip, and a broken down sofa. He must be able to afford something better than this, she'd thought. Maybe he wants to live here. Maybe he wants mum to feel sorry for him; maybe he's trying to make her feel guilty. Maybe, at one time, he even thought she would take him back.

Another detective, lounging lazily against a rotted wooden fence behind the building, had concentrated on trying to roll a cigarette in the gloom. She hadn't seen him and he had taken no notice of her—he had been waiting for Inspector Bliss.

"Dad," Samantha said into the phone, bringing her thoughts back to the present. "Stop worrying about the cat. I know what to do. Is there anything else?"

There was a definite pause as Bliss considered the prudence of disclosing his intended destination. "I need Margaret Gordonstone's address in Canada," he said finally.

"Canada?" she gushed. "You're going to Canada?"

He hesitated, but chose not to tell her that he was already there. "Yeah. I need to talk to Gordonstone's daughter. She's the key to this case, I'm sure. She must know something or he wouldn't have packed her off so quickly after her mother's death. He probably wanted to stop tongues wagging about their relationship."

Samantha caught on quickly. "In case someone suggested he bumped off his wife in favour of her."

"That seems to be the gist of the rumours. Anyway Edwards knows more than he's letting on. I wonder if he suspected the same thing at the time but didn't pursue it. He certainly made sure the file disappeared damn fast for some reason."

"Where am I going to find Margaret's address?"

"Try Gordonstone's lawyer, he must know. The restaurant belongs to her now, so he must be in contact with her."

"He'll probably claim confidentiality."

"Well promise not to tell anyone else then."

She laughed. "Just you."

"Yeah. I'll call you back later."

Mid-day in Toronto and Bliss checked his watch. Five o'clock in London. She should be home by now, he thought, and tried phoning again. Her machine willingly accepted the call and his credit card took another hit. He tried her mobile. The plastic card obligingly dished out some more money enabling him to listen to a complete stranger telling him his call could not be connected at that time. "She's probably on the tube," he said to himself.

He strolled down to the hotel lobby to kill time, and a copy of the previous day's *International Telegraph* caught his attention on the newsstand. He thumbed through it, half expecting to meet himself face-to-face in a grainy blow-up of his warrant card photograph. Nothing. In an effort to remain inconspicuous he found a secluded bar—a smokers' refuge in an otherwise hostile environment of smoke-free lounges—ordered a beer, and wasted another thirty minutes.

His third attempt on Samantha's home phone was successful but she wouldn't discuss anything, fearing the call was being monitored. She insisted he phone her back on her cellphone. He told her she was being ridiculous. She said she knew but was adamant, and he sustained a double hit on his credit card for her canniness.

"Where are you?" she demanded, her tone making it clear she expected the truth.

"Toronto," he confessed, now feeling reasonably safe.

"Oh. What's it like?"

He had no idea. He was still in the hotel where the East Indian taxi driver had taken him the previous night.

The turbaned driver, whose cab, Bliss guessed, would have been condemned as unroadworthy in Bombay or New Delhi, obviously couldn't speak English and was apparently blind to the twenty or so airport hotels, with their huge gaudy neon signs, which they passed on the way to a hotel in the city centre. Bliss had attempted unsuccessfully to remonstrate with him but he had simply given a gap-toothed smile and said, "Sank you," as if he were being complimented on his ability to keep the ancient vehicle more-or-less on the road.

"I haven't had a chance to look around yet," he informed her. "But I'm already fed up with everyone asking me how I am."

"How are you?" she enquired.

"Don't you start," he snapped. "They all do it. They all say 'And how are you today, sir?' Like they care. And if one more person tells me to have a nice day, they'll have a very bad one."

"Don't get excited, Dad. That's just the way Americans are."

"These are Canadians."

"Same difference."

"Sam, this phone is eating my credit card. Did you have any luck with the address?"

She sounded genuinely disappointed. "Sorry, Dad. The lawyer claims he has no idea how to find Margaret, but he's probably lying. Ontario, was all he would say. You'll have to find her yourself."

"Do you know how big Ontario is?"

"As big as Essex?" she ventured.

"Try Europe."

"Go to the police."

"I can't," he replied. "They may have been tipped off by Edwards."

"Try directory enquiries."

"They call it 'directory assistance,'" he said, with an appallingly executed Canadian accent. "And I've already tried. You have to know some sort of area code otherwise they won't help."

"I could ask Chief Inspector Bryan."

"Don't," he screamed.

"I was only joking. Anyway, he's beginning to get on my nerves. He's making vague threats about what he'll do to me if you don't show up." She paused, then her voice darkened a little. "I think he's bluffing but he did say Edwards' wrist is worse than they thought. Damaged nerves or something. Apparently it might not heal properly."

Bliss dismissed the news immediately. "Don't worry about him."

"Oh I'm not." She lifted her tone. "You were right. It is sort of fun being on the other side for a change."

"Don't get used to it. I want to sort this mess out and come home, but I've got to find Margaret first."

"What about a private detective. Do they have those in Canada?

"Brilliant, Samantha."

The hotel bill had grown alarmingly from the original quote and his dismayed look brought an immediate response from the desk clerk. "It's the taxes," she said in a way that made it clear she blamed the government for all things unpleasant. Bliss continued to stare at the bill in disbelief. It was "the taxes," he realized, but it was also the phone calls, a couple of drinks, coffee, breakfast, and the service charge, whatever that was.

"Shall I charge it to your Visa card, sir?" she asked, giving the impression that doing so would relieve him of the financial burden. He nodded and kept his fingers crossed as she ran the card through the machine. His heart was still racing as she handed him the slip for signature. 'Approved,' it said.

Relieved, he sunk into a deep settee in the lobby and mentally totted up the state of his credit card. There had been the boat to France and the train to Paris; he had considered the Chunnel but his excitement at the prospect had been muted by the fear of being spotted by the travelling police officers. Then there was the flight from Paris to Toronto — an absolute rip-off. They must have seen him coming, he reasoned. The young woman clerk at the reservation counter, little more than a hairy French schoolgirl, had explained in broken English that the only last-minute seats available were in first class. His elation at flying first class faded after about ten minutes when he'd correctly worked out the exchange rate. Then there were the phone calls. And the fifty dollars from a cash machine at the airport, almost all of which had been snagged by the taxi driver.

In addition, he figured he needed money for a private investigator, a rental car, food—no, he'd manage without food if necessary—and probably another night in a hotel.

"Shit," he said very loudly, soliciting a sharply indrawn breath and a nasty look from a neat little woman using an adjacent phone booth.

The phone gave him an idea and as soon as the woman left he shoved his credit card into the slot and dialled the toll-free enquiry number printed on the back. A funny burring sound told him the number couldn't be accessed from outside the UK so he called the regular number, and paid dearly for the privilege of hearing an English accent telling him his call would be answered in rotation. He listened to the same message four times before a live operator took his call. Then he waffled—

mother taken ill in Canada, hotels, hospital bills, desperate need of cash. The operator mumbled something sympathetic as he took Bliss's name and account number.

"I realize I'm two months late with payments," Bliss continued quickly, hoping to forestall any hasty decision the operator might otherwise make. "It's been a stressful time, but I've just arranged for my daughter to pay the outstanding amount. She's a lawyer, you know?" He didn't know and did not sound impressed.

"Yes, I'm still in the police," Bliss answered when queried, but didn't add, "I think."

He'd have to consult a supervisor. Hurry, thought Bliss, this call is costing me money—on my Visa!

Keeping his ear jammed to the phone he listened to the muzak draining money out of his account. A minute passed in the space of time he normally associated with ten. "Hello, hello," he shouted, hoping to attract someone's attention, intending to say he would call back. The muzak continued. It was tempting to put the phone down and try again but he didn't know the operator's name. He'd probably have to explain himself all over again.

"Mr. Bliss?"

Finally!—but no hint of a decision. "Yes."

"Hold on, I'm transferring you to a supervisor."

"Wait . . ." Too late, the muzak was back. Money was still dripping away.

The supervisor came on eventually and gruffly made it clear he was putting his job on the line by increasing Bliss's limit by a thousand pounds, on the condition that he pay off the outstanding minimum of four hundred and fifty.

Bliss heaved a sigh. "That's no problem."

But it was a problem; the supervisor demanded the payment up front.

"How can I do that?"

It was, it seemed, simple: the payment would be deducted from the new loan. "That leaves you with five hundred and fifty pounds available credit, and may I suggest you get some sound financial advice," said the supervisor.

"Yes," Bliss said. "Thank you very much. Maybe I should talk to my divorce lawyer and my ex-wife; after all they've got most of my money."

Bliss, dragging his suitcase like a reluctant dog, was hooked by a street bum as he made his way from the hotel to Toronto's Union Station in search of a luggage locker.

"Spare some change, sir?"

Bliss looked down. A mop of matted hair had sprouted from an untidy mound of blankets, a pair of deadpan grey eyes stared right through him. The eyes, like the mound, seemed inert, and he peered closer, seeking life. He found none. No reflection of the piercing blue sky, no sign of glinting sunlight, just a distant, forlorn, numbness. Propped against the dishevelled pile was a sign, pencilled on cardboard torn from the side of a cornflake box: "Old soldier. Unemployed. No food. Please give generously."

Bliss automatically fished in his pocket, but quickly extricated his empty hand. What the hell are you doing, he chided himself indignantly. Giving money to someone who has nothing. You've got less than nothing, nearly twenty thousand pounds less than nothing to be exact. I've got a job, he argued with himself. Maybe not for long, he realized.

He started to walk away but his feet dragged, slowed by logic and not the panhandler's plea. Maybe you should go back to England and put up a defence, he told himself. Innocent men don't run. How many times had he used that very premise to justify an arrest? "If you didn't do it, why did you run away?" In any case, the option of remaining in Canada would soon be out of his hands; he was quickly running out of money. His moment of impetuous behaviour in Edwards' office was going to cost him dearly, and not simply in the potential loss of freedom.

Checking his watch, he gave himself an ultimatum. It's one in the afternoon. Find out where Margaret Gordonstone is by five o'clock today, or go home. Four hours. He had little chance of finding her, he suspected, but maybe that was the point. It had probably been a stupid notion anyway, he reasoned, motivated more by his desire to escape than by any real hope of finding her and getting her to accuse her dead father of double murder. Four hours and not a minute more he decided. After ditching his suitcase in a locker at Union Station, he selected a private investigation agency from the Yellow Pages, based solely on the fact that he recognized the name of the street address.

To his surprise he found an attractive dark-haired young woman in the office instead of the Colombo type he'd anticipated—dirty raincoat *et al*—but she was no less inquisitive by reason of her gender and appearance.

"Why do you want the information, sir?" she asked in a cool tone, accompanied by the steely gaze of a professional.

The question caught him off guard; his immediate reaction was to disclose his identity, but he thought better of it. It didn't make sense. It would, he thought, be impossible to explain why he had not simply gone to the nearest police station with his request. Somewhere in the back of his mind he had a prefabricated story about Margaret being a long lost relative, but the investigator's continued penetrating gaze made it obvious she was watching closely for signs of prevarication, and was becoming suspicious of his hesitation. He finally opted to stick to the truth, more or less.

"She's inherited a valuable restaurant in London and I've been asked by her family to tell her."

"Don't they have lawyers to do that sort of thing?"

"At a price. I was coming over anyway, on holiday," he explained. "So I said I'd try to find her."

She looked at him askance, doubt deeply etched into the lines on her brow.

"What's the problem?" he asked.

"I'll be honest with you," she said. "Men sometimes try to hire us to find their runaway wives or girlfriends so they can harass them or even bump them off."

He felt her sizing up his reaction. "You're kidding."

She shook her head in seriousness. "I could lose my licence if something like that happened."

Her fixed stare offered no room for manoeuvring. He met her eyes and responded icily. "I am trying to find Margaret Gordonstone to tell her about the death of her father and her inheritance."

She challenged him with a stare for a full second before visibly relaxing. "OK. I'll try to find her," she said with a dazzling smile that appeared from nowhere. "Where can I call you?"

"I'm not sure ..." he began. Her smile started to wilt. "I stayed at the Gateway last night," he continued, pulling the receipt from his pocket. Her smile picked up. "You can call me there," he finished.

There was only the question of payment to resolve. "Two hundred dollars upfront," she requested.

"Visa?"

"No problem. Give me a couple of hours. And have a nice day."

The phone was ringing by the time he'd got back to the hotel and re-registered just after four o'clock. He flung himself across the bed and snatched up the receiver. Too late. He had to wait until the message was recorded on the voice mail.

"I have the information you require Mr. Bliss," said the investigator's tinny recorded voice, "if you'd care to give me a call." That was fast, he thought, as he dialled her number and a small part of him was disappointed that he no longer had an excuse to give up and go home. It was nowhere near five o'clock.

"Where is it?" he enquired as he scribbled down the address.

"About a thousand miles north, somewhere called Little Bear Island," she said, as if she were talking about the suburbs.

He whistled through his teeth. "A thousand miles. How long would it take to drive there?"

"Forever, I think," she laughed. "There are no roads."

He found himself whistling again and resolved to stop doing it. "No roads?"

"Welcome to Canada, eh."

"No roads," he repeated. "How can I get there?"

"Fly probably," she sounded vague. "Then it looks like four or five days' hike from the nearest town; three days by canoe maybe." She was obviously tracing out a route on a map and continued after a slight pause. "There are some pretty steep rapids." Then her tone picked up optimistically. "Perhaps you could hire a float plane to drop you on Bear Lake, but you'll have to hurry if you want to get there before winter closes in."

"It's only September."

"Like I said, Mr. Bliss, welcome to Canada. Oh, and have a nice trip."

The hotel receptionist made it abundantly clear by her expression that she didn't believe him when, ten minutes after booking in, he booked out again, claiming he had to rush back to his dying mother in England, but she wished him a nice day anyway as she tore up the credit card slip.

Reversing the charges from a street payphone, and catching an earful of abuse for doing so, Bliss called Samantha and excitedly reported his news.

"Dad. What if you get there and find it's the wrong Margaret Gordonstone?"

"I've thought of that, but she's roughly the right age; and Bryan said she lived in the wilds of Canada."

"Why not phone her first. She might be away."

"She doesn't have a phone, I've already checked. There is no listing for her name or address. By the way, what is Edwards doing?"

"Peter says he's blustering about, ripping into everyone, shouting about getting an arrest warrant, and threatening you with life imprisonment." The line went quiet, Bliss wondered if he'd been disconnected.

"Sam!"

"I'm here, I'm here," she said falteringly, clearly in the midst of serious deliberation. Then she came to a decision. "Dad, Peter says if you are back by tomorrow night and apologize to Edwards, he won't press charges."

He dismissed the offer with little consideration and without comment, but picked up on her familiar use of the DCI's first name. "So how is Peter?"

"He's all right, Dad. I really believe he's trying to help you."

"Yeah. You're probably right, but I'm not sure I can trust him or anybody else just at the moment."

She didn't respond, feeling more than a little wounded.

"How's your mother?" he asked, although he had been determined not to.

"Pissed off with you," she replied spitefully. "She says you still owe her four thousand quid. Four thousand, three hundred and twenty-six to be exact. She made me write it down so I wouldn't forget to remind you."

"Damn!" he swore, reminded once again of money. "Sam, luv?"

"Why is it whenever you say, 'Sam, luv,' like that, I know you're going to ask me to do something I don't want to do."

He ignored her. "There's a couple of small bills I've forgotten to pay. Could you sort them out for me? I'll give you the money as soon as I get back."

She tried to sound exasperated, "Where are they?"

"Under the telly."

"They'd better be small; I'm short this month as well. And what about Mum's money?"

"I still love her, Sam."

"Dad!"

"What?"

"You've got to let go."

"Letting go is the hardest part."

"Fucking right it is."

"Samantha Bliss! I sometimes wonder if you were switched at birth for the illegitimate kid of an east-end dockie."

Laughing, she said, "Luv you," and rang off.

Unencumbered by his suitcase, Bliss temporarily placed his cares in the hands of fate and felt an increasing sense of freedom as he wandered the wide tree-lined boulevards of Toronto, marvelling at the neck-straining cityscape surmounted by the one of the world's tallest towers.

Obtaining Margaret's locality was, it seemed to him, achievement itself, and getting there was almost a *fait accompli*. He walked with a devil-may-care lightness in his step and a feeling that now everything was turning around and all would be right in the end. It was as if Melanie was helping him along. Melanie's memory, guiltily locked away in a compartment of his mind for the past twenty years, visited only occasionally, had now slipped the latch and was determined not to go back until he had appeased her death by uncovering the truth.

The first travel agent he tried was accustomed to pampering people off to Tahiti or the Bahamas, and had never heard of Little Bear Island. The wasp-waisted girl, with more wire in her mouth than teeth, suggested he try a wilderness adventure specialist. Another agency's windows were full of yuppie cruise liners and picture-perfect palm shaded beaches. He didn't bother going in.

The third agency he found, in a backstreet just off the edge of the glitzy downtown core, was squeezed between grocery stores offering a fascinating variety of fruits and produce cascading from the shopfronts, spilling onto the streets in exotic displays. The travel agent was unfamiliar with Margaret's island but would, he said, make enquiries if Bliss could give him thirty minutes. He filled the time by browsing along the street, wondering aloud how certain strange-looking vegetables tasted—or were they fruits? Then he paused for a drink under the shade of a café's flamboyant awning. He was bewildered by the forty-two choices of ice cream, twenty-seven types of coffee, sixteen varieties of bagel, and ten flavours of cream cheese. Deciding that Canada was not for the numerically challenged, he wasn't altogether surprised when his selection of Irish Cream coffee turned out to be only the first in a series of multiple-choice questions.

"Small, medium, large, or jumbo, sir?"

"Medium."

"Milk or cream?"

"Milk please," he replied quickly, then immediately regretted his rashness.

"Will that be all, sir?"

He was tempted to ask for a bagel but felt intimidated by the number of variations on offer so stuck with the coffee.

The travel agent had found the island and mapped out a route by the time he returned. According to him, Bliss was in luck: he could be there in thirty-six hours or so, although the last of three flights would still leave him with a ten-mile stretch of lake to cross, something the agent could not arrange.

The first leg of the trip would leave at eight o'clock the following morning. Did he want a one-way or return flight?

Some quick mental arithmetic left him with few illusions and a stark choice. A hotel for the night or enough money to get back to Toronto after seeing Margaret. He chose the latter and was grateful that at least he had an open ended first-class return to Paris. From there he would hitchhike back to London if necessary.

After retrieving his suitcase, he walked to the lakeshore and sat on the grass for a while, watching the yachts and ferries skimming across the silk-smooth lake to the ring of offshore islands, until they slowly faded into the sunset.

Night came to the city without darkness, and with the night came the creatures: the drunks, drug addicts, and dropouts littering the sidewalks and clogging the well-trodden tourist paths, hands outstretched, mumbling supplications and thrusting hand-written entreaties toward passers-by, as if a few words scribbled on a scruffy card added legitimacy to their solicitations. A few, Bliss noticed, had laboriously scripted their life history onto more elaborate cards, some with hand decorated borders and illuminated capital letters, and had catalogued their downward spiral like a list of professional achievements. These perverse parodies of curriculum vitae seemed to follow a predictable pattern, he noted, as if they were responding to an employment advertisement for which there was a list of required criterion. "Reformed alcoholic," "Unemployed," "Divorced," and "Wrongfully convicted," appeared to be obligatory qualifications, although he noticed that several took obvious pride in proclaiming, "No convictions." Each heading was followed by more detailed explanations, including dates and places where appropriate and, as Bliss meandered from one beseeching figure to the next, it appeared that each had a more compelling cause than his, or her, neighbour. None of the street people bothered Bliss; they seemed to recognize him as one of their own, although he was oblivious to the similitude.

Night wore on, the last of the late-night tourists were shepherded to their hotels or whisked away in limousines, and most of the panhandlers simply crumpled into formless heaps and slept like discarded sacks of humanity dropped carelessly onto the sidewalks. He found a vacant bench in a well-lit piazza and kept himself awake listening to the pulse of the city: the hum of air conditioners, the background buzz of traffic, punctuated occasionally by the screaming siren of an emergency vehicle, the ear piercing screech of cicadas, their mating calls ripping repeatedly through the clear night air like orchestrated dentist's drills, and the constant tinkling of an ornamental waterfall, which added a pleasing counterpoint.

But he started drifting; the balmy Indian Summer air that cozily enveloped him was lulling him to sleep. Jerking himself upright he lit a cigarette. One of the street people was at his side in a second, attracted by the flare of his match.

"Spare a cigarette?" he pleaded.

"It's my last one, mate," Bliss lied.

The grey eyes probed him deeply. "You're new," the man snorted, as if this were an undesirable state of affairs.

Another bundle of rags shuffled into place alongside the first; the burning match had drawn him from a greater distance and he was wheezing heavily with the exertion.

"He's new," pronounced the first man, making newness sound like a sexually transmitted disease.

"What have you got in there?" mumbled the second man, eyeing the old, but solid, suitcase.

Bliss gave them a cigarette to share on the condition they leave him alone.

"You're all right," one of them mumbled as they shuffled away.

"He's new," retorted the other, making it clear that, as far as he was concerned, it might be some time before Bliss could be fully accepted into their society. Then they started sparring over the cigarette and fought, Laurel and Hardy like, as they tottered away.

Realizing that his 'newness' and his suitcase made him a target, he resolved not to risk falling asleep and watched cautiously as shadowy figures drifted in and out of the piazza, picking at the litter bins and scouting under the shrubbery for anything edible or otherwise useful. He kept a firm hand on his suitcase as he carefully scrutinized the stubbly face of those who ventured uncomfortably close, making sure he could identify them later should it be necessary. But most kept their distance, like predatory animals skirting with a watchful eye around the edges of a rival's territory.

The warm somnolent atmosphere closed around him, his eyes slowly drifted shut and his grip on the suitcase loosened. Suddenly, from out of nowhere, they pounced. Hands, pushing him down, holding him down. His face was wet—they were forcing him under the water. It was the suitcase, he realized, clinging to it desperately. It was the suitcase they were after.

"Help! help!" he shouted, but the sound was muffled by the water. Hands were everywhere: big, spongy, powerful hands, holding him down, forcing his head under the water.

Fight back, fight back, he screamed at himself, but it was already too late. A giant soft weight was crushing him down, holding him under the water. He couldn't breathe. Fight, fight, his mind was yelling, but his pinioned arms wouldn't move. Drifting toward blackness, he tried pleading for help, but only succeeded in making a trail of bubbles.

"You're unconscious," said his mind as the hands thrust him deeper under the water. Down, down, down, he felt himself being pushed. "I'm a police officer," he managed to shout. But they laughed at him, and he heard the sound gurgling through the water.

He still had the suitcase, his arms strapped around it, dragging it down into the lake with him. Hands were grappling to take it from him. Let go of the suitcase, his mind was telling him. It's the suitcase they want.

He wouldn't let go. He couldn't let go. Melanie's file was in the suitcase. They musn't get her file, he shrieked. And suddenly she was there, little naked Melanie, descending into the water alongside him. He let go the suitcase and reached out, desperate to save her, but the big pudgy hands held him back, kept her just beyond his reach. Then he looked into her eyes, saw the grey vacant eyes of a panhandler and realized he was too late, she was already dead.

Suddenly he was awake, panting breathlessly; a hand was prodding him and he grabbed the suitcase in alarm.

"Don't worry, it's OK." The voice was warm, calming.

His eyes flickered open and he blinked furiously, trying to focus on his attacker. Sweat was pouring out of neck, his perspiration-drenched shirt clung coldly to his back, and his hands shook from the force of crushing the suitcase to his chest. Realization was swift. It had been a nightmare. He relaxed with an audible sigh and could have laughed in relief.

"Would you like sandwiches or soup?" the chubby-faced woman enquired soothingly. "You can have both if you want."

He had hardly expected room service and shook his head as he tried to control his breathing. "I'm not really on the street," he said, offended that she would think he was.

"Keep believing that," she said sympathetically. "It'll help you to get back on your feet. Here take this." Thrusting a neatly wrapped package of sandwiches in his hands she went to a van at the curbside and returned with a steaming cup of soup. "Now would you like a sleeping bag or a blanket?"

"You don't understand ..." he started, taking the proffered soup.

She shushed him with a little hand wave. "It's OK. I know you need time to adjust, but we'll be here for you." She glanced at the remnants of humanity strewn around the edges of the piazza. "These boys are OK. They'll take care of you, and we come round every night."

Bliss gave up. "Thank you," was all he could think of saying.

"That's better. Now let me get you that sleeping bag."

She was gone and back before he could stop her. "There we are," she said, crinkly-eyed, handing him the brand new sleeping bag still in its original wrapping.

"I couldn't . . ." he started, but he took it when he realized by the look on her face that she would be hurt if he didn't. She smiled with satisfaction; another lost soul had been brought into her fold.

Fear and the haunting nightmare of Melanie's drowning kept him awake until the earth's rotation switched on the sun again. Then, gradually, the huddled night denizens gathered their meagre belongings and, wraith-like, drifted away from the piazza. Clanging delivery trucks, rumbling subway trains, clattering garbage collectors, and the smell of fresh coffee woke the city to another bustling day.

chapter seven

Another day, and a thousand miles, later Bliss awoke in his new sleeping bag, but on an entirely different planet. A land with a bluer sky, a brighter sun, and so many brilliant stars in the night's sky that, although exhausted, he had lain awake on the grassy lakeshore for more than an hour repeating, "I can't believe it," over and over, like a dumbstruck lottery winner.

A brief early-dawn shower had scented the air with the fresh ozone fragrance of rainwater on dry ground. He sniffed deeply and was intoxicated by the freshness. As fresh as a dry white wine with a touch of effervescence, he thought — a blanc de blancs, a Moussec perhaps, or one of the very dry lesser champagnes Sarah had been so fond of. He sniffed again and let out a long satisfied, "Aah." How different from the sticky, thick, Sauternes-like air of the city. On a whim, he delved into his jacket pocket, pulled out his remaining stock of cigarettes, and, in a calculated act of self-defiance, crushed the packet and slung it under a nearby cranberry bush.

He washed in the cool clear lake, defecated guiltily among a clump of small trees, and, a little before nine o'clock, made his way to the airline's office, a small clinker-built wooden hut with barely a memory of paint. Like an abandoned public toilet, it perched uneasily on the end of a short pier jutting out into the mist. The pier rocked with each of Bliss's footfalls and the old float plane, bobbing lightly on its buoyant torpedoes, lightly bumped against the tire fenders. He knocked gingerly on the hut door.

"Come in," shouted a woman and he entered to find the twentysomething office girl, with blond ponytail sprouting from a faded Island Air baseball cap, in an animated discussion on a telephone that looked as old as the hut.

She waved him to the only other seat in the tiny structure, a folding canvas picnic chair, and whipped her hand over the mouthpiece. "Yup?"

"I've got a ticket to Bear Lake."

"I can be there tomorrow Bill," she called into the phone. "Not today, you haven't," she said to Bliss, holding both conversations at the same time.

He held the ticket out and started to rise toward her.

"OK, Bill, tomorrow it is then."

The phone rang again the moment she put it down.

"There must be a mistake," she said dismissively, picking up the phone and announcing, "Island Air," into the mouthpiece in the same breath.

"There's no mistake, I've paid," said Bliss sticking the ticket right in front of her face.

"Bob, yeah, I need fifty litres of gas for Rowan's Point." She scrutinized the ticket and waved it away. "This isn't valid until we've been paid by the agent."

"That isn't my problem," said Bliss.

The look on her face told him it was his problem, and her dual conversations melded into one, leaving him to figure out which part was meant for him. "Yeah fifty litres. You'll have to pay me if you want to go today. Not fifteen, fifty. And Peter needs some engine oil up at Stacy's."

He stabbed a finger indignantly at the 'amount paid' figure on the ticket. "I've already paid."

"You'll have to pay again," she replied with equal resolution.

He argued. She was adamant. He was frustrated. She was unapologetic. They had, she claimed, been ripped off too many times by backstreet city travel agents who booked the flights but never sent the cheques, knowing it would be too expensive, and too troublesome, for a small outfit like hers to sue.

He had travelled half-way around the world, he pleaded. She partially relented and agreed to accept half the fare, saying she would sort the matter out by the time he returned.

"That sounds reasonable," he said, holding out almost all of his remaining money.

When was he coming back, she wanted to know.

"Tomorrow or the day after at the latest, I thought."

Pent up laughter blew out her cheeks until she could hold it no longer and she blurted, "I'll call you back," into the phone. Bliss tried to hold onto the cash but she snatched it playfully. "No refunds," she cried through the laughter. Then she straightened her face and offered him the money back. "You don't have to go if you don't want to." He didn't know what had made her laugh. "We only fly to Bear Lake every two weeks," she explained, noticing his confused expression.

His confusion turned to dismay. "Maybe I should speak to the pilot," he suggested.

She sat rock still. "Yes?"

"You're the pilot?" he said with a surprised lilt. She seemed, he thought, a trifle too happy-go-lucky to be trusted with his life. "What about the owner?"

The look on her face was a picture, thought Bliss as she pointed a finger at herself. "Alice," she said, "Owner, operator and mechanic—plus I make the coffee in our luxury cafeteria."

"You have a cafet ..." he began, before realizing that she was joking; that she was referring to the 6-cup percolator on a small shelf in the corner. "I can't win can I?" he continued, thinking it was not only policemen who were getting younger. "Two weeks," he said vaguely.

She concurred with a nod. "Weather permitting."

"Shit," he mumbled under his breath. "Oh well, I've come this far . . ."

"Don't touch anything," she mouthed as the engine roared into life fifteen minutes later, then they taxied smoothly away from the pier and tripped lightly across the lake's surface, now rippled by a gentle morning breeze.

"How long will it take us?" yelled Bliss above the drone.

"Three hours usually," she shouted, then added jokingly, "Longer if we crash."

"Do you crash often?"

A crooked smile was her only answer.

"It seems like you're the co-pilot today," she had said, inviting him to sit alongside her in the rudimentary cockpit that looked to Bliss as if it was constructed with Meccano. "Don't worry," she'd added. "I usually fly this crate on my own, the co-pilot only comes along to keep me company."

"I can do that," he had said, fumbling with the old canvas seat belt. "But if I'm the co-pilot does that mean I get my fare back?"

Her look was enough.

"OK, I give in," he had laughed.

The twin propellers whisked the tiny wave-tops into spray and with a few sharp bumps they lifted into the air and swung northward. The engine's take-off roar settled into a constant throb that Bliss soon tuned out.

"What brings you here?" she asked when they were safely aloft.

He waffled, muttering about the need to travel, and the word 'adventure' cropped up more than once.

"This is a fabulous place for an adventure," she agreed, then an inquisitive frown spread across her face. "I hope you don't mind, but I've never seen an adventurer carrying a suitcase before. You do know what it's like up here?" The serious way in which she asked the question hinted that some major horrors might await him.

"Wild," he suggested, hoping this all-encompassing evaluation might satisfy her.

"Yeah, you could say that," she replied; a poorly disguised understatement.

He didn't respond. He had no intention of finding out. A few hours with Margaret Gordonstone and, he desperately hoped, he would be on his way back home to a face the music. Although he had no idea how he was going to get back.

Alice felt obliged to enlighten him about the potential dangers. "There's a lotta black bears," she said ominously, then paused to gauge his response. His shrug was noncommittal, so she added, "They often kill for food." The loud snort that followed was somehow meant to convey the creature's ferocity.

"They eat people," Bliss shouted, but he meant it more as a statement than a question.

"Sometimes," she nodded energetically. "But generally they kill folks to steal their food."

Lucky I haven't got any then, he thought.

Alice pressed on, shouting, "Bull moose," in a way that was obviously intended to strike terror. He didn't respond, so she added, "A lotta people 'bin trampled to death by moose. They're enormous." His silence only served to encourage her. "They're the size of a cart horse, but ten times faster."

"I'll keep away from them," he promised.

Feeling that she had at last caught his attention, she regaled him with a zoological catalogue of dangerous creatures he might encounter including packs of wolves and coyotes, man-eating cougars, not to mention rattlesnakes and quill-shooting porcupines. "The insects are the worst," she continued. "Black fly, deer fly, mosquitoes—"

"Thanks for warning me," he said, quickly cutting her off and mentally dismissing her concerns. He had no intention of roughing it or staying long enough to become a victim.

They flew on in silence over a sculpted green carpet of trees dappled with hundreds of lakes threaded on aquamarine ribbons of streams and rivers. And above them, a clear blue sky, uniformly, brilliantly blue, a pure deep blue, not the hazy, ice blue skies familiar to Bliss. An altogether deeper, richer, bluer blue. A colour, Bliss found himself thinking, that would make an excellent television commercial for comparing laundry detergents. The difference between Tide and Sunlight he thought, after umpteen washes.

An apparent trick of the light splashed a blotch of red into the green carpet below and he craned around trying to find the sun.

"What's happenin', Man?" she yelled.

He looked down again, expecting the mirage to have vanished, but found other blotches of red, like angry pimples on an otherwise perfect skin. And ahead, to the north, the forest almost seemed to burn with colour.

Alice realized what had caught his attention. "It's the fall colours."

He gave her a questioning look.

"Don't your trees turn red in the fall?"

"No, they go shitty brown, clog up the gutters, and cause chaos on the railways."

The odd brilliant red blotch became a wide brush stroke as whole valleys of scarlet streaked beneath them. Alice dropped the plane down and flew just above the treetops so that he would get a better view. The scarlet leaves contrasted brilliantly against the blue horizon and the surrounding evergreen firs. "Wow!" was all he could manage to say.

"It's early yet," she explained. "In a few weeks they'll be bright red all the way to Toronto."

A formation of large birds flew directly toward them. "Canada geese," she said, pointing at the perfectly executed wedge of fifty or more birds. "They're starting to migrate. Winter's coming."

"Winter in September?" he queried.

"It'll be snowing in a few weeks," she replied, peering around the clear sky as if searching for signs of advancing snow clouds. Then she swung the plane in a wide loop and pointed at the turquoise lake below. "Bear Lake," she mouthed.

The settlement was at the north end of the lake and as they flew low over the water the tiny plane skipped over a string of tree-covered islands. With a shout Alice sud-

denly swung the control stick over and excitedly pointed down at a small beach on one of the islands. "Bears,"
she shouted. He missed them at the first pass and she
swooped around again, positioning the plane to give
him a better view. Then he saw them. A mother and two
cubs gambolling on the beach. The cubs — "This year's
litter," according to Alice — looked as playful as kittens
as they rolled in the sand, while the mother waded in the
water swiping lazily at passing fish. The noise of the
plane caught the mother's attention and she raised herself up to her full height and opened her huge mouth to
bellow a warning at the sky. Bliss was sure he heard her
above the engine's drone and looked at Alice. "Aren't
they afraid of us?"

"Would you be, if you were that size?"

It had taken him nearly thirty-six hours on three
planes to reach the isolated community perched on the
edge of Bear Lake, much of the time waiting, and as
Alice skimmed low over, what she referred to as "the
town," he wondered if they'd strayed into a foreign
land. Beneath them was a shabby collection of log cabins clinging to a narrow strip of lakeshore edging the
forest. Even from the air he could see there were no
proper roads, just twin tracks of gravel meandering
along the shore, with a spiky dry-grass centre strip to
brush the underside of passing vehicles. And on the out-
skirts of town the gravel gave way to nothing more than
dirt ruts, which faded quickly into the undergrowth.

The lake was smooth and the small plane cushioned
itself onto the water with a soft swishing sound as the
floats skied across the surface. Taxiing slowly toward
the broad wooden dock, where a small pile of goods
waited to be shipped out, Bliss took a closer look at the
collection of tin huts, log cabins, and general store with
a wide covered verandah overlooking the beach. Almost

every property had an enormous satellite dish that looked as though it was worth more than the home. Scattered around the dock was a rusty assortment of trucks, vans, and cars that could have been driven straight off a scrap yard.

"How did they get here?" he wondered aloud.

Alice didn't hear but guessed what he was thinking. "They drive them across the ice in winter."

"What about you?" He meant the plane; she understood.

"Simple. Once the ice is thick enough I swap the floats for skids and land on it."

The place was deserted. The only movement seemed to come from an elderly sinewy man whose individual muscles were clearly defined through his parchment skin. He lazily caught the painter thrown by Alice and tied the plane to the dock.

"How are you, Jock?" she called out of the cockpit window.

"Och, I'm nae so bad lassie," he replied, his soft Scottish brogue catching Bliss totally unawares.

"I've got a passenger, looking for an adventure."

"He should've bin here in thirty-seven then, when we found the gold."

Bliss thought he'd misheard. "You were here in nineteen thirty-seven?"

"Aye. I arrived in thirty-two wi' my folks. Bin here ever since." His accent, not tainted in the least by sixty years in a foreign country, was pure Glasgow Gorbals.

Alice, whose legs, she claimed, had been crossed for the past thirty minutes or so, rushed off to use the facilities in the general store, leaving Bliss an opportunity to confide in the Scotsman. "I was hoping to meet an old friend who lives around here somewhere. Margaret Gordonstone, do you know her?"

"Aye."

"You do?"

"Aye," he replied again, then unaccountably lost interest and began furiously unloading cargo from the plane.

Bliss tapped him on the shoulder. "Can you tell me where I can find her?"

"Depends," he intoned warily, then stopped work and rubbed his thumb and forefinger together under Bliss' nose. "Depends."

Bliss caught on. "Ten dollars."

"Ten does'na go very far these days."

"Twenty," he offered, selecting one of the few remaining bills in his wallet.

Jock whisked the money out of his hand and stared wistfully off into the distance.

"She lives on an island about half a day away."

There were a number of canoes and boats drawn up on the beach. "Could you take me there?" Bliss asked.

"Och, I could." But he seemed less than confident.

Bliss didn't bother checking his dwindling stock of cash. "How much?" he asked, knowing that, whatever, he would be unable to afford it.

The old man was clearly thinking furiously, deliberating how to make the most out of the Sassenach stranger. Then his face fell. "Och. Save your money mon. The wee lassie's in yon store."

Retrieving his suitcase from the plane, Bliss took four steps toward the store, stepped down off the dock, and found his feet frozen to the shale beach.

What would she look like?

Would he recognize her?

Why should he? He'd never seen her before.

Then the big question: Would he see Melanie's angelic face in hers?

He shuffled his feet, the store was only ten yards away. Just ten positive steps. Hesitating with indecision he felt the blood coursing through his temples.

"You've waited twenty years for this," he told himself, forcing one foot forward. Each step brought new thoughts. He had done it before, dozens of times. '"Notification of death,'" it was called. Standing on some mother's, father's, sister's, or son's doorstep, pulling a straight face, practicing a sombre voice. And he had seen all their reactions: the blank stares of disbelief, the deep gasps for breath, the traumatized brain painfully evident in contorted facial expressions. And he'd heard the denials: it's a mistake; impossible; it can't be true. And he'd heard the screams and mopped the tears. But this was different, he reminded himself. She knew. She had known for more than twenty years, about Melanie anyway; she had known about her mother for ten. She had grown up with the pain ... and the fear. She knew they had died — but did she know at whose hands?

A single wooden step led onto the store's verandah; he opened the mesh insect screen and put his hand on the door. Then it hit him: it wasn't Margaret he was expecting to see, it was Melanie.

Melanie was not in the store and Bliss chastised himself for even considering the possibility. If anyone knew that Melanie was dead it was he. But Margaret wasn't there either. His heart missed a beat and he was unsure whether to be elated or relieved. There was only one person in the store-cum-café. An older woman, shaded under a rattan hat, was seated at a rustic bench with her head in a paper. With a dirt-ingrained hand she raised the brim of her coolie hat just a fraction and warily studied him. Her gnarled fingers and chipped nails were no strangers to hard work, Bliss thought, then craned around trying to see if Margaret were in the back room. She was not.

Turning back to the woman, he saw that she had returned to the paper. "Excuse me ..." he started nervously, but her vibes were clear enough — Do not disturb. Then, for just a moment, he wondered if this might be Margaret: sitting alone, confident, self-possessed. Damn, he thought, that can't be her, she looks at least fifty. Then she took off her wide-rimmed hat and suddenly became thirty. It *was* Margaret, he realized with a start. She hadn't aged, she had weathered. Her young features were masked with a mahogany veneer of suntan and wind exposure. With the hat's shadow removed the sunlight lifted her features and what appeared at first to be a slightly receding chin turned out to be delicately carved and finely pointed.

He stared hard, seeking a likeness between her and the dead little girl he'd pulled from the lake. There was something, he thought, or was he imagining it. Then he put his finger on it — it was her hair. She had Melanie's hair. Long, dark, auburn hair. Margaret's untidily scrunched into a sloppy bun and held in place by an eclectic assortment of pins and elastic bands. Melanie's flowed out into the water like a halo. But it was the same hair. It even had a bright glossy sheen that gave it the appearance of being wet.

She looked up and their eyes locked for a nanosecond. Bliss illogically expected some signal of recognition, some sort of reciprocation, some acknowledgement of the twenty years that she had been part of his consciousness. He was disappointed. Her blank face and disinterested glance held no promise of an accord.

There were no formalities; she offered no pleasantries. "You want coffee?" she asked, almost as if she'd been expecting him. It took him completely by surprise. *Had* she been expecting him? Had Superintendent Edwards or DCI Bryan contacted her? Had someone warned her of his impending visit? He quickly dismissed the idea, telling himself that neither of them knew where he was headed, unless ... Samantha! She wouldn't have. She couldn't have.

The woman had risen and reached the counter. "Has the cat got your tongue?" she enquired frostily. "Or do you always stand and stare like a lunatic?"

The ballooning lumberjack's shirt masked her breasts and gave her a manly appearance. The calf-length denim skirt obscured her legs, but it was immediately apparent she had lost the lumpiness the chef at *L'Haute Cuisinier* had scathingly mentioned. But there was something about her which took him by surprise, although, he admitted to himself, there was no reason why he should have been surprised. She had the faintest remnant of a harelip. Good reconstructive surgery — just a fine vertical scar — but the slight lisp in her voice gave it away.

He unfroze. "Sorry. I didn't mean to be rude. Do you know who I am?"

"I've no idea, but Alice says you are English and looking for an adventure."

Alice ... of course. He relaxed. "Coffee would be good."

"You haven't tried it yet."

Pouring the coffee with one hand she grabbed the ringing phone. "Stacy's bar ... No, he's out fishing ... OK, have a nice day."

Her strong Canadian accent disappeared instantly as she turned back to Bliss. "Milk or cream?"

He shrugged. "Either," and was grateful that these were his only choices. Then, as she reached into the fridge, he stepped forward. "Are you Margaret Gordonstone?"

Her head shot around; she gave him a piercing look. "Who wants to know?

"You don't remember me, do you?" he said, stupidly overlooking the fact they had never met.

She squinted at him, her deep brown eyes probing into his. "Are we going to keep asking each other questions or is one of us going to start giving answers?"

"That's another question," he replied, desperately stalling.

Since leaving Toronto he'd turned over a dozen scenarios in his mind to explain his visit and discarded each as being thoroughly implausible. Finally, giving up, he had decided that when the time came he would have plenty of opportunity to trump up a suitable explanation and devise a plan of attack. Now, suddenly confronted by his objective, he was stuck for words. "Just passing," was hardly likely to be believed, especially by this woman, who was clearly a straight talker. He held her gaze and blurted out the truth: "I investigated Melanie's death."

What must she be thinking, he wondered as her face contorted through a range of emotions. Her confidence seemed to drain away. "You're a policeman?"

"Yes. We never met but ..."

Quickly regaining her composure, she challenged him. "What are you doing here?"

Thinking that he could hardly say he just happened to be in the neighbourhood; he sidestepped the question and injected some lightness in his voice. "It's my turn to ask a question." Then enquired in a friendly tone, "Do you work here?"

"Good God, no!"

Alice breezed in carting a mailbag. "Oh. You two limeys have met then. I've got some mail for you, Maggie."

He searched Margaret's face. Would she blow his cover? Stone-faced she turned to Alice, nodded in the direction of the heavy bag, and joked, "What? All that."

"No, idiot." Alice pulled a couple of envelopes from the top of the bag and handed them to the other woman. "These are yours."

"Thanks," Margaret said, but barely glanced at the two letters before stuffing them, unopened, into her handbag.

A touch of excitement swept Alice's face. "And I've got a special package for you, too."

Margaret's face lit up. "What is it?"

Like a conjurer, Alice delved into the Santa-sized bag and brought out a cat's carrying cage. "Look."

There was a shift in the air as three pairs of eyes fought to peer through the ventilation holes. Bliss couldn't distinguish anything and was still trying to focus through the slits when Margaret shouted in delight, "Bald eagle? What's wrong with him?"

"Shot," replied Alice. "Some Native kids, probably trying to prove something. Anyway, Dr. Chaters thinks he got all the pellets out. Here's a note."

Margaret barely scanned the note before swinging back to Bliss and switching her accent back to pure English. "So. Where are you staying?"

Alice was headed back to the plane for another sack before Bliss could reply.

"I would've phoned —" he began.

"I haven't got a phone."

"I was going to say that. I couldn't find your number."

"So you *were* coming to see me then?"

He thought fast. "Sort of. I was going to kill two birds with one ... " He left the saying unfinished and could have kicked himself for the unfortunate choice of expression. Margaret didn't seem to notice so he carried on. "I needed a holiday and my boss thought someone should get a bit of background information about your father."

Her face clouded.

Bliss panicked, put on his 'notification-of-death face' and enquired quickly, "You do know he died?" He was not entirely certain she *was* aware.

She nodded. "A friend of his called. Said he'd had a heart attack." She noticed Bliss's puzzled expression. "They take messages for me here," she explained.

Alice was back, crashing enthusiastically though the front door and flinging the second sack of mail on top of the first. Margaret ignored her. "So what do you plan to do here?"

He felt slightly foolish. "The problem is that I lost my traveller's cheques and I'm a bit stuck for cash."

Alice chimed in. "You could put him up at your place, couldn't you, Maggie?"

Shaking her head vigorously she sat back down to accentuate her unwillingness to help. "The animals," she explained. "They get very nervous with strangers, and Bo wouldn't like it."

"Animals?" enquired Bliss.

"Maggie runs a sort of rehab centre for injured critters. People bring them to her from all over. I often fly them in."

"If it's too much trouble ..." said Bliss politely.

Alice wasn't prepared to let it drop. "C'mon Maggie. I can't take him back now. Anyway, Jock's already loading the furs, I won't get off the lake with all that weight."

"Jock will have to unload some of the furs then. You know I don't like visitors."

Bliss wasn't going to give up that easily. "Perhaps I could stay here and come out to visit you one day."

Margaret's expression made it obvious she didn't want him around. "There's nowhere to stay in town. Anyway I'm really busy at the moment."

"I could help you. I like animals."

"The truth is that people might talk. You now what they're like up here, Alice," she said, turning to the other woman for support.

"C'mon, Maggie," Alice laughed. "They all think you're weird anyway."

"Weird I can live with. A maneater is something else."

At last, thought Bliss, the real reason for her reticence. "I can understand that —" he started, but Alice jumped ahead of him. "Give me a break girl. Let 'em think what they want. I'll put the word out that he's your Dad come for a visit."

Bliss shot Margaret a questioning look. Her deadpan expression suggested she had not widely broadcast the news of her father's death.

He had one more card up his sleeve — the truth, a card he had hoped to avoid having to play. "I've got a confession to make," he said, as calmly as he could. "When I said I didn't have much money, I meant hardly any at all. I'm waiting for some more to arrive but at the moment I can't even pay Alice to fly me back."

"That does it then," said Alice, clearly not intending to fly him anywhere without prior payment.

Margaret caved in. "OK. I know when I'm beaten. But if you upset the animals you'll have to leave."

"I promise."

"And you'll have to work for your keep. I've been meaning to rebuild the dock ever since the ice wrecked it last year. Are you any good with wood?"

"Fantastic," he replied, willing to try anything once.

From the look on Alice's face one might have thought she'd just arranged a marriage. "Yes!" she cried, triumphantly pumping the air with a fist as she set off in search of another mailbag.

"We're going to need more food," Margaret said to herself as she got up and started plucking packets and cans off the shelves with such speed that Bliss wondered if she had any idea what she was grabbing. "Have you got any cash at all?" she asked over her shoulder as she reached into a huge refrigerator.

"About twenty-three dollars."

She clucked disapprovingly. "OK. Stick it into the till and I'll straighten up with Stacy next time." Then she pointed to a Western Union sign over a side counter that bore the red and white insignia of Canada Post. "You can get your money sent here and pay me when it arrives."

"Terrific. I'll have to make a phone call to arrange it."

He searched in vain for a pay slot on the phone and finally enquired of Margaret, "How do I pay?"

"You haven't got any money," she reminded him.

"I will have."

"Write it in the book," she said, pointing to an ancient notepad hanging on string at the side of the counter. "Stacy will work it out at the end of the month."

Was she supposing he'd still be there, he wondered

A few minutes later, phone jammed against his ear, he willed his daughter to pick up. "Pick it up Sam. Please pick up the phone ...."

Samantha's answering machine cost him another call. He was tempted to leave the store's number but decided against it lest Edwards or Bryan had it traced.

"We'll be back in a few days," said Margaret. "We'll need more supplies, you can call again then."

Putting down the handset he turned to the sepia-edged notepad and was not at all surprised to see the last entry was in 1994. Bear Lake settlement was not, he had already decided, the sort of place that attracted visitors out of the blue.

chapter eight

"Where the hell is Bliss?" bellowed Edwards without rising from behind his resurrected desk. DCI Bryan, thinking to slink unnoticed past the superintendent's office, slithered to a halt and stepped cautiously into the room. "I don't know, Sir," he began, but was immediately shushed with a frantic flick of Edwards' good hand. He got the message but hesitated in turning to close the door, searching for an excuse to leave it ajar as an escape route. Not that he would need to escape, he told himself, it was simply comforting to have the option. Edwards impatiently cleared his throat and flicked harder, as if fending off a persistent wasp. The door seemed to shut by itself under Bryan's hand. "He could be almost anywhere," he concluded, uneasily sliding, uninvited, onto the edge of a chair.

Superintendent Edwards, arm in sling, looking as though he'd dressed in the dark, seemed to deflate as he sank back into his chair. "We've got to find him Peter," he began, his voice tinged with anxiety.

You mean *you* want him found, thought Bryan, his eyes fastened on the skewed blue tie and mismatched green shirt, the only one Edwards possessed with sleeves wide enough to accommodate the cast on his wrist. You want to get to him before he says too much, before he goes public with a sob story about his boss blowing up his flat and killing his cat.

"The press are still nosing around," Edwards continued with a nod to his cracked wrist. "Want to interview me. I've told 'em to eff off, it's none of their damn business. But I want to know who grassed."

"Could've been one of the civvies, or even the ambulance men. A lot of people were around when it happened."

Edwards snorted in disbelief. "More likely Bliss, or that lawyer girl of his. Shit-stirring."

"You have to admit, Guv," said the DCI, "the more you read between the lines, the worse it appears. It must look suspiciously like revenge. I mean, Bliss clobbers you and the next thing ..."

"I *know* what happened."

The DCI shrugged, not knowing what was expected of him.

"Anyway, I wanted to warn you," continued Edwards. "The assistant commissioner's been asking questions. Wants to know who gave the order to trash Bliss's flat. I've been trying to protect you, Peter ... " His voice trailed away, dripping with an unctuousness that stank of insincerity. "What about that girl of his, doesn't she know where he is?"

"She may do, but it's too late now, Guv."

"What do you mean?"

"She's upstairs with the divisional commander right now."

"Shit."

Bryan rubbed it in. "She's not very happy either."

He had seen Samantha ten minutes earlier, face set on revenge, stalking up and down the senior officer's corridor, limbering up for a bout with the DC.

"Do you want to wait in my office Samantha?" he had offered tenderly.

"Trust me, you said," she replied haughtily, without considering his offer. "Trust me. I want to help your Dad."

"I did — I do," he interjected.

"Well, what are you planning to do for an encore — blow up his fucking car?"

"Samantha!"

"Oh, I forgot, somebody already stole his car, before you blew up his flat and killed his cat."

He tried mollifying her. "It wasn't my fault ..."

Delving into her briefcase she grabbed a handful of papers and shoved them in his face. "Well, your name's on here as well."

The writs also cited Edwards, the commissioner, and the policeman whose size eleven's had mangled the poor old cat. The documents, hurriedly drawn up by Samantha herself, and liberally spiced with unnecessary but grandiloquent legalese, alleged criminal damage, unlawful entry and search. Then, she had swallowed hard as she'd added a claim for £1 million compensation — for the stress caused by the death of the cat. It was, she told herself, merely a negotiating figure.

Bryan's thoughts were snapped back to the present as Edwards jumped to his feet and stomped across the room.

"You should have realized what Bliss was up to. He's worked you over, Peter."

"It was your idea ..." started the DCI, but stopped when he realized Edwards was coming to the boil.

"Where the hell is he? Wait till I get my hands on him. And that girl of his — lawyer... Humph ... She'll never practice again when I'm finished with her." Megalomania swung to paranoia without coming close to rationality as he fumed. "I bet the bastard did this on purpose."

DCI Bryan let the atmosphere relax for a few seconds as he concentrated on fingering the creases in his trousers, then he gently stoked Edwards' fire again. "If the press find Bliss before we do, he might say something about the Betty-Ann Gordonstone case."

Edwards wasn't drawn, his focus seemingly fixed on something out the window. "So what?"

"He's convinced she was murdered."

"He's wrong," Edwards said, coming back into the room.

Bryan persisted, feeling eggshells crunching underfoot. "Can you be certain, Guv?"

"Yes," he shot back, barely short of shouting, and sat heavily at his desk, intimidating Bryan with a stare.

Undaunted, Bryan persevered. "He was questioning why the file was destroyed so quickly."

In a flash, Edwards' head dropped and his eyes were drawn to the bottom right-hand drawer of his desk. No sooner had he looked, than he jerked his head back to the DCI and, after missing only half a beat, lied, "I destroyed the file in accordance with standing orders." Had the other man noticed his wavering, he wondered with consternation. He searched the DCI's face for clues, but Bryan's expression suggested nothing untoward. The Betty-Ann Gordonstone file could safely remain undisturbed — for the moment.

DCI Bryan was well aware the file had been logged as 'destroyed.' He had already been to central records to substantiate Bliss's story, but, unlike Bliss, he had been circumspect in his dealing with the clerk, ensuring no one would tell Edwards of his visit. Now he raised his eyebrows in mock surprise. "Oh! You destroyed it yourself, Sir."

"So?"

Bryan hesitated, dying to enquire why. "Nothing, Sir," he replied, then cannily decided to ask on Bliss's behalf. "DI Bliss just found it a bit unusual, that's all."

Edwards shook off the insinuation. "Just bloody well find him. He can't be far away."

Bliss was very far away. Leaving the store, he and Margaret walked together in silence along the gravelled shore toward a large freight canoe dragged up on the beach. Margaret's furrow-browed expression suggested she was seriously deliberating some matter of great importance; finally she stopped, dumped her bags on the ground and snapped, "Look, I don't normally take anyone to my place."

She's changed her mind, thought Bliss.

"But," she continued, "I don't have much choice in your case." The coldness in her voice concerned him and he began to say he wouldn't go when she stopped him with the wag of a finger. "I said you can stay, so you will. But I don't want you upsetting the animals, and I don't allow smoking or drinking."

"I don't smoke," he protested, immediately realizing the truth in the statement. But she had already jammed her hat firmly on her head, scooped the bags from the beach, and stalked off, leaving him slightly bewildered, wondering if it was perhaps a hatred of all men that had forced her to leave home and live so far away.

The act of stowing the bags in the canoe kindled in Bliss a sense of adventure and, looking across the picture-postcard lake, he had the feeling that his pilgrimage would be vindicated on one of the islands near the horizon. Looking back, he felt a tingle of excitement as he watched Margaret striding manfully back over the gravelly beach to collect the eagle. I'm going to enjoy this, he thought, ducking the reason for his mission for a millisecond. Then his mind clouded. How would he confront her? When?

"Talk to her now, what's stopping you," he asked himself, struggling with his conscience, knowing he had no need to go with her to the island, knowing he could persuade Alice to fly him back to civilization if he tried hard enough.

She obviously doesn't want you on the island with her precious animals, logic told him. What will you achieve?

"I might upset her if I just blurt out my reason for finding her."

So?

"She might lie."

She'll lie anyway if she's going to. If she's determined to protect her father, she will.

Why are you really going, Dave?

"I don't want to go back ... not yet, anyway."

At last the truth. You're running away.

"No, I'm not running away ... " His mind reached for the alternative. "I'm running toward."

Toward what?

She was back, eagle's cage in hand, while he was still trying to fathom the answer. "What do I call you anyway?" she asked.

"Uh! Sorry, I was miles away ..." Then he dredged her question back up and answered, "Dave. Call me Dave."

The sun was heading low on the horizon before they reached their destination. A few of the brightest stars were shining faintly against the rapidly darkening sky and, in the semi-darkness, she guided the canoe expertly past rocks hiding beneath the slate grey surface. The violent reds of the autumnal trees had slowly turned purple and dissolved in the setting sun, and the day's breeze had died as Bliss and Margaret slipped between the rocks and rounded the island's headland. Only the sound of their paddle splashes echoing off the rocky walls broke the silence and the cliffs loomed so close in the gloom that Bliss fretted the canoe might crash into them. Then, looking skywards, he saw the stars had vanished and dark blobs of trees, like ominous black clouds, now hung low over the narrow channel, turning it into a tunnel.

Breaking out of the tunnel, the last rays of daylight cast a mystical golden glow over the sandy beach below Margaret's house. "Here we are," she said, expertly pulling the canoe alongside and leaping onto the remnants of an old wooden dock. "This is the first job," she added, implying that there were others; for the briefest of moments, Bliss thought she intended starting the repairs straight away. He tugged at his sweat-soaked shirt as he started clambering out of the canoe. "It's warm," he said, hoping to trigger a conversation. But, before she could reply, a giant dark shape detached itself from the shore and lunged at her. Bliss froze, petrified, unable even to cry out in alarm. One foot, still in the canoe, was rooted to the spot and a thousand fears swelled his brain. Then he felt his legs being prised apart as the canoe drifted away from the dock and a singular fear of being dunked in the lake overcame all else. Giving out a terrified shriek, he grappled for a hold on the damaged woodwork and made a leap for the dock.

"Get down, Bo," Margaret shouted in annoyance, and slapped away the huge dog with a double-handed shove.

"It's a dog," Bliss sighed in relief, as he scrabbled aboard the broken jetty.

"What did you think it was?"

"A bear," he admitted sheepishly.

She grunted at his ignorance as the big black dog sauntered over and jabbed his muzzle firmly into his groin. Margaret gave a little embarrassed laugh. "He's only being friendly ... Come here, Bo." The dog obeyed, instantly, and she gave him a rewarding pat. "He's my guardian."

Bliss composed himself as far as he was able and tried again. "I was saying. It's warm."

She gave the darkening sky a cursory glance. "It could snow tomorrow ... You never know in September."

"Are you serious?"

"Sure. It could. But it won't."

"How do you know?"

"I know," she said mystically, as if she were receiving some celestial weather forecasting service.

"What's a nice girl like you doing in a place like this ..." he began, hoping to lighten the conversation, but sensed her eyes narrowing in angry disapproval and shut up.

"I've got to see to the animals," she said, grabbing the bald eagle's cage.

"Can I come?"

The frosty voice returned instantly. "Like I said, they'd be scared. I'll take you to the house."

"Maybe I can see them later."

"Maybe."

The density of darkness shifted as the house materialized out of the forest, its solidity contrasting with the relative openness of the woodland through which he had stumbled, tripping over roots and bungling into branches, clutching a suitcase and two grocery bags. Margaret lit an oil lamp to guide him through the door then eyed him icily in its warm romantic light. "Come in. This is it. And don't expect to be pampered ... I'm not your skivvy."

Bliss laughed, he hadn't heard the expression for years. "Don't worry. I came for an adventure."

She gave him a sideways glance. "Is that all?"

"Yeah," he replied lightly. "That's all." He could have kicked himself; what a missed opportunity. Why hadn't he at least mentioned some of his concerns?

She didn't challenge his reply, saying simply, "I've got to sort our friend out," with a nod to the eagle's cage.

"Can I see him?"

Dropping to her haunches she delved into the cage and caringly lifted the bird out. His ivory coloured head flopped drowsily in the flickering sepia radiance. "The vet gave him a sedative," she explained, as he stroked the bird's silky breast feathers and felt the tiny blip of its heart. He looked up at Margaret and, close to her for the first time, saw the scar on her lip in the soft golden light, and saw the pain in the depth of her eyes.

"Shall we call him Eddie?" he suggested quietly.

"Eddie?" she asked, with an "are-you-crazy" look.

"You remember. That ski-jumper fellow with the beer-bottle glasses and scary hair."

"Oh yeah." She remembered. "Eddie the Eagle Whatsisname ... But he was a bit of a disaster."

"Precisely."

"You look as though you need some sleep," she said, neither agreeing nor disagreeing with his choice of name as she stuffed the eagle back in the cage. Bliss couldn't argue with her assessment and allowed her to lead him through the main room into the only bedroom. "I'll sleep on the couch," she explained, "I've got to be up early to see to the animals and this way I won't disturb you."

Exhausted, he flopped fully dressed on the bed without examining his surroundings. "Why wounded animals?" he pondered as he drifted off, then answered his own question. "Trust." You can trust animals and they'll trust you. Animals won't betray your trust, particularly if you've nurtured and nursed them. That's what she is seeking: trust.

"What are you seeking Dave?" he asked himself. But before he could answer, he thankfully fell asleep in a bed for the first time in three nights.

The steeply slanting morning sunshine woke him just after dawn. Bright shafts of light split by the trees just outside the window poured into the curtainless room. Desperate for a pee, he gingerly opened the bedroom door in search of a toilet and found that his readied apologies were wasted. The couch was bare and his eyes took in a multi-textured mishmash of dog-eared furniture. Nothing matched, even on the same piece: a kinked length of tree branch, bark still attached, stood in for one leg of a plain oak dining table, three differently patterned carpets fought for floor space, and two unmatched couches acted as sentinels for the fireplace. One couch, its Victorian rose pattern almost indistinguishable beneath a dense blanket of shed dog's hair, had lost an arm — and there were teeth marks clearly gouged into the remaining stump. Two bookcases of differing heights, stacked with a disarray of books, took up one wall, and a neat pile of cassette tapes stood on a roughly hewn coffee table. "Mahler," he said, picking up one of the tapes. "More Mahler," he added, inspecting another. Then he bent down and scanned the rest. "All Mahler." His eyes swept the room seeking a stereo; he kicked himself — no electricity.

An old hunting rifle tucked into a corner caught his attention. "Loaded!" he exclaimed, picking it up. Why not, he thought; in fact, it's surprising she doesn't carry it with her. He replaced the rifle and inhaled deeply to ingest the room's ambience. The smell of a wood fire filled his nostrils. Aged smoke — not the morning-after-a-party smell of piled ashtrays — the pleasant smell of smoke-pickled wood. The damp earthy smell of the surrounding forest was also there, in the background, together with the unmistakable scent of an animal. Bo the bear-dog, he guessed.

With his hand on another door, a question suddenly flipped him around. What's wrong with this picture, he asked himself, his brain struggling with the sensation that something was amiss. The lack of television, radio, and computer was obvious, but he couldn't shake off the feeling that the room was not as it should be.

With the question unanswered, he opened the door in front of him and was taken by surprise at the meagreness of the kitchen. Devoid of electrical or gas appliances, it resembled an old-fashioned scullery. Even the tin washboard dangling off an iron hook above the galvanized sink would have been more at home in an anthropological museum. However, the fire glowing inside a wood-burning stove, topped by a gently steaming kettle, gave comforting life to the room.

Then the bathroom, tacked onto the back of the kitchen, took his breath away. He had walked from the nineteenth to the twenty-first century in a single step. An oversized double-ended bath complete with gold-plated taps dominated the room, its deep burgundy richness accentuated by gold-striped wallpaper and gold fleck in the ivory floor tiles. Even the shower curtain patterned with tiny burgundy fleurs-de-lys, hung on huge golden rings, had obviously been carefully matched. Bliss caught his breath and turned the sink's hot tap speculatively, and was stunned when a gush of steaming water poured into the basin. With relief, Bliss used the toilet before continuing his exploration.

Stepping back in time he returned to the kitchen, searched unsuccessfully for coffee, and made tea instead. Cup in hand he wandered back through the main room, stepped out onto a wide verandah, and was startled by the freshness of the air. Clear but not crisp, the air's edge was rounded by a light mist rising off the warm lake. Margaret's house, which he now realized was an elaborate log cabin, was perched precariously on wooden stilts above jagged rocks, without a scrap of flat land anywhere in sight. Ahead, looking out through the trees, the rock face dropped untidily to the lake and, in the distance, heavily wooded islands glowed with a rusty redness in the morning sunlight. Absorbing the view, he lowered himself onto a nearby rock and felt his cares draining away. All thoughts of Edwards and the Gordonstone murders dissolved in the dawn light and a memory of a similar dawn in England, fifteen or more years earlier, took over his mind.

He'd borrowed a bike from a friend. It had ten speeds, but the double-clanger wasn't working, so he managed with five. A dry wheel bearing sang out for oil, and the narrow hard racing saddle sliced into his bum. "I'm going to regret this," he thought aloud.

By the time the early morning sun had kissed the rolling Surrey downs it had surrendered half its warmth to the wispy high cloud, and the other half to a milky mist. But it retained enough brilliance to sparkle on the diamonds of dew trapped on the spiders' webs laced along the hedgerows. The constant buzz of traffic from the nearby motorway was in some strange way comforting as he rode through a beech copse, then he stopped as a stray dog stood firmly on the path, challenging his progress. Eye to eye they stood, testing each other's resolve, for what seemed like minutes and he'd just decided to retreat when the dog slowly turned, flaunted its bushy red tail, and strode off confidently into the undergrowth. "It's a fox," he breathed. He'd seen them before, many of them, all with their guts hanging out or heads pulped — road kill — but this one was so different. A powerful predator marking his ground, making his statement: "I'm not afraid of you." Overhead, the canopy came to life as the fox moved away. Bickering squirrels rattled autumn leaves and dropped the odd nut, and a couple of magpies screeched in alarm at his approach, then relaxed into joyful song behind him.

At the edge of the wood he emerged into a shaggy pasture spattered with blood-red poppies and snowy daises. The mist had cleared and the dazzling sun suddenly burst through the clouds. He dismounted, turned his face to catch the warmth, shut out the hum of the traffic, ignored the drone of a small plane on its final approach to a nearby airfield, blocked out the slightly acrid smell of a local factory firing up for the day, and found himself singing Jerusalem, loudly.

"And did those feet in ancient times
Walk upon England's mountains green."

A feeling of foolishness stopped him. He spun around expecting to find someone watching, but there was no one. But then he recognized a vaguely familiar landscape. The rectangular tower of a Norman church rose above a high blackberry hedge on the far side of the field and Melanie's memory drew him toward it.

He found her grave with difficulty; it had been several years and it was just a neglected little mound with a small, inscribed iron cross put there by the church. No headstone, no flowers, no cherubs.

"I'm sorry, Melanie," he muttered, then found himself singing again, not caring whether he had an audience.

"And did those feet in ancient times
Walk upon England's mountains green.
And was the holy lamb of God
On England's pleasant pastures seen."

Are those words right, he wondered, then thought,
what the hell, and pushed on.

"And did the countenance divine
Walk forth among these crowded hills.
And was Jerusalem. Builded here.
On England's green and pleasant land."

He knew it was wrong but felt it was right.

"Beautiful, isn't it?" Margaret said, startling him
as she squatted on the rock beside him, her moccasins
muffling her approach. He'd been far away — back in
England, back home with Sarah. No — back home,
but not with Sarah, with Melanie. Without responding, he lingered one more second in his daydream and
felt satisfied that he had somehow saluted the land of
his birth, rekindling in himself the feeling he'd had at
the time. The feeling that in some small way he had
been responsible for putting things right with
Margaret's sister while making the day beautiful,
almost God-like.

He put the memory aside and turned to Margaret.
"Why did you come here?"

Her answer, when it came, was not what he'd
expected, not what he'd hoped for.

"I always wanted to be Robinson Crusoe," she said,
confiding in him her childhood fantasy. "Nobody else,
not Barbie or a Bond bimbo." She gazed dreamily into
her memory. "I've read that book a thousand times ...

alone on a desert island, surrounded by wild animals, surviving off the land."

Bliss glanced around, as if searching. "What about Man Friday?"

"You can be Man Friday," she said with a certain lightness of tone.

"I came on Sunday."

Her lips experimented with "Man Sunday" but she shook her head. "It doesn't sound right. You'll have to stick with Friday."

"I suppose Bo is your Man Friday, really," Bliss said, wondering where the dog was.

Margaret's face instantly scrunched into a fiercely probing glare. "What are you suggesting?"

He caught her meaning and unspeakable images invaded his mind. "Nothing. Just wondered where he was," he added innocently, with a disarming smile, quickly moving on.

Her face relaxed. "He's just behind you."

Bliss swivelled, but saw nothing, only trees and rocks.

"Bo," Margaret called, laughing, and the huge animal bounced out of the brush not six feet away, giving Bliss a heart-stopping jolt. The dog, all black apart from a grubby white bib, dropped by her side yet was still shoulder height.

"What kind is he?" enquired Bliss, barely bringing his voice under control.

"A misfit," she replied, as if it were a recognized breed, then she laughed as she gave the huge animal a friendly ruffle. "He was my first patient. Somebody in the town kept him chained up 'cos he got too big and frightened the neighbours. I took him in when no one else wanted him."

I can see why, thought Bliss, warily eyeing the giant's teeth as he yawned with a gape as wide as a rabbit hole.

"Nice dog," he said, still none the wiser as to its pedigree but intimidated by the venomous look in the dog's eyes.

"I wanted to talk to you about your father," he carried on, in a serious tone, but she quickly waved him off.

"Not now," she said, rising. "I'm going for a dip. I swim every morning."

He started to get up, "I wouldn't mind joining you."

A troubled, flustered look took over her face. "The thing is, I don't need a bathing suit here. I don't even have a bathing suit."

"Oh, I see."

Then she cautioned him sharply as she started down the steep path toward the lake: "Now I've told you, I'd appreciate if you didn't watch. You'll be more embarrassed than me if I catch you." There was no hint of a tease, no suggestion she was egging him on, no flirtatious "I bet you can't catch me." Bliss knew exactly where he stood.

The massive dog went with Margaret and together they slipped almost silently into the woodland like a couple of stealthy tigers off to hunt, leaving Bliss to catch his breath. Wow, he thought. She's some tough cookie. Then he carefully reconsidered. Tough or vulnerable? Maybe she's more like a wounded animal, putting up a brave fight, refusing to lick her wounds in public in case a predator might take advantage.

He sat back on the rock, feeling the sun's early blush, listening to the crackle of brittle twigs, deliberating the point at which he might be able to broach the subject that had drawn him there. He would have to proceed warily, he decided; offer tidbits, gain her confidence, encourage her to discuss her past. But when to tell, and what to tell, that's the problem. I can't just come out with it, he realized. I can't just say, was your Dad screwing you as well as Melanie? How did he drown her? Did you see it? Did you hear her cries for help, her pleas for mercy? And, while we're on the topic, how did he kill your mother exactly? Oh, and by the way, did I mention your father was murdered? She must have some idea, he thought, some clue. She's not stupid, clearly. She seems to have survived very well.

The sound of rhythmic splashes from the lake below told him she had reached the water. Why *did* she come here, he wondered. To escape from her father? More likely he packed her off, fearing she might let something slip. Then a chill ran through him. What if I'm completely wrong? What if she knows nothing? Suspects nothing? An image flashed through his mind, of Margaret, completely unknowing, standing in front of him like a wide-eyed kid. "Are you saying my Dad killed Melanie and Mum? Are you suggesting my Dad sexually abused me? Are you trying to tell me that somebody murdered my Dad?"

He brushed the notions aside with a shake of his head. She must know, he thought, at the very least she must have some suspicions. But would she say anything, particularly now he's dead?

The splashes faded gradually as she swam further out into the lake and Bliss found himself tempted to stand and peer through the trees to glimpse the naked young woman, but her parting admonition still rang in his ears. Remaining glued to the rock he wondered why he expected her to tell him the truth about her father when she had never said anything before. Perhaps Samantha was right. Margaret had plenty of opportunities over the years to spill the beans yet had chosen not to do so. Why should she admit it now if not before? In any case, it would be easier for her to deny the truth, even to herself. If false memories of sex assault are possible then, he reasoned, so are false memories that nothing happened.

He was still lost in his deliberations when she swept passed him on her return. Wearing only ripped jeans and a skimpy T-shirt, her hardened dark nipples strained visibly against the flimsy damp fabric. "C'mon," she called. "We'd better get started."

"Right now?" he enquired, hoping they would have an opportunity to talk first.

"I start at sunrise, finish at sunset," she called over her shoulder, as she headed into the house in search of tools. "There's no power, only oil lamps and candles. We have to work when the sun shines."

"I noticed," he admitted, slipping into her wake, intrigued by the pert, self-confident way she held herself — intrigued but not stimulated, feeling that her feminine sexuality was somehow lost in her deep tan. Her skin, weathered brown and prematurely wrinkled with fine but deep creases, encompassed and shielded her like a suit of armour. With a smile to himself, he guessed that, even totally naked, she could walk unconcernedly through a rugby team's change room and, if anyone whistled, kick him in the balls.

He tried again. "I need to talk to you."

She fobbed him off. "We've got to make a start on the dock. We can talk while we're working."

He wanted to stop her, grab hold of her, make her stand still and listen, but there was nothing to catch on to. The bare flesh of her shoulders and arms was well protected with their bronze armour-plate, and the parts barely covered with the T-shirt were clearly off limits.

"Breakfast," he asked hopefully.

She laughed. "It's almost lunchtime."

"It's only nine o'clock," he protested, carefully checking his watch, concerned that he'd miscalculated the time difference.

"Like I said, nearly lunchtime. Anyway, you haven't earned anything yet."

The dock, a jetty of roughly hewn logs set on tree stumps, had disintegrated during a recent storm, she said. Most of the pieces were still there and the reconstruction was as simple as Lego — she said.

"So what did you want to ask me?" she queried, effortlessly dragging a heavy baulk out of the water, swinging it into place, and directing him to hold it. He hesitated, balancing the lump while she hefted a hammer. He didn't want it to be like this, beyond his control. She had dictated the territory and timing and left him off balance. He knew what was happening. Timing is everything, he thought to himself, wanting to set her down somewhere comfortable and prime her to expect the worst. Then he thought, how do I do that? Is anyone ever really prepared for the worst? But now did not seem right at all. He wasn't ready.

"Well?" The hammer hovered.

He stalled. "I'd like to know a bit more about you first. How do you survive here?"

"My needs are few ..." she began, smacking a nail squarely on the head, sending a shiver through the log. Pausing, she looked up. "Oh Christ, that sounds like a literary line. What I mean is: I'm happy enough here."

Bliss caught the qualified nature of her response. Not, "I'm happy here." Only, "Happy enough." Then questioned aloud, "I wonder if anybody is truly happy?"

"I quite like being on my own," she added, interrupting his musing.

There it was again. Not, "I like being on my own," but, "I quite like . . ."

"What about the animals?" he queried.

"Animals?" she asked, vaguely.

"The animals you take care of," he reminded her. "Where are they anyway?"

"Oh," she gave an expansive wave. "All over the island. They're wild."

"You don't keep them in cages?"

She shuddered. "I don't believe in cages."

Showing impatience, she put down the hammer, sat on her haunches and adopted a no-nonsense tone, "Come on Detective, just why did you come here?"

He made it as straightforward as he could. "We think your Dad might have been murdered."

"I wouldn't be surprised. He had a lot of enemies."

"You're not upset," he continued, hoping she would make his job simpler. Anticipating that she might spill everything, expecting her to say something like, "He deserved it after what he did to Melanie, Mum and me." But he was disappointed. She sloughed off his intimation and carried on attacking the nail.

"Don't you want to know how?" he queried.

"Shot," she suggested.

"Poisoned."

"That figures."

"Why?"

"Poetic justice, I suppose. He was a poisonous man. He poisoned people." She smashed the nail with unnecessary force, bending it double, then spat, "He poisoned everything he touched."

Bliss stared at her, alarmed by the violence of her outburst; alarmed but heartened.

Thinking she had read his mind, that he expected her to be devastated, she continued. "If you think I'm going to start blubbering, you'll have a long wait. I did all the crying I was going to do a long time ago."

Hanging precariously over the edge of the damaged dock, he turned away and looked down into the dark lake, digesting her words, considering a response. Then he caught her reflection in the water and Melanie's image swam into view: her long dark hair billowing like strands of weed in a stream. "Melanie," he blurted out. "What happened to Melanie?"

Margaret's face pinched into a puzzled frown. "She drowned. It was an accident. Don't you remember?"

Of course he remembered, how could he ever forget? "What ... What I meant was," he stumbled, "What I'm asking ..." He paused mid-sentence and thought, what I should have asked you twenty years ago... Then he began again, looking her squarely in the eyes. "What I'm trying to say is ... Are you sure it was an accident?"

"Of course I am," she answered without deliberation. "Why?"

Now what? he thought.

They worked most of the day, stopping only long enough to eat the bread and cheese she had taken with her, to drink from a clear spring spouting out of the rocks, and to disappear self-consciously into the bushes from time to time. By mid-afternoon Bliss's hands were screaming for him to stop. Already sore from paddling the canoe the previous day, his palms seared with each baulk of rough timber. Margaret seemed unaware of his suffering and, studying her hands he realized why. Her muscled, sinewy hands, with calloused fingers and ragged nails, were femininely sized but masculine in appearance. They could be the hands of a Peruvian child miner, or a ten-year-old Indian rock breaker, he thought, watching her deftly swing an adze.

Although his city hands, usually wedded to a pen or keyboard, took the brunt of the torture, his back, shoulders, and neck were not unscathed. Eventually he had to admit defeat.

"No problem," she said. "I've got other things to do."

"The animals?" he enquired.

"Yeah. I'd better see how Eddie's getting on."

Intrigued, he was about to ask if he could go with her, but she quickly quashed his unspoken request. "You can cook us some dinner," she said, leaving no room for dissention.

He was asleep by the time she returned. He'd eaten — beef stew with peas and beans. So much for living off the land, he thought, disappointed to find her cupboard stashed with cans, packets, and jars looking remarkably similar to those in Safeway or Sainsbury's, many of them bearing best-before dates that would light up a health inspector's eyes.

Leaving Margaret a note, he slipped exhausted into her bed, feeling a sense of fulfillment, of satisfaction, that he'd not experienced for a long time. But sleep, which should have come instantly, struggled to find a foothold as his conscience continued to nag him. "When are you going to question her? You've put it off for twenty years and you're still doing it." Tomorrow, he promised himself. Tomorrow.

He woke early, refreshed, raring to go, and slipped into the main room. Margaret, asleep on the couch, didn't stir. But Bo, on the other couch, growled a warning and she woke with a start, fighting off the bedclothes, giving him a tantalizing peek at the firm hillocks of her bare breasts. "Sorry," he mumbled, diving into the kitchen. He checked his pulse and was annoyed to find it normal.

A few minutes later, freshly brewed tea in hand, he walked out of the back door straight into the forest. The morning light filtering through the canopy dappled the rocks with a blush as the sun reflected off the crimson leaves. No one would believe it back home, he thought, staring up into the canopy where the colours had gone wild. They would think a photograph had been retouched or taken with a vermilion filter. Mindful of Margaret's warning not to disturb her animals he cautiously scouted around, exploring just the forest's fringe, half expecting to come upon cages or compounds. There were none, But hadn't she said that she didn't approve of cages?

Returning to the small clearing, he stood with his back to the door, cradling his tea and absorbing the freshness of the atmosphere. And he held his breath to marvel at the peacefullness of the surroundings, which contrasted starkly to the noisiness of his concrete block home in London.

"Where's your camera, Dave?" Margaret asked softly, reading his mind as she slid quietly out of the kitchen door behind him.

"Lost it," he replied calmly, grateful a squeaky door hinge had heralded her approach.

"Some adventurer you are."

"It was in the same bag as my traveller's cheques," he lied.

"These are some of the oldest rocks in the world," she said, with a hand sweep, and with the same sense of pride a suburban housewife might have used to describe her fashionably restyled kitchen.

The morning just blew by. Hauling, heaving, sawing, and hammering demanded their full attention; all the while giant red leaves drifted onto the lake from the overhanging maples. The hot sun filtering through the trees was tempered by the coolness of the lake; the spring water refreshed them and soothed their aching hands from time to time. As lunchtime approached, the work was almost complete, and shoals of temporarily evicted small-fry wafted joyously back under the dock, safe again within its tangle of supports and buttresses.

He had procrastinated all morning, hiding behind one excuse after another, deferring the moment when he would have to risk distressing Margaret with allegations against her deceased father. With the work almost completed he judged the time to be right. But, no sooner had he formulated his opening question, than she announced she was going to check on the eagle. With a sense of relief, and a nasty dig from his conscience in response, he called, "Give my love to Eddie," as she slipped into the forest with her canine companion leading the way.

The moment following her departure, Bliss found himself fighting off an irrational impulse to pursue her. "Why?" he questioned himself, but couldn't put his finger on the reason. It was, in any case, out of the question. Margaret moved too swiftly and silently through the bush to permit him to follow unnoticed, and Bo was never far away. The dog's antenna ears, responding to the slightest hint of a cracked twig or rustled leaf, would soon alert her to an interloper's presence. Sitting on the dock, analyzing his thoughts, Bliss realized he was feeling left out, even jealous that he'd been preemptively cut out of Eddie's life so soon after entering it. But was he jealous of being excluded from Eddie's life, or from Margaret's?

"Jealous I can't participate in her life? " he asked inwardly.

"That's preposterous," he told himself. "I'm not jealous. Anyway, I'm helping her rebuild the dock."

"That's not the same and you know it," said the voice in his mind.

Quite illogically, he quit work in retaliation for his perceived abandonment, slung his shirt onto the bank, loosened his muscles, flopped face down on the dock and peered into the lake. In seconds his mind was swimming with the minnows. Swishing lazily back and forth. Drifting with the current. Indistinct images of Sarah and Samantha, appearing more like sisters than mother and daughter, rippled across the surface of his imagination, but Melanie's memory was never far beneath, like a naiad enticing him into the depths. A sudden chill in the air gave him a creepy feeling, making his skin crawl. Melanie's spirit, he imagined, was angry that he was dodging his responsibility yet again. He tried shaking off the spectre by pledging to question Margaret on her return, promising to unravel the mystery of her sister's drowning. But the cold eerie feeling persisted and, in a second, everything changed. The shoal of fish disappeared in a silver streak. The sun faded. The living water died under his gaze. Spellbound, he peered deeper, expecting to spot a prowling predator. Then foreboding menace darkened his mind. He sensed a creature, a hydra of the deep, watching him, sizing him up, preparing to attack.

He shot back from the water in alarm, looked up, and came face-to-face with a real monster — two monsters, actually — just spitting distance away. Two sour-faced, heavy-set men in a canoe, as motionless as if they had just risen from the depths, both with rifles pointing directly at him. Their canoe sat motionless in the water just six feet off the end of the dock. How they got there was beyond Bliss's range of thought. It was one of those How'd-they-do-that, take-your-breath-away illusions. A trick so cunning you end up with a headache if you try to work out how it was performed. He knew it was a trick; it had to be. But the hairs on the back of his neck didn't accept it as a trick, nor did his pulse. All his senses urged him to get up and run, but his limbs wouldn't co-operate.

"Look behind you," he ordered himself, his mind desperately seeking reassurance in the solidity of the island, but the pit-bull glare of the men simply refused to release his gaze. He tried to blink, thinking that they might disappear as quickly as they had materialized, but the muscles of his eyelids refused to respond. His spirit cringed under the malevolent stares of the men and he felt like an intruder. He was an intruder.

"Ojibwa," Margaret whispered in his ear, jolting him back to reality. She had returned. Another illusion? He took a deep breath and risked a quick glance over his shoulder. She was right behind him. "Thank God."

One of the men spoke; fiction became fact. The speaker, in the front of the canoe, an Ojibwa with a braided mane of silver grey hair, a bulbous nose, and fiercely slit eyes, rattled off an angry fusillade. Although his words were directed at Margaret, Bliss had the definite impression that he was the subject. He could have dropped dead when Margaret animatedly replied in the man's own language.

He tugged at her arm in concern. "Don't they speak English?"

"This is their country, Dave. When in Rome ..."

"What's wrong?" he asked, sensing the natives were not happy with his presence.

"Shush. I'll tell you in a minute."

The canoe hovered off the end of the dock. Closer than Bliss would have preferred, but at least the rifles were lowered. The banter continued between Margaret and the front man and Bliss turned his attention to the other. A man with decayed teeth and facial features straight out of the Stone Age. An escapee from a natural history museum in backwoodsman's disguise, complete with camouflage cap, jacket, and jeans.

"What's their problem?" Bliss asked, realizing there was one.

Concern puckered her face. "They're worried about you being here."

"What's it got to do with them?"

"Some of their ancestors are buried on the island. They think you'll disturb their spirits. They're scared you might awaken Windigo."

"Windigo?"

"A cannibalistic monster, according to their legends."

"They don't still believe in that sort of mumbo-jumbo do they?"

"Do you believe evil people are tormented in hell when they die?"

"I used to. I'm not so sure anymore."

"But a lot of Christians do."

He had to agree.

She shrugged, her point made, and returned to her conversation with the Natives. They heard her out, then picked up their oars to indicate the meeting was winding down. The leader, barking a final string of abusive-sounding words, concluded with some methodical finger stabbing. Bliss, uncomfortable, fearful even, attempted a bold stance and kept his attention firmly focussed on the men who, he thought, wouldn't have worn a smile if paid.

Then a hump, under a tarpaulin in the bottom of the canoe, twitched. Bliss caught the movement in his peripheral vision and immediately dismissed it as being part of the illusion. But it moved again. There was something man-sized and alive under the tarpaulin. He had trouble restraining himself, his subconscious screaming for him to demand an explanation, but the Indians silently dipped their paddles and the canoe started moving smoothly away. "Stop," he wanted to shout, but the word wouldn't come out. The aura of darkness lingered. The chill remained. Bliss sought support in Margaret's face, but her pallid complexion and drawn look only served to worry him more. Had she spotted the movement? She must have done, he reasoned. But she calmly bent and picked up her hammer to finish off the last few nails on the dock.

"What was in the canoe?" Bliss asked with panic in his voice.

"I dunno — moose, I expect," she said, confirming she had seen the movement.

"It was still alive."

She walloped a nail. "So? They're hunters aren't they?"

Her lack of concern took the edge off his tension. "What's wampum?" he asked in a lighter tone, seeing that the Natives were now almost out of sight around a headland.

"Where'd you hear that?" she shot back, fighting off a troubled frown.

He played it down. "I thought the Indian said it, but I might have misheard." He hadn't misheard.

"No idea," she lied, with a shake of the head, and heartily smacked the final nail into place.

chapter nine

Peter Bryan left the cryptic invitation on Samantha's answering machine. "I think we've some unfinished business. Off the record. Dinner ... tonight, if possible. Please call."

"I'll meet you there," she said, calling back. "I know the place," she got in quickly, rebuffing his offer of a lift before he could get it out of his mouth, setting her own terms. "And I'll pay my share."

"It's company perks," he lied.

"All right ... But no tricks," she added, wondering what she meant by tricks.

"Samantha!" His tone was hurt, but she couldn't be sure whether or not it was genuine.

"Seven-thirty then."

She considered being annoyingly late in retaliation for her father's mistreatment but, impatient to find out what the detective chief inspector wanted, arrived early. They met in the restaurant's car park, fighting for the same space. He gave way the moment he recognized her car and ended up trudging from an overspill car park in an adjacent field. Set on the banks of a languid river, the converted boat house sat long and low. Scrubbed and repointed turn-of-the-century brickwork, with massive black oak half-timbering, gave it a mock Tudor appearance. The front door had been cleverly fashioned out of the bow section of an old clinker barge.

Lingering politely just inside the vestibule while he parked, she admired a couple of antique skiffs, which dropped from davits secured in the exposed roof timbers and alluded to the building's history. But the heavy nets looping lazily around the walls were, she thought, more suited to Icelandic cod than the tiddlers struggling for survival among the artificial reefs of supermarket carts and car tires in the adjacent river.

"Phew. Sorry. It was a long way." Peter Bryan's breathless apology brought a satisfied smirk to her lips, but she wiped it away as they were led to a table overlooking the aqueous junkyard.

They verbally tangoed while awaiting the first course, neither willing to risk showing their hand too soon. Their common interest in criminal justice enabled them to manage fifteen minutes or more without stooping to the weather.

"You're young to be a DCI," she said, idly stirring a dollop of crème fraîche into her crab and oyster broth.

He beamed, flattered, but his attention was drawn by her distracted look. "You're young to be a lawyer," he parried, wondering what concerned her. She smiled her thanks, but privately regretted mentioning age, fearful he might consider her inexperienced and not take her seriously.

"I suppose this was Edwards' idea," she said, changing the subject with an expansive hand gesture. The single motion summed up both the opulence of the setting and the undoubtedly astronomical bill.

"No. Actually it was my idea. Edwards doesn't know we're meeting."

"Oh, Chief Inspector," she said saucily. "He'll smack your bum if he finds out you're fraternizing with the enemy."

He gagged on his soup. "I like you, Samantha Bliss."

"Well don't think you're going to buy me off with a dinner."

He didn't think so, but would have been pleased if he could. "I can't imagine anyone being able to buy you off."

"So what's this in aid of?" she asked, coming to the point.

"To tell you the truth. I actually think your Dad may have been right. I'm beginning to suspect there's something fishy going on."

"Told you so," she replied, with a look that said, "I know I didn't, but I bet you're too polite to deny it."

She was correct, and a fleeting thoughtful frown was replaced by a look of warm openness in his deep blue eyes. "Now we're on the same side, I thought we might pool what we know and see if there's any answers."

"Try me," she replied, making it obvious she wanted to see all his cards and make sure there was nothing up his sleeve.

"Your father was concerned about a file Superintendent Edwards destroyed."

"The file on the dead girl's mother." She nodded. "Betty-Ann Gordonstone."

"You know about it?"

"Dad told me."

"Well ... No one ever destroys files the very day they become obsolete. Some hang around for years. I'm always getting reminders from admin about defunct files that are still clogging up their cupboards. Edwards wanted that one out of the way for some reason."

"Dad said it was because he was worried he might be proved wrong. That it wasn't a suicide."

"Edwards might think that now, since the husband's murder, but he had no reason to think that three years ago, when he was in such a tearing hurry to get rid of her file."

"I see ... And?"

Bryan hesitated, unsure about whether he was doing the right thing, then took a mouthful of smoked salmon pâté and plunged in. "I think Edwards caused that trouble at your dad's flat on purpose."

"Why? How?"

DCI Bryan edged back in his seat and held his information to ransom. "You tell me what you know first."

She eyed him suspiciously, sizing up his motives, and decided she had nothing to lose. "Basically, all I know is what he told me, which you already know. But I do have something else."

It wasn't much, just a scrap of newspaper, but she drew it out of her handbag like a conjurer's silk scarf. "Gordonstone's funeral," she said, holding the picture in front of his face. "Recognize anyone?"

He scanned it seriously. "No ... I don't think so."

"There," she pointed testily. "Behind a gravestone. Isn't that Edwards?"

He squinted hard. "It certainly could be, but I can only see part of his face."

"What's he doing there?"

"If it is him."

She double-checked. "I'm sure it's him."

Taking the picture from her, Bryan gave it a long thoughtful stare. "Maybe he took a personal interest after the death of Gordonstone's wife."

"But that was ten years ago."

Topping up her glass to indicate that the subject was going no further, he asked, "Have you heard from your dad?"

"What is this, Chief Inspector," she said with a smile, "the old tender trap routine? Soften me up and catch me with my pants down?"

He raised his eyebrows. "You said it —"

She cut him off sharply. "I was speaking metaphorically."

They sat in silence as the hors d'oeuvres plates were swept away by an almost invisible waiter.

"I thought we were here to discuss why you blew up Dad's flat," she continued, her staring eyes reflecting her seriousness.

"I didn't blow up your dad's flat," he protested, moving a small vase of sweet-peas from the table's centre to see her better.

"Well ..." she started to remonstrate, but he stopped her with a wagging finger.

"We used a stun grenade, that's all. It just disorientates someone long enough to stop them hurting themselves 'til we get to them."

"What about his television? You certainly stunned that."

"Collateral damage," he replied with a throwaway gesture. "We'll buy him a new one. The biggest screen Sony makes if he wants."

"What about the fucking ... Sorry, what about his cat? Your guys stunned him all right."

"I'm sorry, but I thought I was doing the right thing."

Her raised eyebrows invited him to explain, if he could.

He tried, sombrely. "When I went to see your dad, he said something that made me think it wouldn't take a lot to push him over the edge. I even got the impression that he was considering ..: " He glanced up at her, checking the effect of his words. Her concerned expression showed understanding, so Bryan left his fear unspoken and continued. "I made light of it, but it worried me. Edwards said your dad had a gun in the flat and when he wouldn't answer the door I thought he might actually do himself in."

"But the flat was empty."

"I didn't know that. The silly sod had left the telly on."

Samantha blushed. "I left the TV on. Not Dad."

"You what?"

"Well, I didn't know you were going to bomb the place."

"We didn't . . ."

"OK, OK. You didn't bomb it. Anyway, I'd left the TV on as company for his cat." She'd almost got the words out before her face crumpled at the memory and tiny tears squeezed down her cheeks.

He handed her his napkin. "I am sorry Samantha. I really thought I was doing the right thing."

"Killing his cat," she sniffled.

"No. That was an accident. He attacked one of the men."

"Wouldn't you if someone had just blown your eardrums to smithereens and smashed down your front door?"

"I suppose I would."

"Thank you for that, Chief Inspector," she said, straightening her face and blowing her nose loudly, oblivious to the grimacing couple at the next table. "But what's this got to do with Edwards?"

"Edwards told everyone your dad had a gun."

"I didn't know Dad had a gun."

"Neither did the firearms department. I checked. He didn't even have a certificate. He wasn't even authorized to carry. His authority was suspended when he went sick."

"So why did Edwards say that?"

Another waiter, young and flashy with a sharp beaked nose and a scary hairstyle, managed to turn a performance of de-boning a Dover sole into a pantomime, giving Bryan a chance to consider his answer. Samantha used the interlude to fix her tear-streaked make-up.

"What do you think?" Bryan replied eventually, as the waiter went in search of vegetables.

She made him wait for a response, seemingly probing among the *poireau a la Milanaise* for a clue. "I don't know," she said finally, flipping a healthy portion of leeks onto her plate. "Maybe he thought Dad did have a gun." Then realization dawned and she slowly raised her head and caught a look in his eyes. "Or ... Are you suggesting what I think you're suggesting?"

"Maybe."

Incredulity strained her voice. "You're saying Edwards wanted somebody to shoot him. To kill my dad?"

"All I know is, Edwards knew that with an armed man in the place we'd have to go in heavy handed.

She digested Bryan's revelation, struggling with a mouthful of fish, her appetite fading. "But there wasn't an armed man in there; just a defenceless old cat." Her tears started again. "I love my dad, Peter."

"I know."

"He can be a bit of a nuisance at times."

"He's a parent, luv. It goes with the territory."

"Are you a parent?"

"Not as far as I know. I'm not even married." He picked up the bottle of Puligny Montrachet. "More wine?" he asked, in an undisguised attempt to change the subject.

She nodded. "So why did you want to see me?"

"To tell you what I know."

"That's a bit lame. You could have told me over the phone."

"Would you be offended if I said I wanted to have dinner with you?"

"Depends."

"On what?"

"Your ulterior motive."

"Do I have to have one?"

"You'd be the first man I've ever been out with who didn't."

"So what are my motives?"

She raised her eyebrows. "I think that's one question we can both answer. Don't you Chief Inspector?"

Margaret had cooked dinner — nothing fancy. Difficult to believe she owns a restaurant, thought Bliss, already bored with tinned stew. They had eaten by the light of an oil lamp in front of a log fire while Bo lay at their feet sharpening his teeth on a giant bone, malevolently eyeing Bliss from time to time, as if to say. "Just practicing—you're next mate."

Margaret and Bliss were two strangers hiding behind barricades, each waiting for the other to crack. Margaret's work-hardened, compact body was still stiffly bound with an intensity that troubled Bliss. The Natives, or whatever she had seen in the bottom of their canoe, still had her gripped.

"You could write a book about your life," said Bliss, attempting to thaw her.

"I've scribbled bits and pieces," she replied unenthusiastically. "I've given it some thought."

"Can I read it?" he asked brightly, hoping to find in her writing some opening gambit on which to pry into her past.

Her shaking head dispelled his hopes. "It's only scratchings. I'd be too embarrassed to let anyone see it."

She caught his look of disappointment and made a decision. "I have written a poem though," she said, rising and making her way toward one of the bookcases.

At last, thought Bliss, heart in mouth.

Returning to the table with a slim leather-bound book, its gilt-edged pages glinting in the lamplight, she sat opposite him, on Bo's couch. "This is a poem I wrote about living alone on an island," she said. "I call it 'Shipwrecked.'" Then she started reading, and he found himself strangely enchanted by her lisp.

"Life passes by with a whisper of breeze,
Rippling the waves and stirring the trees;
But, spurned and rejected, goes on its way:
Life, on an island, holds no sway."

She looked up, checking his reaction. Entranced by the pencil-thin scar on her lip, wishing he could kiss it better, he urged her on with a nod. She bent, as if to read, yet pulled every word straight from her heart.

"Time in the fast lane rushes by
From the time of birth 'til the time you die;
But e'en though the sun sets day after day,
Time, on an island, holds no sway.

"Buy this or that, dog, goat, or cat,
Brand new knickers or a saucy hat,
But here you can put your wallet away:
Wealth, on an island, holds no sway.

"Love of another, abjured and denied,
Lust unappeased with a tear in the eye,
Shipwrecked, marooned, and cast away,
Love, on an island, holds no sway.

"Hope fades fast but lingers long
For the shipwrecked sailor and his plaintive song;
In a search for a saviour both far and away,
Hope, on an island, holds no sway."

She closed the book with sad deliberation.

"That's wonderful," he cried, oblivious to the darkness within the verse. "Have you written anything else?"

"Nothing worth reading," she replied, running her tongue self-consciously over her lip, and quickly returned the book to the shelf, indicating her unwillingness to share further.

Bliss got the message and changed the subject, laying the groundwork for the questions he wanted to ask about her relationship with her father. "I suppose you'll go back to England now your father's gone."

She shook her head. "No."

"What about the restaurant?"

"What about it?" she asked, sitting to face him.

"You could run it now."

"No, I couldn't."

"Of course you can. There's no reason why you shouldn't. Your father's dead. You're his only living relative, aren't you?"

"I said, I couldn't," she enunciated forcefully, her words filled with meaning.

Her seriousness confused him. "Why?"

She was quiet, hesitant. "He had a partner — a silent partner. He left everything to him."

"I'm sorry, I didn't know."

"There are a lot of things you don't know."

He nodded, but his mind was on the murder of her father. At least that eliminates her, he thought. Not that she ever was a suspect. She had no opportunity. Now she had no motive either.

Rising to stand over him, she continued: "Why don't you just tell me who you really are?"

"I'm a detective inspector ..." he began, but she rounded on him furiously.

"That's not who you are. That's what you do. I mean, who *are* you? What the hell are you doing here?" She held up her hand, she was on a roll. "And don't give me that crap about wanting an adventure. You're no more adventuresome than ... than ... than ..." She was stuck. "... Than vanilla ice cream."

Dumbfounded by her attack, he didn't answer. His eyes swept up her boyishly trim body, mentally undressing her, appraising her angrily clenched buttocks and pert little breasts, then focussing on the imperfection of her mouth. Sympathy, compassion, and animalistic desire coalesced and he came up with the classic locker room reaction to all women's ails. What she needs is a good screwing, he thought, then mentally kneed himself in the groin. This was Margaret he was thinking about, Melanie's sister, not some tart or neglected suburban housewife. He still hadn't answered her question though — what was he doing there? She helped him out: "I came here to escape. Why did you come?"

"I guess I'm escaping as well."

"What from?"

"Life, responsibilities, failure, I suppose. Failure mainly."

"Failure?"

"I've lost a lot of things recently," he replied. Explaining everything. Explaining nothing.

"Life's all about losing things, Dave," she said sadly.

The voice of experience, he thought. But what could he have lost compared to her? Sister, mother, father, her entire family — even her inheritance. "My losses are minimal ..." he began, but stopped himself. "Christ I'm beginning to sound like a book now. What I mean is, you've lost everything."

"Maybe," she said. "But what's that to you? You didn't just wash up on my beach by accident."

"No," he admitted, "I wanted to meet you, to talk to you." Then he put on his policeman's voice. "Margaret, I have to ask you some questions. Will you please sit down."

She gave him a questioning look, as if challenging his resolve. "This sounds as if it could be serious," she said, starting to sit.

"It is. Very serious."

She popped back up. "Before we start, would you like a drink?"

Confused, he replied, "I thought ..."

She finished the sentence for him. "That I don't approve of drink. I don't normally," she said. "But under the circumstances ..." She reached down and pulled a bottle from under the couch. "Emergency supplies. Medicinal purposes only."

"Medicinal purposes?"

"I've got the feeling that you're going to hurt me."

At last, she'd opened the door. He gratefully seized the proffered drink, and felt the neat Scotcth burn his throat with a reassuring warmth. "What would you say if I told you I never really believed your sister's death was an accident?"

Deep contemplation glazed her eyes. She stood, grappling with the concept, and poured herself a larger shot. "I would say that you should have mentioned it twenty years ago. It's a bit late now."

Bliss shook his head. "Legally, it's not too late. There is no statute of limitations for an indictable offence."

"Indictable?"

"Serious. Like murder."

"Murder." She tried to get her mind around it. "Melanie ... murdered?"

Bliss bit the bullet. "Yes. I believe your father murdered her."

She was already shaking her head before the sentence was out of his mouth. "That's not possible. It was an accident. You said so yourself."

He cast his mind back. "I never told you it was an accident."

"Didn't you?"

"No. You said it was an accident. I never have."

She dismissed his assertion as inconsequential, "I don't know who told me. I suppose I've always believed it was an accident. That was the verdict wasn't it?"

He admitted it was, then tried a different tack. "But your mother didn't believe it was an accident, did she?"

Bliss watched, almost in alarm, as his words struck home and Margaret's whole being went through a metamorphosis. Intense mental turmoil fiercely entwined her fingers in a twisting, strangling motion, turning them white under the strain. The whirling cogs of her mind contorted her face as she struggled with some inner demon. Her body squirmed and twitched as if fighting off possession by an evil spirit. The battle continued for a minute or more, then Margaret slumped forward and released a flood of tears. The demon had won.

"Melanie wouldn't stop screaming," she bawled. "He was touching her, poking her. I saw him. Kissing her. She screamed, she kept saying, 'Daddy don't, Daddy don't.' He wouldn't stop." Margaret's wide eyes were pleading for help, as though she expected Bliss to stop the horrific memories — maybe even expecting him to travel back in time and stop the assault on her sister. But it was too late to change history; all he could do was stare at her with knowing sadness. His silence urged her on. "They were in the bushes," she continued through the tears. "He pulled down her panties. I saw him. I saw him. Kissing her, down there, between her legs, pushing his tongue in." She stopped, snorted loudly, and smeared the tears across her face. "I saw them, I saw them, I saw them. Melanie kept shouting. 'Don't Daddy. Don't Daddy.'"

Tears flooded her face; sobs shook her shoulders. She looked up at him, her eyes inviting pity, pleading for forgiveness, as if by her confession she had somehow betrayed her father.

"What happened then?" Bliss prodded gently.

Margaret blew her nose on her sleeve and continued quietly, "Melanie stopped shouting and I saw her go under the water. Then I ran to get away from him."

A sense of relief swept through Bliss — he'd been right. All those years, he'd been right. Not that it would do any good now, he told himself. The law may not impose a statute of limitation on serious crimes, but mortality certainly did. But now he knew — it wasn't pain he'd seen in Gordonstone's eyes that day, it was fear. Fear that he would insist on interviewing Margaret and that she would spill the beans. He'd been royally conned — more than conned, he'd been suckered into becoming a co-conspirator. He was the one who'd sworn to God in front of the coroner that he believed Melanie's death had been an accident. He'd been conned because he'd allowed himself to be conned, he realized. And Betty-Ann, fearful for herself and her other daughter, had silently conspired with him and had eventually paid for it with her life.

Margaret clamped her head in her hands and mumbled through her fingers as if trying to blot out the images, as if she'd already remembered too much, and Bliss was surprised when she looked up and answered his original question. "I think Mum knew. He never left her on her own after it happened. He had to give up his job at the stock exchange to stay home with her. That's why he bought the restaurant, so we could live upstairs and he could keep an eye on her. To make sure she didn't wander off and start blabbering things."

"Did he lock her in?"

Margaret looked up, composed her face as best she could, and said confidently. "No. She locked herself in."

"So how did you end up here?"

"After Mum died he didn't want me around anymore. He said I reminded him too much of the past." She lost her composure again and tears streamed down her face. Bliss found himself crying with her, for her, for what she'd lost, for what he'd lost. Wanting to comfort her, to take away her pain, he slid onto the couch beside her and bundled her into his arms. The sudden tension in her body was as sharp as an electric shock and he shrank back as if stuck by a cattle prod. She wasn't used to being touched, he realized. She'd probably never been touched by a man other than her father. She was terrified of being touched. He understood and took his hands away. The tension melted out of her body instantly and she slumped into a ball and rocked herself comfortingly. A thirty-two-year-old virgin, he guessed. Not a virgin by choice. Virginity forced upon her by fear. He didn't speak. What was there to say? The tiny scar that Melanie's death had left in his mind was a gnat's bite in comparison to Margaret's hurt. Her sister's death had chopped off her mother's legs and ultimately lynched her. It had turned her father from a respected stockbroker to a bitter drunken buffoon and had ripped out Margaret's heart, robbed her of her inheritance, and blighted her life. But there was a single unanswered question. The one that had nagged him all those years. Was now the right time to ask? Was there ever going to be a right time? He prodded her softly, persuasively. "Did your father ever ...?"

She followed his train of thought and arrived at the destination before him. "He never touched me," she said, interrupting aggressively.

"Never?"

"Never ... Not ever. He never touched me," she screamed. Then she crashed, blubbering, against his chest.

He gently held her head in his hands, feeling her twitch as she sobbed, wondering why Gordonstone had abused Melanie? Only six years old. Why not Margaret, double her age. Then he figured it out. "Oh my God, " he mused. "The harelip." He studied her distraught face in the dim light and realized that she too must have known — one look in the mirror would have told her. What crushing hurt of rejection in a young girl's mind. No wonder she thought of her father as poisonous.

She wasn't ugly — older than her years certainly, but not ugly. Her taut little body and rough hands had a masculine feel that led him to surmise that sex with her might approximate a homosexual experience. But he had no intention of finding out.

She lay sobbing quietly in his protective embrace, drawing comfort from his presence. Or was he drawing comfort from hers? With the jigsaw beginning to take shape, Bliss ran through it in mind. Gordonstone, a pedophile, found his eldest daughter's disfigurement repulsive and assaulted the younger girl, who screamed — from the assault or because she is seen by her elder sister? He tried to stem her screams but couldn't and, in a panic, he suffocated her. Realizing what he'd done, he dumped her body in the lake to make it look like a drowning. No wonder he didn't search for Melanie before I arrived, Bliss thought, he knew exactly where to find her. No wonder they kept me away from Margaret — Margaret knew. How did they keep her quiet? Where had she been? Locked in her bedroom? No, too obvious; I might have looked. He strained his memory to recall the time he'd spent in the house interviewing Gordonstone and his wife. He'd heard nothing — no cries, no thumps on the wall or floor. He punished himself again for not insisting on talking to Margaret, imagining her bound and gagged, tied to the bed, crammed into a cupboard, or stuffed in the car's trunk in the driveway.

Margaret's soft rhythmic breathing told him that she had fallen asleep in his lap. With her father's dark secret revealed, everything about her seemed to have relaxed. He still wasn't entirely sure how Melanie had ended up in the lake. Did she fall or was she pushed? Or did she jump, intending to wash away the filth? But it no longer mattered. What mattered was that her death was a direct result of her father's action. He was guilty. He killed her, one way or the other. And Betty-Ann knew. For ten years the pain had kept her a prisoner and fear had kept her silent, until one night when she could stand the pain no more... Edwards was right, she had committed suicide. What else was there for her to do? She too had been guilty, in a way. Maybe she deserved the punishment she meted out to herself. She could have spoken out, but he knew why she hadn't. The same reason he hadn't: the malevolent dominance of her husband. Margaret was right — he had poisoned everyone and everything. No wonder she didn't go back for the funeral. He'd exiled her from his life because of her looks and even robbed her of her inheritance; she owed him nothing.

Drawing comfort from the satisfaction of knowing he'd been right — and hating himself for not having done something about it sooner — he bent and gave Margaret a fatherly kiss on the forehead. It was time to go home. Time to face the music. But he could do so with a certain satisfaction. The satisfaction that he had cleared up the only unsolved mystery of his career. But he stopped himself; he knew that wasn't true. There were many unsolved crimes with his name on the dockets, more than he even cared to admit; yet, in some strange way, only the death of Melanie Gordonstone ever stood out in his mind as a failure.

He gently smoothed Margaret's hair as she lay in his lap and memories of Samantha flooded his mind. Memories of how she, as a child, had similarly fallen asleep on his lap. How could Gordonstone have done it, he wondered. What sickness would it take to permit a man to conceive of doing such a thing to his own child? What would drive a man to such behaviour? Bliss squeezed his eyes tight until kaleidoscopic colours swam through his vision, trying to imagine what it would have been like to touch Samantha, his own daughter. But the images wouldn't take shape. He could picture her, a joyous six-year-old, with frothy blonde hair, playing in the suds at bath-time or building sand castles on a secluded beach. But every time his mind reached beyond, to envisage touching, exploring, poking, it would swerve off, like a record needle slipping an LP's worn groove, skidding across the surface to lodge on the next track. He kept bringing his mind back, but over and over again the thoughts got away from him. For him, even the thought was impossible. He tore his mind away, managing to change the focus if not the topic, and thought only of Melanie. Seeing her tiny corpse lying on the grassy bank. Her father's disgusting secret destined to be buried with her. He felt Margaret's head under his fingertips. If only he had questioned her twenty years earlier, how different life would have been for all of them — all but Melanie. Nothing would have brought her back.

In the morning light the house seemed brighter, the ceiling higher. More at ease than he'd previously seen her, Margaret's brittle edge had softened. The tenseness of her parched skin relaxed—the lines a little less deep; her eyes a little wider. If her self barricades had not caved in altogether, the defences were certainly beginning to weaken.

Bliss chanced his arm. "I'd really like to have a look around the island.

A cloud returned to her face instantly. "Like I told you, Dave, I worry about the animals. The whole point of a wildlife refuge is to keep them away from people. They're scared of people in the wild, that's what keeps them safe from hunters. If they get used to seeing people who don't shoot or trap them they become vulnerable."

His crestfallen look clearly touched a nerve. "OK," she capitulated, "but only the parts where there aren't many animals."

He brightened.

"As long as you promise not to wander off."

It was an easy promise.

"And I don't want this to become a habit."

"I won't be here much longer anyway."

"I thought you'd have to wait for Alice to return."

"There's nothing keeping me here now. I'll work out some way of getting back."

They chatted companionably as they strolled through the undergrowth. Margaret revealed that her father had picked up the island as an investment in a stock deal believing that it would one day be a real estate gold mine; giving it to her after her mother's death, making it clear that she was expected to live here.

Bliss, for his part, felt he owed her something, and told her about his ex-wife and her newfound love; making her laugh with "Gangly" George's nickname. He even mentioned that he had more or less decided to quit the police, but skipped the part about attacking Edwards.

"So what are you going to do now, Dave?"

"What do you mean?"

"Well, if you had your choice."

"I'd go back."

"To where?"

"Not where. When."

"When?"

"Before Sarah ... " He gazed skywards with a detached look. "Before she left."

Margaret shook her head. "You can't. You've got to keep going, keep moving forward. You can't go backwards. Life doesn't work in reverse."

"If I could get Sarah back, that would be going backwards."

She chewed a thumbnail in deliberation. "No, it wouldn't. Sarah, your Sarah, isn't the same now as she was when she left you. She's moved on without you."

"So?"

"So, going to her now would be moving on, for you anyway. You'd be going on to a different person. The old Sarah has gone forever. You can't get her back. She doesn't exist anymore."

Acceptance of her assertion was difficult for him and he contended that Sarah would be going back as well. "We'd be going back together," he claimed.

Margaret shook her head. "No. She'd be moving forward as well, because you're different now. You've changed as well."

"I have," he admitted.

"So, she would be moving forward then."

"Yes ... " he hesitated, then added, more to himself than Margaret, "But she might be worse off with me than she was before."

She heard. "Nobody says the future has to be better than the past."

"Isn't it supposed to be?"

"Only for people who believe in fairy stories."

Bliss closed his eyes for a moment. Did he believe in fairy tales? "It wouldn't work anyway," he concluded, without finding an answer. "Sarah wouldn't take me back."

"So what do you intend to do?"

"If I had my choice at this particular moment, I'd quite like to stay here with you."

"You can't do that."

"I thought you'd say that."

"You were right then."

Kicking himself for getting drawn into disclosing his personal problems, annoyed that she had turned the conversation around, he plunked himself down on a fallen tree trunk and said, "What about you?"

She thought hard for a second as if contemplating telling him to mind his own business, then sketched in the details of her life in half a dozen words, steering well clear of any mention of Melanie. School? "Hated it."

Friends? "None really." Likes? "Swimming and Bo."
Dislikes? Her simple shrug could have meant nothing,
or everything. Life in general? "All right."

"Mahler?" he enquired.

She screwed up her nose. "I don't like Mahler. He's
too painful."

"Oh. I thought ... I noticed your tapes."

She froze momentarily with a puzzled look then
caught on. "Oh, those. I got them years ago. I saw a
movie once ..." She shrugged off a brief attempt to
remember the title. "Anyway, some snooty character
said 'I could die for Mahler' in a terribly posh voice and
I thought it was so chic I went out and bought the lot.

He laughed. "Tell me about your work."

"I don't work ..." she began, then backtracked.
"Oh. You mean the animals."

He nodded and stared into the undergrowth. He
was disappointed by the lack of furtive scurries. Where
he had expected to find a teeming menagerie, he'd
walked into a movie-set forest and was waiting for the
director to shout "Action."

"Yeah. What have you done with all the animals?"
he enquired light-heartedly and was stung by the sharpness of her reply.

"What do you mean?"

"I just wondered where they were, that's all."

"Oh," she waved vaguely, "all over the place. They
keep out of the way when they hear someone coming."
She spent the next few minutes chatting animatedly
about her animals. A family of orphaned mink were
apparently doing very well. A porcupine with a broken
leg was on the mend. Squirrels, chipmunks, skunks, and
white-tailed deer were all recuperating in the relative
safety of the island paradise.

"And Eddie the eagle?"

"Oh yes. He's fine."

"What will you do with him?" he asked innocently. Her crustiness returned. "What do you mean?"

"Well ... When he's better, what'll happen to him?"

"Oh, I see. I'll release him in the wild."

Bliss's attention was caught by the rising sun glinting off the lake through the trees. He was hopelessly lost; the tangled woodland was more confusing than Hampton Court maze. For all he knew they could have been walking around in circles. He chided himself. It was an island. That's exactly what they had done.

"We should get going," she said, as he made a move toward the lake.

"Just a sec," he shouted, pushing a path through the thick bush to a secluded cove with a white sand beach carved into the rocks.

"C'mon, Dave," she cried, agitated, not following. "We have to go."

He hopped down onto the fine sand and skimmed a few pebbles. "Five," he counted triumphantly.

"Dave, please," she implored.

"Hang on, I want to try for seven," he called, flipping another stone.

She perched on a rock above him, hugged her knees and playfully called, "Try for eight," momentarily forgetting the time.

Bending to grab another pebble his eye was caught by a cigarette butt just six inches from the waterline. Margaret's, he thought stupidly, even going so far as to check the end for lipstick before realizing that she neither wore lipstick nor smoked. But hadn't she also claimed not to drink?

He picked up the stub reflectively. Fresh, he noted with surprise.

"Let's go," she called, already on the move.

Flicking the butt into the water, his attention was drawn to a long groove in the silt just below the surface. "A canoe's been here," he shouted.

She was already in the forest and he rushed to catch up. "Must've been those Indians from yesterday."

"No," she replied adamantly. Then she softened. "Probably some picnickers up from the city."

They must be brave, he thought, remembering the hand-painted sign firmly planted in the middle of the beach. "Private: No hunting, fishing, or trapping." And the words, "Trespassers will be shot," had been underlined with such ferocity that Bliss, for one, believed she would do it.

As they wormed their way back along the twisted trails, concern distracted him and he wandered off the track. Realizing his mistake and seeing that Margaret had changed direction he veered at a tangent to head her off.

"Stop!" she screamed.

He took another step.

"Stop! Stop! Stop! Stand still. Don't move,"

"What is it? He shouted, his eyes frantically searching for a cougar, rattlesnake, or bear. A hundred imaginary claws ripped into his back and spun him around. A swaying stalk became a venomous fang biting his leg and making him leap.

"Don't move, Dave. Stay still," she yelled. "I'm coming."

Nothing she said allayed his terror and he glued down the hair on his neck with a perspiring hand and his face tingled with tension. Then she was behind him.

"Come this way," she called soothingly.

"What is it?" he enquired, his voice barely controlled.

"A bear pit."

"A what?"

"Just ahead of you there's a deep pit. To catch bears. I didn't really worry about them until two people were mauled to death on Onongo Island," she waved vaguely off into the distance. "They were trapped with a big male that hunted them, stalked them. Set out to kill them for invading his territory. So, if a bear gets on this island . . ."

He didn't move. "Show me," he said.

Selecting a sinewy switch from a nearby bush, Margaret stepped forward with the breathtaking care of a ballet dancer, prodding the ground as if searching for a land-mine. Ten feet ahead of him the switch sank into the ground. Bending down she carefully brushed aside a thick layer of skeletal leaves and debris revealing a lattice of slender branches. "Be careful, Dave," she called motioning him forward and parting the branches.

"Shit," he breathed peering into the deep pit to a floor spiked with sharpened stakes.

"Eight feet," she said, guessing his next question.

"This is scary. Are there any more?"

"They're all over the island."

He gulped, recalling his unescorted foray into the forest's fringe the previous morning.

"That's why you shouldn't leave the house without me."

He had no intention of doing so again.

"We must get a move on if we're to get to the settlement and back today," she continued, steering him back to the trail.

"I just hope Samantha's at home." he said, falling in behind, carefully placing each foot exactly where hers had been.

chapter ten

The fleet was in when they reached the settlement. Dozens of canoes and motorboats littered the beach. Fishing nets swung in the breeze. Bloated cats siesta'd on the shore.

The men, after a hectic morning fishing, took their siestas more earnestly, over a few pints in Stacy's store. Bliss's arrival a few days earlier had not gone unnoticed in the isolated community and speculation was rife. Jock, the Glaswegian odd-job man, knew little but fantasized freely. According to him, Bliss was Margaret's estranged husband, from whom she had fled shortly after her wedding, having realized the folly of marrying an older man. Alice's assertion that he was Margaret's father had been offhandedly dismissed; there was little entertainment in the arrival of a father.

Bliss's mind exploded with nostalgia as he stood framed in the store doorway. The smells from inside transported him back to the corner store in Dorking, just six houses from their terraced house at a time before supermarkets, with their hospital-corridor odours of floor polish and disinfectant, aircraft hangar lighting, 'in-your-face' displays, and financial advisor personalities. Closing his eyes for a second, vivid recollections flooded his mind. Eight years old again, he mentally walked back into the corner store and smelled the pungent bouquet of traditional herbs — parsley, sage, and thyme — the ace-tone of pear drops, the flowery fragrance of perfumed candles and soaps, and the earthy scent of vegetables. Fruit —oranges in particular, some on the turn — wafted the air with heady sweet fragrance. And golden, ripe bananas, not rock-hard green sticks, hung in cascades from bright steel hooks. Their were no cucumbers in con-doms, no plastic-skinned sausages, spray painted apples, flavour-injected chicken, or hormonally inflated toma-toes. Only real food with real smells

Leaping back to the present he opened his eyes and met the stares of twenty men. The air quivered with ten-sion, but a shove from Margaret propelled him forward and broke the spell. Conversations, temporarily inter-rupted, recommenced. Glasses, paralyzed mid air, unfroze. Time paused, then moved on.

"Hi Maggie," mumbled a cacophony of voices.

"Pete, Ross, Gill, Buck," she intoned with a nod and worked her way around the room, acknowledging each in turn, ending with the man behind the counter. "Stacy."

"This is Dave," she said to the room without elaboration.

Stacy waddled out from behind his counter to greet him. He looked, thought Bliss, as though he'd suffered a catastrophic internal collapse, as though his lungs and heart had crashed into his belly leaving a sunken chest and slumped shoulders. He was all gut, with a wide leather belt buckled under the mass, and the crotch of his trousers hung round his knees. Giant's suspenders looped up and over the bulge of his stomach, like a couple of bungee cords, straining to hold it in place. Bliss waggishly wondered if he removed the swelling at night, like a store Santa Claus, and extended a hand in greeting.

"How are you?" asked Stacy ignoring the outstretched hand. "You wanna coffee?"

"Please," said Bliss, his eyes taking in the room, examining it properly for the first time. His previous visit had been an unreal affair, with his mind focussed exclusively on Margaret, but now he had a different perspective. He drank in the scene like an artist preparing to sketch. The streaks of autumn sunlight, turned ochre by years of window grime, were augmented by a few sixty-watt light bulbs under white enamel shades. Smoke from a dozen cigarettes hung in the air and gave the picture a fuzzy edge. The aroma of beer and spirits, combined with fruity, spicy smells, somehow rustled up the aura of Christmas. The twenty or so occupants — all men, most misshapen, many in lumberjack shirts and jeans — were clumped around the long counter and could have been partygoers, Bliss thought, were they not so serious, surly almost.

Stacy busied himself with a hissing espresso machine while he talked to Margaret but tried to include Bliss. "Are you two goin' back today?"

"Uh huh," she nodded.

"You shouldn't leave it too late — Could be a storm."

A Forrest Gump-like figure, with a Blue Jays baseball cap tightly jammed on his head, parroted, "Could be a storm."

"How're doin' Bob?" enquired Margaret, turning to him with an encouraging smile.

The man's careful consideration of several possible responses was accompanied by a variety of facial gri-

maces as though he were giving clues in a game of cha-
rades. With his reply finally selected, he adopted an
appropriate face and spoke in a slow vibrato, sounding
like a cheap bass loudspeaker. "I'm doin' real good
Maggie. Who's your friend?"

Time stopped. Life was suspended as twenty men
awaited the answer.

"Just a friend," she intoned after a thoughtful pause,
giving nothing away.

Bliss moved to the phone, dragging twenty pairs of
eyes across the room with him, and dialled Samantha's
number. Her answering machine greeted him cheerily as
the room behind him held its breath. ·

"I'll call again in half an hour," was all he said, realizing it was barely six o'clock in England. He turned back
to the room. Eyes scattered, conversations were forced
back to life. Margaret chatted to a couple of the men,
sipped her coffee, and scanned an old newspaper that was
on the bamboo table where he'd first seen her. Bliss killed
time browsing around the store, his eyes drawn to the
ornate ceiling along the old wooden shelving that climbed,
ladder-like, on all four walls. But the stucco ceiling turned
out to be fraudulent under closer scrutiny, nothing more
than whitewashed, embossed tin-plate tiles. A forerunner
of Styrofoam, he guessed, though certainly more attractive. Then he surveyed the familiar products and brands
on the shelves and felt a sense of belonging. Cadbury's,
Kellogg's, Nestle's, and Heinz vied for display space with
Lipton's, Maxwell House, Nabisco, and Knorr.

A turn-of-the-century Morse code key stamped
Marconi & Co. caught his eye, its finely knurled adjust-
ing screws and mother of-pearl finger plate turning a
purely functional instrument into a work of art.

"How much?" he called to Stacy, holding it out for
him to see.

"What's it got on it?"

"The label says \$2.20," he replied, with no expectation of negotiating a price anywhere near the original.

"Give me two bucks then," said Stacy, cheerfully taking a ten percent mark down on a ninety-year-old artifact. Bliss, bemused but not inclined to argue, stared hopefully down at the top of Margaret's head.

"Put it on his tab," she called to Stacy, without looking up from the paper. "He already owes you fifty so another couple won't make a difference."

Forrest Gump, eyebrows raised, loudly grunted his amusement at a foreigner crazy enough to pay for something as old and useless as a Morse key. The men around the room smirked in agreement. Men, Bliss suspected, for whom the notion of collecting *objets d'art* was irrelevant. Men for whom Toronto was as exotic as Acapulco or Bombay.

He finally got through to Samantha at seven-thirty London time.

"Dad," she said, with a sigh of relief. "Where are you?"

He picked up the concern in her voice. "Is everything all right?"

The memory of his cat clawed at her mind, she fought it aside. "Fine. What's happening?"

"Did you pay those bills?"

"Bills?"

"Under the telly."

The telly — blown to pieces — the bills and their memory swept away with the debris.

"Oh yes," she lied. "Don't worry about it."

"You can tell Peter Bryan I'll soon be home. I've got all I need."

"When will you be back?"

He put a forlorn tone into his voice. "I'm stuck here for two weeks if I can't get some money."

"How much?" she asked.

"Uh ... " She'd caught him off-guard. Psyched up for an argument, assuming she would refuse, he had not bothered estimating his needs. He waffled. "I mightn't be able to pay you back for a while."

"It's a gift — early Christmas present. Just tell me where to send it and how much."

"Are you sure everything's all right?" he queried, sensing that she had something heavy on her mind.

"Dad ... " she started hesitantly. "You should be careful. Peter says he thinks Edwards set you up." Her voice cracked. "I just want you to come back."

I'm not coming back, he thought, recalling Margaret's words, I'm going forward. "I should be home by the weekend with any luck, if you send the money today."

"Today! It's nearly eight o'clock here."

"Tomorrow then." Thursday, he said to himself, and quickly calculated: Saturday evening in Toronto, night flight to Paris arriving Sunday morning. "I should be back late Sunday afternoon. I'll call you as soon as the money arrives and let you know definitely."

He dictated the address off the Western Union sign and was about to end the call when he had an idea. "Could you make some enquiries for me, Sam?"

"What?"

Explaining that Margaret had not inherited her father's restaurant, he asked her to find out the identity of the silent partner.

Samantha agreed to assist if she could, then enquired. "So what's this Margaret like?"

Bliss became suddenly conscious he was being overheard by several patrons and cut his voice to a whisper. "She's very tough, but she looks after sick animals."

She envisioned a Beatrix Potter figure in a house teeming with small creatures. "Dogs and cats, that sort of thing?" Her voice wobbled over the mention of cats but she held herself together.

"No. Wild animals. We've got a bald eagle called Eddie."

She laughed. "It's 'we' now, is it?"

"Nothing like that, it's just ... Oh, never mind. Anyway, send the money and see what you can find out. See if there's any loophole in the ownership. I bet it's not straightforward. You're a lawyer, see if you can get Margaret some sort of compensation. She deserves it after what she's been through."

"You sound quite chirpy."

"I am," he said. "Oh. One more thing."

"What now?"

"There was a video taken by some bloke the night Gordonstone died. I left it on the side table or on the telly in my place. Didn't get a chance to watch it. It might be useful. Have a look will you. You'll have to take it back to your place, I haven't got a VCR ... George has it," he added vitriolically. "And my telly's only black and white."

Black and black now, she thought, but kept it to herself. "OK." she promised.

"Oh, and tell Peter Bryan I'm still on the case whether Edwards likes it or not."

"Will do."

"That's all," he said, but waited on the line.

"I love you, Dad," she said finally, knowing how much the words would mean to him.

"I love you too, Sam. See you soon."

Bliss's luck held. Alice was in her office when he called a few minutes later. "Yes," she would return for him the following afternoon. By coincidence her scheduled route was a mere fifty miles away and she would detour — for a fee.

"Six o'clock precisely," she warned. "If you're not there, tough luck, you won't see me for another two weeks." He assured her that he'd be at the settlement.

"How's the bird?" she enquired as he was about to put the phone down.

"Doing well," he replied, and laughed. "It'll soon be able to fly home by itself. It won't need you. See you tomorrow then."

They left almost immediately, Bliss grumbling that it was a hell of a long way just to make a couple of phone calls.

"Stop moaning," Margaret chided light-heartedly. "It was for your benefit."

"And yours," he replied. "I thought you wanted to get rid of me."

"I was just getting used to you, " she said, catching him by surprise with a sideways look that, from any other woman, he would have taken as a sexual come-on.

Darkness fell early, hastened by the storm's approach. No lights guided their path, no moon lit their way, but Margaret paddled confidently and drove the canoe forward at full speed. As the bow sliced cleanly through the darkening water the constant high-pitched swishing was the only sound, even the lightning above the horizon was silent. There was no thunder and no needle-sharp crack of a lightning strike. Just a wash of brilliance flashing through the clouds, flickering on and off like a defective florescent tube.

"Harder, Dave," she called over her shoulder. "It's going to be a big storm. The animals will be terrified."

What about me, he thought. "Do you think I'm not scared?" he yelled.

She half-turned and threw him a life jacket before struggling into her own. "This is your bloody fault," she shouted above the strengthening wind.

"Sorry," he called, with more sincerity than he intended, though less than she expected.

"You don't bloody sound it," she retorted. He let it go.

They raced toward the storm and collided with its leading edge long before reaching the island. Under the black cumulus canopy the electrified air crackled with energy and the lightning was devilishly transformed. Jagged spears now stabbed earthward with such rapidity their eyes couldn't recover from one before being zapped by the next. One roll of thunder crashed headlong into the next. Squalls ripped up the lake's surface and sloshed it into the canoe in great bucketfuls. Bliss alternated paddling with bailing. Margaret doggedly pounded her oar into the surf. Then a beacon appeared directly ahead — a beacon of fire. She saw it first and froze. Bliss, sensing disaster, screamed at her back, "What's the matter?" Then he saw it too. A brittle-dry pine on her island had been turned into a flaming torch by a stab of lightning and the parched trees surrounding it were feeding frenziedly on the flames.

"Row," he commanded, flinging down the bailer, grabbing the oar.

Ten frantic, adrenalin-filled minutes later Margaret, blinded by hysteria, smashed the half-submerged canoe straight onto rocks. Bliss felt the crunch as a jagged boulder chiselled a hole in the hull right under his foot.

"Fuckin' hell!" he shouted as the boat jarred to a unexpected halt, slinging him forward into her, dumping them both into the water-filled bow.

"Get off!" she yelled, almost as if he'd done it on purpose.

The canoe sank away beneath them leaving them floundering a couple of pool-lengths off the beach. Striking for the shore, on a path lit by the fire's angry glare, Bliss suddenly realized the danger. Far from being a safe haven, the beach was a fire-trap. The trees hanging picturesquely over the water's edge were next in the firing line and stray sparks were already raining down on them. Margaret, in her frantic efforts to reach the island had made a beeline for the nearest shore, but they were downwind of the fire. The wind-fanned smoke and flames were coming straight at them and they were trapped in the cove by ragged headlands. It was no longer a question of saving her precious animals. The tide had turned; they had to save themselves.

"Stop!" he yelled, she streaked away from him. "Come back!"

Head down, oblivious to his shouting, intent only on getting to the beach, she raced through the water.

"This is crazy," he shouted. "We'll be killed."

He took off after her with a fast crawl; he couldn't stop himself. And he couldn't stop her. Within minutes she was clawing her way up the beach under an onslaught of sparks. As he neared the shallows the absurdity of the situation struck him — What would he have said ten days earlier if a clairvoyant had told him that he was about to risk his life for a complete stranger five thousand miles away. But Margaret wasn't a stranger. She had been part of his consciousness for twenty years. She had, in some small way, influenced the investigation of every case he had handled since her sister's death. Whenever he was inclined to take the easy road, to embrace the simple explanation, to accept a witness's uncorroborated statement, the injustice he had done to Margaret and her sister spurred him on in search of more evidence, and the truth. She was no stranger, she had been with him every day.

He hung back, just off the beach, his mind a whirlpool of improbable ideas for fighting the blaze. In a normal world there would be extinguishers, hoses, pumps and ladders.

She'd reached the sand and was standing under a cascade of sparks, paralyzed by indecision. Her island, her animals, and her life were going up in flames around her, yet she couldn't move. Suddenly, from twenty feet away, Bliss caught the unmistakable stench of singed hair.

"Cover your face! Your hair!" he shouted, making a megaphone out of his hands. Rushing forward he grabbed Margaret, dragged her, protesting, back into the water and forced her head under. Then he roughly yanked up her shirt, held it over her nose and mouth, and clamped it in place with one of her hands. "It's not the fire that kills," he yelled. "It's the smoke. Breathe through this and keep it wet. I'm going to get the bailing buckets!"

"Bo," she cried, making to rush back ashore. "I've got to save Bo."

"Stay here," he commanded, his fingers biting painfully into her arms, restraining her.

"You're hurting," she protested.

"Stop struggling then."

Obediently she went limp and he relaxed his grip, then, slipping from his grasp, frantically took off toward the beach again. He tackled her into the surf just as a burning branch crashed onto the beach a few yards ahead of them. It shook her up and brought her to her senses. "OK. Get the buckets," she said, subdued.

It was the rain that finally quenched the fire, though not before they'd exhausted themselves, furiously flinging bucket after bucket of lake water at the blaze. The downpour, when it came, seemed anxious to make amends, quickly drenching the flames and cooling the embers. Then Bo bounced through the scorched bush and flung himself joyously at his mistress, flattening her into the mud, slobbering over her face. She grappled with him, laughing in relief.

Margaret easily found her way through the forest in the gloom and outside the house they stripped off their ripped and burnt clothing. Although their mutual triumph over adversity diminished personal shyness Margaret coyly kept on her white knickers and, in a way, he wished she hadn't. Dripping wet, they clung to her contours and no matter how hard he tried, he couldn't avert his gaze.

"I'll get you a towel," he said, making for the bathroom, anxious to get his eyes and his mind off her.

She followed him and within seconds an explosion that had been brewing ever since his arrival burst all over him. As he slung the towel around her shoulders she yelled, "Why didn't you leave me alone?"

"I'm going tomorrow . . ."

"You should never have come!"

She stripped half a dozen books off the shelf and showered them across the room in anger. Bo, thinking it was a game, barked for more.

"Just calm down," he said, using his policeman's voice.

"Calm down? This is all your fault."

"Sorry."

Sorry wasn't good enough. "Sorry?" she screamed mockingly, slapped his face, and lost the towel in the process.

He tried battling back, pinioning her bare arms, shouting into her face. "It wouldn't have made any difference. It would have been worse if I hadn't been here. You would have had to fight the fire alone."

Logic had no place in her argument. She was determined to be ungrateful. "It was your fault," she spat, squirming against his grip.

Stupidly, he tried sticking to logic. "The lightning would have struck anyway, whether I was here or not."

She twisted away angrily. "You never get anything right do you?"

Then it dawned on him. She wasn't attacking him for the fire, she was attacking him for what he'd done to her life. *That* was his fault, he conceded. How different her life would have been had he treated Melanie's death properly? While he had often considered the impact of his actions upon the families of criminals he'd arrested and sent to prison, he had never given thought to what happened to those he didn't catch. That's an interesting perspective, he was thinking, when a stack of cassettes whizzed across the room in his direction and crashed around him in a symphony of broken plastic. Typical of Mahler he thought: unpredictable, a volcanic eruption one minute and morbid depression the next.

Ducking, he made a grab for her arm, missed, and felt his hand brush a naked, hard nipple. "Leave me alone," she screeched. "Leave me alone. You're pathetic. You couldn't survive ten minutes in a place like this."

"Don't talk to me about survival. You'd be dead on that beach ..." He bit off the rest of his reply; there was no point. She didn't need this.

You've no idea what it's like being on your own," she sobbed.

She was right, it was beyond the scope of his imagination that anybody would volunteer for a life such as hers. "I can't imagine —" he began, but she cut him off angrily. "You're damn right you can't. So keep your fuckin' nose out."

Her rage inflamed the little scar and puckered her upper lip, drawing his eyes, capturing his heart. She misunderstood and her hand flew to her mouth. "Don't look at me like that!"

"Like what?"

"You know."

He didn't know. All he knew was that he was very near to planting a kiss smack on her mouth. Then her face suddenly changed. The anger evaporated, replaced with distress as she relived the fire in her mind. She paled, and began shivering violently. Bliss recognized the clinical signs of delayed shock — the autonomic nervous system spinning out of control. She'll throw up in a minute, he thought, or faint.

"You need a drink" he said, drawing a blanket warmly around her then scrabbing under the couch for the bottle, knowing very well that he shouldn't give her alcohol, but feeling the need to do something. His hand collided with a small book then he found the bottle and pressed it to her lips.

"Drink this," he said solicitously. She swallowed obligingly then choked in a paroxysm of coughing.

Cradling her protectively he waited until she seemed asleep on the couch then crept into the bedroom and fell exhausted onto the bed.

Later, though not much later, the squeak of the slowly turning door handle grabbed his attention. It stopped. The unseen hand hesitated. "Dave," she called, tapping lightly.

He looked up. "Yes." The door opened slowly revealing the iridescent whiteness of her panties in the glow of smouldering log fire from the main room. She slid into the bed beside him.

"Hold me," she said, turning her back and pertly sticking her backside into him. His pulse went from sixty to one hundred and twenty in a beat but his arms instinctively enfolded her, his blistered fingers stinging at the touch of her bare flesh. His mind spun. Was she giving herself, offering herself, in gratitude? What on earth did she expect to happen? Maybe the locker-room sex-maniacs were right, he thought, maybe she does need a good screw. Maybe it's what I need as well. Apart from a couple of false starts that had ended disastrously, there had been no one since Sarah. And now celibacy was part of his overall plan in preparation for Sarah's eventual return. To prove his love for her. There would be no-one else, he'd decided. He'd show her. Gangly George's novelty would wear off eventually, then he'd be there waiting for her, still unsullied. Maybe Samantha had been right. "Get over it Dad," she had said, and now he lay, marvelling at the amazing twist of fate that had stuck Margaret's hot round bum into his groin.

Was she giving, or was she taking? She lay still, offering no clues, but her presence seared into his mind and her backside burned into his lap.

She doesn't want to, he decided finally, she simply feels obliged to offer herself as a reward. She had hung a "do not disturb" sign on her heart a long time ago. Then he flattered himself: maybe she does want me. I'm not bad looking, especially considering the competition: the two Indians, Stacy and his obscene paunch, the rest of the shaggy-haired freaks hanging around his store.

Weighing this all up he wondered whether she would be more offended if he did make a move, or if he didn't, but he failed to reach a sensible conclusion. Or, he wondered, would she wake in the morning and accuse him of rape? "Margaret," he crooned softly.

She was asleep, her breathing still deep from exertion. Her heart still raced, bumping up against her ribcage and pulsing through his fingertips as they rested under the fold of her breasts.

He tried to take his mind off her by reliving the battle against the forest fire in his mind. Branches whipping their faces, flames licking their clothes, sparks searing their flesh, fear burning their minds. They had fought the elements together — fought and won. The memory of the fire's noise beat in his brain, a terrifying whooshing, pounding sound, as if he'd stuck his head in a coffee grinder. But now he was fighting his own fire.

There was something tantalizing about her, he admitted. He'd felt it from the first moment of meeting her; the seductive allure of the unattainable he had assumed. But now he brushed the thought aside. She's just a lonely woman living on an island seeking physical support at a traumatic time. But that's it, he realized: she isn't just living on an island, she *is* an island. Just as her mother had turned herself into a prisoner, Margaret had become a hermit and, in the process, fulfilled her own prophecy. If her own father hadn't wanted her, why should any other man? She's dug a moat around herself, and tonight, possibly for the first time in her life, she's lowered the drawbridge. But what did she want, what did she expect? A knight in shining armour, charging with his lance?

He had second thoughts. Was she asleep or just feigning? Was this her way of surrendering her virginity without volunteering herself? A ploy to avoid responsibility; blaming him or blaming the heat of the moment. Enabling her to remain a virgin in her own mind regardless of the state of her hymen. Was she desperately hoping to 'wake' with his lance pumping away inside her, too late to protest? Or was she merely seeking the warmth and comfort of another human?

"Go on, touch her," he told himself. "Feel her. Squeeze her. Hug her. It's what she wants."

"Leave her alone," another part of him wanted to shout. "She's suffered enough." But he couldn't unstick his fingers from her breasts.

You're going home tomorrow, he told himself. Margaret won't leave her island and animals. In the long run it would just make things worse for her. More rejection, more loss. Just another kick in the crotch. Anyway, you're in enough trouble with everyone already. Haven't you done enough damage?

chapter eleven

The storm had passed in the night stealing the remains of the summer. Bliss woke just before dawn, at a time eager newlyweds engage in passionate re-runs of the night's activities, and errant husbands test the plausibility of prepared alibis as they slink back to sleepy wives. He drowsed awhile, probing his thoughts for what had occurred during the night, letting the music of Margaret's breathing keep him on the edge of sleep. He felt the rhythm of her heartbeat under his fingertips, and the silkiness of her panties teased the length of his erection. He needed a cold swim in the lake, a piss, or ... Quelling all thoughts of the third alternative he settled for the swim, slid out of bed, shielded his embarrassment with a hand, and skulked into the living room. Bo, on his couch, opened one eye and stared at him insolently, letting him know he was not worthy of the effort it would take to raise his head, let alone growl. Grateful, Bliss cloaked himself in the blanket from

Margaret's couch, slipped outside, and was jolted by the coolness of the atmosphere. The morning air, freshened by the presence of the lake, gave him goosebumps and he had second thoughts about the swim. The vision of Margaret's body in bed suddenly seemed particularly inviting but he steeled himself and made his way down the trail to the beach.

Leaving the blanket bundled in a heap atop a reasonably dry rock he swam naked in the lake, wishing she was with him, glad she was not. The water's coldness was iodine to his burnt hands and arms, yet he held them under, anaesthetizing the pain, washing away the smell of the fire and the scent of Margaret. He tried to wash away the memory of the night, but found himself wishing it could happen again, while hoping it would not. A tingle of freshness rippled through him as the cool water scrunched his testicles in spasm. He looked back at the island; everything had changed. The oppressiveness of the forest had lightened. The wind had bared the trees, clearing away the red shroud, leaving only bones. Everything was spotless. The smoke-filled air had been filtered and the lake, rejuvenated by rain, sparkled.

A golden sunburst spread across the lake from the horizon as suddenly as if someone had switched on a searchlight and a flashbulb went off in his mind. This was what life was supposed to be: bright, cool, fresh and clean and above all, free of stress. A toothpaste commercial.

His mind cleared in one cathartic moment and he took a mental leap forward. The past puddled around his ankles like a dropped pair of dirty pyjama bottoms, all he had to do was step out of them and walk away. His life could begin again. The martyr's chain binding him to Sarah had snapped with the realization that he had slept with another woman, that he could have had sex with her if he had chosen to and, when he got back to the cabin, he would, if that was what she wanted.

Tipping back his head he floated with his eyes shut, revelling in the freshness and his newfound freedom. I will miss this, he mused, feeling like a vacationer making the most of a last minute dip in some idyllic setting, delaying the inevitable return to the daily grind, etching the experience permanently into their mind lest they should never return. I'm leaving today, he thought. Then reality struck. No, he wasn't. The canoe! Repairing it would have to be a priority. How? He had no idea. But without a boat or a phone he could be stuck for days, or forever! Alice would be pissed off, he thought, as would Samantha and, with his daughter uppermost in his mind, he scanned the horizon. Surely he would be able to hail a passing boat and bum a ride to the settlement, although, he told himself, apart from the Indians' canoe, he'd not seen any others — not near the island anyway.

Thoughts of the Indians made him jumpy and he swam warily for a while, watchfully keeping his head above water, concerned they might have seen the fire in the night and returned to investigate. It wasn't every day he had a couple of rifles trained on him by hostile Natives.

Bo was gone when he got back and although he poked his head into the bedroom for confirmation he knew what to expect. Bo wouldn't go anywhere without her. Without bothering to dress he flopped onto the couch, irrationally feeling let down. It was as if she had slunk away as soon as his back was turned. Why? They hadn't done anything shameful — yet. Maybe she regretted sleeping with him. Even allowing a man to touch her would have been a traumatic turnaround if his assessment of her had been correct. Then he pulled himself together; she's gone to check on the animals, you idiot. He half rose, tempted to find her, wanting to share news about his catharsis, but fear of the bear pits quashed the notion. He could wait.

With time on his hands he began to explore. An old dictionary caught his attention and he looked up the word he thought one of the Natives had used. "Wampum — Algonquian Indian for money." Then he remembered the book under the couch, the one that had brushed his hand as he searched for the whisky the previous night.

The word "Private," stencilled heavily across the front cover, struck him as soon as he dug it out and his first instinct was to return it unopened, but his inquisitive side wouldn't allow that. After all, it wasn't as though he was unused to delving through other people's confidential papers; he had done so numerous times in the hunt for information and clues. But this was different, he argued to himself, this was just being nosy. Despite a creepy feeling that he was betraying her hospitality, he was eventually able to pretend that what he was doing was in the line of duty; he even managed to convince himself of the need to discover more about this eccentric woman in order to aid his understanding of her father's murder. "Nonsense," he declared aloud to himself, but nonetheless struggled to untie the intricately knotted shoelace that was bound so tightly around the book it had eaten into the binding.

Two unopened envelopes fell out. Strange, he thought, recognizing them as the ones Alice delivered on the day of his arrival. He scrutinized them with a practised eye. One, an ordinary white Bond, had no return address but was postmarked London, August 14th. "That was the day after her dad died," he remembered aloud. He studied the small neat handwriting with its aggressive forward slope, which suggested that the writer had been in a determined hurry to reach the end of each line. He unsuccessfully tested the flap with his finger then balanced the envelope in his hand, speculating about the kettle on the stove.

The other letter he would have easily recognized as from a solicitor even without the embossed crest and legend. He even knew the name. Gosforth, Morgan, and Mitwich, the same firm Gordonstone had used at the time of Melanie's death, with an address near enough to hallowed chambers of Lincoln's Inn to add a hefty surcharge to any bill, yet sufficiently far away not to put off potential clients. Why she had not opened the letters was beyond him; he could only assume she had forgotten them in all the kerfuffle of the past few days.

Putting the envelopes aside for future consideration he turned his attention to the book itself. It was straightforward, so far as he could see: a personal scrapbook like millions of others. A series of photographs celebrating life's stepping stones, with a short handwritten notation under each. "Me, aged 30 minutes." The harelip clearly visible. His heart sank for her mother and he sat for a moment thinking how glad he was that Samantha had been perfect. Then he shuffled through the scrapbook's first few pages — just pictures of Margaret and her sorry little smile. No shots of mother and daughter. No raw pictures of Betty-Ann with eyes still bloodshot from the birthing pains; face still bloated from the tears. What, he wondered, would she have looked like? She would have smiled in relief, of course. But it would have been a forced smile nevertheless, her joy tempered by a deep pang of jealousy, her smile wracked with guilt and tainted by failure. "Why wasn't my baby perfect like the others?" she might have asked herself. "Was it something I did during pregnancy? Is it something to do with my genes? Why couldn't I have produced a normal kid?"

Bliss sat back and studied an early picture of Margaret, her cracked little mouth holding his attention

There was something so defining about the mouth, he realized, every one marginally different despite fulfilling the same multiplicity of functions. From rosebuds to letterboxes, round, square, or slashed, every mouth could allure or repel, attack or entice. Life in the absence of most bodily organs could at least be tolerable, but life without a mouth ...? But Melanie's mouth had not helped her survive. Losing himself in the picture, Margaret's deformed little mouth became Melanie's, and he saw only the tiny dead lips that he had pursed his own around in a vain attempt to rekindle her life.

Bliss shook his mind clear of the image and returned to the book. One ill-conceived photograph had been shot through the bars of the hospital cot turning Margaret into a mutilated little prisoner, and he wondered how the usual stream of visitors had been prevented from registering shock at such a sight. Waylaid, he guessed, probably by the ward sister or staff nurse. Whispered warnings in the vestibule or ward office: "Harelip. Don't mention it, don't upset the new mum."

"What lovely eyes," visitors would have cooed. But not the mouth — anything but the mouth.

Every photograph, it seemed, was a commemoration of something new in Margaret's life: new trike, new dress, new school. Then came Melanie. Bliss turned the page and flinched in horror. There was a picture a tiny baby not unlike Margaret, only this one didn't have a split lip. This one didn't have any lips at all. Someone — Margaret, he assumed, without overtaxing his investigative prowess — had painstakingly cut the entire face out of the picture with a scalpel or craft knife. He gagged. There was something sinister and repulsive about the tiny faceless body and he shivered uncontrollably. Even a grotesquely mutilated face could be loved, but not even a mother could love someone without a face.

Revolted, he quickly flicked to the next page, and the next. More horrors. Margaret had painstakingly cropped Melanie's face out of every picture, as though she were trying to cut her sister out of her life. If only life were so simple, he thought; how he would love to be able to carve George's face out of Sarah's life's pictures.

The parade of horrifically mutilated photographs ceased after Melanie's sixth birthday, a day on which twenty or so other six-year-olds in party dresses and bow ties had posed smilingly around a cake, with the flames of six candles flexing spookily from the breath of the mouthless, faceless creature in the centre.

Bliss skimmed back through the book. Something else was missing in addition to Melanie's face. There were no pictures of Betty-Ann. Had she been ashamed of posing with her disfigured daughter or had Margaret dispensed with her altogether, not content just to eliminate her face from the scrapbook?

Then he came to the last page and there was a picture of Melanie's face, the only one. A picture so macabre that Bliss caught his breath, tasted bile in the back of his throat, and had to swallow hard. Slamming the book shut he held it away from him like a dirty diaper while he prepared himself for a second look.

He had seen worse, he said to himself — much worse, in real life, not just pictures. Still, he steeled himself before re-opening the book. Curiosity finally overcame his distaste and he found Melanie's cherubic little face peeping out at him through a hole in the lid of a coffin. It was one of the decapitated heads from an earlier picture, though he didn't know which, and had been pasted within a carefully drawn of a casket. The words "That will teach you," had been scored with a sharp pen and heavily outlined in black, like an engraved legend, below the coffin. Only Margaret could have done this, he realized, but why? He looked closer and felt himself going cold. A thin black pen line scarred Melanie's upper lip. Immediately the scene at Melanie's post-mortem sprang into his mind. The pathologist had made light of it — a little jagged ink line drawn to resemble a faint scar above Melanie's lip. "She's been mucking about with a pen," he had said. "Punk make-up." Bliss, unaware of Margaret's deformity at the time, had thought nothing of it; he had not even noticed it while trying to resuscitate her. Indeed, had he not been standing beside the pathologist under the bright operating room lights he might never have seen the tiny mark. No mention was made of it in the pathologist's report to the coroner; it seemed hardly worthy of comment at the time. Kids were always drawing on their faces; it usually wasn't fatal.

His mind now reacted in slow motion. He digested each morsel of information, and could draw only one reasonable conclusion, but he delayed acknowledging it for as long as possible. In another life, in another world, at another time, he might have cottoned on. But here, on Margaret's island, in Margaret's house, his mind refused to admit that he had been so totally wrong about her. The notion of little schoolgirls murdering each other was so entirely out of context with his experience of life that he momentarily found himself worrying about his cat. Just thinking about Margaret holding her sister's head under water gave him a jolt. He needed something to steady himself; a cigarette would come in handy. Coffee? There was none. Whisky? He stretched his hand back under the couch and came up with the bottle — empty. She must have finished it before she slipped into his bed and his arms the previous night. Dutch courage? he wondered.

Feeling numb, he forced himself to re-evaluate the morbid picture and finally dismissed it as surrealist doodling. Perhaps it was merely a strange way of commemorating Melanie's passing; Margaret's way of dealing with the survivor guilt, he concluded. She might even feel that it should have been her who died. Maybe she would probably have been happier to die than Melanie.

With the grotesque picture rationalized, he closed the book and turned his attention outward, scanning the now familiar room. Far from comforting him, the depressingly decrepit surroundings weighed him down further. He was missing something and he knew it. Then it dawned on him what was lacking in the room — everything. The detritus of life. The trinkets of success and failure, the baubles of existence. Family photos, plastic mementos, plaster dogs with chipped ears. More especially, for someone living so far from home and family, there was nothing on which to hang memories. Apart from the books and cassettes, it could have been a hotel room, albeit a dingy one.

Bo barrelled in announcing Margaret's approach. Bliss stiffened, feeling traitorous. Snatching the fallen envelopes off the floor he started to cram them back into the scrapbook. Which way? Which page? He didn't know. She won't notice, he told himself. She must have stuffed them in the book hurriedly on their return from the settlement. Why? But he did not have time to work out an answer before she called, "Dave," with an excited tone that suggested she had something interesting to divulge. In a panic he jammed the envelopes back into the book haphazardly, hastily retied the shoelace thong, shoved the whole package back under the couch, and readied his face to greet her.

"Dave," she called again as she entered the room.

He turned with a fixed smile. "Hello," he said. Every impulse in his body attempted to pull his face into a different expression. She sensed something was amiss and her eyes narrowed questioningly.

"Hi," she responded guardedly, her excitement lost, then she busied herself fussing with Bo. A fog instantly clouded the atmosphere between them. Bliss, assiduously avoiding eye contact, found himself absorbed by her hands as she stroked and soothed the dog, and he imagined them throttling her sister. His brain was a whirlpool of thoughts. Images flashed through his mind faster than film falling on a cutting room floor.

Margaret's body language, fluid and carefree when she arrived, was now calculated and sluggish. In a few seconds of silence they had become strangers again.

"We both know what we nearly did, but let's pretend otherwise," she seemed to be saying as she kept her eyes averted and her attention focussed on the animal.

Attempting to avoid confrontation they ran out of conversation before they even started. "I should get dressed," he said, looking sheepish, suddenly feeling vulnerable wrapped only in a blanket.

"I'll make some tea," she replied unenthusiastically.

Consternation drew him toward the bedroom; he needed space to think, to plan. She knows, he thought — feminine intuition. "Don't follow," he silently implored. She didn't.

He sat on the bed, analyzing Margaret's demeanour and concluded he was simply being melodramatic. She's probably just wondering what happened in the night. She was physically and mentally exhausted from fighting the fire; she was frightened and tipsy. But surely she would know whether or not she'd had sex?

He pulled himself up sharply. "What are you playing at? Frigging mind games, prevaricating, thinking about anything other than ...Can't you see what she's done?"

Challenging himself to do something positive, to find some evidence, he whipped open the closet and picked through the clothes. These aren't her clothes, he reluctantly admitted. They aren't anybody's clothes — certainly not anybody living in today's world. It was full of Salvation Army rejects. His eyes scanned the room, taking in the few scraps of old furniture and the bare walls. It was a bachelor's bedroom — his bedroom *après* Sarah. A male's temporary shelter, unworthy of lavish attention — of any attention — just waiting for a woman to step in and take command. Like the living room, there was nothing personal, nothing feminine. No gummed-up cosmetic bottles, no perfumes, no collection of creams.

"Is there any part of your body that doesn't have its own cream?" he had once griped to Sarah during a discussion about her spending habits "Yeah, my ass," she'd shot back. "And you make it so sore I'd better get some."

They had collapsed in laughter onto the bed, but Bliss wasn't laughing now. His mind raced through the house. Apart from the bathroom it was a time capsule from the 1950's. Cobwebs and dust as thick as icing sugar plastered everything. The books on the bookshelves were just a job lot from a flea market put there to entertain guests on a wet weekend. The cassette tapes — Mahler — were hers, she had admitted as much, but she had no tape deck and she'd claimed to hate them. The food in the kitchen's store cupboard was nothing more than emergency rations. "Dog food!" he mentally exclaimed, with the sudden realization there wasn't any.

Then the clincher — sanitary pads. None!

Two and two had finally made four. Margaret was as much a visitor as he was. This was nothing more than a holiday cottage. She didn't live here. No one lived here. The realization disheartened him. If this wasn't really her home then everything else about her was suspect.

By now his world was beginning to tilt. Conscious from the moment of his arrival that there was a degree of unreality in his surroundings, the whole universe now seemed to be spinning out of control. What should he do? Go back out there and confront her? Ask her outright, "Where do you live?" Pull out the book, stick it under her nose, and say, "Explain this if you can." But then he cautioned himself. "Remember the lawyers' rule: never ask a question to which you don't know the answer." His whole world was turning black again. What was going on? He felt as if he had got onto an icy hill and whichever way he spun the wheel or applied the brakes he couldn't prevent himself from sliding toward a brick wall at the bottom.

He made up his mind; he needed answers, however unpleasant. Plus, he needed to straighten out his own feelings. He felt dirty, he shouldn't have shared a bed with her. It had been wrong in any circumstances. It was as if he had deceived her although he couldn't explain why. Delving back into his suitcase he pulled out his detective's uniform of blue pinstripe suit, even began brushing off the jacket before asking himself whether he intended to interrogate her or make her wet herself laughing. Slinging the suit back into the case he hurriedly dressed in shirt and slacks and marched confidently back into the living room.

She was gone. He fished under the couch. The book was gone and with it the letters. He glanced around the room and his testicles scrunched again. "Oh, shit." The rifle was also gone. Another fire ignited — this time in his mind.

chapter twelve

Detective Chief Inspector Bryan warily nudged the café door with his shoulder, reluctant to grasp the handle for fear of contracting something nasty. This must be the place, he thought, recalling Samantha's description: "That brown-collar greasy-spoon on Snuff Street where Dad used to meet his grass. It's the *Hurricane* I think."

The sign on the door read *Typhoon Café*; calling itself a greasy spoon would have been false advertising.

"Over here," she shouted, half concealed behind a high-backed plywood bench.

"Nice place," he said, turning up his nose as if he'd caught the scent of a bad fart.

"It was close," she replied, keeping her head down, obsessed by her skirt, repeatedly smoothing the shiny fabric over her thigh. For her dinner with Bryan she had dolled herself up, telling herself, the way her mother would have, that she should try to look her best. But this time worry overcame her desire to impress and she had thrown on a tired polyester skirt and sloppy brown sweater to match her dowdy mood. Her face was so taut she looked as though she'd left on a face-pack. Her hazel eyes, just too far apart to be considered stunning, were dulled by a lack of sleep. "Do you want something to eat?"

"In here!" Bryan exclaimed.

"Don't be so stuffy. It's not that bad."

"I've closed down better places," he joked, wrinkling his nose. "What is that damn stink anyway?"

Samantha's churning mind couldn't be bothered with such trivia galloped away with her mouth leaving Peter Bryan breathless and confused. "He hasn't called ... It's Sunday and he hasn't called. He definitely said he'd call as soon as he got it. It's Sunday," she repeated, as if Bryan should understand the monumental significance of the day. "I sent it Thursday morning for fuck's sake. First thing. He promised to call when it arrived ... It's not like him ...Well all right, it *is* like him. I called the bank, 'No record,' they said. No record? 'How can you say that?' I said. No record! 'Administrative error,' they said. I said, 'Fucking sort it then.' D'you know what they said?" Bryan, dazed by the verbal onslaught, had been left standing at the start; his bewildered expression clearly said so. "They said they'd need a week to find out what happened. 'A week?' I said, 'He could've starved to death by then!'"

A stick-man hiding inside a shredded raincoat and clutching a large carrier bag obligingly interrupted as he shuffled fussily into an adjacent booth. His vulture-like head protruded forward and his watchful hooded eyes surveyed the floor as if seeking prey. He ordered a drink without a word, just an upward flick of his chin in response to the waitress's shouted proposal: "Tea?" Then he animatedly leapt up and stormed around, probing for treasure, seizing a used wooden stir-stick off the floor with the delight of a herring-gull swooping down on a half-eaten salmon sandwich. He snatched tidbits off an uncleared table, picked through the litter bin, and came up with a find so rewarding he squirrelled it into his bag with a twitter of laughter.

Samantha chuckled briefly in response, but caught herself as her mind substituted her father for the demented man. Anxiety pulled her to her feet. "I've got to go," she said to Bryan, starting to pace like a four-year-old desperate for the toilet.

"Hang on. You asked to meet me, have you forgotten? I haven't got a clue what you've been talking about."

She was headed toward the door. "I've got to go."

"Where?"

She hovered. "I don't know."

"Stop stressing and sit down then."

She half-sat then leapt up again. "I can't ... You don't understand."

"Understand what?"

"He's in trouble, I know he is."

Bryan caught her hand and eased her to a standstill. "Let me help ... I mean it."

She sensed the flow of sincerity through his touch and let him guide her back to her seat. "Tell me where he is and I promise to help him," he said.

"Canada."

She could see the cogs clicking into place. "The daughter?"

"Yes," she nodded. "He said he'd got the evidence he needed and was on his way back as soon as he got the money. It's Sunday, he should have been here by now."

"You're worrying unnecessarily ... What money?"

She let go with a sudden burst of aggression directed at the ceiling. "I bet Edwards has got him.

Had him arrested at the airport. Whisked him off to some secret dungeon."

"Now you're being ridiculous," he said, glancing around the room disconcertedly. "And you're causing a scene."

"Don't be ridiculous," she continued shouting. "You couldn't cause a scene in here if you tried. Only posh places have scenes. You could have a fuck on the floor here and nobody would take any notice." She spun around, feeling the f-word had attracted some attention. She was right, several men were leering at her, obviously considering the possibility of testing her theory. With a snort of disgust she bent over the table toward Bryan and peered accusingly into his face. "You said Edwards wanted him killed."

"That's going a bit far. I only said it was possible. But anyway, how could he? He didn't know where your dad was any more than I did."

"Are you sure?"

"Absolutely. Edwards calls me at least four times a day asking if I've found out."

"And you didn't tell him?"

"How could I? I've only just found out myself."

"Sorry," she said. "I suppose you think I'm being paranoid?"

"Let's go somewhere half decent and think about this logically. We could check the bank again. I could put some official pressure on them to hurry their enquiries along."

She flicked her wristwatch pointedly in front of his face, as if it gave the day as well as the time. "It's bloody Sunday."

Samantha felt better as she drained her coffee and rose to leave. Venting at Bryan had released some of her pent-up concern. It was the second explosion in a day. Her mother had caught the blast from the first when she adamantly refused to lend Samantha the money to hop on a plane to Toronto in search of her father. "Don't you give him any more either," Sarah had shouted. "If you've got some spare you can repay what he owes me."

They left the café in the midst of deliberating strategy.

"What about the place in Canada where you sent the money?" Bryan enquired. "I know it's Sunday but someone might be there." He checked his watch. "They must be three or four hours behind us.

"Five, I think," she said, remembering her last conversation with her father.

"Right. Your place or mine?"

"Mine," she replied. "Just in case he's phoned."

"Maybe we should go to his place first, just to make sure he hasn't slipped home without telling anyone."

Their eyes signalled agreement. "I've still got his key," said Samantha.

"So have I," said Bryan, and produced one from his pocket.

Puzzled, she probed, "How did you get a key?" She held hers up to his; they were different.

"Come on." He left no room for discussion. "My car or yours?"

"My car's a 79 bus or a taxi."

"Mine then," he said, grabbing her arm and guiding her to his Porsche, not allowing her to protest. Who was going to protest?

An ethnically diverse huddle of teenagers scattered like rats as Peter Bryan climbed from the car outside the apartment block. Everyone in the neighbourhood had been jumpy since the raid on Bliss's flat the previous week. "Fuzz," rang through the air. Little wads of dubious substances disappeared into cracks and crevices where few would venture to explore.

The door, a flashy new door, had a new lock — bright and brassy. Samantha's eyes, drawn to his sensuously long fingers, watched in horror as he slid his key into the keyhole and she felt the blood drain from her face. It was as though someone had pulled a plug in her neck and let the blood out of her head. She seemed to be looking down at herself and watching it happen. Close to fainting she grasped his hand. "Don't." It was the cat, she convinced herself as her head swam. Memories of Balderdash prevented her from going in.

"What's the matter?" Bryan asked, pausing long enough for her to explain, if she wanted to. If she could.

"You'll think I'm being stupid," she replied, her slurred voice sounding muffled to her ears, like an old tape recording.

"No."

"You will."

"Try me."

She told him it was the death of the cat — she feared its spirit. But it wasn't the cat that caused her fright, and she knew it wasn't. She'd had a sudden premonition that her father, not the cat, was dead. When else would you enter your dad's place without knocking? Why else would you turn up on his doorstep with a policeman?

"Why are you looking at me as though I'm an imbecile?" she asked, then felt angry at herself for being upset with him.

"I'm not."

"Knock then," she said and, feeling as though she were regaining control, removed her hand from his.

He started to turn the key. "Don't be silly. He's not here."

Her hand shot back and her nails bit into his fingers in terror. "Knock." It wasn't a request.

He didn't say, "This is stupid," but she saw it on his face.

"Out of the way," she ordered, pushing him roughly aside. "Dad, are you there?" she called, banging loudly, then she stuck her ear to the door.

The key turned easily a few seconds later and they entered a different world, one she barely recognized. The apartment, redecorated beyond recognition and refurbished beyond capacity, was palatial compared to its former self. "He'll love it," said Bryan, proud of the way he'd got things moving in the twelve days since Bliss's disappearance.

Samantha was unsure. "He probably won't even notice," she said, awed by the newly papered walls and the abundance of matching furniture, but knowing her father better than anyone. "There's no television," she added, noting immediately the one deficiency that would bother him.

"Surprise," said Bryan, flashing a memorandum authorizing the purchase of both a television and a video cassette recorder.

"Dad didn't have a VCR ..." she started.

"Shhhhh. Do you want to get me shot?"

They laughed, then her face straightened. The television — the bills under the television, she had completely forgotten them. She looked around hopefully. "I don't suppose you noticed some bills under his old telly did you? I was supposed to take care of them."

He glanced around with little hope. "Nope, I can't say that I did."

"What's that smell?" she asked, catching a whiff of something strange.

"New paint," he suggested.

She snuffled around noisily, "No. It's cat — dead cat."

He sniffed, as loudly as he could, just to ensure she would know he was taking her seriously, then gave her a shrug accompanied by a blank expression.

But she was determined to find something wrong, illogically annoyed with the police for trying to wriggle out of their responsibilities by putting everything right before she could sue the pants off them. "It's cat shit," she announced with triumph in her voice.

He scented around. "Impossible. We had the carpet replaced professionally."

She dropped to all fours, sticking her bottom in the air and her nose to the floor. "I bet the poor old bugger shit himself when your copper kicked him to death."

"Don't exaggerate," he said, his eyes glued to her backside.

She looked up, and caught him. Inwardly she smiled, but managed to put a scowl on her face. "I bet you'd shit yourself if someone kicked you to death." She looked around for something else to moan about, knowing she wouldn't get far with a vague complaint about an odour. "Where are his boxes?"

Bryan tried getting his own back. "That stinking load of junk ..." but he got no further.

Scenting the brush, she adopted a tone long practised for her Old Bailey debut. "Chief Inspector. That junk, as you describe it, contained many valuable personal belongings, heirlooms — "

It was his turn to cut in, mockingly: "It's in protective custody. You don't think I would have left his 'valuable' belongings unattended in this neighbourhood?"

"Protective custody?"

"My place."

She readied herself for another attack, but he saw what was coming. "Don't worry, I haven't pried," he said, blocking her with the wave of an outstretched hand, and added, "I wouldn't want to catch anything."

She knew when to quit and graciously allowed him to pull her to her feet.

"Samantha," he crooned. "Can we stop fighting, please? I'm not the enemy."

"Pax," she said, holding out a hand.

He laughed at her childlike gesture but stuck out his hand anyway. "Pax."

Their hands met for a brief shake then Bryan headed toward the door. "Back in a jiff. Gotta get something from the car," he said, leaving her perplexed as he disappeared out of the apartment. He returned in seconds, slipping her a manilla folder. "I shall deny ever seeing this," he said, his eyes roaming the ceiling.

"What is it?"

"I've no idea. I've just told you, I've never seen it before it my life."

Her face was a picture as she gingerly opened the folder. She looks as though a tarantula might leap out, Bryan thought.

It was the Betty-Ann Gordonstone suicide file. "Where did you get it?" she breathed.

"I don't know what you're talking about," he called from the newly decorated kitchen as he wandered around pretending to admire the handiwork.

She slid up behind him. "Liar," she said with so much laughter in her voice it bubbled over and infected him.

"OK. But not a word, promise?"

She promised.

"From the Coroner's Court archives. When I discovered Edwards had destroyed the original, I thought someone was bound to have a copy, and I was right."

He took the file back from her and shuffled through it. "It's not all here. Only the copies of statements lodged with the coroner. The original file would probably have a lot more, statements from the casualty doctor ... Oh, correction," he said, "there is a statement from the doctor." He quickly ran his eye down the witness list. "That's interesting, there's no statement from her daughter."

"Margaret," Samantha suggested.

"Yeah. The one in Canada."

"What is in there?" she enquired excitedly, straining to look, temporarily forgetting the loss of her father.

"I'm not sure. I only picked it up this morning."

"Sunday morning?"

"Well, it's not exactly kosher," he said, weighing the file in deliberation. "But as long as my contact gets it back tonight, no one will know. Now, if your dad is right and Gordonstone did kill his wife we're going to have to find something in here to justify going over Edwards' head."

She snuggled up to him as he opened the file. "You really are on Dad's side aren't you?"

"He's going to need any help he can get when he gets back."

"What are we looking for?" she asked. "Something absolutely bizarre like a tiny RIP tattooed on her left breast by the murderer using a rusty hatpin?"

"You're just being fanciful."

"OK. What about a piece of ripped thumbnail embedded in her right earlobe, or ... or ... or ..." she clutched herself round her throat and gasped, theatrically, "or one of his hairs stuck in her throat as she struggles for a final breath."

"Oh come on, Samantha, you know better than that. 'Bizarre' usually happens only in novels. Anyway, if there was something obviously pointing to third party involvement Edwards would never have got the coroner to bring in a suicide verdict. No, I would prefer to find something more down-to-earth."

"Like what?"

He didn't know. He couldn't know what he was looking for without finding it, so he turned the joke on himself. "Like a death threat penned in blood and pinned to her petticoat."

"Now you're being facetious."

"I know, but sometimes it isn't what you find that matters. It's what isn't there that's important."

"Such as?"

"A suicide note." He ran his finger down the list of exhibits as she peered over his shoulder. "There was no suicide note," he said, very pointedly.

"Do suicides always leave notes?" she breathed, leaning over his shoulder, her breath smouldering in his ear.

"Usually. Not always, admittedly, but usually. But this was no spur-of-the-moment, chuck-yourself-under-a-truck suicide. She could have lynched herself on that chandelier any time, she had plenty of opportunity to think about it. So why not leave a note explaining why?"

"Maybe there was a note," Samantha replied with a gush. "Think about it, Peter. What would she have written?" She answered her own question without giving him a chance to get his breath. "'You bastard, Martin. I saw you drown Melanie and I can't live with that knowledge any longer.' And," she continued, the puzzle already solved in her own mind, "what do you think Gordonstone would have done with the note if he'd found it before Edwards arrived?"

"Chucked it on the fire," Bryan suggested, catching up.

She nodded. "Wouldn't you?"

"In his place? You're damn right I would."

"So how long did he have before Edwards arrived?"

Peter Bryan leafed through the slender file and located Edwards' statement. "That's interesting ... He was off duty at the time — he says so." He recited Edwards' words: "'I was off duty in the vicinity of *L'Haute Cuisinier* restaurant when I heard an appeal on the radio for assistance.'" Bryan shuffled a couple more papers. "He must have been very close. Look," he said as he pointed to two places in the file, comparing Edwards' time of arrival on the scene with the time the call went out. "According to the control room log he got there in two minutes flat."

Samantha looked puzzled. "So Gordonstone only had two minutes to destroy the ... No!" she cried in frustration, "He could have found the suicide note before he dialled 999. He had as long as he wanted. He could have found the body, searched until he found the note, burned it, then phoned."

"Let's see what he has to say," replied Bryan, scanning Gordonstone's statement and throwing out snatches aloud for Samantha's benefit so she wouldn't have to read over his shoulder. "Went out at eleven ... Staff locked up ... Got home about ten past one ... Had been drinking with friends."

"Which friends?" asked Samantha. "Who?"

"Doesn't say," he continued, "...Found wife hanging from chandelier."

The identity of Gordonstone's friends niggled Samantha. "Why didn't Edwards ask? Surely that was important," she said. "They were Gordonstone's alibi." She hung onto Bryan's shoulder as they both reread the statement, searching in vain for information about his drinking partners.

"He didn't really have an alibi," concluded Bryan eventually. Apparently, he hadn't needed an alibi; the self-appointed officer-in-charge, Detective Inspector Edwards, had taken him at his word and embraced his account of the discovery of his wife's body. A story later accepted by the coroner.

"It doesn't prove she killed herself, though, does it?" Samantha said, implying by her tone that her father's postulation about murder could be correct.

"No. It doesn't," replied Bryan, shaking his head. "Gordonstone could have been home by one, murdered her, and called the police ten minutes later. It only takes a minute or two to kill someone; it's much faster than giving birth."

Though not as fast as conception, thought Samantha, recalling her very brief encounter with Mr. Wrong.

"So what have we got?"

"The lack of a suicide note is definitely suspicious, and unless Gordonstone's 'friends' can back up his story he would certainly be in the frame. But it's been ten years. It might be a job to find them now, and I doubt they'd remember exactly what happened."

"We've also got to find Dad," she reminded him, then remembered the videotape her father had asked her to view. "Oh. I nearly forgot. Dad said something about a videotape of the night Gordonstone was murdered. He said it was on the tele..." Her voice tapered as she realized the folly of even asking. "OK. Well we had better get back to my place just in case Dad has called."

He hadn't called ... He couldn't call. Margaret had shot him on Thursday.

Following the shooting, Margaret stomped around the clearing angrily, bursting twigs like firecrackers. "I told you not to come." Bo pranced delightedly, thinking the shooting was a huge game.

"I warned you," Margaret continued, making no effort to help Bliss as he fought to stem the flow of blood from his leg.

"You didn't say you were going to shoot me."

She sounded almost apologetic. "I wasn't going to; I didn't want to."

"Like you didn't want to drown Melanie," said a stranger's voice from inside him.

She started turning away. "I didn't drown her."

He could feel the bullet — it was huge — a missile deep in his thigh, grazing the bone. "Aagh," he cried as it moved under his probing.

"I saw them together. I saw him kissing her ..." she stopped and stared up through the leafless spokes of a maple tree at the clear blue sky, as if searching for a word or an image to complete the phrase.

He felt himself becoming woozy. "Losing blood," he said, recognizing the symptoms.

"She teased me. 'This is what Daddy does,' she said."

"Help me," he muttered drowsily.

"'Like this,' she said."

"The blood ... stop ... help." He was fighting the grogginess.

"'Stop it,' I said. 'Don't.' 'It's nice,' she said. 'I like it.' But she didn't mean it. She was just getting at me."

"Margaret ...Please, I'm dying."

"'Shut up, or I'll smack you!' I told her."

Bliss was reaching out to her. "Margaret ..."

"But she kept on and on. 'I'll tell mum,' I said."

"Marg…"

"'Mum knows,' she said."

The light was dying. "Please …"

"I watched them — I saw them together — I saw what they did."

Bliss's eyes glazed and closed. Night descended. His struggle was over.

"Even after she'd gone, he still didn't want me."

She glanced at Bliss with the realization that his sagging body had ceased to move, then sat cross-legged against a trunk, head slumped, gun by her side, recalling the times following Melanie's death when she had slipped almost naked into her father's bedroom late at night on the flimsiest of pretexts. *"Dad … I'm too hot, or too cold. I'm scared of the dark — of thunder — of ghosts,"* or, *"I feel sick. Will you cuddle me?"*

"Go to bed Margaret," he would say coldly. "You'll be all right."

"I wanted to scream, 'Love me, Dad,'" she said to Bliss, as if he could still hear. "'Why won't you love me like you loved Melanie?' But he didn't want me; he wanted Melanie back. He didn't want me. He called me a whore." Her voice rose in a crescendo of anger. "After what he'd been doing to Melanie, he called *me* a whore! He wouldn't even hit me. I wanted him to."

She pleaded with the unconscious Bliss. "Do you understand? I wanted him to hit me. To hit me and do with me the things he did with Melanie. 'Do it to me, Daddy — do it to me like you used to do it to Melanie.' But he never did."

Suddenly conscious of the surrounding silence, Margaret lowered her voice to a whisper. "Even you didn't want me," she mumbled, then she stood and drifted soundlessly into the inert forest.

Although it had died, the forest's resurrection was only a season away. Bliss's resurrection came much sooner; a matter of hours not months. Bo's tongue stirred him as it rippled across his face like a warm wet flannel, but full awareness was still way over the horizon as he lay on the wet leafy ground, drifting through a misty, unreal landscape trying to get his head around everything that had happened,

A warm salivating sensation in his mouth made him retch and he turned his head and vomited. Margaret, who had been standing close by, moved discreetly away; he saw her through a gummy haze, gun in hand, urging Bo to her side. With an inexplicable feeling that it might be safer to appear unconscious until he got his act together, he lay still again, struggling to remember what had happened, but the events were as nebulous as if they had occurred in a trance. He vaguely recalled falling asleep as Margaret was speaking, but her words were as faint as a barely remembered dream, although the message "I didn't drown Melanie" seemed to stand out, like the headlines on a newsagent's billboard.

So if she hadn't killed Melanie, what had happened to her sister? Nothing, he thought. That's untrue: she was murdered by her father, as you have always known. Removing the images of Melanie's face from the photographs was merely Margaret's way of dealing with the loss.

I'd make a good psychiatrist, or is it a psychologist, he thought, running through the scenario in his mind. Unable to protect Melanie from her father's abuse, Margaret protects herself from the guilt by eliminating any trace of her sister's image.

But a niggling thought persisted. What if she did do it? *She didn't.*

But what if she did? What would you do?

Arrest her.

You'd look bloody foolish asking her to mend the canoe so you can take her in.

What's the alternative?

Let her go. What difference will it make now? Melanie's been dead for twenty years. Edwards was right — why dredge up the past? The only one who will be hurt will be you. In any case, you've got no hard evidence, and the only two witnesses are both dead. And, as Samantha had said, a good lawyer would punch holes in anything Margaret herself said, putting it all down to the survival guilt and false memory syndrome of a traumatized child.

He had to agree with himself. The mutilated photographs, especially the one with the coffin, might simply have been her interpretation of what happened, a manifestation of a conscience permanently marred by her sister's death.

Pull yourself together you idiot, he yelled at himself. If that's true, then why did she shoot you?

"I've been shot!" Bliss jerked awake and stared at his leg in disbelief. His trousers had been pulled down to his ankles and a scruffy bandage had been tied around the wound. A ruddy blot was already seeping through the cloth.

"It's the tranquillizer," she explained as she bent to examine the dressing, realizing he was having difficulty focussing. "It'll wear off in a while."

Everything was fuzzy; he watched her re-bandage his leg as if it belonged to someone else. Maybe all this belongs to someone else, he thought, looking around, his mind muddled. Maybe I've strayed into somebody else's life.

"I've got the dart out," she continued. "But it's made a bit of a mess."

The tranquillizer dart, designed to penetrate the thick fur and tough hide of a bear, had done more than make a bit of a mess, it had carved a crater into his leg the size of a carrot.

Bliss' mind drifted. The vision of Gordonstone thrusting Melanie's cute little face underwater had plagued him for twenty years; it was difficult to dispel even with the stark evidence staring him in the face and burning into his leg. He still found himself excusing Margaret, thinking that she must simply blame herself for Melanie's death. Perhaps she felt guilty that Melanie was the one who suffered at her father's hands. Perhaps she even believed that it should have been her he drowned. But now an alternative notion pounded in his brain,

It couldn't be, he thought. But he vacillated — maybe it could be. The light finally clicked on; Margaret drowned her sister, not Gordonstone. But why?

He felt Margaret's hands working on his leg but didn't need to look at her face to understand. The hare-lip! Margaret had envied Melanie for being perfect. Margaret had killed her sister because of everyday sibling jealousy. The axe that cleaved a million families; the nick in a child's heart that festers until it becomes an open sore. Two sisters, conceived in the same womb, sharing the same genes, bickering over toys that neither really wanted, squabbling over one-eyed teddy bears and armless dolls, battling over bed-times and boys. Each demanding fatherly attention; Melanie getting more than her fair share.

Bliss succumbed to the effects of the tranquillizer again and floated sleep thinking how easily the petty rivalries of childhood — more often based on perception than reality — could turn siblings, parents, and partners into mortal enemies. Drug-induced dreams washed over his mind, morning turned to afternoon, and the narcotic eventually wore off. He woke and felt the sting of sunlight as he pried open his eyes. Margaret hadn't noticed him stir; she was lost in concerns of her own, staring off into the future. Bliss contemplated making a grab for the gun, which was idly propped against a tree, but one look at Bo lying protectively by Margaret's side convinced him he would never make it. Closing his eyes again he weighed his limited options and concluded his best bet was to simply forget what he'd discovered — he had no proof anyway. He should just go back. He checked himself; he couldn't go back, she had taught him that. "Life doesn't work in reverse," she had said. Go home then. He could lie, even to himself if he wanted, it wasn't difficult. All he had to do was stick to the original script she had given him: her father had sexually abused Melanie, then drowned her when he thought he might be caught. It was, after all, what he himself had always suspected.

With the decision made he opened his eyes, praying that the scene had changed; that the real world and normality had returned. He was dismayed to see Margaret checking the bandage again. But he would let her go, he decided. There was no point in doing anything else; she had suffered enough. He'd tell her she had nothing to fear, that he was only interested in her finding her father's killer. And as for the hole in his leg, he could explain that away as a hunting accident.

Watching Margaret as she carefully re-tied the bandage, it struck him that it was no wonder her mother had committed suicide. Ten years of living with the knowledge that one of your daughters killed the other was far more than any mother should have to bear. What could she have done? Informed the police and lost the other daughter as well.

"What about your mother?" he asked, expecting her to shatter yet another of his illusions and confirm that Betty-Ann did indeed commit suicide.

Startled, her head shot up as if she'd been stung. "I didn't kill her," she protested, with indignation.

"I didn't — " he started, but she picked up the gun threateningly and froze him into silence.

"Don't look at me like that," she said.

"Like what?"

"Like you pity me. I don't want your pity."

"What *do* you want?"

"Nothing from you. I just wanted you to leave me alone but you couldn't, could you?"

"Your mother?" he tried again tenaciously. There was something he had not grasped, and he was determined to get to the bottom of the matter despite his perilous situation. "What exactly happened that night? You were there weren't you?"

She sat back on her haunches and weighed her response carefully. "I put her out of her misery, if you must know," she said finally, then warned him against responding with a cautionary wave of the rifle. "And before you say anything — There is a difference."

Too flabbergasted to respond, he lamely enquired, "So what happens now?"

"I don't know. I've got to talk to someone."

That's interesting, he thought. "What happens to me in the meantime?"

"Stay here, you're safe enough. Don't wander around; I don't want to have to save your life again." Her tone suggested she actually believed what she was saying, that after shooting him, she had saved his life.

"I'm hardly likely to run away," he said. "Could you help me to the house?" he added, hoping to have a chance to grapple the gun away from her.

She eyed him from a watchful distance, her forehead creased in deliberation, making him wonder if she was contemplating putting him out of his misery as well. "No. Just stay there. I'll be back."

Then she and her dog evaporated into the trees and left him to wonder once again if any of what was happening was real. Pinching himself was useless, he reasoned; if this was an illusion, it was so well constructed he would expect to feel pain. However, if everything was fabricated, the designer of the subterfuge had apparently fallen down in the background noise department. The soundtrack was missing and he was struck by the utter silence and stillness. He was also stunned by the lack of wildlife. It wasn't just the absence of Margaret's animals that perturbed him, it was the absence of any creatures of any kind. No birds tweeting in the treetops, not even a butterfly noisily beating its wings against the air. He almost laughed at the thought of hearing a boisterous butterfly, then realized that in this deathly still forest he just might. That was it, he realized, this forest was deathly still, as if frozen in time — petrified. It was a sound stage without the sound. His mind swung back to his previous expedition through the forest, when Margaret had exposed the bear pit. There had been no animals then either — none.

Bliss made up his mind; he wasn't going to wait like a wounded duck for her return. She'd killed her sister and mother, even if she had managed to rationalize their deaths. Surely she'd rationalize his death as well if she so desired. He had to escape or somehow summon assistance, and his initial instinct was to wait until dark and take the canoe, then he remembered the smashed hull. Swim then ... Crazy. Build a raft? It would take weeks.

Was there a better idea?

The design of a raft was already taking shape in his mind when a faint buzzing sound cut through the forest and interrupted his deliberations. He was so immersed in his own thoughts it took a few seconds for him to catch on. It's an engine of some sort, he deduced dreamily and had almost dismissed it before jerking himself alert. "It's a plane you fool!" he said aloud, and snatched a look at his watch: it was nearly six-thirty. Alice was returning to the settlement to collect him.

"Down here," he shouted, peering up through the spindly canopy. He drunkenly pulled himself upright against a tree, cautiously testing his weight on the injured leg, and waved frantically as the small plane hopped over the island. She'll never see me, he realized, but ripped off his shirt and flagged it around his head anyway. Within a second the little plane had zipped across his field of vision and his spirits plummeted. He was almost certain she had not seen him; he recalled what difficulty he'd had spotting things from the air on his arrival, how he had even missed the family of bears playing in the open on the beach at their first pass. The beach! That's it, he thought, I must get to the beach. Then she'll see me on her return. Which way? He panicked. Where's the beach? Which beach? Any beach.

Steeling himself against the pain he crashed through the forest. Dismissing the threat of an ambush from Margaret or her dog he cursed his dragging leg and ignored the danger of a bear trap. His good foot, pounding the ground with all his weight, thudded dully on the rain-softened earth and suddenly the forest was vibrant with noise — but only his noise. Twigs crackled underfoot, dried leaves rustled, branches whooshed back into place behind him, and the sound of his own breathing seemed deafening as the sharp breaths whistled in and out. Sounds that would have been swallowed amid the music of a normal forest resounded in his sensitive ears. And in the background the constant drone of the plane's engine faded slowly into the distance.

Stopping for a moment to catch his breath, Bliss anticipated the resurgence of silence but was surprised to hear the engine growing stronger, deeper, and richer. It was louder now — much louder. The plane was returning; momentary confusion clarified into joyous relief. She's coming back. She's landing, coming to pick me up.

Drawn by the booming engine he thrashed his way through the last of the trees toward the beach. He was going to make it, he realized, spying the lake ahead. What luck, he thought, assuming he had misunderstood about meeting at the settlement. Alice must have meant she'd pick me up here. I can still make Toronto by Saturday. Rushing excitedly through the final few yards of bush, eyes and mind on the heavens, he tripped headlong over an exposed root and flailed wildly at spindly shoots, fearing for just an instant that he was falling into one of the deadly bear traps. Be more careful, she'll wait a few minutes, he cautioned, pulled himself upright, and reached the shore in a few strides. The droning of the engine thudded with a sound so palpable that even with his hands clamped over his ears it still beat into his brain, yet he stood transfixed, bamboozled, staring skyward. The vacant planeless sky, as sterile as the forest, stared blankly back at him. His wounded leg crumpled slowly under his weight and he closed his eyes and sank to the sand, now firmly convinced everything around him was a hallucination.

chapter thirteen

Superintendent Edwards wore the mantel of martyrdom with a superior air at the Monday morning prayer meeting. Remaining at his post, arm encased in plaster, had, he believed, bolstered his credibility over that of Bliss, whose disappearance clearly proved his culpability.

After nearly two hours of crime stats and arrest reports, the room cleared of officers faster than a scuttled ship, but DCI Bryan lingered over the dregs of his coffee.

"Is Mr. Bliss still AWOL?" asked Edwards, falling neatly into the trap. Bryan put down the cup with a clatter and nodded.

"Give him another day or two, then start the ball rolling," continued Edwards with a glance toward his plastered arm. "Forget this, let's just get rid of him on an AWOL charge."

I'd bet you'd love that, Bryan thought to himself, knowing that a disciplinary charge for being absent without leave wouldn't offer Bliss a public pulpit from which to broadcast his side of the story. "Have you a few moments, Sir?" he asked, defying Edwards to protest.

Edwards waved him to a chair. "What's on your mind?"

"A couple of things that Bliss said. He couldn't understand why no witnesses were brought forward to provide Gordonstone with an alibi after his wife's death."

Edwards jerked upright in his seat. "How did Bliss know that?"

"Search me." He let his face play dumb.

"Well, Chief Inspector," Edwards insisted defensively, "you can take my word for it. Martin Gordonstone had a cast-iron alibi. He could not, and did not, kill his wife." With that, he started to rise, the words "Now push off" written all over his face. Bryan was unmoved, carefully counting the grounds of coffee in the bottom of his cup. "He was also concerned about the absence of a suicide note."

Strike two, he thought as Edwards deflated like a stuck balloon. "It happens," he replied sinking back into the chair.

"True, but most people on the verge of topping themselves usually made it fairly obvious to friends and family beforehand." He looked up with a scrutinizing stare. "Had she?"

"Are you questioning me, Chief Inspector?"

"It seems that way, Sir," Bryan said with deliberate insolence, then decided that Bliss should give Edwards something else to consider. "Inspector Bliss also says that there was no evidence of booze or drugs. Most suicides —"

Edwards cut him off, yelling, "I know what most suicides do, Chief Inspector, I've dealt with enough of them."

"So did anyone come forward to say she was contemplating doing herself in?"

If looks could castrate, thought Bryan, yet was surprised by Edwards' submissiveness as he answered, "Not as far as I remember."

"Did you ask?" Bryan probed, feeling that he had the upper hand. "It's just that Bliss was so certain. He was also sure that Gordonstone killed his daughter."

"Kept it to himself though, didn't he?"

"He had his reasons."

"How do you know so much? That girl of his been blabbering?"

"She's concerned that's all. And I'm beginning to think that Bliss should be considered a missing person, not AWOL."

Edwards grunted in disbelief. "Misper my eye. The coward's fucking hiding."

"I hope you've got good news," Peter Bryan enquired when Samantha called a little later.

"No. I've spoken to the bank again. The money was definitely returned on Friday afternoon. Apparently the Canadian bank said that they had no knowledge of Dad."

"What sort of place is it, do you know?"

"The sort of place where everybody would know everybody and all their business from what I can make out."

"It doesn't make sense. Why don't you call the place — ask 'em what's going on."

"I'm in court ..." she started.

"Let me have the details then and give me a bell when you're free."

Stacy was not in the best of moods when Bryan called enquiring about Bliss. "Geez man it ain't light yet," he complained, and added that he had never heard of any-one with that name. "An English cop out here, you gotta be kidding," he declared, though his tone said, "You gotta be mad."

"His daughter sent some money last week."

Stacy's silence marked a moment's deliberation. "Oh yeah. I remember," he said eventually, as if he had just had a brainwave.

"You do?"

"Yeah. I sent it back. Thought it must be a screw up. Sorry, you've got the wrong place." The impatience in Stacy's voice suggested he was about to hang up, so Bryan shouted, "Wait a minute, there's obviously been some mistake."

"Your mistake bud."

"What about Margaret Gordonstone?"

"Who?"

"Margaret Gordonstone."

Another moment's silence. The transatlantic delay, Bryan assumed.

"No one here by that name...Sorry bud." He had finished, the inflection in his voice made it absolutely clear the conversation was over. A foreign-sounding buzz in Bryan's ear reinforced the point.

"The case has been adjourned *sine die*," Samantha said when she returned Bryan's call. She sounded more relaxed, he thought. She was more relaxed; a simple negative pregnancy test had taken a huge weight off the rest of her life. "The police claimed that they needed more prep time," she added with obvious disbelief. "Anyway, that gives me all day to find Dad."

"You might need more than that."

Panic filled her voice. "Why?"

Bryan sighed. "The bank in Canada say they've never heard of your dad or the Gordonstone woman."

"Impossible."

"I can't argue now, meet me for lunch."

She would have persisted but the battery on the cellphone was warning her that it was tiring. "OK," she agreed.

"Not that Tornado place..." he started.

"The *Typhoon*. No, you choose. It's your turn to pay anyway."

That's a change, he thought, but offered willingly. Then he stuck his toe in the water, adding a hint of laughter so that he could make out it was a joke should it backfire. "Maybe, when this is over, we could have a romantic dinner somewhere without having to worry about your dad?"

"Maybe" she said tentatively, then kicked herself for not being forthright. But what should she have said: "I'd love that and if you behave yourself, you've got a good chance of a fuck?"

"Indonesian, Italian, Chinese, or Indian for lunch?" he asked.

Doesn't anybody eat English anymore she thought but cast her mind back to the *Typhoon* and understood why. "Italian," she suggested, figuring it would be difficult to disguise cat or kangaroo as fusilli.

He knew a little place off Oxford Street.

"Doesn't everyone?"

"Meet me at Piccadilly Circus then. Midday."

She'd come straight from court. The grungy dress of the previous day had been exchanged for a working uniform — dark grey skirt and a virginal blouse — and she breezed straight past him at the subway exit.

"Sam," he called, startling her from a daydream. She turned, wondering how she could have missed him. Then it struck her: he looked older. No, not older, more mature, more trustworthy, in a hand-tailored suit that had never been near Marks and Spencers. They walked to the restaurant, fighting for pavement space among the hordes of hunters stalking lunchtime edibles.

"I thought you might like this place," he said as they were guided to the table he'd reserved.

"Don't tell me," she laughed. "This is just another excuse to take me out for a meal."

"Oh, dear — do I need an excuse?"

She sidestepped the question and her face clouded. "What are we going to do?"

Before he could answer she marched off to hang up her coat.

"He's in big trouble, I know it," she said, returning to her chair.

"Leave Edwards to me."

"I didn't mean Edwards ..." she started, then interrupted herself. "Back in a mo." She was up again. The call of the loo, he realized, as she disappeared down the backstairs.

He ordered in her absence, hoping she wouldn't mind the lobster primavera. Who would mind?

No sooner had she sat than she was off again, retrieving her cellphone from her coat.

"Samantha, for God's sake sit still," he called, "Stop popping up and down like a jack-in-the-box."

"Sorry," she blushed, resuming her seat. "I've been thinking ... That bank place you called, maybe I should call. There must be some mistake."

"You could try. But there's no mistake; the bloke was adamant. He'd never heard of your dad or Margaret. Plus the fact your bank said the money wasn't delivered."

"Oh yes. I called them again this morning," she said, forgetting in her consternation that she'd already told him. "They said that the money wasn't accepted and I can have it back." A momentary relief spread over her face. "That's probably why he hasn't come home: he has no money."

Bryan was less easily mollified. "That isn't why he hasn't phoned though, is it?"

Her face tensed again; her emotional pendulum was in full swing. Bryan continued, "He had every reason to phone if he hadn't received the money. Maybe he's in hiding?"

"He's not hiding from me. He never has."

"You've known where he was all the time?"

She nodded, then saw the look of admonishment of his face. "What are you going to do Chief Inspector — slap me in handcuffs and charge me with obstruction, aiding and abetting a fugitive?"

"No. But you lied to me," he pouted, irrationally feeling hurt. He knew it was irrational; knew that everybody, himself included, would lie if the situation demanded it. But it still stung that she hadn't trusted him.

Samantha, sensing his chagrin, slipped off a shoe and ran her foot up his shin under the table. "Never mind. I'll make up for it."

She gave him a complete account, interspersed with mouthfuls of lobster and pasta, beginning with her father's gnawing belief in Gordonstone's guilt, and continuing through his discovery of Margaret's whereabouts and his assertion that he'd found the evidence he was looking for and was anxious to return to duty. "I know this sounds crazy," she concluded, "I just can't help feeling that I should go and find him."

"We could go and find him," said Bryan. But he wasn't serious. Neither was she really, but there was a certain satisfaction in articulating the possibility.

"Are you really serious?" she asked, knowing he was not; she could recognize a smooth line when she heard one.

What the hell, he thought. "Yeah. Give me your phone. Can you get your things together in an hour?"

"Hold on, slow down," she said, her spinning mind throwing up a roadblock. "He's not in Toronto, he's on an island somewhere."

"We'll get a boat then. You've got the address."

"Dad said something about a small plane."

"We'll get a plane."

"You mean it!"

"I do."

Samantha and Peter Bryan were still rushing through their cappuccinos in London as the frost-glazed treetops of Little Bear Island hovered above the swirling lake mist, sparkling in the early morning sunlight. Winter's glacier was already sliding down from the arctic and the sharpness of the air signalled the approaching season. But much more had changed than the air. The island's soul had veered around. Yet to an outsider, nothing had changed. The day, as usual, had dawned without a chorus; the forest's waking silence echoed only with the roar of the breeze and the occasional crash of a falling leaf.

But, witnessed or not, there had been a fundamental shift in the island's atmosphere since the previous Thursday, when the very real pain in his leg had drawn Bliss back to earth on the beach. He had opened his eyes and stared in disbelief with the realization that the noise he had assumed to be Alice's plane was actually a powerful speedboat, its wake showing it had come from around the next headland and was headed out into the lake. Although already some distance from the shore he had no difficulty making out the solitary figure at the helm — Margaret. It was, he thought, the final nail in this coffin of unreality. Absolutely nothing was at it appeared. He had spent three days in a fool's paradise, living in a house that wasn't a home with a victim who was the villain, and torturing himself paddling a canoe with a woman who owned a speedboat. To say he had misjudged Margaret was like saying the Texan who bought London Bridge believing it to be Tower Bridge was a dab hand at picking a bargain.

Unarmed and wounded, Bliss sat on the sun-warmed sand for a while, mulling over what had happened, and had difficulty suppressing a feeling of relief; at least he'd finally got to the root of the matter. But a chill ran through him as the night's shutters started to descend. It was nearly eight o'clock and there was still no sign of Alice's plane returning from the settlement. Thinking that she would not see him in the twilight, he was on the point of building a fire on the beach when his heart sank with the realization that she had been leaving, not arriving, when he had seen her fly over the island. She had left without him and he had wasted much of the evening, and a great deal of hope, in anticipation of being rescued.

"Now get out of that," he said to himself, comprehending the seriousness of the situation but unable to formulate a plan of escape, as he sat mesmerized by the tiny ripples that barely ruffled the fine white sand. Ideas came and went but the only thing of which he was certain was that once he made it to safety he would return with reinforcements and take Margaret into custody. But, to start, he would need to find out where the boat had come from. There had to be a dock and probably a house, and maybe — with luck — a telephone or radio.

Sticking to the safety of the beach he set off toward the headland but had not dragged himself far when a sudden whiff of something raised the hairs on the back of his neck. Fearing the presence of a bear or Bo, he froze and inhaled deeply. The meat and shit smell of an abattoir turned his nose and drew him inland away from the beach. With the feeling that the odour might somehow hold the key to his survival he inched forward, pulling himself from tree to tree, painfully dragging the wounded leg. The source of the smell became visible in the form of a black phantom hovering just above the ground. A creepy background murmur increased in volume as he inched forward and, as he watched the black mass constantly morphing from one eerie shape to another, he had the feeling that the tranquilizer might be taking over again. "It must be the drugs," he told himself as he watched the spectre slowly spiral, like smoke on a still day. Suddenly, as if sensing his presence, the apparition simply melted and silence returned. He rushed forward, as fast as his leg would permit, and discovered a small deserted clearing with a leafy woodland floor. There was no bag of bones, no chunks of stinking carrion, no pile of rotting vegetation, but the overpowering smell hadn't dissolved — something dead lay close by. The vanishing black spectre, a cloud of insects and flies, knew a thing or two about rotten smells and were clearly not all deluded.

He was on the point of venturing forward into the clearing itself when memory of the bear pit struck him and he dropped slowly to the ground to scrutinize the area ahead of him. Some of the startled flies were still disappearing into small holes in the ground. There was something smelly underground! The stench was so strong it made him retch. It must be a dead bear, he decided, nothing living could smell that bad.

Leave it, he said to himself, and started to inch away. *What if it's just wounded?*

Are you crazy, he thought. You can't save yourself. What are you going to do with an enraged injured bear full of gangrene?

Oh, God, he thought, looking at the bandage on his leg, which now leaked like a rusted burst pipe. Gangrene!

He racked his brain — what did he know about gangrene? Nothing — only that it was fatal. But so was Margaret, he'd concluded.

The Canadian Mountie at Pearson International Airport listened to Peter Bryan's explanation for their visit with growing skepticism. When Bryan finished talking, Sergeant Gdowski turned to Samantha. "You came all this way just cuz your dad didn't phone. Are you guys crazy or what?"

"We are crazy," admitted Samantha, who wanted to tug her co-conspirator's arm and say, "Let's go home."

"Crazy or not," added Bryan, "we're here now, so can you tell us how to get to Bear Lake?"

"You should've called ahead," the sergeant complained, sweeping his hand across a map on the wall behind him. "I bet there's upwards of fifty Bear Lakes in Canada. Do you know there's so many lakes in this country that no one's ever counted 'em. Many of 'em don't even have names."

They didn't know, didn't care, and shrugged simultaneously. "Can you help us find him?" appealed Samantha.

Gdowski turned to Peter Bryan. "I'd have to get clearance, Sir."

"It's sort of unofficial, Sergeant."

"How come?"

"Officially he's AWOL, but we think he's in trouble."

"He sure is if he's AWOL."

"Come on, Peter, we'll get a cab," said Samantha, feeling they were getting nowhere.

"Hang on. I ain't trying to be funny, Miss. It's just that I don't know where to start."

"We've got the address my dad gave me over the phone. He even gave me the postal code." She delved into her purse and came up with her note pad.

"OK. Now we're talking. If we've got the postal code we can pin it down right away."

He pinned it down all right — straight to Stacy's store. "Shit, there's gotta be some mistake," he said, massaging his forehead in disbelief. "There's gotta be lots of simple answers."

"One will do," said Bryan.

"Eh?"

"Sergeant, we would be very happy to have just one of your explanations."

"Yeah," the sergeant said. "Just give me a second." He picked up the phone and made a few hurried calls, then turned to address Bryan and Samantha. "Boy are you folks lucky. We're sending someone out near Bear Lake first thing tomorrow to investigate a plane crash 'bout a hundred kilometres away. I can get you a ride if you want."

They wanted. "But what about the extra sixty-odd miles?" Bryan asked.

"No big deal, the pilot can run you over there while our guy investigates the wreck."

"Great."

An hour later, as guests of the Mounties, they relaxed over dinner at their hotel, unable to believe their good fortune.

The *Lego Hotel* on the airport strip could have been in Sydney, Singapore, or Sheffield, but it was bright and clean.

"Do you folks want one room or two?" the sergeant had enquired as he introduced them to his friend at the front desk.

"Two —" started Bryan, but Samantha's shout of "One," trumped him.

"I don't know what came over me," she apologized a few minutes later. "It's not too late if you'd prefer to be alone."

"It's fine with me."

"I don't usually do this," she prattled on, still nervously apologizing as the elevator took them to the seventeenth floor. "I just didn't want to be on my own. Are you sure you don't mind?"

Is this attractive, desirable woman crazy, he thought. "I really don't mind," he said, "The room has two Queen-size beds, so it would be silly to have two rooms."

"How come you never married?" she asked, then searched his powder blue eyes for an answer.

"I'm only thirty-six, not past it yet. How old are you, anyway?"

She gave him a saucy wink. "Frightened of accusations of cradle snatching are we?"

"No. I was actually wondering if you could introduce me to a younger sister."

"Oy!" she exclaimed, digging him in the ribs. "I'm twenty-five, if you must know."

"Wow, that means your dad was ..."

"Seventeen," she said, with a certain pride. "Mum and Dad were only seventeen."

"Did they love each other?"

"I think they still do, really. Mum just wanted a change that's all. Twenty-three years having dinner in the same restaurant with the same menu might be too much for most people."

"So she found a different restaurant?" Gangly George's, he knew, Bliss had told him. "Does she like the menu there?"

"There's more pasta than steak," Samantha said, summing George up succinctly. "But that's the trend nowadays."

Bryan nodded knowingly as he let her out of the elevator and headed to their room.

"Dad was a bit tough to take at times, being a cop and all. George is pretty soft. I suppose it's easier to digest soft food as you get older."

"Your dad's not so tough at the moment."

She looked up, tapping her arm meaningfully. "I don't know if Edwards would agree with you."

"True."

"Mum's leaving hit him hard. That's the trouble with steak — overdo it and it falls to pieces eventually. Pasta just goes on soaking up more and more and gets softer and softer until you can mould it into any shape you want."

"This is it," he said, sliding the electronic key through the magnetic strip reader and opening the door.

Bryan had presumed little and was consequently not at all disappointed when, following dinner, Samantha flopped onto one of the beds, pulled herself into a fetal position and said, "I hope you don't mind Peter ...I'm really tired ... The flight ... You understand."

He understood. Anyway there was something deliciously teasing about sharing a bedroom with a virtual stranger, especially an attractive one. "We've got a very early start," he reminded her, wondering what she was like about getting up, hoping she was not a morning monster. He kissed her cheek lightly as she drifted off.

Bliss had been about to leave the fly-infested clearing when a thought struck him. Bo would scent him out easily when Margaret returned, but maybe he could evade the dog by confusing the animal with a stronger smell than his own. The stink of a dead bear, perhaps. He steeled himself and, armed with a stout stick, snaked forward rodding the earth. He wasn't surprised when the stick seemed to melt into the ground just ahead of him. Another bear pit, he guessed, and a new fear entered his mind: what if a wounded, enraged male were to leap out snarling and ripping?

He shrank back, mentally testing the wisdom of his actions. Wait, he thought, common sense prevailing. The animal, whatever it is, must be dead. It couldn't have replaced the cover by itself if it had fallen into the trap. There would be a hole where the branches had given way, and there was no sign of a hole. A human had re-covered the trap. Clenching his teeth with renewed vigour he gradually eased the latticework of branches apart and was almost on the point of seeing into the pit when a swarm of insects, startled by the sudden light, darted angrily out and caused him to jerk back in alarm. He was covered in seconds, a stream of black, biting bugs, attacking his eyes, and filling his nostrils, mouth, and ears. He rose and wildly smashed himself around the face and head, but his frenzied activity lured even more of the creatures from the hole. Then he looked down at his leg in horror — the bulk of the insects had been attracted like vampires to the blood seeping through the bandage. Stooping to swipe them away he lost his balance and barely avoided falling into the pit. So much for that, he thought, retreating hastily into the forest, beating away the insects and exhausting himself in the process. It will have to be plan "B" then, he thought, making his way carefully through the rapidly darkening forest in search of the cabin, food, and a night's sleep.

chapter fourteen

Four-thirty Tuesday morning and Samantha's world was dizzyingly out of control as she woke to Peter Bryan's gentle prodding. "Samantha, we've got to get a move on."

"What?" Who is this man? "Where am I?" This is a dream — right? Where's Dad?

"We've got to be ready in twenty minutes," Bryan added.

It all came back in a rush and she leapt out of bed and headed to the bathroom. Peter Bryan was already dressed, ready to roll, but she caught up in ten minutes and they were whisked back to the air-port police office in a waiting police car. Then their troubles began.

"Who the fuck authorized this?" Detective Sergeant Phillips of the RCMP demanded, angrily slamming down his beaker of coffee when he learned that he was to be accompanied by Bryan and Samantha.

"Authorized?" murmured Bryan, feeling slightly cowed under the onslaught from a man who looked capable of eating little boys for breakfast.

The plane's pilot chimed in to make matters worse. "I can't take a civilian, I'd get shot."

Bryan shrugged. "It was all approved last evening by Sergeant Gdowski."

"Gdowski ... I might have known. I'm sorry, Sir," said the detective, "But he had no right ..."

Bryan headed him off. "Well, he made several phone calls, he obviously got clearance from someone."

The detective raised his eyebrows. "In writing?"

"No idea," replied Bryan, who now realized that without triplicate or quadruplicate memorandums, each signed by the right person, they were unlikely to get off the ground. Damn regulations, he thought, recalling the fuss that Edwards had made the previous day when he had requested taking two weeks leave to which he was entitled.

"Fourteen days prior notice in writing, Chief Inspector, you know the rules," he had said.

"It's an emergency, Sir," Bryant had riposted, and thinking at a gallop he'd invented an ailing relative. "It's my Aunt Maud, Sir. She's had a nasty accident."

"Call an ambulance then, that's what they're for."

Bryan had whipped up the pace. "I can't do that, Sir, she's somewhere in the mountains."

"Where, for God's sake?"

He'd taken a deep breath. "Everest. Well the foothills anyway. I said I would go to co-ordinate the rescue. I knew you would understand." Then he had flown out of the superintendent's office, saying, "Thank you very much, Sir," before the other man had got his mouth into gear.

"Something like this should be cleared through Interpol anyway," the detective sergeant continued, adding weight to his argument, his mind clearly made up. They were not going.

Samantha started to cry. Softly, more of a whimper at first, but building to a crescendo of snotty sniffles. Bryan cradled her, "C'mon, Sam, he'll be alright."

"He's dead, I know he is," she bawled.

"He's not. He's just lost ...I expect."

She turned on him, blubbering. "How can you say that? He's been missing nearly a week." Then she spun on the troublesome sergeant. "He's a detective the same as you. How would your family feel if you were missing in a foreign country and nobody would help find him?"

That did it. "OK. You win."

But the pilot had other ideas. "Sorry, Sir," he addressed Bryan. "Even if I took you, as a visiting police officer, I couldn't possibly take the young lady."

Samantha's anguished cries filled the small room and Bryan was inclined to tell her to shut up before conceding that she'd been successful before. But it didn't work on the pilot.

"Sorry, Miss," he said, "But that's final; I've gotta cover my ass. Service personnel only."

Peter Bryan leapt into action. "Have you got a Bible?"

They had — a Gideon's. Placing it firmly in Samantha's right hand and ad-libbing like crazy he declared, "In my capacity as a DCI in the Grand Metropolitan Police Force, I hereby appoint you to the rank of special constable. Do you swear to protect life and property and to serve Her Majesty the Queen?"

"I do," she replied, hardly thinking.

"I now pronounce you man and wife," said Phillips, and they all laughed, including the pilot. "Let's go then," he said, easily satisfied.

"Can you really do that?" whispered Samantha on the short walk across the tarmac to the small plane, which was equipped with both wheels and floats.

He shook his head and stuck a finger to his lips. "Shhh. They don't know that."

Bliss had spent Thursday night somewhat uneasily back at the cottage; fearing he might die of exposure without shelter. Although he'd not heard Margaret's boat returning, he had blocked the door with his bed just to be on the safe side.

Friday morning dawned with a foretaste of the rapidly approaching winter: a crust of frost as thick as snowfall brightened the dreary trees. He awoke shivering in the unheated house and was horrified to find his wounded leg had become paralyzed during the night. The muscles strained painfully to move but nothing happened and he lay staring blankly at the ceiling, his mind tortured by wartime stories of men who had amputated their own limbs. It's one thing to chop off a few mangled fingers in the heat of the battle, he reasoned, but a whole leg! But his hysterical mind was already working out the details: a saw, sharp knife, boiling water, alcohol. Then he reigned back on the hysteria, telling himself that amputation was out of the question. There was no alcohol left, no hot water unless he rekindled the fire, and, with the wound high up the thigh, the leg would have to come off from the hip joint — clearly impossible.

"So, what's the alternative? What are you planning to do, lay here and die?" he said to himself. He threw back the blankets and, trying harder, willed his leg to move with all his might. His toes wriggled inside his socks, he saw them moving, although for a second thought he was looking at the wrong foot. He tried even harder, cold perspiration trickling down his forehead. If he couldn't move he was a sitting duck and was already regretting that he had returned to the house; not that he'd had much of an alternative choice. It's the first place she'll look, he realized. Finally his leg moved — stiffly and not far, but it moved. With an audible sigh of relief, he realized it wasn't immobilized at all, it was glued to the mattress by the congealed blood and pus that had saturated through the dressing.

Bliss could have laughed, but freeing the bandage and unpeeling it from his thigh revealed a situation as distressing as paralysis. Livid tentacles of infection were spreading in all directions from the ugly crater like the radials of a spider's web and he panicked, speculating that the wound might also be infested from the insect attack. The thought that his flesh could soon be crawling with maggots made him shudder and he hustled to the bathroom in desperation, stinging the wound with a deluge of icy water and wrapping it in the cleanest towel he could find. He knew he needed antiseptic and antibiotics quickly if he were to survive. He also knew he wouldn't get any on the island.

The flight to the scene of the crash would take five hours, the pilot informed Samantha and Peter Bryan as they clambered into the rear seats of the small twin-engine plane.

"Wait," cried Samantha, worming her way back out. "I can't go five hours without a loo."

"Don't worry, Miss," said the pilot, patting her backside with unnecessary familiarity as he urged her forward. "We've got to land a couple of times before we get there. We'll stop for breakfast and fuel in an hour or so."

Offended by his wayward hand, but not anxious to upset the pilot lest he should change his mind about taking her, she joined her compatriot in the back of the plane. "Here goes," she said, as the engines roared to life and the two men in the front chatted to each other through their headphones.

"Samantha," started Bryan, with a look of seriousness. "Don't get your hopes up too much. He might not be there."

"What d'ye mean? How can you say that? Of course he's there."

He was shaken by her determination and backtracked a little. "I'm not saying he isn't. I just think you should be prepared. I don't want you to be devastated if there has been some sort of foul-up and we don't find him today."

The little plane roared into the pre-dawn sky. Samantha gave Bryan's concerns some thought before dismissing them lightly and without explanation. "Of course he's there."

"But why would the bank and that man Stacy lie?" he said, hoping to plant a seed of doubt.

"Why are we going then?" she challenged, to which he had no answer.

Bliss was expecting Samantha to come to his rescue, although not in person. She'll probably call Stacy, he thought, working out the scenario that would most likely follow his failure to pick up the promised money. Samantha will call Stacy and badger him or Jock to take a trip to the island to find me. All I've got to do is stay alive long enough to be rescued. Dealing with Margaret will come later. And he *would* deal with her, he decided, feeling solace that fate had granted him an opportunity to right such a significant wrong.

What will Edwards' face be like, he wondered, when I return with Margaret and the evidence to show she also murdered her mother? "He'll be sick as a dog," he mused, already drawing up Margaret's extradition papers in his mind.

"Damn," he thought. Where's the evidence? I've only got her word for the whole thing. I don't even have any proof she killed Melanie. Even the scrapbook full of photographs had gone missing

With his spirits somewhat dampened he turned his attention back to hopes of rescue. So, when would Samantha call? Friday...today! No, she'll probably wait until Saturday or even Sunday. "Survive until Sunday then; maybe Monday, just to be sure," he told himself and set about making preparations.

He already knew where to hide for the weekend. His biggest dilemma was that Bo could easily track him wherever he went on the island. But he already knew the solution to that problem as well. All he needed was to distract the huge hound with a smokescreen of scent more potent and compelling than his own. And he knew exactly where to find that.

A few minutes later, his wound bound with a strip of fairly clean shirt, and his suitcase hastily re-stuffed with blankets, sheets, canned foods, and a selection of cutlery, he left the house and painfully hauled himself toward the stinking clearing.

Keeping to well-worn trails, hugging the trees and tiptoeing across clearings as if they were mine-fields, he dragged his damaged leg and battered case through the freshly fallen leaves, plowing a trail like a giant slug. "Shit," he muttered glancing behind him at the scraped furrow. Even a seven-year-old Brownie would be able to track him, yet he could only press on with his ears constantly pricked for sound of the returning launch and his eyes alert to the possibility of a canine ambush.

The familiar unpleasant odour guided him the last hundred yards or so, but thankfully the frost had rendered torpid both the stench and the bugs. Retrieving the stout stick he'd used the previous evening, he jabbed the ground until he found the edge of the pit and without concern started tearing at the matted covering. The intensity of fetor increased nauseatingly as the hole developed, but he stuck to the task and within a minute had pulled aside a sizeable chunk.

Bliss had given the probable contents of the pit a great deal of consideration since finding it and, although he was fully braced to encounter the mouldering carcass of a dead bear, nothing could have prepared him for the carnage he actually found. Shrinking back, he steadied himself against the nearest tree while he vomited and mentally fought against horrific images.

At least half a dozen partially decomposed bear carcasses had been flung willy-nilly into the pit and were heaving with maggots and insects, as if the food chain had been slammed into reverse. He slumped to the ground and stared in horror as the bloated white grubs crawled in and out of eyeless sockets and greasy looking beetles clambered around gaping wounds. This is the life of death, he thought, feeling sorrow for the once giant creatures. In life, the bears would have easily clawed away the revolting bugs, but in death the roles were reversed. The tiny predators had nothing to fear from these bears' paws — they were clearly missing, all roughly chopped off at the wrists.

But his eyes and mind had reserved the most sickening sight for last, hoping perhaps that it would go away. It would not. Dumped atop the rotting heap was the body of a bald eagle — Eddie, without a doubt. Bliss easily recognized the stout beak and the blood-spattered, lolling head, but someone had ripped out all the raptor's wing and tail feathers, reducing the magnificently plumed predator to a scrawny battery hen. He shook his head in horrified disbelief, wondering how Margaret might attempt to rationalize such butchery. No wonder she discourages visitors, he thought, and vomited again.

If ever Jung needed proof of his theorem of synchronicity, this would be it, thought Bliss, as he recalled how, just a week or so earlier, he had been wandering the deserted concourse of Toronto's airport late at night, scavenging for reading material as he waited to get hold of Samantha. Bored, willing to read anything, he'd been through a stack of tourist information pamphlets (settling on a visit to Niagara Falls when his mission was accomplished), and had studied the airport bylaws and fire regulations in full, twice. In desperation, he had picked up an environmentalist group's leaflet about the illegal trade in wild animals. Casting his mind back, he recalled what he'd read about bears. "Bear paw soup is sold for as much as $2,000 a tureen in specialist Korean restaurants," it had claimed. Written by a bunch of lefty apocalyptic enviro-holocaust types in torn jeans, he had assumed as he sceptically scanned the article, but now one sickening glance down into the chamber was all the confirmation he needed.

"Bear's gall bladders," the pamphlet had disparagingly reported, "are wizard aphrodisiac according to some Chinese, and are imbued with magical abilities to cure sclerosis of the liver and dislodge gall-stones, according to others who pay $45,000 or more for each one." The bears' hacked open stomachs, now fly-blown and blackened by decay, were all the proof he needed that Margaret's father had not been conned — this island was indeed a gold mine.

Samantha and her companions landed for breakfast at a small airfield an hour and a half north of Toronto, just as the sharply angled sun was becoming unbearable through her side window.

This looks like a scrap yard, she thought, noticing that one corner of a rust-streaked corrugated iron hangar appeared to be dissolving back into the ground, and several small planes with chunks missing had been abandoned where they had fallen. As they walked across the crazy-paving runway to the old wooden crew hut, Samantha wondered aloud if the Wright Brothers might still be around.

"This is Canada," said the pilot huffily. "Not the States."

They were expected. The detective sergeant had radioed ahead and ordered breakfast.

"I'll pay," offered Bryan, feeling that he owed them.

Phillips refused with a dismissive wave. "It's taken care of."

Samantha, overwhelmed by lack of sleep, jet-lag, post-partum blues, and the trauma of dealing with a delinquent parent, folded her arms on the table and crashed out for the entire twenty minutes. The bulky detective sergeant, clearly a happy eater, concentrated on his four fried eggs, deck of sliced ham, and a mountain of French toast while begrudgingly responding to Peter Bryan's attempted conversation.

"The plane crash ...What sort of plane; how many passengers?" asked Bryan, imagining something the size of an Airbus.

"Prop," said the detective, circling a loaded fork in the air. "Four."

"Fatalities?"

"Humph." Which could have meant yes, no, one, or two, but Bryan let it go.

"One, for sure," interpreted the pilot helpfully after a two-egg silence.

"Possibly two, maybe more," the detective added in between bites of ham.

They were soon back in the air, heading north, leaving behind the red carpet as the northern forests yielded to the approaching winter.

"I brought some croissants and coffee," said Bryan to the drowsy Samantha as they took off, but she was already asleep, having shrewdly switched seats without a word.

Four days earlier Bliss, gagging continuously, fished out a lump of rotten bear flesh from the open grave and smothered himself with it, then covered the pit and made off toward the bear trap into which he had almost stumbled just three days earlier. Three days that now seemed a lifetime. The bear trap, he had decided, would provide an ideal hiding place, but to find it he had first to locate the cove where he had skipped pebbles.

With a hunk of rotten bear flesh dripping from one hand and his suitcase in the other he painfully lurched from tree to tree, dragging himself over promontories and jutting headlands, and crawling across beaches until coming to the sign in the sand warning of fatal consequences to trespassers. Standing lopsidedly on the shore-line he sought the groove in the lake bed, which, he now realized, had been made by the keel of a boat æ Margaret's boat, perhaps. The clearly cut trench was as he remembered it, but now there were additional tracks and he saw that a boat trailer with treaded pneumatic tires had been wheeled across the dry sand to the place where a boat had been launched. Following the tracks back up the shallowly sloping beach he discovered a trailer concealed in a thicket of brush. No wonder Margaret tried to guide me away from the cove, he said to himself. Although that still didn't explain the cigarette butt he'd found — maybe it did. She couldn't have caught and butchered the bears on her own; some of them were twice the weight of a man.

Then the whole picture clicked into place. Margaret was in cahoots with the Indians! In hindsight it was obvious: they'd had a sedated bear in the bottom of their canoe. That was what was under the tarpaulin. Margaret buys captured bears from the Natives, pays them wampum, and they help her with the slaughter and disposal of the bodies. Then she makes a killing from the sale of the paws and gall bladders on the Asian market. It is so obvious, he thought, when you know the answer.

The solution to Melanie's murder had also been obvious, he now realized, as he sat brooding, staring out over the darkening lake, wondering where Margaret could be. If only he had looked for the answer twenty years earlier, how different life would have been, and not just for Margaret and her parents. Looking back on it now, it would have been so simple to crack the case. Just two minutes with the twelve-year-old Margaret would have been enough to alert him to the probability of her guilt. Gordonstone knew that of course, hence his determination to keep Margaret out of harm's way. In retrospect it was so obvious. Who was the only witness? Margaret. The two girls were supposedly playing together prior to Melanie's disappearance, yet he had dismissed her involvement as lightly as brushing off a Mormon at the door.

"Never dismiss anything," he had been taught at detective training school and had even quoted this maxim to Peter Bryan, yet he had done it again and again. He'd never stopped doing it. He'd dismissed Margaret as a suspect on her father's say-so, dismissed the glaring evidence that Margaret's house and island sanctuary were a sham. Even where his own family was concerned, he'd dismissed Sarah's concerns that Samantha needed his guidance. And he'd dismissed Sarah altogether. She didn't flee to Gangly George because he was better looking, or even a better lover (he liked to think). She went to him because he had shown her more attention, that was all.

Intrigued by the discovery of the trailer, he rose to scout further into the bushes just off the beach and uncovered the entrance to a cave. The entrance was concealed behind a closely woven mat of slender branches and in the encroaching gloom, even uninjured, he might have balked at entering without a flashlight. Mentally tossing a coin, he won — or lost — and ventured inside.

By Tuesday afternoon, as Samantha and Peter Bryan were landing for fuel at the last airstrip for five hundred miles, Superintendent Edwards sat at his desk building steam.

Bryan's impromptu excuse had backfired when Edwards, with just a hint of suspicion, had pulled his chief inspector's personnel file and called his aging mother — his next of kin — to offer condolences for the injured relative.

"I'm sorry to hear of his Aunt Maud," he had started, unsure to which branch of Bryan's family she belonged. Sister, or in-law, he wondered.

"Thank you, Superintendent," she replied, confused. "But my sister's been gone three years now."

"In the Himalayas?" he asked with feigned innocence.

"No ... Hillingdon crematorium," she replied, nonplussed, assuming he had misspoken. "But she was ninety-four, so our dear Lord gave her a good long stretch."

Not as long as I'll give Bryan, Edwards thought, then quickly recovered. "Do you happen to know where Peter is?"

"Canada, I think."

"Canada," he breathed as a small alarm bell sounded somewhere deep in his mind.

"Yes — I think that's where he said they were going."

"They? Mrs. Bryan," he queried with growing distress, "I don't suppose you know who he's with?"

That, she hadn't known. In fact she would not have known anything had her son not needed a plant-sitter at short notice. "I'm not sure," she continued, then added sotto voce, "Although I suppose it was a young lady. He thinks just because I'm eighty-three I've forgotten what a dirty weekend's like —"

Edwards, impatient, cut in. "How long has he gone for?"

"A few days, maybe a week, he said, but the state he left his place ..." she tutted. "I would say he was in a tearing hurry. Wouldn't surprise me if he hasn't eloped with the woman. Mind you, like I was saying to —"

Edwards butted in again, too querulous for idle chit-chat. "Did he give you a phone number or address?" Then he added gravely, in case she had been cautioned against revealing information, "It is something of an emergency,"

"No, I've no idea," she replied guardedly, indignant at being checked. "Who did you say you were?"

"Just a friend," he said, dropping the phone as if it were a fizzing firework.

The bottom drawer of his desk lay open. Betty-Ann Gordonstone glowered accusingly out at him in the guise of a dog-eared folder. His shredder buzzed briefly, grated reluctantly on the hard-to-digest file, and she was gone.

As Margaret's island drifted into the sunset on Thursday evening, Bliss pressed his eyes against the curtain of blackness in the cave and inched forward, gripping himself against the desire to run, anticipating that at any second some giant snarling creature — or maybe Margaret herself — would lunge at him from the dark depths. Concentrating fearfully on what lay ahead, he stopped and held his breath. The noise of his heartbeat was deafening as, motionless, he strained to hear the slightest scuff of a paw, or the controlled breathing of a creature readying to pounce.

With his fists held at the ready, he froze and waited for the sinister shroud of darkness to lift. A low black mass solidified out of the void in front of him, and he was forced to gasp for air as a shape gradually formed in the blackness. The square corners of a giant steel table protruded out of the murk. With a tremendous sigh of relief his eyes took in the fact that the cave was shallow, no more than a scrape in the rock, and the table occupied most of it.

With his vision adjusted, and fear of imminent attack removed, he searched around the table top and found huge steel shackles chained to each corner. He understood immediately: the environmentalist leaflet had explained, "Buyers of bear's gall bladders usually insist on having a video showing the bladder being removed from a living bear as proof of provenance."

"So would I," he had mused at the time, "If I were paying $45,000." Now he shuddered with the realization that he had found Margaret's killing field, complete with the instrument of butchery — a large knife jammed into a fissure. Grabbing the weapon by its curved bone handle, he turned to retreat, but was stopped by a chilling rebuke. "You could have prevented all this," said something deep inside him.

Shooting back outside, with the ghosts of a dozen bears in his wake, he was appalled to discover how suddenly the day had dissolved. Another night was falling and the cove was already deep in shadows.

The bear trap, with its promise of shelter and safety, turned out to be trickier than he had imagined. A drop the height of a bungalow's eaves would have been daunting to a man with two good legs in broad daylight. For an injured man in twilight it was fearsome. But, thinking quickly, he knotted a rope of the sheets and blankets taken from Margaret's cabin and anchored one end to a tree root on the lip of the crater and lowered himself and his suitcase.

Once he had patched the roof darkness descended on the pit and, although the silence in the forest outside had been eerily unsettling, the black silence in the pit bottom hung over him like an anvil on a thread. The reason for the island's deathly silence and dearth of wild creatures had become all too clear with the discovery of the burial pit. Nature's instinctive aversion to death, he concluded. He couldn't count the number of times he had arrived at the scene of a road accident to find a mangled body dumped on one verge and a huddle of sombre witnesses across the road, on the other. It was, he knew, a primeval protective response to shy away from death, lest the attacker should be skulking in the bushes, seeking another victim. Even the birds have steered their migrations around Margaret's gruesome mortuary he theorized, realizing that he had not even seen a sparrow in nearly a week.

The first two hours in the pit dragged with the eternity of an avant-garde opera and he began to think that hiding here was a mistake. Would he not be safer at large in the forest, he wondered, but quickly dismissed the idea, shuddering at the notion that all of his effort had been for nothing. But the silent loneliness nibbled at the edges of his mind, fraying his nerves and causing him to twitch in alarm at the slightest sound. Alone, truly alone, for the first time in his life, Bliss felt desolation sapping his spirit.

With Mrs. Bryan's admissions neatly woven into a tapestry of lies and deceit, Superintendent Edwards unofficially sought the ear of the divisional commander over lunch in the officers' mess.

"Got a spot of bother with Peter Bryan, Kenneth," he began with airy nonchalance, manoeuvring himself alongside his senior officer at the self-service counter.

"I've managed to swing those three new motors you wanted," replied the commander, as if he had not heard.

Edwards gushed. "Thank you, Kenneth, I appreciate that." Then he carefully shaded his tone. "About Peter Bryan ..."

"And I want your blokes to look after these ..." the divisional commander continued, and Edwards tuned him out as he reeled off a longstanding litany of injuries which had been inflicted on police vehicles. " ...cigarette burns, coffee stains, and a used johnny under the seat," he was moaning as Edwards switched him back on. "And the bloody mileage. What are they doing — laps around the M25? It all comes off our budget you know."

"I'll look into it Kenneth," Edwards promised without sincerity, then added like a school tattletale, "But I wanted to have a quiet word about DCI Bryan. I suspect he's gone walkabout with Bliss's daughter."

"What are you saying, that your DCI has gone AWOL now as well as Bliss?"

"Not exactly AWOL, no."

"But he's done a runner with Bliss's girl?"

He nodded. "Seems likely, yes."

"That's careless of you, Mr. Edwards, you should keep better control of your staff," the commander said, placing Edwards firmly in front of the fan. "Let's just hope for your sake they turn up soon ... before I find out officially."

"Kenneth, I —" started Edwards, but the commander refused to get involved.

"Sorry old chap. Must dash," he said, dumping his empty tray, all thoughts of lunch evaporating.

Edwards had lost his appetite as well and opted for a KitKat and coffee.

Thirst eventually forced Bliss out of the pit and dragged him back to the lake. Although his suitcase contained rust-spotted cans of food taken from the cottage kitchen, he needed water more than anything and was still lucid enough to know that his fever would progress and he would need more and more. If his revulsion hadn't driven him so quickly away from the killing cave he might have thought to take some lake water with him. Now, with a copper saucepan swinging from his belt, he hauled himself up his makeshift ladder and hobbled back to the beach in the moonlight.

A furtive movement among the trees was lost in the gloom, the sound swallowed by the swishing as he played the saucepan in the lake before bringing it to his lips and drinking noisily, revelling in the freshness of the cool clean taste. Oh for a toothbrush, he thought, regretting that he had omitted to collect his from the cottage's bathroom. Then he stopped, ears pricked, hackles raised. Had he heard something? The silence was palpable. He knew instinctively that there had been sound, but could not reproduce it in his mind. He drank again, the deafening gurgle of water down his throat blotting out another sound. He stopped and an envelope of fear enclosed him as he warily refilled the saucepan and set off back to his hiding spot.

As he left the beach for the forest, a cacophony of disturbing noises crowded in on him, yet, every time he paused, so did the sounds. He froze, trying to stop the blood roaring through his temples and the breath whistling through his nostrils. He listened — nothing. But the moment he set off again, he was instantly surrounded by sound. Every movement brought with it a polyphony of terrifying noises. Each swish of his clothing became the snorting breath of a bull moose, every sigh of the breeze in the uppermost branches a vampire bat, and every snap of a twig underfoot the crack of a gunshot. Danger lurked everywhere in the thin light. A shadowy figure hid behind every tree, every twisted stick became a rattlesnake, every spiky bush took the form of a porcupine, and every creaking branch bore the weight of a cougar.

The nearest he had come to such feelings of perilous isolation was early in his career, walking the deserted London streets at three or four in the morning with only his radio for comfort, knowing that around the next corner or up the next alley he might stumble across an armed lunatic. But now he had no radio — he was truly alone.

The eyes of the faceless forest were everywhere, bowing him under their weight and slowing his progress to a crawl, as he moved haltingly, constantly searching for the slightest movement or sound. But the fever was already jangling his nerves. Shadows followed him, keeping abreast, then, in the milliseconds between movements he heard an animalistic snuffling, as a giant's snout scented the air. Bo, he thought, sensing the glare of the dog's watchful eyes. He spun round.

"Don't bugger about Margaret!" he shouted, almost willing her to shoot him; anything to relieve the tension. "You can always say you put me out of my misery," he jibed, not knowing what reaction to expect.

With a heart-stopping *crack*, a twig snapped in front of him. He whipped backwards and the dark shade of forest turned into a black wall. It wasn't Bo. A giant bear had stepped into his path and stood like a rock. Run, he thought ludicrously. "Never run," Margaret had warned. "You can't outrun a bear. Running just triggers a chase response. You have to stand up to them and be ready to fight."

The huge bear reared up and barked hoarsely, like a Rottweiler with laryngitis. Bliss might have sneered at the pathetic roar had he not been so terrified. His precious pot of water was the first casualty as it thudded to the soft woodland floor.

"Shit," he muttered under his breath, too scared to let the sound out. He backed up half a pace, pulling the butcher's knife from his belt, knowing it would be useless against the huge creature. What about a tree, he thought, sizing up the nearest, considering whether he could climb with his damaged leg, but Margaret's words came back: "Bears climb trees for fun."

Everything went into slow motion. His mind, overloaded with snippets of absurd and ineffectual escape plans, rooted him to the spot. The bear, calculating the wisdom of taking on a meal the size of Bliss, hesitated and dropped back to all fours.

"Attack!" Bliss's mind told him. "Rush him — catch him unawares. Stab him in the eye or kick him in the goolies." His mind may have been willing, but his heart wasn't in it. The bear was as big as a tank and looked twice the size in the darkness. Then, almost without thinking, he got behind a low springy branch and retreated, pulling back on it with all his might.

The bear made up his mind to attack and, huffing with a hacking warning cough, pawed the ground like a playful dog. Bliss had no intention of being the toy for a three-hundred-pound sheepdog and, as the bear advanced, let go of the branch, thwacking it straight into the creature's face. Feinting from tree to tree, leaping out of the way as the half blinded animal swiped madly at the air, he worked his way, one tree at a time, toward his haven. The enraged bear blundered after him chopping a swath through the undergrowth, ferociously pawing at everything that moved, grasping at swinging branches, huffing and barking in anger, clawing at the pain in his face as if to remove the cause.

In a deadly game of cat-and-mouse, Bliss scrabbled for sticks and rocks and tossed them clattering off into the bush, keeping the animal disoriented as he slipped from tree to tree. Closer and closer he got to the relative safety of the pit with the bear floundering from one decoy to the next, but he had no plan, and no time to think of one. Survival from moment to moment occupied every fibre in his body. Getting into the pit, replacing the cover, and preventing the bear from following were issues so enigmatic that his mind refused to even consider them.

The bear was gaining ground. Using his nose instead of his ears, the wily male homed in stealthily and the unexpected silence disoriented Bliss, who lost his bearings in the darkness. Although the pit could not be far off, his sanctuary had suddenly become a trap again. With every movement he expected the ground to cave under him and drop him onto the sharp spine of stakes. The bear's continual snuffles echoed directionless through the silence, leaving Bliss twisting and turning in alarm. An envelope of fear squeezed so tightly around him he didn't even dare to breathe for fear of giving himself away.

Then, with a satisfied snort, and for no apparent reason, the bear ambled off into the darkness and the deathly silence of the forest returned. Bliss sank to the ground trembling. "I'm too old for this," he breathed, and couldn't understand why he wasn't having a heart attack.

A few seconds later he jumped back into the pit, barely breaking his fall with the makeshift rope. He patched the roof above him as best he could then crouched, terrified, expecting the giant creature to crash through the roof and drop on him at every moment.

chapter fifteen

Nursing his hugely swollen leg, Detective Inspector Bliss of the Metropolitan Police sat in the dark, damp pit waiting for Armageddon and wondering what had happened to his life. "At my age I thought I would have had everything sorted," he mused, speculating on the speed his life had free-fallen since Sarah had let go. And, although Margaret hadn't exactly picked him up, she had certainly given him cause to rebound. Some rebound, he thought, surveying his gloomy circumstances. I suppose they would call this a dead-cat bounce, he thought, wondering who "they" might be. He also wondered how his old cat was faring without him

Every minute was a day. Every moment he expected the stealthily moving Margaret to rip off his roof and peer down at him. And where was the bear, he wondered, imagining it to be skulking impatiently above like one of its white coated cousins waiting for a seal to pop out of an ice hole.

And what would Margaret do if she found me, he worried. Just pray she won't, he told himself. Stacy or Jock will soon arrive with the cavalry, he thought hopefully, but his trust in salvation lasted only a minute before he started worrying again. Would she shoot? Could she shoot? It would be cold-blooded murder.

"She's murdered before," he said aloud, unaware the sound had escaped, then reflected on the incident that triggered the chain of events binding him to Margaret. How had she killed Melanie? Did she drag her sister screaming and kicking to the water's edge and hold her under? Or did Melanie run from her and accidentally fall?

"Stop it," he said, knowing he was trying to excuse her again. She killed her mother. He couldn't get away from that. She was quite forthright about that. That was no accident. Even Edwards had not claimed it was an accident. And euthanasia was no defence — not in law anyway. So, she was perfectly capable of murder, he decided, staring up at the lattice roof, imagining her standing above it with a rifle. It would be like picking off an elephant in a circus ring from the front row, he realized; a kid could do it with a spud gun. Maybe this isn't such a good place to hide, he thought, maybe I would be better off in the forest. At least there I could run. He slumped back. With this leg?

But his tormented mind, flying back and forth between pessimism and optimism picked him up and flung him down a hundred or more times as he lay in the dark awaiting the executioner, while trying to imagine a fitting eulogy for himself. "He wasn't a raging success but he was generally good at avoiding calamitous disasters."

"Until now," he said, wondering why he was still alive. She could have killed him easily had she chosen, especially when he was unconscious. So why didn't she? Maybe she is not a cold-hearted killer after all.

"There you go again," said his alter ego, "dismissing the obvious because you don't want to accept the reality. This woman is a pariah who killed her sister, mother, and God knows how many innocent creatures to get her own way, and you think she cares whether or not you live."

But the fundamental question uppermost in his mind remained unanswerable. Would she deliberately murder him or would he simply die before help arrived? Maybe that's her plan, he concluded. She'd just let him die of exposure and septicaemia. But, how would she explain that to the authorities? The troops will come eventually, he thought; Samantha will contact someone, surely. But, even then Margaret wouldn't need to explain his disappearance, he decided, not in any defensive way. "Nosy old codger," she could say. "Came poking around my island, trespassing. He must have wandered off and got lost. He's probably been eaten by a bear or fallen into the lake and drowned."

And if they search, and they probably will, using dogs and infrared heat detectors, what will they find? Visualization of the maggot-infested bear carcasses in the burial chamber was enough to give him the answer. Margaret had dug out the dart from his thigh while he was tranquillized, and not very gently by the look of it, leaving a wound that even now could be mis-diagnosed as having been caused by him falling on a jagged rock or stake. A week or so of putrefaction and infestation would make it certain to be overlooked.

He had a nagging feeling she was going to get away with it again, her conscience salved by the fact that she didn't actually kill him. Unlike her mother, there was no need to put him out of his misery. How strange, he pondered, that only two weeks ago he was seriously considering that suicide might be the only alternative to life without Sarah, and now he had got over her, ironically thanks to Margaret, he wanted to live more than ever.

Saturday was lost to a delirium of frightening hallucinations and terrifying nightmares. As a finale, an aberrant vision of Sarah swooped down into the pit sometime during the evening, flying in on plucked wings. She was carrying Samantha — baby Samantha.

"Why did you leave me, David?" she asked accusingly.

Had he left her, he wondered, his lightheaded mind struggling to make sense. "I didn't want to, didn't mean to ... When did I leave you?"

"You left me with the baby," she said, holding Sam out to him.

He looked at the baby and saw a naked little girl — Samantha, his little girl. But she had grown. Still a baby, she had real little beasts with tiny pert nipples. He reached out to touch them but the flesh dissolved and he found himself touching the bare ribs. His clothes were awash with perspiration. His body and mind were on fire.

"Samantha," he called, holding out his hands, beckoning her to him.

"Come to Daddy, Samantha."

Sarah dragged her away. "This is George's little girl."

"George's daughter? No that's impossible, it's Samantha."

"Look," she said, spinning her around. "It's George's girl."

He looked. She was right, it wasn't Samantha, he knew what Samantha looked like, and this naked little girl was faceless. Then it dawned on him as he looked at the faceless girl: it was Melanie.

"It's Melanie," he said, but Sarah laughed at him.

"Wrong again, David," she cackled. "You don't know one girl from another."

"Stop this. Stop this," he shouted, and Sarah disappeared.

Relieved, he looked down, but the faceless baby was still there. "Sarah," he called. "Sarah, you've forgotten the baby."

Sarah's voice drifted out of the ether. "You look after her. It's your turn. It's time you did your share."

Panicking, he picked up the baby, expecting to see Melanie. But it was Margaret. Margaret, who hadn't had a face when Melanie died. Margaret, her face unseen at Melanie's inquest and absent from her little sister's funeral. And Margaret, whose guilty, deformed little face had never been put into the frame of her mother's death. Melanie's face may have been missing from her sister's photographs, but it was Margaret's face that had been hidden from the real world.

Reaching out to feel the blank screen that substituted for the face of the child in his arms, his fingers sank into bland, gelatinous flesh. He touched off a ripple that expanded slowly outward, like the effect of a stone dropped into a pool. But not just any pool. He did not need to search his mind to know which pool.

"I'm sorry, Melanie," he said, though no one would ever hear. But the faceless child heard, and the ripples stopped expanding and contracted, smaller, smaller, and smaller until they formed a perfect pair of rose-bud lips.

"Help," whispered the lips.

He choked himself awake, his thirst-swollen tongue filling his mouth, his sweat-soaked body limp from fever.

"Water ... Water," he muttered, but he had no water and there was no one to hear his pleas. He started sinking back, saw Melanie's face swimming back into view and forced open his eyes, desperate to make the images disappear. But Sarah was still there in front of him, although he knew she wasn't real. "What happened to Samantha?" he asked.

"Samantha's gone," Sarah replied and slowly evaporated until only her mouth was left. Then her lips puckered into a goodbye kiss and vanished into the darkest corner of the pit.

It was Sunday and the island woke to the sound of voices. The world had returned, although Bliss, exhausted by fever, slumbered on the verge of unconsciousness and awaited death. But raised voices, close by, ate into his soporific senses. "Dave? Where are you?"

It's another dream, he persuaded himself, hoping to avoid the Herculean task of waking.

"He's not here," someone shouted, apparently eliminating another thicket from a string of potential hiding places.

"What's that over there?" said another.

"Looks like a saucepan."

"It must've come from the house ... He's got to be here somewhere ... Dave? Where are you?"

"Are you sure you're dreaming?" asked a voice deep inside Bliss's mind.

"We should have brought the dog," said someone far outside his world, but the sound penetrated fuzzily into his atmosphere.

It's not a dream, he decided. It's Stacy. He tried to force his consciousness to surface.

"Dave? Hello? Are you there?"

Clawing his way toward wakefulness he fought to stand, but his legs buckled and he pitched headlong on to the pit's muddy floor. Fighting to haul himself upright he became entangled in the blankets and ended up trapped in a muddy shroud. Realizing the urgency of the situation he bellowed, "Down here, Stacy!" Immediately he knew something was wrong. He would have sworn he had shouted — the effort had hurt his throat — but he hadn't heard a whisper.

"Help," he tried again, screaming with a growing hysteria, but the silent forest above the pit turned a deaf ear.

"Come out, Dave, we're here to help."

"Stacy, Stacy, I'm here," he called, but not even a squeak escaped.

The voices were closer, and there were other noises. Noises he recognized — the noise of sticks being thrashed through the undergrowth in search of bodies. He had thrashed his way through thickets in many a murder case, though had never been the object of the search before. Wait until they are close enough to hear, he said to himself, trying to calm his impatience. Don't waste your energy.

But the voices were already fading. "He's not here," said one.

"Where is he then?" said another.

Is that a woman's voice, he wondered. There were two voices, he thought — two at least.

Shout, now, he ordered himself, but his throat had closed. He fought to get up, knowing it was his last chance. If Stacy doesn't find me he'll go away.

"He's gotta be here somewhere," called the woman.

It *is* a woman. It's Samantha, he thought with utter relief. "Samantha — I'm down here," his mind sang out, but nothing came out of his mouth; he found himself mentally crying in frustration. "Samantha, Samantha," he breathed, desperately trying to stand, to struggle out of the blankets. But even standing, what could he do? The ceiling was eight feet high. He had untied the rope of blankets to keep himself warm; now he'd have to retie it, and they were wet and slippery. Working frantically, his lips miming, "Samantha ... Stacy," his numb fingers fumbled the knots. But the voices drifted away, exploring another part of the island, and he would have screamed in frustration if he could.

"Don't go away. Don't leave. Please," he pleaded inside, and remembered a line from Margaret's poem "Hope fades fast but lingers long." How long will I linger, he wondered. If I can't get out now, how will I ever get out? How long can I last — a day or two? The clotted brown bloodstain which had spread through his makeshift bandage told an ugly truth. If he didn't get out now, he never would.

"Come on out, Dave," the woman's voice floated back through the barren woods and a thunderflash exploded in his mind.

That's not Samantha; she wouldn't call me Dave!

Nothing in his psyche wanted to believe the obvious. I must be dreaming, he reasoned. It can't be Margaret ... It mustn't be Margaret. But the turmoil in his mind spun his thoughts so fast he was left wondering if he was even alive. That's why I can't shout, why they didn't find me, why my leg doesn't hurt anymore. Oh God. I'm dead.

You're not dead, he said to himself, trying to rationalize what was happening. But he was thinking through a layer of molten chocolate. Thoughts dissolved before they formed, murky images swam into view but never coalesced, and all the time a thin voice was telling him, "It is Margaret. She's returned to finish you off. Get to the beach, escape in her boat, leave her stranded on the island."

With a dull throbbing in his leg and a feeling of lightheaded drunkenness, he hauled himself out of the pit and lay on the woodland floor for several minutes trying to catch his breath. With his energy zapped he couldn't stand, and had to crawl toward the beach, conscious of the terrible row his body made as he slid through the dried leaf debris. It was no further than a kindergarten's three-legged race, but with only one leg it took him a painful ten minutes and, when he reached the cove, he got another jolt. It wasn't Margaret's boat, it was a float-plane laying at anchor just off the beach.

"Alice," he breathed aloud, his spirits jumping. "Alice came back for me. Good girl."

"Thank God," he whispered and slithered down the short beach toward the water. He lay by the water's edge for some time, watching the unattended plane rocking gently just twenty yards or so offshore, worried she might somehow return and take off without seeing him.

Realization that something was wrong came as slowly as a Sunday train, and even when he saw what was coming around the curve he still refused to believe it. The plane was the wrong size, the wrong make, and the wrong colour to be Alice's, but he tried convincing himself that she could have had it repainted. When his mind rejected that possibility, he quickly switched tack and decided it was Alice's *other* plane.

"Dave — this is your last chance. Where are you?" called a familiar voice from the bush behind him and his heart stopped. It was Margaret. Now that he was out in the open he had no difficulty recognizing her voice, but he was trapped on the beach between her and the plane. And, in his haste to escape he hadn't re-covered the pit; she would have found his suitcase.

"Dave."

Forced forward by fear he slithered into the water with no clear idea of what to do. The cool water soothed his leg and bore his weight, but the coldness clamped his chest as he scrambled toward the plane with a vague notion of climbing aboard and escaping. But, working his way closer to the floats, he soon realized the impracticability of the scheme. He couldn't fly. The one time in his life that he'd found himself taking the controls of a plane in an emergency, he'd crashed. He wouldn't even be able to start the engine.

"At least you can stop them," he said to himself.

How?

"Cut fuel line, the ignition wires, the control cables — anything. You've got the knife, for God's sake, he told himself, use it."

Margaret's voice was gaining ground. "Dave. C'mon out. This is your last chance. Where are you?"

Swimming now, fighting against the drag of his useless leg, the splash of each stroke invited the zing of a rifle bullet.

"Dave!" she screamed, all patience lost. "I'll bloody kill you if you don't come out."

Reaching the torpedo floats he hung on, waist deep in water, and risked a look back to the shore. She was there, on the beach, still shouting his name. With her were two men, two complete strangers, neither of them wearing Stacy's pear-shaped torso.

Ducking behind the float he watched as the men went to collect an inflatable dinghy that had been drawn ashore further along the beach. He'd not noticed the boat in his anxiousness to get to the plane and, realizing that if he'd taken the dinghy he could have got away, he could have cried.

Margaret was helping the men now as they dragged the small boat back to the water.

"Get aboard the plane and hide," his mind was screaming as he pulled himself to the far side of the float.

What if they find me?

"It's a faster death than gangrene."

Margaret and her companions were loading boxes into the dinghy, their backs to the lake.

"Now, quickly," his turbulent mind overwhelmed him with panic. "Get aboard! Get aboard! Get aboard!"

Too late. The dinghy was headed his way and two faces on the beach were following its progress.

"They're Chinese," he breathed, the final cog dropping into place as he trod water trying to work out how to climb aboard unseen.

"The annual eight billion dollar international trade in body parts of endangered species is largely controlled by the Chinese," the environmentalist pamphlet at Toronto airport had advised him. Information which, at the time, he'd found as compelling as counting the number of Maple Leaf flags hanging from the rafters. But synchronicity had struck again.

They must be the dealers, he decided, here to purchase and collect bear parts. And possibly eagle parts, he thought sadly — Eddie's parts.

"Get aboard and stop them," every nerve in his body was telling him, but just clinging to the float was draining all his energy. Climbing aboard would be Herculean. Anyway, he realized, just in time to stop himself wasting his energy, sabotaging the plane might not be such a good idea. It had been bad enough sharing the island with one homicidal maniac, he didn't need the company of another two.

"Get aboard and escape with them, then." That makes more sense, he thought. Then his ears picked up the sound of paddle splashes. She's coming. Dive! Dive! Dive!

He dove, but his feverish lungs forced him back to the surface in a couple of seconds. "Don't do that again," he lectured himself. "That was crazy, could have had a coughing fit."

Heaving himself up, he peeked over the float. The dinghy was closing on him — Margaret and the cargo of boxes and bags. Fortunately she had her back to him as she rowed. The two Asians squatted on the beach awaiting her return. There's not enough room for all of them, he realized and dropped silently back in the water with so many ideas in his head they tripped over each other. Attack Margaret, get aboard, sabotage the plane, use the radio to send an SOS.

"Slow down," he thought to himself. There was no way he could get aboard, he'd never be able to climb up there.

The dinghy bumped the other float and Margaret scrabbled aboard. Bliss slunk behind the opposing float and pressed himself hard against the cold metal as his mind almost exploded in frustration.

Margaret was heaving the cargo into the plane.

"What's your plan," he asked himself. He needed a plan.

Another heavy thud marked the arrival of another box.

Think, for Christ's sake, think.

Several more thuds, then the dinghy was pulling away.

"You've got to get aboard," he said to himself., "Hurry. Get aboard and make a plan. She'll be back with the other two and it'll be too late."

Heaving himself up the float he immediately realized his mistake.

Margaret was looking straight at him as she rowed back to the shore.

"Shit!" he spat through clenched teeth. His knife dropped to the water.

Did she see me? he worried.

Logic told him that it didn't matter; he had to retrieve the knife.

His tortured mind was soporific. Dappled sunlight on the shiny blade was a flashing beacon as the knife sank, but he was mesmerized into inactivity.

"It's gone — the knife's gone," he said, like an imbecile, too stupefied by his ordeal to realize that he could reach out and grab it.

Time warped; the dinghy was back with all three people and he was still staring at the knife. He could see it clearly in the clean water but his lungs wouldn't let him dive again. He made a couple of false starts, but it was too late. The inflatable was being pulled onto the other float and deflated for stowage. Suddenly the knife became the most important thing in his life; he would have died to get it, and, as he dived, the plane's door shut and the engine burst into life.

The spluttering engine drowned his coughs as he surfaced and fought for air, but he had the knife. Too late. The plane was already inching ahead and he felt the rush of air as the propeller spun into life, kicking up spray. He felt the pull as the float started creeping forward. Margaret, the villains, the evidence, and his only hope of escape were getting away.

In a moment of lunacy he considered hanging on and escaping aboard the float. But the thought of landing at nearly one hundred miles an hour put him off, although he couldn't help feeling that Sylvester Stallone would have done it.

Frustrated and disheartened by his inability to prevent her escape, Bliss stabbed angrily at the float as it picked up speed. He held on, grasping a safety line, losing his temper, viciously slashing at the thin-skinned float, ripping into the sheet metal, digging the knife in like a can opener then twisting, gouging, and cleaving.

The plane picked up speed as the throttles opened and the engine roared overhead. The float, bouncing and bucking, washed him with spray and bashed him against the waves, but he held on and lunged maliciously at the bulbous torpedo, imagining it to be Margaret. Faster and faster the plane tore over the water and he kept stabbing and jabbing, until the knife was suddenly wrenched out of his hand as it struck deep and held. Letting go of the float he was swallowed in the wash and he sank back into the water, and his spirits sank at the loss of the knife. Now he had nothing to fight off the bear.

chapter sixteen

They were running late, explained Phillips over his shoulder as they neared Bear Lake. "We more or less fly right over the place, so we'll drop you off and pick you up on our way back," he added. "That'll give you four hours or so to find your father."

Bryan glanced at his watch. "That's fine. We'll check out the bank and find a nice restaurant for lunch."

"We could do a bit of sightseeing," chimed in Samantha, convinced that locating her father was already accomplished merely by their arrival. "And shopping," she added, realizing that in her haste to pack she had forgotten that, no longer pregnant, she was due on at any moment.

The pilot had been to Bear Lake before and couldn't hold in a short guffaw.

"What's up?" said his partner.

"You'll see," he laughed, dropping down onto the lake.

A few minutes later Jock released the rope as the plane glided away from the short wooden pier.

"Where would we find the bank?" asked Samantha as soon as the noise of the departing plane permitted.

Peter Bryan had already sussed out the situation. "This way, Samantha," he called, his size tens already pointing to Stacy's.

"Mr. Stacy, I presume?" he announced without hesitation as he swung open the door and clonked across the bare wooden boards.

"Stacy," said the lone occupant cagily. "It's just Stacy."

"Like Lovejoy," suggested Bryan and got an unexpected nod of familiarity.

"Yeah. The antiques guy. We get him on the satellite."

"Oh," replied Bryan with surprise. "So, Stacy, I called you yesterday morning about a friend of mine — David Bliss, the policeman."

The look on Stacy's face, bottled, would have outsold any proprietary laxative. "Um ...aah ...agh," he floundered, then coughed repeatedly to clear a tenacious frog.

"So where is Mr. Bliss, Stacy," the DCI continued, in a '"don't muck me about"' interview room manner.

Stacy gathered together his Humpty-Dumpty figure as best he could and tried again. "I ... I've ... I've never heard of him."

"This is definitely where I sent the money," called Samantha, scouting behind Stacy and finding the Western Union sign on the wall.

"I sent it back," Stacy protested, fearing he was being accused of theft.

"We know that," said Bryan. "But what I want to know is why Mr. Bliss gave this address if he wasn't here?"

"I ...I ..." Stacy was still bumbling. "I don't know, but you can check my records."

With his hands steadying his prolapsed torso, Stacy wobbled across the room to the mail counter and retrieved a war surplus ledger with a ripped calico cover. Flopping it open onto the counter he needlessly checked his own entries. "No record," he shook his head gravely.

"Give me that," demanded Samantha, coming up from behind and roughly snatching the book out of his hands. She futilely ran her finger down the last few lines before giving Bryan a blank stare that pleaded, "What the hell do we do now?"

Old Jock had shuffled into the store at a discreetly nosy distance and perched himself in the window overlooking the lake. Samantha swung on the old man. "Have you seen him?"

"Och, I dunna ken, lassie. What's he look like?"

"Tall — tallish, anyway," she began, then wavered. What does he look like? "Hair ...?" Her mind was out of focus; she froze indecisively.

"Light brown," chipped in Bryan.

"Yeah," she continued, annoyed with herself for not remembering, then she realized with horror that she really didn't remember what he looked like at all. Of course you know what he looks like, she told herself, it's just difficult to describe him as though he were an object, as though he were a missing person. Yet, simply attempting to describe him to a stranger seemed to be an admission of loss and she suddenly found herself fighting back tears. Bryan finished the description while she struggled to grasp the prospect that her father was actually missing and that the return of the money wasn't some silly error.

The old Scotsman said they must be mistaken, then Samantha was lifted by a moments optimism. "There must be another bank ..." she started, but Stacy quickly squashed the idea.

"Nope."

Perplexed beyond annoyance, Samantha searched for some way to relieve her frustration and found the telephone. "I'd better phone Dad's place," she began. "Maybe he's home now." Then she added with a vitriolic glower at Stacy, "If he's not here."

Bliss was not at home either; at least he wasn't answering his telephone. Samantha hung on, listening to the persistent brr, willing with all her mind that he should pick it up, wondering if the handset she was holding was the same one he had held nearly a week earlier. Finally she put it down in dismay.

The arrival of a strange aircraft had caught the eye of many in the small settlement and an advance party of housewives, suddenly finding themselves short of sugar or salt, slipped into the store and promptly forgot what they had come for as they stood around discussing well-worn topics. A crumple-spined old man, skillfully flipping his dentures in and out in time with his breathing, shuffled up to Samantha. "Hi. Where a'ya from?"

"England ... I'm looking for my father, have you seen him?"

"Oh yeah."

"You have?" she shrieked. "When? Where?"

"Don't take no notice —" started Stacy, but she shocked him into silence.

"Shut up, you."

"When did you see him?" she demanded of the shrunken pensioner.

"All the time," he mumbled. "Will ya git me a drink, eh?"

Stacy tried again. "Bob'll tell you anything you want for a drink."

"Give him one then," stepped in Bryan, feeling it was time to be less confrontational in the hope of garnering support from the locals. Then he addressed the assembly. "We're looking for an English policeman who was supposed to be here last week. Did any of you see him?"

Seemingly taking their cue from Stacy, the small band shook their heads and remembered the bread they had left in the oven or the lure they had left unattended in the lake. One rough man with a gut capable of concealing twins, even triplets, and looking as though his major contribution to society was doing one armed press-ups and vomiting down his shirt, spat, "Cops," as he headed out the door; he needed to add nothing to let them know where he stood on the subject.

Peter Bryan spun back on Stacy. "What about Margaret Gordonstone?"

"Never 'eard of her. Now did you want to buy something?"

Bryan looked at Samantha but she shook her head, unable to bring herself to ask for Tampax in such a hostile environment.

"That's four bucks for Bob's scotch then."

"Wait," said Samantha, still unable to come to terms with the situation. "This must be the place."

Stacy took the proffered bill from Bryan and spoke to Samantha as he handed him the change. "Sorry, dear — you're just confused, that's all."

"C'mon" said Bryan, but she stomped her foot with the petulance of a thwarted child in a sweet shop.

"No, I won't leave. I want some answers."

"We've had all the answers we're going to get here," Bryan said, physically dragging her out of the store and leading her to the beach.

The glassy lake shimmered under the early afternoon sun and, like a mirage in the distance, the nearest of the islands swam in and out of their vision. Margaret's island was hiding in the haze.

Samantha sat cross-legged on the sand, sullenly plopping pebbles into the lake. "I've let him down. I must have got the wrong postcode — written something wrong. He must be frantic, wherever he is. He must think I don't care — that I didn't send the money."

Bryan would have loved to be able to tell her she was wrong but couldn't, so he kept quiet.

"I'm sure he thinks I do things just to annoy him," she said.

"Like what?"

"Well, he always thinks I'm getting at him because I take defence cases, but I don't have any choice. Anyway, I enjoy defending people."

Bryan gave it some thought as he soaked in the warm midday sun.

"He's caught in a deadly embrace," he said, eventually.

She looked up with surprise. "What do you mean?"

"Well, he wants you to be a successful lawyer by winning cases, but inwardly he's sickened by the thought of you helping villains get off. So his mind is screaming 'Win,' and 'Lose,' at the same time, and whichever side wins, he loses. It must be very difficult for him."

"I'd never thought of it like that, I thought he was just bloody-minded."

He can be that as well, thought Bryan, absentmindedly humming a few bars of "The Laughing Policeman."

"I never do anything right for Dad," she continued morosely after some reflection. "I left his telly on so you could kill his cat."

"Samantha, please don't. I feel bad enough about that without you continually rubbing it in."

She sniffled, close to tears. "You'd better get used to it." She carried on, "I didn't pay his bills ...Didn't watch the video. I didn't even find out who owned the restaurant."

"What video? What restaurant?"

"Someone took a video the night Gordonstone died. Dad left it on top of his telly. You remember — the one you blew to pieces when you murdered his cat."

"Oh, Christ."

"What?"

"That video might have been evidence in a murder case."

"Well, you shouldn't have blown it up then, should you?"

"Your Dad shouldn't have had it at home. It should have been in the evidence cupboard."

"That's right, put the blame on him," she said, rising, addressing the lake histrionically. "Good old Dave Bliss — let's shit all over him. Everybody else has shit on him. Mum shit on him —"

"Samantha!"

She spun round. "Don't Samantha me!" she shouted, then carried on. "Edwards shit on him. I shit on him, and now you. Brilliant. Just fucking brilliant." Then she stormed off along the beach kicking up a cloud of sand.

He trailed after her. "What's this about a restaurant?"

"Don't talk to me!" she screamed, angrily swinging a fist behind her and missing by several feet. He backed off and let her take out her frustration on her shoes.

The beach was gradually swallowed by the encroaching forest and finally she dropped onto a fallen log and burst into tears. "I'm sorry," she spluttered after a few minutes, sensing him beside her.

Cupping her face in his hands he touched his lips to her tear-swollen eyes then bundled her into his arms.

"It's OK Samantha, I understand. We'll find him; I know we will. Now what's this about a restaurant?"

"He wanted to know who owned Gordonstone's restaurant," she mumbled into his chest. "Apparently there was a partner who now owns it all — not Margaret. Whoever inherited it obviously had the best motive for killing him."

As her anger gradually subsided under Bryan's soothing touch, Samantha gave thought to his assessment of her father's confusion over her success, concluding that he had often been faced with similar dilemmas. He brought me up to be a free spirit, she thought to herself, allowing me to find things out the hard way, yet constantly worried to death I would become independent. It was the same with Mum, she realized with reflection. Dad always wanted her to be her own person, to have her own life, and look what had happened: George. It was the same with his job. He fought and struggled for promotion, then resented the responsibility that came with it and yearned for the days when he had pounded the beat without a care. Every time in life he thought he had won, he'd lost.

"He's a good man," she said aloud and was surprised to hear the words. She had meant it only as a silent tribute. "You are right," replied Bryan, knowing immediately whom she was referring to. "But where on earth is he?"

"Wherever I was supposed to have sent the money," she replied guiltily.

Bryan struggled with that proposition. "But what I still don't understand is, if he didn't get the money, why didn't he phone?"

She lifted her head and spoke as if talking to a child. "Because Margaret doesn't have a phone."

"So why didn't he go back to wherever he phoned from before?"

She didn't reply but her fixed glare along the beach, toward Stacy's store, indicated her beliefs. Bryan interrupted her pre-occupation, dropped to his knees in front of her and, holding her hands tightly in his, delved into her eyes. "Could your dad have lied to you?"

"No!" she insisted, trying to jerk her hands away.

He held on tightly. "Just think about it. Maybe he wanted to get away completely — from everything."

"No. He was here, I know he was."

Bryan wanted to believe her.

"He even told me about an eagle, a bald eagle I think. Margaret had rescued it. He couldn't have made that up. They had even given it a name — Eddie ..." She paused, peering intently into his eyes, noticing how the colour had deepened under the sapphire sky. "Do you know what this is like?"

He raised an eyebrow questioningly.

"This is what an innocent man must feel like when he's accused of a crime and all the evidence points directly at him. He knows very well he didn't do it, but because he hasn't got a cast-iron alibi the bloody police won't listen to him."

Bryan felt the sting. "It's not that I don't believe you Samantha, it's just ..." he dried up.

"Precisely. There is no evidence on my side, so you'll go with the opposition."

Bryan stood and slouched across the beach to let a few handfuls of sand trickle through his fingers into the lake while he mulled over the situation.

"Have you ever prosecuted an innocent man, Chief Inspector?" she called without getting up.

He turned quickly, emphatically. "No."

"Do you think any policeman would admit to prosecuting an innocent man?" she continued.

He could see which way she was headed and didn't like it. "Possibly not."

"Possibly?" she queried

"All right. No, they wouldn't. And, yes, before you ask, I would agree that sometimes innocent people are convicted. So what do you expect me to do?"

"I expect you to believe me when I say that Dad phoned from that place."

"OK. Let's say I believe you."

"No. No. No," she shook her head irately. "You don't get it, do you? I don't want you to say, 'Let's say I believe you.' I want you to say, 'Samantha, I believe you, — now how can we prove you're right?'"

"But we've spoken to people at the store and looked at the books. I don't know what else you expect." He dropped his voice an apologetic notch. "I'm sorry, Samantha, but he's not here."

But she wouldn't let him off the hook. "I'm not some silly complainant who needs to be humoured. When that plane comes back you are going to be getting onto it alone. I'm not leaving here till I've found him. Oh," she had an afterthought. "And you can forget that cozy tête-à-tête you've planned, and the post-prandial bonk."

"That's not the most romantic proposal anyone's ever made to me," he laughed, walking back up the beach. "But I wouldn't say no."

She stood, aggressively. "Well you won't get a chance to unless you start getting serious about finding Dad."

"Gone fishing," read the sign on the store door when they returned for another go at Stacy.

"It's locked," cried Samantha in dismay. Apart from a couple of mongrels play-fighting in the scrub just off the beach, there was no sign of life. "Keep watch," she whispered.

"What are you doing?"

"I'll see if I can get in round the back."

"Samantha ..."

"What are they going to do — shoot me?"

She was back in a flash. "It's tight as a virgin's fanny," she complained, slumping disconsolately on the verandah.

"Wherever did you learn that language?" he laughed, finding her expressions so incongruous with her lawyerly accent.

"My clients mainly." She switched topics and pointed to the hastily scribbled sign on the door "I bet that sign was put up for our benefit."

"How do you work that out?"

"Deduction," she said, swinging an arm in a wide arc around the village. "There's no more than twenty houses in the whole place; everyone would know where Stacy was if he wasn't at the store."

"So, what are you suggesting?"

"Dad was here. I know he was. He probably still is."

"Well, let's examine the evidence," he began, holding up his hand to stem her anticipated protest. "I'm not doubting you. I'm just trying to establish if there are any clues to his exact whereabouts. Now, how do you know your Dad was in Canada — for sure?"

She played the game reluctantly. "His phone calls."

"Now, don't get upset, but you know as well as I do that he could have been anywhere when he phoned, unless ... Did you call him?"

"No," she shook her head, disappointed. "Wait, I remember." Her excitement bubbled over. "He reversed the charges once. I gave him hell, but the operator said, 'Will you accept a transfer charge call from Toronto, Canada?'"

"Fab. Now we're getting somewhere. He was in Toronto, anyway. Now, what do you know for certain about Margaret?"

"I know he got her address from a private detective in Toronto."

"Brilliant," he said, and meant it. "If a PI can find her, then the local police shouldn't have a problem. Now, what else do we know about her?"

"He told me about the eagle."

"But that's not admissible evidence, it's hearsay."

"I know," she nodded. "But he couldn't have made that up — not Dad. He's not that creative."

Bryan conceded the point with a nod. Bliss's flat had been a testament to his creative ability.

"What about Stacey's address and postcode? I wrote it down," she said, grubbing around in her purse to find the scrap torn from the corner of a scratch pad.

He wrinkled his nose in a less-than-encouraging expression as she handed it to him.

"This is good evidence," she insisted. "It's a note made at the time. I wrote down exactly what he said, I'm sure I did ... Bear Lake Post Office, Bear Lake, Ontario, Y3Z 4R1."

Bryan scrutinized the scrap carefully for several seconds then made up his mind. "Why are they lying? All of them."

"You believe me," she shouted, flinging her arms round his neck and kissing him.

"Well, you present a very compelling case, Miss Bliss."

"Thank you, Chief Inspector."

"Does this mean the dinner is back on?"

She looked askance. "You're not just ..."

"No. I'm not just agreeing with you to get you in the sack." He smiled. "I do believe you — honestly.

Although I still don't know why these people would lie about a complete stranger, and I don't know how we're going to get them to tell the truth."

chapter seventeen

They tried Stacy again, when he eventually returned in his aluminum fishing boat. "Lake trout," he called cheerfully, holding up a string of mottled lapis-lazuli fish as he ran the boat ashore. "Like a couple?"

They were both hungry, and the plane wouldn't be back for another hour. "Why not," Bryan whispered out of the corner of his mouth. "We might get him talking."

Samantha agreed. "Will you cook them for us?" she called as he waddled his way up the beach.

"Sure thing. Barbecued with loads of butter and a mound of fries, that's how I like 'em." His belly gave testament to that. Some of the fish were still kicking as he unlocked the door and let Samantha and Bryan in. "Freshest fish you ever had," he stated conversationally. "You just help yourself to seats and I'll have these beauties ready in a flash."

"Thanks," they mumbled.

Samantha, totally unconvinced by his swagger of innocence, stuck her mouth to Peter Bryan's ear as they followed him into the big room. "I still think he knows where Dad is."

They sat in the window, looking out over the lake, marvelling uneasily at the utter peacefulness, wondering how long it would take for consummate boredom to turn into insanity, and thinking how different it would be if they were back amidst the freneticism of London.

"What's the time in England?" she asked out of the blue.

"About eight o'clock," Bryan answered vaguely.

She looked around at the deserted store cum café. "That's odd."

"What?"

"When Dad called last week to ask for the money it was about this time, but I remember a background 'rhubarb' of voices and chinking glasses. I thought he was in a bar; it sounded like a bar."

"Maybe we have got the wrong place," he said, looking round at the empty turn-of-the-century store with its incongruous nineteen-fifties' freezers. "My father had a freezer like that," he announced, pointing to the massive American machine, which could have been a tank if it had tracks. "He bought it from a GI and always called it his 'Third Reich' freezer."

She screwed up her nose confusedly.

"Bloody cold-hearted and built to last a thousand years," he laughed.

"There we go folks," said Stacy, producing the two plates of trout and chips with a flourish as he came from behind the counter. "Now, can I get you a drink?"

"Beer," they agreed. "And please join us," insisted Bryan.

The trout was delicious, but Stacy gave nothing away as he balanced, overflowing, on an adjacent stool, professing his willingness to help, promising to put the word out, pledging to do all he could, vowing to call Samantha with any news, however meagre.

"It's quiet today," said Samantha, still thinking about the noises she had heard on the phone. Like a freed hostage trying to help the police locate the place they had been held captive by recalling the ambience.

Stacy stared slowly around the empty room, as if he needed to check that he hadn't been suddenly inundated. "About usual," he said. "I don't get many folks in as rule."

Stacy refused to accept payment as they readied to leave, saying, "It don't cost me nothing." He reassured Samantha with his greasy, stubby fingers on her forearm that he would call the moment there was any news. Her flesh crawled from his touch but she didn't jerk away, thinking that, in some way, she might be able to judge his sincerity through his fingertips. But she only felt the grease and tried one last time. "You are certain you've never seen him?"

He shook his head sadly. "Sorry, Miss. Like I said, I'll call."

"That's good timing," said Bryan as they walked toward the wooden dock and saw the small police plane streak across the lake in the late afternoon sun. "What do you want to do?" he asked. "You said you wouldn't leave without him."

"I don't know anymore. I've sort of burnt out my neurosis. I'm running on empty."

Bryan summed up the situation pragmatically. "There's nowhere for us to stay here and we haven't got clothes or anything. Let's go back, find out Margaret's address and call on her tomorrow."

It sounded simple enough and Samantha felt a tingle of excitement as the Mounties' plane churned up the unnerving tranquillity by swooping out of the sky and skimming to a standstill with the grace of a swan. But the excitement turned to consternation with the thought that she would be leaving without her father. "I suppose another day won't make a lot of difference," she said, more to appease her conscience than to please Bryan.

The pilot kept the propellers turning as he leant out of the cockpit window, shouting above the engines. "Any luck?"

Bryan shook his head. "No. He's never been here."

Old Jock, holding open the door, proffered his shoulder for Samantha to lean on as she boarded but, on an impulse, she stepped back. "Wait a minute."

"What?" said Bryan.

"I ought to have checked my answering machine at home."

"You've had all day."

"It didn't occur to me," she called, angry with herself. "He's probably left a message to say where he is, wanting to know where the hell is the money. That's it, that explains everything."

The pilot was mouthing irritably, "What's happening? We've got to go. We're late already." His words were whipped away by the propellers' wash. But Samantha shut her ears and was already running back down the short wooden dock toward the store. "I won't be a sec," she shouted over her shoulder.

"What's my number," she asked herself, searching her mind frantically, phone in hand. This is ridiculous, I can't remember my own phone number. "How often do you call yourself?" she asked out loud, and felt foolish, realizing Stacy was hovering.

"What's the international operator number?" she called.

"Zero," he replied, moving away a little.

Feeling stupid she dialled and asked for international directory enquiries, then, feeling even more stupid, gave her own name and address as if she were a stranger.

"Hold the line," said the Canadian operator and suddenly Samantha found herself talking to a familiar voice — an English operator. She gave her name and address again and flicked idly though the notebook hanging on a string by the phone while waiting. The operator was back in a second but Samantha's mind wasn't focussed, it was glued to an entry in the little book and, as the woman slowly recited the digits, she found herself reading the number — her number — in the book.

"Did you get that, Miss?" asked the operator.

Samantha's silence signalled a problem. "Miss? Miss?"

"Oh. Sorry," she said, her mind on another planet. "I missed that, would you mind giving it again."

Clearly annoyed, the operator started reciting the number a second time, then paused. "Are you writing this down?" she asked, unwilling to waste more time.

"Yes," Samantha lied, then traced the numbers in the book with her finger as the operator spoke. Dazed, she put down the phone, omitting to thank the operator, unable to quite comprehend what was happening. Turning toward Stacy with a question poised on her lips she heard a warning bell ring deep inside her. "Thank you," she muttered as she left the store and walked back to the plane in a dream, her face ghostly white.

"Hurry up," called the pilot testily.

"Anything?" asked Bryan as she started to climb aboard.

Her zombie-like mind still hadn't really worked it out. "Peter," she started with a gush, then saw that Jock, the Scotsman, was still close enough to hear, his old ears cocked.

"Are you OK?"

"Hold my hand," she said, seeking confirmation of reality, and waited until they had taken off to straighten her thoughts.

"What!" he exploded when she told him.

She told him again, repeating exactly what had happened, in a rush, but missing nothing.

Bryan tapped the pilot's arm. "We've got to go back," he shouted, then turned to Samantha. "There must be some explanation."

"Don't look at me like that, Peter. I know what I saw."

"You're just a bit overwrought, that's all."

"And I imagined it. Is that what you're saying?"

"Mistaken, perhaps. Probably a similar number, that's all."

"Too stupid to know my own telephone number, is that what you think?" Then she realized with some embarrassment that that was exactly what had happened.

"Not exactly."

"Exactly!" she screamed. "That's exactly what you are suggesting. You said you believed me. Didn't you?"

"Well, I ..."

"Did you say that?" she demanded with a dig.

"I did."

"Well, believe me then. I am telling you, Dad wrote my phone number in the book at that place. No one else could have."

Bryan was still fighting for a rational explanation. "What about when you called ...?"

"You called. Not me," she shot back. But maybe there was an explanation. "Did you give Stacy my number?" she queried.

He only gave the question some consideration because he felt he should, but then shook his head. "No — I didn't give him your number. Why would I?"

"Right, that does it then. He was there — they're lying."

"Excuse me," shouted the pilot, agitated. "Can you make up your minds before we run out of gas?"

Samantha ignored him in her anger. "I bloody knew it," she cried in relief. "I knew that address and post-code were right."

"Where is he then?" called the detective from the front.

"Where is *she*?" added Bryan, still sceptical. "They said they had never heard of her, either."

"Who is *she*?" asked the detective, making it clear from his tone that he was unaware a woman was involved.

"A woman Dad came to find, a witness to a murder."

"What's her name?" said the pilot, reaching to flick on his radio to make enquiries.

"Margaret Gordonstone."

"Oh, God," said the DS, staying the pilot's hand. "I know where she is."

"You do?"

The detective would have said, "I think you had better sit down," if it had been relevant but, as they were all strapped firmly in their seats, he was left fumbling for an alternative way of verbally presaging disastrous news. In a half-second's silence the already stretched atmosphere reached snapping point; he ran out of time and had no choice but to blurt out the cold facts. "She was killed on Sunday in the plane crash."

The plane lurched as Samantha and Bryan both leapt forward at the same time. "That's not the bad news," added the detective with a note of foreboding.

"It's not?" queried Bryan.

The big man sucked in a long, deep breath that seemed to draw everything and everyone towards him as he physically and mentally steeled himself. "There was a second person in the plane, possibly two others. Badly injured judging by the blood, but they escaped."

"Badly injured," echoed Samantha in a dream, or a nightmare.

"Where is he?" demanded Bryan.

"I don't know ... I've no idea," the detective said, lying. He had lots of ideas — drowned or taken by a bear were at the top of the list.

"Hold on," said Bryan, realizing what thoughts were in the air. "We don't know it was your Dad. Why would he be in a plane with Margaret? We don't even know it was a man, do we?" he asked the detective.

"No, Sir," replied the sergeant, acknowledging Bryan's rank for the first time. Feeling that things were becoming serious enough to warrant officialdom.

Samantha had already made up her mind. "I knew he was dead. I had a premonition."

The pilot, quiet for sometime, now piped up. "What the hell do you want me to do?"

"The settlement," said Bryan "Those people must know something. He was obviously there."

Although the detective had set his mind on getting home, he felt that the site of the plane crash was the most likely place to find Bliss, and said so.

But the pilot ruled it out immediately. "I can't land there in the dark," he said, pointing to the rapidly setting sun. "It's too dangerous; there's no lights and I don't know the waters."

"It's either the settlement or civilization then," said the detective, already knowing he would be outvoted and the chief inspector would insist on returning to investigate Samantha's claims.

"Take us back to the settlement," demanded Samantha, sounding like a hijacker, "We're not going anywhere without him."

Samantha, relieved at her vindication, found herself staring at the scrawny neck of the pilot in front of her and the hulk of the man in the other seat and wondering, of all things, if the pilot had to keep the controls over to counteract the weight. Would they fly round in circles, she wondered, if he took his feet off the rudder?

In the few minutes it took to return to the settlement Phillips filled in the missing details. They knew the deceased was Margaret because they had found some of her belongings in the plane's cargo compartment, and she had ID in her purse. The plane had crashed, he said, because one of the floats ripped open on landing and flipped it over.

"Accident?" asked Samantha.

The detective nodded. "It must have hit a log or something sharp in the water as it came in to land. It happens."

"We'll tell them our plane has a malfunction," said Bryan as they skidded back onto Bear Lake. "That'll give us an excuse to stay."

The detective sergeant had more direct plans. "I'd rather kick Stacy's butt 'til we get some answers."

"They must have a good reason for lying," suggested Bryan, unable to think of one.

Following the plane's departure an assortment of men had come out of the woodwork and the bar was buzzing with excitement as the inhabitants speculated on the foreigners' visit. Nothing this interesting had occurred since a couple of tourists were ripped to shreds by a bear a few years earlier, although Margaret's arrival had certainly caused a stir ten years ago.

A dropped pin would have been deafening on the old plank floor as the detective and the others marched smartly into the store with Jock sheepishly in tow.

"Leave this to me," the policeman had said confidently as they mounted the wooden steps to the verandah, but Samantha had other ideas. "Where's my father?" she shouted at Stacy in the moment of hiatus following their entry.

Stacy, stunned, shrank away. "I ... I don't know."

"Explain this then," she screamed, ripping the notebook off its string and forcing it under his nose. "That's my fucking phone number ... There." She stabbed her finger at the book. "How'd that get there?"

Forrest Gump gave the game away. "Maggie said ..."

Samantha whipped around. "Who said that?"

Someone dug the simpleton in the ribs to shut him up, but he took it as a cue to keep going. "Maggie said we'd never seen 'im."

The detective sergeant flew across the room, gripped Stacy round the throat, and flung him against the wooden shelves. "Who's Maggie? Who is she?"

Stacy didn't hesitate. "Maggie said he was an old friend in trouble. Said you might come looking. Said he was on the run."

"On the run from what?"

"The law ... Perverting justice ... Murder, she said."

"When was this?"

"Last Thursday evening. She came over in her boat and said we should keep quiet about him. The money came when she was here. She said I had to send it back; said to say I never heard of him. So I did."

"And that was the last you saw her?"

"Yeah … Maggie said they were going away for a bit and she'd take care of him. He'll be all right if he's with Maggie, Miss. She'll look after him, she's really good with critters in trouble."

Samantha looked into his piggy eyes. "You don't know what's happened do you?

"What?" said Stacy.

Bryan told them about the crash and Margaret's death. The expressions on the men's faces caught Samantha by surprise. It was more than just the shock or hurt someone might register on losing a neighbour or co-worker, more like the almost disbelieving dejection displayed by a family member. No one cried, but Old Jock shot off to the toilet pretty quickly.

The pony-tailed Indian stepped forward and peered closely into Samantha's eyes. "I have heard the voices whispering through the trees," he said with religious overtones and the worst case of halitosis she had ever withered under. "It is Windigo that has taken them."

"Who the hell is Windigo?" demanded DS Phillips, readying himself to put out an all points bulletin, and giving Samantha an opportunity to slide out from under the Indian's gaze and breath.

"Windigo," the Indian began, addressing the air with a sing-song voice. "He is the great monster of the north who roams the lands of the Algonquian and feeds upon our people."

"Crap," mumbled someone at the back, but most of the store's occupants knew the Indian legends well enough not to mock them.

"We must hold a 'shaking tent' ritual right away if we are to find your father before Windigo swallows him up," continued the Indian, addressing Samantha with the positiveness of a surgeon announcing the need for an immediate tracheotomy. "And we must call upon Mishipi-zhius, the god of the lake, to help us."

Phillips had heard enough and pulled the Indian roughly to once side. "Samantha, don't listen to this garbage. I know where your father is. All we have to do is get back to the crash site in the morning and start a proper search."

"Windigo must be appeased," continued the Indian, refusing to be silenced. "Do you have anything belonging to your father?" he pleaded of Samantha. "The Shaman will need something to focus on."

"C'mon Samantha," called the sergeant, preparing to leave.

"Wait a minute," she said, touched by the man's sincerity. "What is a 'shaking tent' ritual? Who is the Shaman?"

"It is the way we ask the spirits to find lost things or help someone in trouble. The Shaman is our holy man."

Bryan, sensing Samantha's need to do anything to help her father, interceded. "What do we have to do?"

The remains of the Indian's smoke-stained teeth looked like a row of rusted stanchions as he laughed. "Nothing. You must do nothing. It is the Shaman who will do everything. We will place him in a tent with something of your father's. If the spirits are listening the tent will shake and the Shaman will be told where we should look."

Samantha was already rummaging in her handbag. "I've got this," she said, pulling out the door key to her father's apartment..

"You don't believe that, do you...?" started the detective, but Samantha's look shut him up.

"Here, take this," she said. "It's his door key."

The Indian, his hands as filthy as his teeth, held the key like an orchid and whispered an incantation over it, then he studied the ceiling and spoke with the absurd seriousness of an amateur actor reciting a line from an equally amateurish play. "My name is Running Moose. I will take this key to the Shaman and as the sun rises over the great lake he will ask the spirits to seek out the spirit of your father."

"This is getting ridiculous," the detective sneered.

Running Moose ignored the jibe and charged ahead with his plan. "We must hold the ritual where he was last seen."

"King's Cross railway station," said Samantha, immediately realizing the impracticability of the location. "Wait a minute, where does Margaret live?" Nobody had thought to ask in all the fuss. "That's where he must have been seen last," she continued positively.

The Indian paled noticeably under his thick brown skin. Samantha looked around at the blank faces. "Well, where does she live? Sorry, I meant where *did* she live?"

Stacy answered straightaway. "Little Bear Island."

"That's the place then," she announced, and was amazed by the speed Running Moose took flight.

"Maybe it is not so important," he said, his voice shaking nervously. "Maybe we should hold the ceremony right here."

"No way," said Samantha. "We've come this far so we might as well go to her island. Where is it?"

chapter eighteen

Superintendent Edwards, in London, asked the same question of Laslow Mitwich, Gordonstone's solicitor. Furtively calling from a payphone in an alleyway behind Canon Street station, even hiding under a rarely worn trilby, he was put straight through to the solicitor's chamber.

"It's only a postal address I'm afraid, Michael," said Mitwich, happily obliging with Margaret's location. But, to Edwards' disappointment, he had no phone number for her. "Never needed to phone her old chap," said the solicitor. "And I don't think Martin kept in touch."

"How d'ye fancy bashing a ball about on the greens sometime?" Mitwich asked, catching Edwards by surprise.

"Oh, I'll give you a buzz," said Edwards, preoccupied. "I'm just a bit tied up at the moment."

Edwards thanked him and was lost in thought as he went to replace the receiver. Edwards wandered back to his office for an afternoon of discussions and briefings about the Gordonstone murder. Under pressure from the divisional commander a full team had been assigned to the task — the commander pulled no punches when he told them that the officer previously assigned to the case had "fucked up and fucked off." Even the file was missing, the commander complained.

"Stolen with his car, so the burke claims," Edwards added, without naming names. But everyone knew the story of Bliss's lost car and exploding cat.

Samantha was stomping around Stacy's store demanding action, exhorting the detective sergeant to call in the army, insisting that the search commence immediately. But the pilot ruled that out. There were no more than twenty minutes daylight left; he wouldn't go until the morning — and that was final.

Hysterical speculation about her father — injured, probably dying, alone in the forest — was beyond Peter Bryan's consolatory ability, particularly as he had been so reluctant to believe her in the first place. And Samantha's fractiousness was aggravated further by Phillips, who had taken a seat at the bar.

"We can't just sit here," she screamed. "We've got to do something."

"Look around you, Miss," the detective sergeant said. "This isn't London. The plane crashed Sunday. The Indians who found it were ten miles from their reserve and didn't report it 'til Monday."

It had taken more than two hours for the Indians to trek around the densely wooded bay to reach the upended plane. Margaret's body, still strapped in her harness, hung upside down with her long, dark hair dangling into the water. The blood-spattered interior and open door led the Indians to search for survivors but they had given up as night fell. Instead they trudged back to their reservation to report their grisly find.

"The best thing — the only thing — we can do is join the search in the morning," added the detective with his eye on a beer.

But Samantha had other ideas. "There's nowhere for us to stay here," she pointed out. "At least we could stay in Margaret's house if we went to her island."

"I thought your plane was broke," said the Gump figure, too stupid to realize it was a ruse.

"We lied," said Bryan with defiant pride, and he turned to the detective. "Samantha's right. Plus, I'd like to be there at sunrise just in case that Indian witch doctor shows up."

Running Moose had already left the store, after agreeing reluctantly that the Shaman would hold the "shaking tent" ceremony on Margaret's island at dawn.

Samantha piled on the ammunition. "I definitely want to be there," she said, although in truth she had little faith in the ancient ritual.

The flight to Little Bear Island took no more than ten minutes; the detective used the time to radio his office and inform them of his whereabouts and intentions. He also relayed information about his passengers, then turned in his seat as far as is bulk would permit.

"They want to contact your office in London," he said to Bryan.

"Why?"

"Just to confirm what you're saying."

"That could be a bit of a problem. They think I'm in Nepal."

"Nepal," breathed Samantha.

"Yes ..." he continued. "Leading a rescue mission on Everest actually," thinking as he spoke that, although sounding impressive, the story was totally unbelievable.

The detective certainly wasn't fooled. "You're kidding — right?"

"I'm afraid not. That's what I told my boss."

"Good for you, Peter," said Samantha.

Little Bear Island was silhouetted against the setting sun; they found it easily, but landing was a hair-raising experience in the twilight. Rocks the size of cars shot out of the shadows and God-knows-what lay just below the surface waiting to snag a float as they touched down. The pilot cursed Samantha freely under his breath. Every time he thought he had found a clear stretch of water he would spot a boulder or a floating log at the last minute, or imagine that he had done so. But he had to land. Returning to the settlement was not an option; it would be even darker by the time they got back there.

The dark stain of water rushed up at them for the fourth time. The pilot strained against his seat belt, the floats fizzed as they kissed the surface, and then, with a yelp, he yanked the stick back and rammed open the throttles. "Rocks," he yelled, perspiration dripping down his face. "This was stupid," he continued to no one in particular and they all felt the tension. "You'd better put on life jackets," he added once they'd gained a few hundred feet, scaring them further. He tried landing again. This time the oily surface picked up a reflection off the floats and sent the pilot into a dizzying climb as his nerve cracked at the apparent sight of logs in the water. "Shit," he spat through clenched teeth. "Hold tight folks," he added swinging away from the island, "I've got an idea."

He landed far offshore, away from the rocks, then idled the small plane toward the shore at a snail's pace, using a hand-held spotlight to guide the way.

"Here's Dad's suit," shouted Samantha, stumbling into Margaret's bedroom in the light from an oil lamp and finding his discarded clothing.

"How can you be sure?" challenged the detective poking his head into the room.

She slipped her hand into an inside pocket of the rumpled clothes, pulled out the return ticket from Paris, and flapped it under his nose. "What the hell do you call this? Look," she screamed, jabbing it with a finger. "D.A. Bliss. See."

"Sorry, dear."

"And don't call me dear."

Bryan gave the detective a look of condolence as he slunk back into the living room.

Samantha slammed the door behind him and slumped on the bed in tears. "Poor sod," she cried, stroking one of her father's ties with the sort of idolatry with which a fan might finger one of John Lennons', and brushing out his suit with the care of an acolyte preparing a Bishop's vestments — as if some Godliness had been absorbed into the fabric.

"Supper's ready," called Peter Bryan with a muted knock a little later. The men had lit the fire in the stove and heated food from the plane's emergency rations. They sat on the couches in the flickering light, forcing the conversation as much as their appetites.

"When I said romantic candlelight dinner," Bryan laughed, determined to keep Samantha cheerful, "this isn't exactly what I had in mind."

She tried a smile but wasn't satisfied with its authenticity so let it drop.

"So why did Margaret lie to Stacy about your dad?" enquired the detective, still trying to fathom out how he had got caught up in such a convoluted scenario.

"I think they'd fallen in love," she replied, still with a choke in her voice.

"But why the lies?"

Samantha was still trying to work that out herself and her face went blank with inner thought. Finally she said, "I'm sure he wasn't lying to me on Wednesday when he asked for the money to get home. But then," she clapped, "Bam! Love struck, and they must have decided to disappear together to start a new life." She paused, the memory of a pregnancy testing kit uppermost in her mind. "New love makes you do stupid things," she added. "But it solved all Dad's problems: Mum, George, Edwards — even his stolen car. It even eliminated problems he didn't know he had."

"Like what?" asked the pilot.

"Someone trashed his apartment and murdered his cat," she replied, coldly staring at Peter Bryan.

Bryan rolled with the punch. "But how can you be sure they went off together?"

"Consider what he left behind," she said, in a Sherlock Holmes manner, counting off the items on her fingers. "His working suit, five ties, best shirt, brogues, braces, and his return ticket to Paris. And he wasn't on any day trip — he took his suitcase."

"I'm not sure that proves anything —" started the detective, but Samantha cut him off with an expansive wave.

"Well, look around here. What is there of hers? Nothing, only some jumble sale clothes. Check the bathroom cabinet. God knows, my bathroom isn't an Iraqi chemical depot like Mum's, but the toiletries she's left behind wouldn't cover a pimple on her bum. There's virtually no food in the kitchen and they even took the sheets and blankets off the bed."

"So where were they going?"

She shrugged and turned to Bryan. "What do you think, Dr. Watson?"

"I think we all need some sleep," said Bryan, unwilling to commit himself in case he should be proved wrong again.

The early start and exhausting day had taken their toll and they turned in as soon as supper was finished. Samantha and Bryan took the bedroom without discussion, leaving the other two to fight over the couches. After turning the mattress to avoid the nasty brown stain, they lay together fully dressed with a couple of blankets from the plane's emergency kit spread over them. But Samantha couldn't sleep, her mind tossed and twitched with memories, thoughts, and ideas. "I'm sorry," she whispered into the darkness, realizing she was disturbing him.

"It doesn't matter, I don't know if I can sleep, anyway."

"I suppose the real tragedy is that he had just found love again."

"With Margaret?" he said, noticing the surprise in his tone, not knowing why.

"Yeah ... It was in his voice the last time he called. It was just the way he said, 'We've got an eagle.' He denied it of course, but I knew." She almost added, "Randy old bugger," but changed her mind. "Poor old devil," she said. "I see what you mean though — every time he wins he loses, and ..." she broke into tears. "He's lost it all this time."

Bryan cuddled her in the darkness, smoothing her hair the way a parent might soothe a testy child.

Samantha had sobbed them both slowly to sleep. It was sometime later when Bryan woke and sensed emptiness beside him. Creeping past the sleeping figures in the main room he stepped quietly onto the verandah and felt a chill through his socks. She was there, sitting as still as a statue on a rock, hugging her knees and peering through the skeletal trees to the darker splodge of lake in the distance. The moon was as bright and yellow as a forty-watt bulb, and the stars were so close through the window of unpolluted sky he felt as if he could touch them. Samantha hadn't moved; lost in her grief, she was unaware of his proximity. He spent a moment marvelling at the Milky Way as it cut a wide swath from horizon to horizon, then he called softly, "Samantha — are you all right?"

Awareness of his presence filtered through the fog of her anguish. "He's out there somewhere," she mused, resigned to her father's fate.

"You're freezing," he said, shocked by the paleness of her hands and face. "How long have you been out here?"

She shrugged, the relevance of time lost.

Dropping to her side he tried to mould her body into his but she resisted stiffly, preferring to freeze, to accept nature's punishment — wanting to feel the pain her father had endured as he struggled, injured and dying in the frigid water. "I knew he was dead on Sunday, I had a premonition at his flat. Do you remember?"

"We don't know he's dead."

"I think he should have died when Mum left," she went on, hating herself for saying so. "He's been like someone with a terminal illness ever since. It seems trite to suggest it, but I wonder if he attacked Edwards on purpose. Maybe he was so frustrated that he didn't consider or care about the repercussions. He never used to be like that. Nothing would get to him, he'd shrug off anything. 'Like water off a duck's ass,' my mother used to say.

"I think it's a duck's back," corrected Bryan gently.

Giving it some thought she answered seriously, "No ...I think she meant a duck's ass."

Peter Bryan smiled and attempted optimism. "There's really no reason to believe he's dead. Like the detective said, he got away from the plane, so he can't be too badly injured."

"Please Peter, don't humour me. I'm a big girl now. I can feel it, like I felt it Sunday, like a hollow space in my heart." She peered questioningly into his eyes. "It sounds very melodramatic, doesn't it?"

"No," he replied, but at that moment would have said anything to please her.

She looked wistfully back at the lake. "The strange thing is I really don't know if I want to find him now. Isn't that weird?"

Bryan waited patiently for the explanation he felt coming.

"He's gone," she continued. "Finding his body is going to bring him back, and I'm going have to lose him all over again. Plus the fact that I actually think he found happiness here. I got the feeling he might have stayed if he could. Now we're going to find him and stick him in a hole in the ground in Wimbledon or ..." Her sobs got in the way and she melted into Bryan as he clutched her to his chest.

"Your dad's a fighter Samantha, I haven't given up hope. If anyone could survive, it would be him."

She sniffed snottily into his sweater. "Do you really think so?"

"I do," he lied, thinking that his words may well have been true before Sarah had dumped Bliss in favour of George and he'd suffered a few other setbacks.

Samantha perked up at his words and looked at him seriously. "Isn't this the part in the movie where we have a frantic fuck just to convince each other that everything will turn out all right in the end?"

"You're unbelievable, Samantha Bliss," he sniggered. "But if you think that I'm going to take my trousers off and freeze my backside out here you've got another think coming."

Wiping the last of her tears she stared into the bright moon. "It is kind of romantic though isn't it? At least, it would be if Dad was here."

Peter Bryan's laugh rippled through the silent woods. "I'm not sure you meant that."

She smiled. "You're right," and their lips met and melded into a kiss. Then she broke away. "Did you really tell Edwards you were going to the Himalayas?"

"Yeah. It just popped into my mind and was out of my mouth before I could stop it."

"I really like you, Peter," she said, and mashed her lips back to his, giving him something else to chew on.

"The Shaman is wearing a new headdress," Running Moose explained as they stood on the beach waiting for the sunrise, watching the Indian priest ready himself for the ceremony. The cascade of bald eagle feathers, a male bird's entire trousseau, had been stitched together over the weekend for an upcoming tribal gathering; Samantha couldn't help wondering if it was entirely appropriate for the man to test drive a new bonnet while searching for her father.

The little band of Indians had arrived before day-break, their noisy twin-engine powerboat failing to disturb any animals as they manoeuvred just off the dock in the gloom.

"What are they doing?" asked Samantha rhetorically as she and Bryan stood on the shore and watched a heavy birch canoe being lifted off the boat and placed in the water. When a fragile old man was helped into it, her vivid imagination and irascible sense of humour briefly overcame concern for her father. "Shall we cast him adrift, Mr. Christian?" she said under her breath with a West Country drawl. Bryan heard. "It is a bit like *Mutiny on the Bounty*, isn't it?"

Ten minutes later fiction became farce as Running Moose and two other Indians struggled to erect an army surplus pup tent on the beach. The Shaman, the old medicine man in the canoe, could not come ashore until everything was prepared, they said, and then he would have to paddle silently so as not to frighten off the spirits from the beach. That makes a lot of sense, thought Samantha, considering the dreadful noise they'd made arriving.

They were joined by the detective and the pilot as the Shaman, a sixty-year-old in a two hundred-year-old's body, stooged around in his canoe ten feet off the beach shouting tent-raising instructions.

"I was in the Scouts," offered Bryan, following the third aborted attempt. He recognized the tent as the type designed to be pitched by a ten-year-old in a hurricane. One of the Indians, a willowy man with a truly red face and permanent gap-toothed smile, explained with great seriousness that the tent could only be erected by believers. Bryan quickly withdrew his offer, then noticed the look of dissatisfaction on Samantha's face. She had expected a teepee or something sturdy made of birch bark and chewed hides, not a backpacker's special from Discount Deals.

With everything finally in place, Running Moose padded over to the small group of white people. "The Shaman says that the spirits are demanding an offering."

The detective coughed cynically. "I might've guessed."

"If they're expecting the blood of a naked virgin they're wasting their time," mumbled Samantha, her faith in the process already diminished by the fiasco over the tent.

"What do they want?" asked Bryan, anxious to try anything within reason, for Samantha's sake.

The spirits felt that one hundred dollars, American preferably, was appropriate. But DS Phillips scoffed, "This is ridiculous. It"s fraud. I've told you where he is, why are we wasting time with this bunch of con-men?"

Running Moose, sensing the wind's direction, quickly dropped the spirit's asking price to fifty dollars and Bryan dug into his pocket.

"Don't bother," whispered Samantha. "This is nothing but a pantomime. I still can't believe we actually came here, but I am sure Dad wouldn't want us to do this. Let's just go to the crash site and find him."

"I'll give you twenty," said Bryan. "Take it or leave it." Running Moose took it.

With the spirits apparently appeased, the Shaman paddled ashore, carefully adjusted his new headdress, and without disembarking the canoe took up a chant. Two Indians, costumed in Levi jeans and Chicago Bulls sweatshirts, seated themselves cross-legged on either side of the tent flap and began beating tom-toms with no particular rhythm, while Running Moose, with a great sense of occasion, held Bliss's front door key high above his head to await the first rays of sunlight.

"The Shaman is calling the sun," explained Running Moose over his shoulder, as the drumbeats and the Shaman's chant coalesced into a continuous undulating wail, then faded into an eerie stillness as an aura of anticipation surrounded them, as if the spirits were really there, holding there breath, waiting to be released by the sunrise.

"This is just silly," whispered the detective sergeant and, although Samantha may have privately agreed, she was gradually mesmerized by the old brass key, which started glowing in the morning light as if drawing power from the sun. The key slowly turned gold and dissolved into the solar rays. No wonder the Druids flock to Stonehenge for the solstice every year, she thought, as the Shaman slipped unnoticed from the canoe and was bundled, bound hand and foot, into the tent, together with the key and the money.

The drummers started again, their beats now hypnotically in tune with the beat of a heart, and the Shaman's high pitched wailing struck the nerves and chilled the spines of everyone on the beach. Then the tent trembled — just a flutter of movement, but it sent a ripple through the canvas from one end to the other. Though almost imperceptible, no one disputed that the movement had occurred.

"Does that mean Dad's still alive?" Samantha breathed, hastily shelving her scepticism.

"He will always be alive," said Running Moose. "What you call life, in a warrior's body, is only one step in life. When your body dies your spirit stays alive. Maybe he is a caribou or a cougar now."

"He *is* dead then," she cried. "I knew it."

"Wait until the spirits have spoken," insisted the Indian as the ripples of vibration grew in intensity.

DS Phillips had seen enough. "This is crap!" he

exploded, but couldn't tear himself aware from the increasingly violent motions of the tent.

But something seemed to be wrong. The Shaman's chant had become a terrifying wail. The drummers lost their rhythm and looked at each other in alarm — this wasn't part of the act. The tent wasn't just shaking, it was writhing like a flag being wrenched from its pole in a gale.

The drummers stopped, but the beat continued as the canvas slapped and banged as if caught in a tornado. The Shaman's wail became a scream. He shot out of the tent and made a dash for the water, but crashed headlong as his hobbled feet sent him tumbling into the sand. Clearly terrified, the drummers dragged the old man to his feet, whipped off the bindings, and helped him into the canoe.

"I'm sorry, Miss," said Running Moose without explanation, though Samantha knew what he meant.

"This is crap," shouted the sergeant again.

"You saw it shaking," insisted Running Moose.

"Come off it, he was kicking the pole. Let's see him do it again."

But the Shaman was already pulling rapidly away from the beach, still yelling and screeching, and the drummers were hastily ripping the tent pegs out of the soft sand.

"He says we should leave quickly," said Running Moose heading toward the small dock and the powerboat.

"But where is my father?" Samantha called after him.

"He doesn't know. He says that Windigo is here on the island. We must leave. There is much evil here. He is calling for O-Ma-Ma-Ma, the great Earth Mother to help us."

The key, wrapped in the money, fell at Samantha's feet as the drummers tore down the tent and rushed after Running Moose. She bent to pick it up but the heat from the bundle almost burnt her fingers and she dropped it quickly onto the sand.

"Look at this Peter," she said with a mixture of confusion and distrust in her own senses. The notes had welded themselves together like papier mâché; he had to let them cool for a few seconds before he could separate them. As he did so, he felt the hackles rise on his neck and the blood pulse in his temples. The old brass key had shattered into a dozen pieces.

"It's a trick," said Phillips with a shaky voice. "Like that Yuri Keller or something."

"Don't stay here. It's dangerous," shouted Running Moose as the powerboat's engines roared into life, and the boat leapt backwards under the panicked hand of one of the men. "Shit," he shouted and slammed the engines into forward, but the stern line was still attached to the dock. Within seconds the powerful boat was dragging a huge chunk of it out into the lake.

While everyone's attention focused on the mangled dock, wondering how they would now board the float plane, Bryan pocketed the remains of the key. He had a friend at the forensic lab who he was sure would be interested in taking a look.

chapter nineteen

"Someone's leaked," spat the divisional commander, flinging a copy of *The Daily Mirror* at Superintendent Edwards.

Edwards paled. "Gordonstone: It Was Murder," shouted the headline.

"Read it," commanded the Commander.

"Controversial restaurateur Martin Gordonstone, (51 yrs), whose untimely death last month was attributed to his boisterous lifestyle, may have been murdered ..." he read, zipping through the details. "...Sources also link a recent explosion at the lead detective's home to this rapidly deepening mystery."

"Sources! What sources?" the commander demanded.

Edwards immediately put his money on Samantha.

"Bring her in, let's talk to her. She's got a bloody nerve. I suppose this is her way of putting pressure on us to settle. Bring her in Michael, let's have a word with her."

"Ah ..." Edwards started uneasily and was grateful for the commander's interruption.

"Oh. By the way, what's this about Peter Bryan being on leave?"

"I told you yesterday, Sir," Edwards said with a rush of confidence, but then had an apprehensive feeling he was walking into a trap.

The commander spun on him with a puzzled frown. "No, you didn't."

"In the messroom, Sir. At the lunch counter."

"As far as I recall, all we spoke about was the new allocation of cars."

Edwards felt the rising breeze of an ill wind. "I definitely told you, Sir."

"Well, you'll have a copy of his written application, won't you?"

Edwards waffled: an emergency, family problems, no time to submit, but he prudently avoided repeating the Everest story. Even the 'big lie' had its limitations.

"But you did authorize his leave?"

Snap! The trap shut. What to do? Admit he'd been conned — that Bryan's mother had let the cat out of the bag, that he had authorized leave on such a blatant falsehood — or admit that he had willingly approved the leave despite Bryan being in the midst of a murder enquiry that required delicate handling.

He opted to save his skin with an outright lie. "I didn't actually authorize anything. As far as I'm concerned, DCI Bryan is AWOL and I've no idea where he is."

Peter Bryan, Samantha, and the Canadians were nearing the crash site where Margaret had been killed. Disturbed by the episode with the Shaman and the shaking tent, they had wasted no time getting away from the island,

and fifty minutes later dropped out of the clear blue sky over a group of men huddled around a fire on a beach. The little knot of searchers and their dogs hardly took any notice as their plane slid onto the glassy lake and nudged in among a small flotilla of launches and planes.

"What's happening?" called Phillips out of the cockpit window, making a megaphone with his hands. "Why aren't you searching?"

"We found them," shouted one man, breaking away from the warmth of the fire and wading a little way out. "Both dead. Exposure."

Although Samantha had known what to expect she still gave a little cry. "Dead," she breathed. The plateau of despair on which she'd been balanced collapsed and she found herself falling again.

"Where are they?" shouted the detective sergeant.

"The chopper's taken them to Goose Bay."

The pilot grabbed his maps. "It's only twenty miles or so," he said with a glance, then added insensitively, "We might as well go, we need fuel anyways."

Samantha had reached another level of depression, and had the feeling she was headed lower. Every time she had thought things couldn't get worse, they did. Bryan caught her hand in an attempt to comfort her but she whipped it away. Only her father's warm hand would have been a comfort.

Goose Bay, like most northern trading posts, was simply a grander version of Bear Lake settlement with the addition of a tin shack hospital. The tiny mortuary was overflowing. Six month's worth of bodies from a single plane crash had stretched the refrigerator beyond bursting point; Margaret's body, surrounded by bags of ice from the local store, had been left on a gurney.

Samantha had made up her mind that she would identify her father's body — it was her duty. But when it came to it she asked Bryan if he minded doing it for her.

"I have to do the identification, anyway," he said. It was force policy ever since one enterprising officer's wife had bilked the Force's insurance company out of millions with a forged death certificate from some remote holiday isle. "Let me see him first and I'll see what he looks like," he added, hoping for his own sake that he wasn't about to walk into a real-life version of a chain-saw massacre.

The mortuary's rubber doors had hardly swung shut behind him when he bounced back out and gave her a smile that was sort of crooked and confused. "It's not your dad."

"Not Dad?"

"Not unless he's turned into a Chinaman."

"What?"

"They're both Chinese."

But Samantha had already accepted the fact of her father's death; it wasn't that simple to twist her mind around such a diametrically opposed concept. "You must be mistaken?" she said, not even daring to consider that Bryan might be right. She was not even willing to hope that he might be right.

"Look for yourself then," he said, swinging the rubber door wide.

Illogically sensing that Bryan was deliberately winding her up she barged past him.

As she stood over the body of the Asians she was left with the feeling that someone was playing Russian roulette with her mind. *Click* — another empty chamber spun into place. But what would happen the next time?

"Where is he?" she mumbled, more confused than ever.

The local policeman, a multi-chinned, grand-father-ly figure with a crew-cut, who took every wheezing breath as if it were his last, had seized the Chinese men's possessions: bloody lumps of bears, and accompanying videotapes, all sealed in heavy-gauge plastic bags.

"We should watch the videos," suggested Bryan. "There might be some clues."

Samantha was in no mood to watch videos. "How can you, Peter?" she stomped. "I want to leave now. Dad's still out there somewhere; he could be alive."

The town's policeman was shaking his furry-football head. "He wasn't in the plane, Miss. There would-n't have been room for another passenger."

"Are you sure?" queried Bryan, having difficulty believing.

"Dead sure," he replied, with a poor choice of words. "And the trackers only found two sets of foot-prints."

"What about his suitcase? An old brown —" Samantha began.

The policeman was already shaking his head again. "There was no suitcase, and no room for one either."

"That does it," said Bryan. "We're watching the videos."

There was something artistic about the opening shot as the lids of a dopey black eye flickered in response to the touch of a finger. "See, this bear is still alive," said the voice of the commentator, though none of the viewers understood the Cantonese. The shot widened to take in the rest of the animal as the big knife hov-ered over the bear's belly. It could easily have been a clip from *All Creatures Great and Small* if the charac-ters had been speaking with Yorkshire accents, but

James Herriot could never have stomached what was about to happen.

"I don't want to watch any more," said Samantha, retching, as the knife dug into the still moving bear, then she escaped from the doctor's office to the near-normality of the mortuary waiting room.

"Samantha. Are you all right?" asked Bryan, finding her slumped on a bench in the waiting room with her head buried in her hands.

"Feeling a bit faint actually. I think I should eat something." She looked up, her tight face showing the scars of mental torture. "What day is it Peter?" What time, what year, what century, she wondered, staring at her fingers. She hid them quickly — the nails had gone.

"Stop the world, I want to get back on," she added listlessly, as if she'd had enough.

"It's Wednesday."

"Where the hell is he?" she screamed, as if someone had just plugged her fuse back in. Annoyance was rapidly overtaking concern and she broke down in frustration. "I feel like I'm playing chess on a dartboard," she sobbed, and he caught her in his arms. She twisted away. "What happened to the bear?"

"Ah ..."

"Don't tell me, I don't want to know." But feminine inquisitiveness got the better of her. "Did they kill it?"

"Yes, they killed it," he said, deliberately neglecting to tell her how the knife had sliced open the living bear's gut and how the Chinese commentator had broken into an excited babble. "Whoa — take a look at that," he seemed to be saying as a small latex hand poked around inside the pulsating mass. "What a stomach, and look at that duodenum. Get a load of that peritoneum. Is that the gall bladder? Yes, I think it is, I think we've found the gall bladder. Wow, would you take a look at that beauty. A real snip — if you'll pardon the pun — at only forty-five thousand bucks." Then something the size of a human thumb was dangled in front of the camera and an identification tab was tied around it. Movement stopped for a few seconds as the bear's heart gave up, then the camera swung to each of the giant paws in turn as they were butchered at the wrist.

Samantha's mind was all over the place. A sinister knife-wielding man was carving up bodies while her father was being chased by a bear.

"Hang on," she shouted, pulling herself together as thoughts clunked into place like a row of cherries. "Do you realize what this means?"

Bryan wasn't even in the same book, let alone the same page.

"He's still on Margaret's island," she continued with absolute certainty.

"But we were there, Samantha. We would have seen him, or heard him."

She was shaking her head. "No. No wonder the Indians were spooked. He *is* there — at least his spirit is."

Peter Bryan realized what she was saying. "You mean he's ..."

"Dead, Peter. I can see it all. He must've discovered what the Chinks were up to and tried to arrest them. They killed him and were trying to get away when they crashed."

"But where does Margaret fit in?"

"I'm still working on that," she said after a thoughtful pause. "But she must be involved or she wouldn't have got Stacy and the others to lie."

"Unless ..." Bryan breathed, catching on. "Unless

the dealers were holding your dad hostage and made Margaret go to the settlement with the message."

"Possible ... But we must get back to the island."

DS Phillips was still in the doctor's office, embroiled in a turf war with the local policeman who was insisting on retaining the videotapes as evidence. Unswayed by the detective's argument that smuggling was a federal offence, the local man could see media headlines and an almost certain promotion coming his way if he kept control of the case.

Samantha exploded through the door and burst into the conversation. "We have to go back to Margaret's island immediately."

"But ...I ..." Phillips floundered. He had expected to be investigating a straightforward plane crash and had been unprepared for Asian smugglers, Indian rituals, and female lawyers with errant fathers and PMS. He put his foot down. "I'm not doin' anything more until I've got clearance," he said, and meant it.

Time dragged for Samantha and Bryan while the detective sergeant sought permission to return to the island, but breakfast in the hospital's homely cafeteria was a diversion from their concerns. Samantha appeared on the verge of collapsing from hunger, but said she couldn't eat a thing when a plateful of scrambled eggs, ham, and hash browns was placed in front of her. Bryan had other ideas and threatened to force it down her throat. She ate, insisting that she was going to throw up. She didn't.

The cafeteria was a revolving door of coffee snatchers; no one lingered long enough for more than a cheery, "Hi! How'ya doing?"

"OK," replied Bryan to the first enquirer, feeling

anything but OK; realizing he and Samantha were the talk of the hospital, he switched to, "So-so."

DS Phillips popped in to grab a coffee and said, "I'm still waiting folks," forestalling the inevitable query.

Samantha wanted to scream.

"Thanks," said Bryan getting up and wandering around the cafeteria walls to browse an exhibition of modern landscapes by a local artist; to raise funds for a new ambulance according to the note attached to a Maxwell House collecting tin.

"What do you think?" called Samantha, turning her nose up at bubble-gum pink hills and trees that could have been puddles of projectile vomit.

"They are by someone called Louisa Martini Corella Thornton-Fink," he read off a handwritten biography taped to the wall.

"But what's your opinion?"

He sat down with a shake of his head. "Anyone who needs that many names has little else to offer. Anyway," he added, "I like to think that the artist can do better than me; I've seen five-year-olds do better than that."

The detective sergeant had taken his coffee, leaving them depressed in their private thoughts. Samantha wanted to think about her father but she couldn't get the bear video to leave her alone. She found herself looking into Bryan's eyes, wanting to ask, "What happened?" Wishing now that she had forced herself to watch it.

Bryan, his mind mired in images from the video, picked up the unspoken inquisitiveness in her look and broke the ice.

"They were after the gall bladder and the bile ..." he started, as if she should know where his mind was.

"Bile!" she gulped, tasting it in the back of her throat. "Whatever for?"

"It's a hundred times more valuable than gold in the

Far East," he said, repeating the local policeman's words. "Five hundred quid a gram."

"But what the hell do they do with it? It's puke, they can't make it into jewellery?"

"Some of it's used for treating gall stones and liver disease apparently, but most of it's taken as an aphrodisiac."

"I'd expect to fuck for a fortnight at that price." She shook her head disbelievingly.

Bryan might have laughed, but he was surrounded by too much darkness; Miss Thornton-Fink's weirdly distorted windows on the world weren't helping.

The counter assistant wandered smilingly to their table with a steaming pot. "More coffee, folks?"

"Thank you," Samantha nodded.

"Saw you looking at the pictures," she said to Bryan brightly. "What d'ye think?"

As if needing to make a final re-evaluation, he looked around for an appropriate half-truth. "Overpriced rubbish," he said, giving up; he'd had enough of half-truths.

"Oh!" Louisa Thornton-Fink's face slipped faster than a share in a dodgy gold mine and she tramped back to the counter without refilling his cup.

"Boyfriend trouble I 'spect," Samantha whispered knowingly, with a nod, as Louisa's sobs reached them from the kitchen a few seconds later.

DS Phillips returned. " 'Kay folks. The boss has given the green light, so I'll just grab a coffee for the pilot and we'll head back to the island."

The instant screech of their chairs on the polished linoleum floor set teeth on edge.

"It isn't a big island, so you two and the pilot should be able to check it out in a couple of hours," he carried on as he poured the coffee himself, the distraught artist still hiding out in the kitchen. "Meantime, job number one for me is to see if I can find anything to ID the Chinamen."

chapter twenty

Monday and Tuesday had been one long nightmare for Bliss. In the cave's darkness he had fought off demon after demon, real and imagined. The real ones were only insects and, although they lanced and stung him in the most painful places, none was dangerous. But the demons in his mind were deadly, more than once bringing him to the verge of lunacy. Margaret, the bear, and Superintendent Edwards conspired to keep his mind in turmoil, but Margaret was his biggest adversary and he fought her off repeatedly.

Sometime Tuesday a vision of Sarah drifted back, but the omnipresent spectre of Margaret chained her to a bed and pulled off her limbs, one by one, blood every- where, then she ripped off his ex-wife's head, leaving only her naked torso, dumped, like Eddie, on a pile of rotting carcasses.

Margaret had flown away a million times in Bliss's mind after killing Sarah on Sunday. She had escaped.

She'd killed her sister, mother and Sarah, then flown away with the Asians. He had watched them go as he'd dropped back into the water. "Dive, dive, dive," he'd shouted to himself, certain one of the Chinese men would look down out of the cockpit window and see him floundering in the water, but his lungs hadn't recovered from either the exertion of retrieving the knife or his frenzied attack on the float and all he could do was pray.

The plane had risen effortlessly into the sky stealing his precious knife, and he'd slumped despondently into the water watching it all the way to the horizon before dragging himself back to the beach, exhausted. His sanctuary in the pit was so impossibly far it might as well have been on the moon and, too drained to be concerned about the frightful images of mutilated bears, he'd crawled into the cave, made a nest of leaves under the killing table, and squirrelled into it.

Wednesday — a little after midday, although time had lost meaning — the crack of a pistol shot jerked him awake. Voices, on the beach just outside his hiding place, forced him deeper into the shadows and he scrunched himself into a tight ball under the steel killing table. Someone sounding like Samantha called, "Dad! Dad!"

"It's a trick," he said to himself, remembering the previous time he'd heard someone calling. Margaret was back — it was his turn to die. First Eddie, then Sarah, now him. He held his breath praying that Margaret wouldn't find him.

Outside, in the sunshine, Detective Sergeant Phillips slipped his .38 back into the shoulder holster as a big male bear loped off along the beach, stopping every few yards to glance back ruefully. Losing one good meal would have been bad enough but he'd already seen himself through the winter on what Bliss had to offer.

It was the bear that had caught their attention as they'd skipped the lake's surface, choosing a landing place. With a steady north wind flicking up the waves and bringing an early taste of winter, the pilot had searched for a sheltered cove.

"Bear!" he'd shouted, shying away from landing. They'd looked, and were thrilled, forgetting for a moment the morbidity of their mission. The huge black creature, just off the beach, had paused at the sound of the plane then carried on lumbering back and forth expectantly outside the killing cave, knowing Bliss was inside, but too frightened by the dreadful aura of death to go in and get him. He had worn a deep path in the sandy soil since Sunday evening and had survived on the blueberries and cranberries ripening on the surrounding bushes, but he could wait for Bliss; thirst and hunger would force him out eventually.

In his more clearheaded moments, Bliss knew the bear was outside his refuge, but to him it was just another demon. Its huffing and pawing had tormented him for three days, and at times he had been tempted just to quit and walk into its waiting claws. But there was nothing quick about being clawed to death by a bear, he realized, not like a single shot in the head. And he'd seen enough gunshot victims to know that even that wasn't guaranteed.

The crack of a second pistol shot confirmed Bliss's suspicions as he cowered in the deepest corner of his hiding place. If only he hadn't lost his knife he would have had some protection, but weak and unarmed all he could do was to clamp his hands over his ears and pray he wouldn't be found.

"Dad! Dad!" Samatha was yelling as the search party walked the beach. "Shoot again," she called to Phillips, "And keep shooting. He must hear it if he's still ..."

"Dave! Dave!" Peter Bryan took up the shout, stopping Samantha from uttering the unthinkable.

Several shots reverberrated through the forest and kept the bear on the move, but in the quiet darkness of the cave Bliss heard only his own rasping breaths and the thumping of blood coursing through his temples. He knew they were closing in him; Margaret and her cohorts he assumed. Days and nights of playing cat and mouse with a bear on a desrted island had honed his animalistic instincts and he felt the vibes of the searchers, but he had nowhere to run. Another shot went unheard as he cowered deeper.

Outside on the beach the search party had turned away Samantha, close to breaking, was pleading, crying, "Da...ad. Please Dad. Where are you?"

Bryan and the others join in. "Dave! Dave!"

But Bliss, in the silent blackness of his hiding place, was back in a nightmare and imagined himself being strapped to the table; having his guts ripped out, his hands chopped off, and his remains dumped in one of the burial pits along with the bears.

She wouldn't kill me here, he tried telling himself. But wasn't this the place where most of Margaret's murderous activities took place?

The search party had split; Samantha and Bryan probing the fringe of the forest while the pilot and DS Phillips kept the bear in sight as they scoured the beach.

"Over here. There's a cave," called Samantha a few minutes later as she stumbled over the entrance.

"Dad! Are you in there?" she called, and Bliss heard. It was Margaret — he was certain, and he stilled his breathing and willed himself into a state of torpor. Perhaps he could cheat Margaret's murderous intent by dying.

Samantha, Bryan, and Phillips continued calling as the pilot ran back to the plane for a flashlight but their voices faded as Bliss sank into unconsciousness.

"Hurry up! Hurry up!" Samantha screamed close to hysteria as the pilot waded toward the plane. Then she turned to the cave entrance. "Dad! Are you in there ... Dad! Dad!"

"Dead!" The word soured the air in the tiny plane's cabin like a fart in an elevator. "Dead? Are you sure?"

"Yes, quite sure. Absolutely certain," said Peter Bryan, "Probably died fairly quickly, according to the doctor.

The buzz of the float plane's engines dropped to a hum, waiting for a response.

"I can't believe it ..." started Bliss, his speech slowed and slurred by his still-swollen tongue. "I'd say pinch me, but I know it's real, I saw it happening."

"We'll soon get you to the hospital, Dad," said Samantha, tears streaking down her cheeks as she tenderly stroked her father's face. He lay jammed in the centre between her and Bryan in the rear of the plane. He should have been on a stretcher but, according to Phillips, it could take a day or more for an air ambulance to reach them.

"How are you feeling now?" asked Samantha as they lifted clear of the lake

"I'll be better when I've had some coffee. But what happened to Sarah? What have you done with your mum's body?"

Samantha tenderly took her father's hand and swivelled around in time to see Little Bear Island sinking into the horizon behind them. What happened back there? she wondered. "It's Margaret who's dead, Dad ... Not Mum."

"It's all right, Luv ..." he said, his eyes faraway. "I'll look after you now."

"But, Dad ..."

"Better leave him," whispered Bryan. "He's had a nasty shock."

Bliss closed his eyes; he couldn't muster the energy to argue. He knew he was right.

Tears continued to trickle off Samantha's chin but she didn't wipe them away. She wouldn't let go of her father's hand and resolved never to let go of it again — ever.

Samantha had only her father's pulse to tell her that he was still alive and the flight dragged toward eternity until the pilot finally announced they were nearing Goose Bay.

Bliss stirred. "Where are we?"

"Won't be long, Dave," replied Bryan. "We'll soon get you that coffee."

Samantha squeezed his bruised and bloodied hand and attempted to cheer him up. "Good news, Dad: we've got your car back."

He remembered, at least he seemed to. "That's not good news — I needed the insurance money."

"Don't worry, I've been negotiating damages and compensation on your behalf."

"Compensation," he said vaguely, desperately trying to make sense of what was happening. "What for?"

Oh Christ, she realized, he doesn't know about the apartment — or the cat!

"Don't worry about it now."

"About what?"

Samantha looked to Bryan for help. He gave her a vacant look, then looked at Bliss, then back at her, like an umpire. "F'kin' thanks," she muttered from the corner of her mouth.

"Never mind, Dad. You just get better and stop worrying about money. Everything's going to be all right."

"Good."

Not bad, she agreed, but how the hell am I going to break the news about his trashed flat and Balderdash? Then she looked ahead and found a colossal white mountain blocking their way. "Where did that come from?" she breathed, then realized it was a cloud. "Rain," she said, pointing it out to the pilot, like a back-seat flyer.

"Snow, probably," he said, peering into the billows as if searching for a pathway.

"Snow? — What's the date?"

"October first."

Bliss was unconscious again, this time by design, under the operating lamps at Goose Bay General Hospital.

"Nothing too serious," the surgeon assured Samantha. "Physically, he could go home tomorrow."

"And mentally?" she asked.

That was a whole other can of worms, he told her.

Bryan was amused by the hospital's pompous title; the only hospital for four hundred miles and they call it a "General." Samantha, worrying about her father, was slow on the uptake and looked askance.

"Arthritic? Spinal injuries? Geriatric?" he mused on the possibilities. "Can you imagine travelling four hundred miles through the forest with a broken leg and a fractured skull, and they turn you away because it's a burns unit?"

She laughed — really laughed — for the first time in three days.

"Let's get some tea," he suggested. "Then find the police station and see if they have any more information."

They took paper cups and drank as they walked, neither could stomach sitting in the canteen with Miss Thornton-Fink's vomit splodges on the wall.

"They were Chinese ... Either from Hong Kong, Canada, or the States," said the constable, acquiring an authoritative voice as he dealt passports onto his table one after the other like stud cards.

Bryan shuffled through the assortment. "They look genuine enough."

"Probably are. With the sort of money these guys make, they could buy themselves a diplomat anywhere in the world."

"What about Margaret Gordonstone?"

"Only one alias as far as we know. From her things, we've worked out that she goes under the name of Melanie Brown, and she's got a place in the bush not far from Bear Lake settlement."

"Little Bear Island," said Samantha helpfully. "That's where we found Dad."

"No, Ma'am, not according to what we found, although it's not far from there. I'm going over to take a look in the morning. You're welcome to come along if you want."

Samantha gave Bryan a look. "What about Dad?"

"We'll see."

Samantha sat back and let the two policemen discuss the deplorable state of the criminal world. She cast her eyes over a rogue's gallery of photos covering one wall. But she soon realized there was only one rogue: the policeman himself, in dozens of manly and heroic poses. An egotist's portfolio of "Me" mug shots. Me with my hat on crooked. Me wearing a new uniform. Me with a big dog. Me with an even bigger dog. A bigger me, no dog. Me with my foot on a dead moose. Me with my foot on a dead bear.

She listened in on the conversation.

"Thefts?" asked Bryan.

"What could you steal here? There's mebbe fifty

cars in the town, and folks 'ud be mighty suspicious if you got yourself a new TV the day after the neighbours lost theirs. There's sometimes fightin' over women — sometimes the other way 'round."

"What do you do? Arrest them?"

"Nothing — you crazy or what? I jus' lets 'em fight it out and make sure I'm around to take 'em to the hospital. That way they all put me down as the good guy."

That explains the photos, thought Samantha, distaste causing her to rise. "I think we should get back, Peter."

"Where are you folks staying? I could offer you a room ..."

"We've made arrangements, thanks," said Samantha, grabbing Peter's hand and tugging him toward the door."

"What arrangements?" he whispered, aside, before they got as far as the pavement.

"I don't feel like being polite; I can't be bothered to sit around comparing the weather, prices, jobs, lying politicians, and everything else we have in common. I want to go to a hotel, strip off these dirty clothes, relax in a hot bath, and work off my stress with the man who found my dad."

He gave her hand a squeeze and her lips the brush of a kiss. "I think I'd like that as well."

Disappointment struck at the local store after they had bought underwear, matching lumberjack shirts, and a bagful of toiletries: there was no hotel in the town. What now: go back to the cop, cap in hand?

"But you might wanna try the fishing lodge," the storekeeper suggested.

"This is ..." Samantha wanted to say beautiful, but the word seemed so inadequate, so she reached for his mouth instead.

"Who needs an aphrodisiac here?" he mumbled through the kiss as they waltzed slowly back and forth along their private verandah with the rhythm of the lake making music beneath their feet.

Their fisherman's cabin, as quaint as an oil painting, etched itself into the forest bordering the lake and stared into the sunset. The verandah, jutting out on stilts, seemed to float on the surface and sway with the drift of the rippling waves.

"Dad's lost his marbles," she said eventually, pulling away, her mind still troubled.

"No, he'll be fine."

They stood shoulder to shoulder, his arm protectively round her waist, soaking in the tranquil mood of the aquamarine lake.

"You never explained why you told Edwards you were going to Nepal," she said eventually, feeling uneasy about interrupting the silence.

"It was the first thing that came into my mind. I wasn't going to tell him Canada."

"You did that for me?"

"And your dad."

"Edwards could have you shot at dawn."

"I'm pissed off with the man. Everybody kow-tows to him like he's some sort of God — me as well, I'm ashamed to admit. Anyway, I had a vested interest."

"What?"

"My credibility. I told Edwards your dad could handle the Gordonstone murder. Edwards reckoned he couldn't. So where does that leave me?"

"I guess he was right. Dad came here to salve his conscience, to prove that Martin Gordonstone killed his daughter. Now look what's happened: he's proved nothing, even his prime witness is dead. And he nearly killed himself. What a disaster. Edwards is going to have a bloody field day with both of you."

Dad and his bloody conscience, thought Samantha, as they drifted back and forth on the cabin's verandah after dinner watching the sun sink into the lake. A rustic verandah swing pulled at their tired limbs. A loon cried with the clarity of a clarinet and they mistook it for the mating howl of a wolf in the twilight.

"That sent shivers up my spine," said Samantha, as the sound of the sexually sonorous note died away.

"Like this," he said, running his hand soothingly up and down her back.

"Ummmm ... You never did tell me why you hadn't married."

"You make it sound as though I've missed the boat," he said, searching deep into her eyes and finding a hint of the aquamarine lake. "Maybe I never met the right person before."

The message was clear. She touched a finger to his mouth then reached with her lips. "Maybe you have now," she breathed.

The log fire in the stone fireplace had been lit for them and gave all the light they needed as they teased and toyed with each other, playfully shedding clothes — strip poker without cards.

With only her bra and knickers left on, and the contents already explored, she whispered, "Bathroom," and slipped out of Bryan's arms.

"Peter," she called from the bathroom a few seconds later.

"Yeah?"

"You're not going to believe this."

"What?"

"Could you bring me my bag, please?"

"Why?"

"I need something."

"What?"

"I hate to tell you this ..." she began.

"Oh, shit." He'd got the message. "Good job I didn't take a dose of bear bile then, isn't it," he called in laughter. He slipped into the bathroom with her bag and they laughed together.

chapter twenty-one

"Ah. Mr Edwards, Sir. Nice of you to come," said Bliss, his fist plumping his pillow with a soccer hooligan's gusto.

Niceness was neither on Edwards' face nor in his mind. "I hope you didn't expect flowers," he snarled, his tousled hair and crumpled tie-less shirt giving him a boyish, late-for-school appearance.

Bliss already had flowers, shoved into a vase by a nurse with the artistic bent of a bricklayer. Sarah had delivered them, together with a minimal dose of sympathy, while George nervously swanned about in the corridor, protecting his interests. It was a fairly modest bunch of yellow chrysanthemums, nothing smushy like roses or orchids. It's the thought that counts, he mused, not knowing precisely what thought yellow mums were supposed to convey.

"Just because you've been banged up a bit doesn't mean I've forgotten," Edwards continued, thrusting his damaged arm into Bliss's face.

"I can see that," said Bliss with a satisfied glow. "How's the forehead, by the way?" he added, unnecessarily opening an old wound.

"Cut the pleasantries. What do you want?"

Bliss let him dangle. "How are things down at the station?"

"Same as usual."

"Chief Inspector Bryan tells me someone broke into my locker while I was away."

Edwards feigned disinterest, studying the drip in Bliss's arm. "Really. Why are you telling me?" he asked, wondering what would happen if he squashed the bag and pumped a large dose of saline solution straight into Bliss's vein.

"I wonder what they could have been after?" continued Bliss, winding Edwards up.

"How the hell should I know?"

Bliss carried on twisting. "It's not as though I'm on the porn squad. Those blokes are always getting their lockers screwed for dodgy videos."

Edwards snapped. "I'm sure you didn't drag me here to discuss a missing video, or did someone nick yer Mars bar?"

It was a video Bliss wanted to discuss, although not one that had been in his locker. But that could wait; Edwards could have time to stew over it.

"I thought you might be interested in this," Bliss said, pulling Margaret's family photograph album out of his bedside drawer.

Edwards flicked through the gruesome faceless photographs dispassionately; they were not his skeletons, they belonged to Bliss. Samantha and Peter Bryan had retrieved the book from Margaret's real house, the one she owned in the name of Melanie Brown. Samantha had told him about it excitedly, asking, "Why did she call herself Melanie Brown?"

"Easy," replied Bliss. "She didn't want to be Margaret. Melanie was perfect, Melanie got the attention, Melanie was a favourite. But Margaret wasn't a very nice person and inwardly she knew it."

"And Brown?" Samantha was still wondering.

"She didn't want to be a Gordonstone after what her father had done, so she took her mother's maiden name."

A little message board in his brain lit up as he spoke. He could do that; he could change his name. What to, he wondered. Gangly George? Not fucking likely. I'm happy the way I am now, he thought, now that I know the truth.

A nurse with endless legs and a sloppy pin-cushion of golden hair poked her smile around the door, snapping Bliss back to the present. "Everything all right, Mr. Bliss?"

"Fine thanks, Evelyn," he said, looking past Edwards. She could be the world's worst nurse, but legs like that could keep you alive for weeks, he thought, as she bent to check his chart.

"Did you know that Gordonstone was a pedophile?" he began as soon as Evelyn was out of sight.

Edwards tossed the disgusting book onto the bed with a casual gesture. "How the hell would I know what he did in his spare time? I hardly knew the bloke. If it hadn't been for his wife's suicide, I would never have met him."

"Is that true?" Bliss asked. His undertone said, "Bloody liar."

Edwards bit indignantly. "Of course it's true. What's this all about?"

Bliss put the photograph album back in the drawer with a calculated delay and drew out exhibit two:

Margaret's diary, also from her house. He found the relevant page and read. "Melanie's dead. Drowned. — It was her own fault. — I told her to stop but she wouldn't. Dad licked her to death." Bliss paused, letting the meaning sink in.

"You knew, didn't you?" he said. "You knew that Margaret killed her sister. Not at the time, obviously, not until her mother died. But you did know."

"You can't prove that."

"Maybe I can't. Maybe I can. But I say you knew, and that's why you didn't want me to re-open the case. You didn't want me on the Martin Gordonstone murder."

"Why should I care? You were the copper that screwed that case up. I wasn't even in the same division when Melanie died. It was your neck, not mine. What difference would it make to me?"

"I couldn't figure that out, until I found you'd destroyed the file."

"What file?"

"Don't give me that crap."

"How dare you ..."

"There's the door. If you don't like what I'm saying ..."

Bliss's cockiness was worrisome. "Like I told you before, his wife's death was suicide," said Edwards, staying close to the big red emergency call button.

"Did you consider murder?"

"Of course I did. But he couldn't have killed her."

"How can you be so sure?"

"He had a cast-iron alibi."

"I've blown plenty of cast-iron alibis to smithereens. Some people will say anything for a few hundred quid, you know that. Anyway most alibis have nothing to do with money, it's a question of loyalty. Almost any mother'll swear on her life that her kid was —"

"This was different," Edwards butted in, sticking his nose into Bliss's face in frustration. He wished he knew where Bliss was leading. "Just take it from me. He couldn't have killed her. It was impossible."

"Not good enough."

"OK. If you must know, he couldn't have killed her because he was with me at the time."

This was unexpected. "You?"

"Yeah, me. We were at a lodge meeting."

Bliss grated his fingernails down Edwards' blackboard. "Do you mean the funny handshake brigade?"

"The Freemasons to you ..." he started, then unexpectedly lost steam. He deflated into a chair and buried his head in his hands as Betty-Ann's grotesquely mutilated body swung into his field of vision. His voice dropped to a confessional whisper. "We had a few drinks afterwards and got back to his restaurant about two in the morning."

"What about before you left?" Bliss asked. "Could he have done it then?"

Edwards looked up. "No. The place was still open. Fifty people having dinner might have noticed a woman dangling from the ceiling."

"So why not just admit you were together and give the bloke a proper alibi?"

"I had my reputation to think of. I was only a DI at the time; the publicity wouldn't have done me much good. Besides, I thought it would make things easier for Martin if I was the investigating officer. After all, there was no chance of me treating him like a suspect and giving him the third degree. I told him to ring 999 and waited outside in my car until the call went out on the radio. I said I was in the area and would attend, then went back inside until the uniformed lads arrived. There was nothing I could do. She was obviously dead, poor bitch swinging from the ..."His eyes drifted to the ceiling as he looked into the past for an awful second, then he exclaimed defiantly, "Martin didn't do it. Martin could not have done it. There was no way he could have murdered her."

"I know that."

"You do? So why the hell are you jerking me around?"

"I know that now, but if you'd told me the truth in the first place then I probably wouldn't be here today."

"What difference would it have made? She committed suicide whether or not I was there to give him an alibi."

"Are you certain?"

Edwards' face caught fire. "Yes."

"What if I said that I know she was murdered?"

"How? The place was all locked up and the alarms were set. I checked it myself. All the staff had alibis, and they all left together."

"And Margaret?"

Edwards was stumped. Margaret was there, asleep upstairs, he'd woken her with the news himself. He'd put on the sad face, adopted the slightly stooped, apologetic stance, used the hushed undertaker's tone, held her sobbing body, poured brandy down her throat, and said the right things.

"What did Margaret say in her statement?" Bliss continued, realizing that the other man's mind was preoccupied with decade-old visions.

"What was there to put in a statement? I spoke to her — she didn't see or hear a thing. She was asleep upstairs. It's a big place, in case you hadn't noticed."

"But she did make a statement," said Bliss.

"She did not."

"I've got it here," he continued, taunting Edwards with an old exercise book that he pulled slowly from under his pillow. He started to read.

"The new kitten was just purr-fect the other creatures agreed ..."

Edwards was already halfway to the door. "I haven't got time for this. They were right: they said you'd need treatment."

Edwards had second thoughts about leaving and tried to snatch the book away from Bliss. "Give me that," he shouted as Bliss whipped it out of reach.

"If you don't listen now, I promise you'll read it in the papers tomorrow," Bliss said with what appeared to be suicidal indiscretion.

The comment stopped Edwards in his tracks. "You're barmy — you think the press'll be interested in that crap?"

Let's see who's bluffing here. "I'm willing to take the chance. Are you?"

Edwards wouldn't dignify the question with an answer, but nevertheless waited while Bliss started reading again.

"The new kitten was just purr-fect the other creatures agreed.

"'I adore the feel of her long silky fur,' snorts the old pot-bellied pig, irritated by her own scratchy coarse hair.

"'I love the way her slender body slinks,' howls the pit-bull, who had never slunk anywhere himself.

"The master was away, somewhere in another galaxy — on another construction job.

"'Oh my,' barks the pit bull, 'You're all messy Miss Pussy, come let me preen you.'

"'That's nice,' purrs the pussy as the pit-bull's rough tongue tickled her fur.'"

Edwards was pacing with the frustrated impotence of a hit and run victim, but Bliss continued.

"A pair of green eyes watches from the trees.

"'Time for lunch,' grunts Mrs. Piggy.

"The pit-bull bares his teeth and gives a terrifying snarl. 'Not now, Mrs. Piggy.'

"Never mind. I'll keep it warm,' she squeaks."

Edwards finally burst, "What the effin' 'ell ..."

Bliss closed the book and started to shove it under his pillow. "Press it is then."

"Oh, for Chrissake get on with it."

Bliss came close to overstepping the mark. "Should I start at the beginning?"

"'Time for bed,' sighs Mrs. Piggy," Bliss continued reading, taking Edwards' warning growl as a no.

"'Not now,' grunts the pit-bull.

"'Never mind. — I'll keep it warm,' squeals Mrs. Piggy.

"The pretty little pussycat was nowhere to be found, but green eyes saw her.

"Mrs. Piggy was so angry she ate and ate and ate until her pot-belly was so big she couldn't leave her sty; couldn't see the sky; couldn't see the stars; couldn't see the snake.

"The snake slides out of the shadows and slips silently around Mrs. Piggy's neck.

"'Oink,' squeals Mrs. Piggy in alarm.

"'Go to sleep,' hisses the slithery snake.

"'I'm feeling tired,' snuffles Mrs. Piggy.

"'Go to sleeeeeeeeeep,' sings the snake.

"And Mrs. Piggy flew away."

Edwards sank to the chair in relief. "So what the hell were you going on about her statement for?"

"That's it — Margaret's statement in her own handwriting. Her confession to murder."

"This is crap. Whose murder?"

"Betty-Ann Gordonstone, of course — Mrs. Piggy."

"Snake? What fucking snake?"

"Margaret — the harelip. Snakes have a split upper lip. She was writing about herself. Doesn't the truth mean anything to you?"

"Truth," Edwards spat. "Kids' stories about poxy pussy cats?"

Margaret was hardly a pussy, thought Bliss, reminding himself to ask Samantha about Balderdash. "She admitted it to me," he said, casting his mind back to the nightmare island experience, which he might have put down to a bad batch of beer if it hadn't been for the book in his hand and the hole in his leg. "She told me she'd put her mother out of misery, and she was pointing a rifle at me when she said it."

Edwards' face was speaking on his behalf. "This guy's crazy," it said. And Bliss suddenly realized who *they* were: a couple of white coats with swinging stethoscopes who'd ignored the hole in his leg and spent most of their time with an ophthalmoscope trying to peer into his brain.

"You still don't believe me, do you?" Bliss said. "You think I'm barmy."

Edwards folded. He had no evidence that Margaret had done it, although he had his suspicions. But what was he supposed to have done? Gordonstone had been distraught. His younger daughter had died in a terrible accident, his wife was a basket case whom he'd looked after for ten years. How would he live with loss of Margaret? Anyway, it was easy to believe that Betty-Ann had wanted to die, from what Gordonstone had said.

Bliss was still waiting; Edwards felt his eyes probing. "Melanie's accident —" he began.

"It wasn't an accident," shot back Bliss.

"Yeah. Well, that was your fault; you were the one who told the coroner it was. I've read the bloody file."

"True."

"Anyway, I felt sorry for the poor bastard and, yes, if you must know, I did think Margaret might have done it. But I'll deny ever saying so. But what's this got to do with Gordonstone's death? That's what you were supposed to be working on, not something that happened years ago."

"I *was* working on that, Guv. In fact, I now know for certain who killed him."

"So who did it?"

"You did."

Edwards could have murdered him — smacked him round the head with his plastered arm or pumped a pint of saline straight into his heart, if Evelyn hadn't returned.

"Your tea, Mr. Bliss," the nurse said. "Would your friend like one?"

Bliss said, "Yes," just for the pleasure of watching her backside go out into the corridor and return, then go out again. He could also watch Edwards build steam.

The pressure cooker in Edwards' brain exploded just as Evelyn's behind disappeared. "How dare you!" he shouted.

"Well, you had the best motive."

Edwards went as white as a sheet. "What d'ye mean?"

"Greed. Why own half a restaurant when you can have all of it? It is yours isn't it?"

Edwards lost steam. "How did you find out?"

"I didn't — I guessed, but you've just confirmed it."

"What? How dare you? You repeat that and I'll sue for defamation."

"You can't sue if it's true."

"You're doing it again. You're saying I killed Gordonstone."

"You were in the restaurant the night he died?"

"You can't prove that."

"You don't deny it, though."

"Are you interrogating me?"

"Call it what you like, but I still want to know why you were there when he died, but didn't do anything to help him, and certainly didn't come forward as a witness."

"Mind your own damn business."

"Ah, but it is my business. You see, I was given the job of finding his killer, and I have. Like I said, it's you."

"I shall pretend I didn't hear that."

"You needn't bother. I shall tell everybody, unless I start getting some straight answers."

"Like what?"

"Like, how long have you been a television reporter?"

Edwards' expression made it clear he was about to deny the accusation. Bliss saved him the breath. "I could get Mr. George Weston to attend an identification parade if you like. What did you do — wear glasses, false beard, and a borrowed raincoat from lost property?"

"How did you find out?"

"I had plenty of time to think about it, then" he whipped open his bedside drawer, "I watched a copy of the videotape — the one I got from Mr. Weston. The one he took at the restaurant the night Gordonstone died. You didn't know he'd made a copy, did you? Anyway, I watched it and ... Bingo! Who is that sitting all by himself in the corner by the kitchen door but our Mr. Edwards? What is he doing there, I said to myself." Bliss reached back into the drawer and pulled out the newspaper clipping of Gordonstone's funeral. "And I saw our Mr. Edwards at the funeral and I thought to myself, 'There's something fishy going on here.' So, I got someone to make a few enquiries with all the television stations, and they all said that they had never heard of Weston or his videotape. So, who else might have known about it?"

He opened his eyes wide, offering Edwards the opportunity to respond.

He declined.

"Well. Lo and behold, when someone asked Mr. Weston why he had contacted the television people about the videotape, he said he hadn't. He claims he only called our police station, and was taken by surprise twenty minutes later when a reporter turned up and offered him a hundred quid for the tape. He was so taken aback he forgot to mention the copy. He probably griped about the restaurant so much that the reporter was happy to get out of there. Anyway, apparently the reporter was in a tearing hurry, desperate to get the tape back to the studio for the mid-morning news, or so he claimed. Strange that, considering it was never shown. But it wouldn't have been, would it, considering the tape was in your bloody desk drawer."

"I shall deny it. You can't prove any of it."

"I can prove you were there," Bliss said, waving the videotape in the air. "And I can get Weston to ID you as the man who claimed to be a reporter."

In a flash, Edwards ripped the videotape out of Bliss's hand, threw it on the floor, and stamped it to shreds. Bliss watched impassively.

Peter Bryan and Samantha came in, hand in hand.

"Oh, Christ," said Bliss. "That's all I need."

"Shut up, misery," Samantha laughed. "You're always telling me I should find a nice man with good prospects. I have."

"I give up."

"Is this what you want, Dave," said Bryan, passing him a copy of the letter addressed to Margaret from Gosforth, Morgan, and Mitwich. The letter she had left unopened in the cottage.

Bliss scanned the single sheet then looked at Edwards. "This appears to be confirmation that you do own *L'Haute Cuisinier*. According to Gordonstone's solicitor, his shares passed on his death to a Michael Edwards."

"So, you really did have a motive," said Samantha.

"I didn't," Edwards protested, squirming. "There must be dozens, hundreds of Michael Edwards. I'm not the only Michael Edwards in the world."

"But you're the only Michael Edwards who investigated his wife's death," said Bliss. "The only Michael Edwards in his restaurant the night he was poisoned, the only Michael Edwards at his funeral."

"It looks pretty bad, Guv," said Bryan sagely.

"Oh, it's worse than that," said Bliss, loving every minute. "Look," he said to Bryan, pointing to the dismembered videotape on the floor.

"What happened?" cried Samantha.

"Mr. Edwards —"

"I don't have to listen to this crap," said Edwards heading for the door.

"I suggest you do, or you may hear the rest of it from the comfort of a cell," said Bliss, causing Edwards to stooge about near the door while he nervously considered his best course of action. Bliss carried on speaking as if Edwards were a disobedient child. "As I was saying, Mr. Edwards took exception to that videotape you gave me, Samantha."

"Not the ..."

"Yes, that one."

Samantha swung accusingly on Edwards. "Why did you do that?"

"Look, I've got nothing to hide. All right, all right, I admit it, I was there the night he died, and I was at his funeral."

"And you own the place."

"Legally, no."

"According to the solicitors ..."

"They are out of date. When I found out you were sniffing around I knew there'd be a problem, so I transferred all the shares into my wife's name. So legally she owns the place now."

"When did this happen?" demanded Bliss.

"Yesterday, if it's any of your damn business."

"But you were the silent partner weren't you?" said Bliss. "You inherited his shares on his death. That's why you didn't want anyone re-opening the Betty-Ann investigation; in case your name came up and someone put two and two together."

Edwards weighed the odds. "He offered me a partnership. Out of gratitude, he said."

"For the considerate way that you covered up his wife's murder."

Edwards was back up to full steam in a millisecond. "How dare you, Inspector? It was suicide. I've told you before."

Wrong, thought Bliss, but let it pass. "OK. So what were the shares in the restaurant for?"

"He said he was doing me a favour, said it was a gold mine —"

Bliss cut in, "He seemed to have a knack for investing in duff gold mines."

"He needed money. Quite a lot actually. I assumed it was something to do with his wife's estate; death duties perhaps. Maybe she'd borrowed the money and he had to pay it back when she died. I don't know. I didn't ask. All I know is that he was looking for an investor, a silent partner. He wasn't a drunk then. He owned a very successful restaurant — at least it appeared successful, it was always packed. Anyway, he needed some cash and I happened to have some, though I had to borrow a fair bit as well."

Bryan stepped in with an official air. "But you know a police officer can't legally own licensed premises, or even be involved in the running of licensed premises."

"I know the Licensing Acts, you don't have to tell me, but I thought by the time anyone found out I'd be so rich that I could just quit the force and ..." he paused, close to meltdown. "It's a disaster. The place is bankrupt. Half my bloody wages have gone into that place for years. Gordonstone drank himself and the business into the ground."

"So you're not a wealthy man?" said Bliss.

Edwards snorted. "Lost my shirt. His drunken antics made good publicity, but we were always being sued for assault, damages, libel — you name it. Nothing criminal — always had to settle out of court. I couldn't afford to have my name in the papers. I was going to quit the force ten years ago. Give it six months, he said, just to get everything sorted out, then I'd quit and ..."

"He never got it sorted," helped Samantha.

Edwards shook his head. "More and more debt. I'm up to my neck in bloody debt and the interest is crippling me. I couldn't get rid of him."

"Somebody did." suggested Bliss.

"It wasn't me."

"Strikes me that what you've told us makes you even more of a candidate."

Edwards would have hit him had he thought he could get away with it. "Killing Gordonstone doesn't do me any good. I'm saddled with a restaurant that loses more money than John DeLorean. I can't even go bankrupt without publicly admitting I own it. Then I'd lose my job on the force.

"Wait a minute," said Samantha. "This is all very well but it still doesn't explain."

"Explain what?" said Edwards.

She bent down and picked up the remains of the videotape. "It doesn't explain why you ripped up Dad's favourite Barry Manilow tape."

Bliss opened the small bedside cabinet and extracted a small white envelope addressed to Margaret Gordonstone in Canada. "This envelope contains the real proof of who killed Gordonstone." He held it aloft, almost daring Edwards to snatch it out of his hand and rip it up, but Edwards didn't intend to be caught a second time.

"Perhaps Mr. Edwards would care to open it," he said, handing it to him.

"It's from Gordonstone to his daughter," explained Edwards slitting it open and scanning it. Then he read: "'I don't know why you have written to me. I thought I made it perfectly clear that I never wanted to hear from you or see you ever again. You are an evil woman. You will never get another penny from me, and if you ever contact me again I will go to the police and tell them everything.'"

Edwards flipped the letter in his hand, searching unsuccessfully for more information. "I thought you said that this would explain who killed him?"

"It does."

He reread it. "How?"

"Whose handwriting is that on the envelope?"

Edwards compared the handwriting on the envelope with that in the letter. "It's not Gordonstone's, that's for sure."

"A woman's?" queried Bliss.

"Possibly."

"Could it be Margaret's?"

"Makes sense, I suppose. She sent a self-addressed envelope to make sure she got a reply."

"No, not to make sure she got a reply."

"What then?"

"To make sure he licked the flap."

"Shit," shouted Edwards dropping it faster than a hot brick and dashing to the sink. "Why didn't you warn me?" he shouted frantically washing his hands under scalding water.

"Don't worry, Guv." Bliss was enjoying himself. "Gordonstone must have licked most of the poison off."

"The scheming witch!"

"By the way, how's old Balderdash?" enquired Bliss of his daughter after Edwards disappeared in search of a doctor.

Samantha's downward glance and shuffled shoes told the story.

"The poor old sod's dead isn't he?" Bliss said resignedly.

"Yes, but ..."

"I sort of expected it. He was quite old. He probably missed me and pined away."

Peter Bryan silently pleaded with Samantha not to disillusion her father.

Samantha was cradling a cardboard shoe box. "But look what we've bought you."

"What is it?"

Bliss peered in and his eyes were met with a pretty pair of kitten's eyes. "I don't really know," he began, obviously not keen.

"I thought you loved Balderdash," Samantha said. "I thought you'd want another."

"To be absolutely honest, I only kept him to annoy your mother."

"Oh, Dad."

"Why don't you have him, Sam? You've got a garden for him to play in."

Samantha looked for Bryan's approval. "OK."

"Anyway, you two are all dolled up. Something special?"

Samantha gave Bryan's hand a squeeze. "We're going out for a romantic dinner. And Peter's got something he wants to show me afterwards, haven't you?"

Bryan felt a blush rising and kicked her on the ankle.

"Ow!" she said, with a laugh.

"Do you know the worst thing about this entire affair?" said Bliss."

"No," they said in unison.

"The possibility of ending up with a son-in-law as a boss."

"As long as you don't expect me to call you 'Dad,'" sneered Bryan.

The End